J.G. Lockhart

Memoirs of the Life of Sir Walter Scott, Bart

Vol. IV

SALZWASSER
VERLAG

J.G. Lockhart

Memoirs of the Life of Sir Walter Scott, Bart

Vol. IV

Reprint of the original, first published in 1862.

1st Edition 2022 | ISBN: 978-3-37503-344-6

Verlag (Publisher): Salzwasser Verlag GmbH, Zeilweg 44, 60439 Frankfurt, Deutschland
Vertretungsberechtigt (Authorized to represent): E. Roepke, Zeilweg 44, 60439 Frankfurt, Deutschland
Druck (Print): Books on Demand GmbH, In de Tarpen 42, 22848 Norderstedt, Deutschland

MEMOIRS

OF THE

LIFE OF SIR WALTER SCOTT, BART.

BY

J. G. LOCKHART, ESQ.

VOL. IV.

EDINBURGH:

1862.

WALTER SCOTT.

1808.

CONTENTS

OF VOLUME FOURTH.

CONTENTS.

CHAPTER XXXII.

CHAPTER XXXIII.

MEMOIRS

OF THE

LIFE OF SIR WALTER SCOTT.

CHAPTER XXV.

The " Flitting" to Abbotsford — Plantations — George Thomson — Rokeby and Triermain in progress — Excursion to Flodden — Bishop-Auckland — and Rokeby Park — Correspondence with Crabbe — Life of Patrick Carey, &c. — Publication of Rokeby — and of the Bridal of Triermain.

1812–1813.

TOWARDS the end of May 1812, the Sheriff finally removed from Ashestiel to Abbotsford. The day when this occurred was a sad one for many a poor neighbour — for they lost, both in him and his wife,

very generous protectors.   In such a place, among
the few evils which counterbalance so many good
things in the condition of the peasantry, the most
afflicting is the want of access to medical advice.
As far as their means and skill would go, they had
both done their utmost to supply this want; and
Mrs Scott, in particular, had made it so much her
business to visit the sick in their scattered cottages,
and bestowed on them the contents of her medicine-
chest as well as of the larder and cellar, with such
unwearied kindness, that her name is never mentioned there to this day without some expression of
tenderness.   Scott's children remember the parting
scene as one of unmixed affliction—but it had had,
as we shall see, its lighter features.

Among the many amiable English friends whom
he owed to his frequent visits at Rokeby Park, there
was, I believe, none that had a higher place in his
regard than the late Anne Lady Alvanley, the widow
of the celebrated Chief Justice of the Court of
Common Pleas.   He was fond of female society in
general; but her ladyship was a woman after his
heart; well born, and highly bred, but without the
slightest tinge of the frivolities of modern fashion;
soundly informed, and a warm lover of literature
and the arts, but holding in as great horror as himself the imbecile chatter and affected ecstasies of the
bluestocking generation.   Her ladyship had written
to him early in May, by Miss Sarah Smith (now

Mrs Bartley), whom I have already mentioned as one of his theatrical favourites; and his answer contains, among other matters, a sketch of the " Forest Flitting."

" *To the Right Honourable Lady Alvanley.*

" Ashestiel, 25th May 1812.

" I was honoured, my dear Lady Alvanley, by the kind letter which you sent me with our friend Miss Smith, whose talents are, I hope, receiving at Edinburgh the full meed of honourable applause which they so highly merit. It is very much against my will that I am forced to speak of them by report alone, for this being the term of removing, I am under the necessity of being at this farm to superintend the transference of my goods and chattels, a most miscellaneous collection, to a small property, about five miles down the Tweed, which I purchased last year. The neighbours have been much delighted with the procession of my furniture, in which old swords, bows, targets, and lances, made a very conspicuous show. A family of turkeys was accommodated within the helmet of some *preux* chevalier of ancient Border fame; and the very cows, for aught I know, were bearing banners and muskets. I assure your ladyship that this caravan, attended by a dozen of ragged rosy peasant children, carrying fishing-rods and spears, and leading poneys, greyhounds, and spaniels, would, as it crossed the Tweed, have furnished no bad subject for the pencil, and really reminded me of one of the gypsey groupes of Callot upon their march.

" Edinburgh, 28th May.

" I have got here at length, and had the pleasure to hear Miss Smith speak the Ode on the Passions charmingly last night. It was her benefit, and the house was tolerable, though not so good as she deserves, being a very good girl, as well as an ex‑ cellent performer.

" I have read Lord Byron with great pleasure, though pleasure is not quite the appropriate word. I should say admiration—mixed with regret, that the author should have adopted such an unamiable misanthropical tone.— The reconciliation with Hol‑ land-house is extremely edifying, and may teach young authors to be in no hurry to exercise their satirical vein. I remember an honest old Presby‑ terian, who thought it right to speak with respect even of the devil himself, since no one knew in what corner he might one day want a friend. But Lord Byron is young, and certainly has great genius, and has both time and capacity to make amends for his errors. I wonder if he will pardon the Edinburgh reviewers, who have read their recantation of their former strictures.

" Mrs Scott begs to offer her kindest and most

respectful compliments to your ladyship and the young ladies. I hope we shall get into Yorkshire this season to see Morritt: he and his lady are really delightful persons. Believe me, with great respect, dear Lady Alvanley, your much honoured and obliged　　　　　　　　　　WALTER SCOTT."

A week later, in answer to a letter, mentioning the approach of the celebrated sale of books in which the Roxburghe Club originated, Scott says to his trusty ally, Daniel Terry:—

"Edinburgh, 9th June 1812.

" My Dear Terry,

" I wish you joy of your success, which although all reports state it as most highly flattering, does not exceed what I had hoped for you. I think I shall do you a sensible pleasure in requesting that you will take a walk over the fields to Hampstead one of these fine days, and deliver the enclosed to my friend Miss Baillie, with whom, I flatter myself, you will be much pleased, as she has all the simplicity of real genius. I mentioned to her some time ago, that I wished to make you acquainted, so that the sooner you can call upon her, the compliment will be the more gracious. As I suppose you will sometimes look in at the Roxburghe sale, a memorandum respecting any remarkable articles will be a great favour.

" Abbotsford was looking charming, when I was obliged to mount my wheel in this court, too fortunate that I have at length some share in the roast meat I am daily engaged in turning. Our flitting and removal from Ashestiel baffled all description; we had twenty-four cart-loads of the veriest trash in nature, besides dogs, pigs, poneys, poultry, cows, calves, bare-headed wenches, and bare-breeched boys. In other respects we are going on in the old way, only poor Percy is dead. I intend to have an old stone set up by his grave, with ' *Cy gist li preux Percie,*' and I hope future antiquaries will debate which hero of the house of Northumberland has left his bones in Teviotdale.[*] Believe me yours very truly,   WALTER SCOTT."

This was one of the busiest summers of Scott's busy life. Till the 12th of July he was at his post in the Court of Session five days every week; but every Saturday evening found him at Abbotsford, to observe the progress his labourers had made within doors and without in his absence; and on Monday night he returned to Edinburgh. Even before the Summer Session commenced, he appears to have made some advance in his Rokeby, for he writes to Mr Morritt, from Abbotsford, on the 4th of May—

[*] The epitaph of this favourite greyhound may be seen on the edge of the bank, a little way below the house of Abbotsford.

" As for the house and the poem, there are twelve masons hammering at the one, and one poor noddle at the other—so they are both in progress";—and his literary labours throughout the long vacation were continued under the same sort of disadvantage. That autumn he had, in fact, no room at all for himself. The only parlour which had been hammered into anything like habitable condition, served at once for dining-room, drawing-room, school-room, and study. A window looking to the river was kept sacred to his desk; an old bed-curtain was nailed up across the room close behind his chair, and there, whenever the spade, the dibble, or the chisel (for he took his full share in all the work on hand) was laid aside, he pursued his poetical tasks, apparently undisturbed and unannoyed by the surrounding confusion of masons and carpenters, to say nothing of the lady's small talk, the children's babble among themselves, or their repetition of their lessons. The truth no doubt was, that when at his desk he did little more, as far as regarded *poetry*, than write down the lines which he had fashioned in his mind while pursuing his vocation as a planter, upon that bank which received originally, by way of joke, the title of *the thicket*. " I am now," he says to Ellis (Oct. 17), " adorning a patch of naked land with trees *facturis nepotibus umbram*, for I shall never live to enjoy their shade myself otherwise than in the recumbent posture of Tityrus or Menalcas."

But he did live to see *the thicket* deserve not only that name, but a nobler one; and to fell with his own hand many a well-grown tree that he had planted there.

Another plantation of the same date, by his eastern boundary, was less successful. For this he had asked and received from his early friend, the Marchioness of Stafford, a supply of acorns from Trentham, and it was named in consequence *Sutherland bower*; but the field-mice, in the course of the ensuing winter, contrived to root up and devour the whole of her ladyship's goodly benefaction. A third space had been set apart, and duly enclosed, for the reception of some Spanish chestnuts offered to him by an admirer established in merchandise at Seville; but that gentleman had not been a very knowing ally as to such matters, for when the chestnuts arrived, it turned out that they had been boiled.

Scott writes thus to Terry, in September, while the Roxburghe sale was still going on:—

" I have lacked your assistance, my dear sir, for twenty whimsicalities this autumn. Abbotsford, as you will readily conceive, has considerably changed its face since the auspices of Mother Retford were exchanged for ours. We have got up a good garden wall, complete stables in the haugh, according to Stark's plan, and the old farm yard being enclosed with a wall, with some little picturesque additions in front, has much relieved the stupendous height of the Doctor's barn. The new plantations have thriven amazingly well, the acorns are coming up fast, and Tom Purdie is the happiest and most consequential person in the world. My present work is building up the well with some *debris* from the Abbey. O for your assistance, for I am afraid we shall make but a botched job of it, especially as our materials are of a very miscellaneous complexion. The worst of all is, that while my trees grow and my fountain fills, my purse, in an inverse ratio, sinks to zero. This last circumstance will, I fear, make me a very poor guest at the literary entertainment your researches hold out for me. I should, however, like much to have the Treatise on Dreams, by the author of the New Jerusalem, which, as John Cuthbertson the smith said of the minister's sermon, must be neat work. The Loyal Poems by N. T.* are probably by poor Nahum Tate, who associated with Brady in versifying the Psalms, and more honourably with Dryden in the second part of Absalom and Achitophel. I never saw them, however, but would give a guinea or thirty shillings for the collection. Our friend John Ballantyne has, I learn, made a sudden sally to London, and doubtless you will crush a

* The Reverend Alexander Dyce says, " N. T. stands for *Nathaniel Thompson*, the Tory bookseller, who published these Loyal Poems." [1839.]

quart with him or a pottle pot; he will satisfy your bookseller for ' The Dreamer,' or any other little · purchase you may recommend for me. You have pleased Miss Baillie very much both in public and in society, and though not fastidious, she is not, I think, particularly lavish of applause either way. A most valuable person is she, and as warm-hearted as she is brilliant.——Mrs Scott and all our little folks are well. I am relieved of the labour of hearing Walter's lesson by a gallant son of the church, who with one leg of wood, and another of oak, walks to and fro from Melrose every day for that purpose. Pray stick to the dramatic work,* and never suppose either that you can be intrusive, or that I can be uninterested in whatever concerns you. Yours,   W. S."

The tutor alluded to at the close of this letter was Mr George Thomson, son of the minister of Melrose, who, when the house afforded better accommodation, was and continued for many years to be domesticated at Abbotsford. Scott had always a particular tenderness towards persons afflicted with any bodily misfortune; and Thomson, whose leg had been amputated in consequence of a rough casualty of his boyhood, had a special share in his favour from the high spirit with which he refused at the

* An edition of the British Dramatists had, I believe, been projected by Mr Terry.

time to betray the name of the companion that had occasioned his mishap, and continued ever afterwards to struggle against its disadvantages.   Tall, vigorous, athletic, a dauntless horseman, and expert at the singlestick, George formed a valuable as well as picturesque addition to the *tail* of the new laird, who often said, " In the Dominie, like myself, accident has spoiled a capital lifeguardsman." His many oddities and eccentricities in no degree interfered with the respect due to his amiable feelings, upright principles, and sound learning; nor did *Dominie Thamson* at all quarrel in after times with the universal credence of the neighbourhood that he had furnished many features for the inimitable personage whose designation so nearly resembled his own; and if he has not yet " wagged his head" in a " pulpit o' his ain," he well knows it has not been so for want of earnest and long-continued intercession on the part of the author of Guy Mannering.*

For many years Scott had accustomed himself to proceed in the composition of poetry along with that of prose essays of various descriptions ; but it is a remarkable fact that he chose this period of perpetual noise and bustle, when he had not even a summer-house to himself, for the new experiment of

* Mr Thomson died 8th January 1838, before the publication of the first edition of these Memoirs had been completed. — [1839.]

carrying on two poems at the same time—and this too without suspending the heavy labour of his edition of Swift, to say nothing of the various lesser matters in which the Ballantynes were, from day to day, calling for the assistance of his judgment and his pen. In the same letter in which William Erskine acknowledges the receipt of the first four pages of Rokeby, he adverts also to the Bridal of Triermain as being already in rapid progress. The fragments of this second poem, inserted in the Register of the preceding year, had attracted considerable notice ; the secret of their authorship had been well kept ; and by some means, even in the shrewdest circles of Edinburgh, the belief had become prevalent that they proceeded not from Scott but from Erskine. Scott had no sooner completed his bargain as to the copyright of the unwritten Rokeby, than he resolved to pause from time to time in its composition, and weave those fragments into a shorter and lighter romance, executed in a different metre, and to be published anonymously, in a small pocket volume, as nearly as possible on the same day with the avowed quarto. He expected great amusement from the comparisons which the critics would no doubt indulge themselves in drawing between himself and this humble candidate ; and Erskine good-humouredly entered into the scheme, undertaking to do nothing which should effectually suppress the notion of his having set himself up as a modest rival to his friend. Nay, he suggested a further refinement, which in the sequel had no small share in the success of this little plot upon the sagacity of the reviewers. Having said that he much admired the opening of the first canto of Rokeby, Erskine adds, " I shall request your *accoucheur* to send me your *little Dugald* too as he gradually makes his progress. What I have seen is delightful. You are aware how difficult it is to form any opinion of a work, the general plan of which is unknown, transmitted merely in legs and wings as they are formed and feathered. Any remarks must be of the most minute and superficial kind, confined chiefly to the language, and other such subordinate matters. I shall be very much amused if the secret is kept and the knowing ones taken in. To prevent any discovery from your prose, what think you of putting down your ideas of what the preface ought to contain, and allowing me to write it over ? And perhaps a quizzing review might be concocted."

This last hint was welcome ; and among other parts of the preface to Triermain which threw out " the knowing ones," certain Greek quotations interspersed in it are now accounted for. Scott, on his part, appears to have studiously interwoven into the piece allusions to personal feelings and experiences more akin to his friend's history and character than to his own ; and he did so still more largely, when

repeating this experiment, in the introductory parts
of Harold the Dauntless.

The same post which conveyed William Erskine's
letter above quoted, brought him an equally wise and
kind one from Mr Morritt, in answer to a fresh application for some minute details about the scenery
and local traditions of the Valley of the Tees. Scott
had promised to spend part of this autumn at Rokeby
Park himself; but now, busied as he was with his
planting operations at home, and continually urged
by Ballantyne to have the poem ready for publication
by Christmas, he would willingly have trusted his
friend's knowledge in place of his own observation
and research. Mr Morritt gave him in reply various particulars, which I need not here repeat, but
added—" I am really sorry, my dear Scott, at your
abandonment of your kind intention of visiting
Rokeby—and my sorrow is not quite selfish—for
seriously, I wish you could have come, if but for a
few days, in order, on the spot, to settle accurately
in your mind the localities of the new poem, and all
their petty circumstances, of which there are many
that would give interest and ornament to your descriptions. I am too much flattered by your proposal
of inscribing the poem to me, not to accept it with
gratitude and pleasure. I shall always feel your
friendship as an honour—we all wish our honours to
be permanent—and yours promises mine at least

a fair chance of immortality. I hope, however, you will not be obliged to write in a hurry on account of the impatience of your booksellers. They are, I think, ill advised in their proceeding, for surely the book will be the more likely to succeed from not be-ing forced prematurely into this critical world. Do not be persuaded to risk your established fame on this hazardous experiment. If you want a few hundreds independent of these booksellers, your credit is so very good, now that you have got rid of your Old Man of the Sea, that it is no great merit to trust you, and I happen at this moment to have five or six for which I have no sort of demand—so rather than be obliged to spur Pegasus beyond the power of pulling him up when he is going too fast, do consult your own judgment and set the midwives of the trade at defiance. Don't be scrupulous to the disadvantage of your muse, and above all be not offended at me for a proposition which is meant in the true spirit of friendship. I am more than ever anxious for your success—the Lady of the Lake more than succeeded —I think Don Roderick is less popular—I want this work to be another Lady at the least. Surely it would be worth your while for such an object to spend a week of your time, and a portion of your Old Man's salary, in a mail-coach flight hither, were it merely to renew your acquaintance with the country, and to rectify the little misconceptions of a cursory view. Ever affectionately yours—J. B. S. M."

This appeal was not to be resisted. Scott, I believe, accepted Mr Morritt's friendly offer so far as to
ask his assistance in having some of Ballantyne's bills
discounted : and he proceeded the week after to
Rokeby, by the way of Flodden and Hexham, travelling on horseback, his eldest boy and girl on their
poneys, while Mrs Scott followed them in the carriage. Two little incidents that diversified this ride
through Northumberland have found their way into
print already; but, as he was fond of telling them
both down to the end of his days, I must give them
a place here also. Halting at Flodden to expound
the field of battle to his young folks, he found that
Marmion had, as might have been expected, benefit-
ted the keeper of the public house there very largely;
and the village Boniface, overflowing with gratitude,
expressed his anxiety to have a *Scott's Head* for his
sign-post. The poet demurred to this proposal, and
assured mine host that nothing could be more appropriate than the portraiture of a foaming tankard,
which already surmounted his door-way. " Why,
the painter-man has not made an ill job," said the
landlord, " but I would fain have something more connected with the book that has brought me so much
good custom." He produced a well-thumbed copy,
and handing it to the author, begged he would at
least suggest a motto from the tale of Flodden Field.
Scott opened the book at the death scene of the hero,

and his eye was immediately caught by the " inscription" in black letter—

> " Drink, weary pilgrim, drink, and pray
> For the kind soul of Sibyl Grey," &c.

" Well, my friend," said he, " what more would you have? You need but strike out one letter in the first of these lines, and make your painter-man, the next time he comes this way, print between the jolly tankard and your own name—

> " Drink, weary pilgrim, drink and PAY."

Scott was delighted to find, on his return, that this suggestion had been adopted, and for aught I know, the romantic legend may still be visible.

The other story I shall give in the words of Mr Gillies. " It happened at a small country town that Scott suddenly required medical advice for one of his servants, and, on enquiring if there was any doctor at the place, was told that there was two—one long established, and the other a new comer. The latter gentleman, being luckily found at home, soon made his appearance ;—a grave, sagacious-looking personage, attired in black, with a shovel hat, in whom, to his utter astonishment, Sir Walter recognised a Scotch blacksmith, who had formerly practised, with tolerable success, as a veterinary operator in the neighbourhood of Ashestiel. — ' How, in all the world !' exclaimed he, ' can it be possible that this is John Lundie ?'—' In troth is it, your honour — just *a' that's for him.*'—' Well, but let us hear ; you were a *horse*-doctor before ; now, it seems, you are a *man*-doctor ; how do you get on ?'—' Ou, just extraordinar weel ; for your honour maun ken my practice is vera sure and orthodox. I depend entirely upon twa *simples.*'—' And what may their names be ? Perhaps it is a secret ?'—' I'll tell your honour,' in a low tone ; ' my twa simples are just *laudamy* and *calamy !*' — ' Simples with a vengeance !' replied Scott. ' But John, do you never happen to *kill* any of your patients ?'—' Kill ? Ou ay, may be sae ! Whiles they die, and whiles no ; but it's the will o' Providence. *Ony how, your honour, it wad be lang before it makes up for Flodden !*' " *

It was also in the course of this expedition that Scott first made acquaintance with the late excellent and venerable Shute Barrington, Bishop of Durham. The travellers having reached Auckland over night, were seeing the public rooms of the Castle at an early hour next morning, when the Bishop happened, in passing through one of them, to catch a glimpse of Scott's person, and immediately recognising him, from the likeness of the engravings by this time mul-

* Reminiscences of Sir Walter Scott, p. 56.

tiplied, introduced himself to the party, and insisted upon acting as cicerone. After showing them the picture-gallery and so forth, his Lordship invited them to join the morning service of the chapel, and when that was over, insisted on their remaining to breakfast. But Scott and his Lordship were by this time so much pleased with each other that they could not part so easily. The good Bishop ordered his horse, nor did Scott observe without admiration the proud curvetting of the animal on which his Lordship proposed to accompany him during the next stage of his progress. "Why, yes, Mr Scott," said the gentle but high-spirited old man, " I still like to feel my horse under me." He was then in his 79th year, and survived to the age of ninety-two, the model in all things of a real prince of the Church. They parted after a ride of ten miles, with mutual regret; and on all subsequent rides in that direction, Bishop-Auckland was one of the poet's regular halting places.

At Rokeby, on this occasion, Scott remained about a week; and I transcribe the following brief account of his proceedings while there from Mr Morritt's *Memorandum:* —" I had, of course," he says, " had many previous opportunities of testing the almost conscientious fidelity of his local descriptions; but I could not help being singularly struck with the lights which this visit threw on that characteristic of his

compositions.   The morning after he arrived he said,
' You have often given me materials for romance——
now I want a good robber's cave and an old church
of the right sort.'   We rode out, and he found what
he wanted in the ancient slate quarries of Brignal
and the ruined Abbey of Eggleston.   I observed him
noting down even the peculiar little wild flowers and
herbs that accidentally grew round and on the side
of a bold crag near his intended cave of Guy Denzil ;
and could not help saying, that as he was not to be
upon oath in his work, daisies, violets, and primroses
would be as poetical as any of the humble plants he
was examining.   I laughed, in short, at his scrupu-
lousness ; but I understood him when he replied,
' that in nature herself no two scenes were exactly
alike, and that whoever copied truly what was before
his eyes, would possess the same variety in his descriptions, and exhibit apparently an imagination as bound-
less as the range of nature in the scenes he recorded ;
whereas——whoever trusted to imagination, would soon
find his own mind circumscribed, and contracted to a
few favourite images, and the repetition of these would
sooner or later produce that very monotony and barrenness which had always haunted descriptive poetry
in the hands of any but the patient worshippers of
truth.   Besides which,' he said, ' local names and peculiarities make a fictitious story look so much better
in the face.'   In fact, from his boyish habits, he was

but half satisfied with the most beautiful scenery
when he could not connect with it some local legend,
and when I was forced sometimes to confess with the
Knife-grinder, ' Story! God bless you! I have none
to tell, sir'—he would laugh and say, ' then let us
make one — nothing so easy as to make a tradition.'" Mr Morritt adds, that he had brought with
him about half the bridal of Triermain — told him
that he meant to bring it out the same week with
Rokeby — and promised himself particular satisfaction in *laying a trap for Jeffrey;* who, however, as
we shall see, escaped the snare.

Some of the following letters will show with what
rapidity, after having refreshed and stored his memory
with the localities of Rokeby, he proceeded in the
composition of the romance :—

" *To J. B. S. Morritt, Esq.*

" Abbotsford, 12th October 1812.

" My Dear Morritt,

" I have this morning returned from Dalkeith
House, to which I was whisked amid the fury of an
election tempest, and I found your letter on my
table. More on such a subject cannot be said among
friends who give each other credit for feeling as they
ought.

" We preregrinated over Stanmore, and visited the

Castles of Bowes, Brough, Appleby, and Brougham
with great interest.   Lest our spirit of chivalry thus
excited should lack employment, we found ourselves,
that is, *I* did, at Carlisle, engaged in the service of
two distressed ladies, being no other than our friends
Lady Douglas and Lady Louisa Stuart, who over-
took us there, and who would have had great trouble
in finding quarters, the election being in full vigour,
if we had not anticipated their puzzle, and secured a
private house capable of holding us all.   Some distress occurred, I believe, among the waiting damsels,
whose case I had not so carefully considered, for I
heard a sentimental exclamation — ' Am I to sleep
with the greyhounds?' which I conceived to proceed
from Lady Douglas's *suivante,* from the exquisite
sensibility of tone with which it was uttered, especially as I beheld the fair one descend from the
carriage with three half-bound volumes of a novel
in her hand.   Not having in my power to alleviate
her woes, by offering her either a part or the whole
of my own couch — ' *Transeat,*' quoth I, ' *cum cæ-
teris erroribus.*'

   " I am delighted with your Cumberland admirer,*
and give him credit for his visit to the vindicator of

---

   * This alluded to a ridiculous hunter of lions, who being met
by Mr Morritt in the grounds at Rokeby, disclaimed all taste for
picturesque beauties, but overwhelmed their owner with Homeric
Greek ; of which he had told Scott.

Homer; but you missed one of another description, who passed Rokeby with great regret, I mean General John Malcolm, the Persian envoy, the Delhi resident, the poet, the warrior, the polite man, and the Borderer. He is really a fine fellow. I met him at Dalkeith, and we returned together; — he has just left me, after drinking his coffee. A fine time we had of it, talking of Troy town, and Babel, and Persepolis, and Delhi, and Langholm, and Burnfoot; * with all manner of episodes about Iskendiar, Rustan, and Johnnie Armstrong. Do you know, that poem of Ferdusi's must be beautiful. He read me some very splendid extracts which he had himself translated. Should you meet him in London, I have given him charge to be acquainted with you, for I am sure you will like each other. To be sure, I know him little, but I like his frankness and his sound ideas of morality and policy; and I have observed, that when I have had no great liking to persons at the beginning, it has usually pleased Heaven, as Slender says, to decrease it on further

---

* *Burnfoot* is the name of a farm-house on the Buccleuch estate, not far from Langholm, where the late Sir John Malcolm and his distinguished brothers were born. Their grandfather had, I believe, found refuge there after forfeiting a good estate and an ancient baronetcy in the *affair* of 1715. A monument to the gallant General's memory has recently been erected near the spot of his birth.

acquaintance. Adieu, I must mount my horse. Our
last journey was so delightful that we have every
temptation to repeat it. Pray give our kind love to
the lady, and believe me ever yours,

WALTER SCOTT."

" To the Same.

" Edinburgh, 29th November 1812.

" My Dear Morritt,

" I have been, and still am, working very hard,
in hopes to face the public by Christmas, and I think
I have hitherto succeeded in throwing some interest
into the piece. It is, however, a darker and more
gloomy interest than I intended ; but involving one's
self with bad company, whether in fiction or in reality, is the way not to get out of it easily ; so I
have been obliged to bestow more pains and trouble
upon Bertram, and one or two blackguards whom he
picks up in the slate quarries, than what I originally
designed. I am very desirous to have your opinion
of the three first Cantos, for which purpose, so soon
as I can get them collected, I will send the sheets
under cover to Mr Freeling, whose omnipotent frank
will transmit them to Rokeby, where, I presume,
you have been long since comfortably settled—

' So York may overlook the town of York.'
3d King Henry VI. Act I. Scene 4.

" I trust you will read it with some partiality,
because, if I have not been so successful as I could
wish in describing your lovely and romantic glens,
it has partly arisen from my great anxiety to do it
well, which is often attended with the very contrary
effect. There are two or three songs, and particularly one in praise of Brignal Banks, which I trust
you will like—because, *entre nous,* I like them myself. One of them is a little dashing banditti song,
called and entitled Allen-a-Dale. I think you will be
able to judge for yourself in about a week. Pray,
how shall I send you the *entire goose,* which will be
too heavy to travel the same way with its *giblets* —
for the Carlisle coach is terribly inaccurate about
parcels? I fear I have made one blunder in mentioning the brooks which flow into the Tees. I have
made the Balder distinct from that which comes
down Thorsgill—I hope I am not mistaken. You
will see the passage; and if they are the same rivu-
let, the leaf must be cancelled.

" I trust this will find Mrs Morritt pretty well;
and I am glad to find she has been better for her
little tour. We were delighted with ours, except
in respect of its short duration, and Sophia and
Walter hold their heads very high among their
untravelled companions, from the predominance acquired by their visit to England. You are not
perhaps aware of the polish which is supposed to

be acquired by the most transitory intercourse with your more refined side of the Tweed. There was an honest carter who once applied to me respecting a plan which he had formed of breeding his son, a great booby of twenty, to the Church. As the best way of evading the scrape, I asked him whether he thought his son's language was quite adapted for the use of a public speaker? to which he answered, with great readiness, that he could knap English with any one, having twice driven his father's cart to Etal coal-hill.

" I have called my heroine Matilda. I don't much like Agnes, though I can't tell why, unless it is because it begins like Agag. Matilda is a name of unmanageable length; but, after all, is better than none, and my poor damsel was likely to go without one in my indecision.

" We are all hungering and thirsting for news from Russia. If Boney's devil does not help him. he is in a poor way. The Leith letters talk of the unanimity of the Russians as being most exemplary; and troops pour in from all quarters of their immense empire. Their commissariat is well managed under the Prince Duke of Oldenburgh. This was their weak point in former wars.

" Adieu! Mrs Scott and the little people send love to Mrs Morritt and you. Ever yours,
WALTER SCOTT."

" *To the Same.*

" Edinburgh, Thursday,
10th December 1812.

" My Dear Morritt,

" I have just time to say that I have received your letters, and am delighted that Rokeby pleases the owner. As I hope the whole will be printed off before Christmas, it will scarce be worth while to send you the other sheets till it reaches you altogether. Your criticisms are the best proof of your kind attention to the poem. I need not say I will pay them every attention in the next edition. But some of the faults are so interwoven with the story, that they must stand. Denzil, for instance, is essential to me, though, as you say, not very interesting; and I assure you that, generally speaking, the *poeta loquitur* has a bad effect in narrative; and when you have twenty things to tell, it is better to be slatternly than tedious. The fact is, that the tediousness of many really good poems arises from an attempt to support the same tone throughout, which often occasions periphrasis, and always stiffness. I am quite sensible that I have often carried the opposite custom too far; but I am apt to impute it partly to not being able to bring out my own ideas well, and partly to haste — not to error in

the system. This would, however, lead to a long
discussion, more fit for the fireside than for a letter.
I need not say that, the poem being in fact your
own, you are at perfect liberty to dispose of the
sheets as you please. I am glad my geography is
pretty correct. It is too late to inquire if Rokeby
is insured, for I have burned it down in Canto V. ;
but I suspect you will bear me no greater grudge
than at the noble Russian who burned Moscow.
Glorious news to-day from the north — *pereat iste!*
Mrs Scott, Sophia, and Walter, join in best compliments to Mrs Morritt ; and I am, in great haste,
ever faithfully yours,   WALTER SCOTT.

"P. S. — I have heard of Lady Hood by a letter
from herself. She is well, and in high spirits, and
sends me a pretty topaz seal, with a talisman which
secures this letter, and signifies (it seems), which one
would scarce have expected from its appearance, my
name."

We are now close upon the end of this busy
twelvemonth ; but I must not turn the leaf to 1813,
without noticing one of its miscellaneous incidents —
his first intercourse by letter with the poet Crabbe.
Mr Hatchard, the publisher of his " Tales," forwarded a copy of the book to Scott as soon as it was
ready ; and, the bookseller having communicated to

his author some flattering expressions in Scott's letter of acknowledgment, Mr Crabbe addressed him as follows : —

" *To Walter Scott, Esq., Edinburgh.*

"Merston, Grantham, 13th October 1812.

" Sir,

" Mr Hatchard, judging rightly of the satisfaction it would afford me, has been so obliging as to communicate your two letters, in one of which you desire my ' Tales' to be sent; in the other, you acknowledge the receipt of them; and in both you mention my verses in such terms, that it would be affected in me were I to deny, and I think unjust if I were to conceal, the pleasure you give me.   I am indeed highly gratified.

" I have long entertained a hearty wish to be made known to a poet whose works are so greatly and so universally admired; and I continued to hope that I might at some time find a common friend, by whose intervention I might obtain that honour; but I am confined by duties near my home, and by sickness in it.   It may be long before I be in town, and then no such opportunity might offer.   Excuse me, then, sir, if I gladly seize this which now occurs to express my thanks for the politeness of your expres-

sions, as well as my desire of being known to a gentleman who had delighted and affected me, and moved
all the passions and feelings in turn, I believe —
Envy surely excepted—certainly, if I know myself,
but in a moderate degree. I truly rejoice in your
success; and while I am entertaining in my way, a
certain set of readers, for the most part, probably, of
peculiar turn and habit, I can with pleasure see the
effect you produce on all. Mr Hatchard tells me
that he hopes or expects that thousands will read my
‘ Tales,’ and I am convinced that your publisher
might, in like manner, so speak of your ten thousands ;
but this, though it calls to mind the passage, is no
true comparison with the related prowess of David
and Saul, because I have no evil spirit to arise and
trouble me on the occasion ; though, if I had, I know
no David whose skill is so likely to allay it.   Once
more, sir, accept my best thanks, with my hearty
wishes for your health and happiness, who am, with
great esteem, and true respect,

Dear Sir, your obedient servant,

GEORGE CRABBE.”

I cannot produce Scott’s reply to this communication. Mr Crabbe appears to have, in the course of
the year, sent him a copy of all his works, “ ex dono
auctoris,” and there passed between them several
letters, one or two of which I must quote.

" *To Walter Scott, Esq., Edinburgh.*

" Know you, sir, a gentleman in Edinburgh, A. Brunton (the Rev.) who dates St John Street, and who asks my assistance in furnishing hymns which have relation to the Old or New Testament — anything which might suit the purpose of those who are cooking up a book of Scotch Psalmody? Who is Mr Brunton? What is his situation? If I could help one who needed help I would do it cheerfully — but have no great opinion of this undertaking. . . . . . .,

" With every good wish, yours sincerely,

GEO. CRABBE."

Scott's answer to this letter expresses the opinions he always held in conversation on the important subject to which it refers; and acting upon which, he himself at various times declined taking any part in the business advocated by Dr Brunton :—

" *To the Rev. George Crabbe, Muston, Grantham.*

" My Dear Sir,

" I was favoured with your kind letter some time ago. Of all people in the world, I am least entitled to demand regularity of correspondence; for

being, one way and another, doomed to a great deal
more writing than suits my indolence, I am sometimes tempted to envy the reverend hermit of Prague,
confessor to the niece of Queen Gorboduc, who
never saw either pen or ink. Mr Brunton is a very
respectable clergyman of Edinburgh, and I believe
the work in which he has solicited your assistance is
one adopted by the General Assembly, or Convoca-
tion of the Kirk. I have no notion that he has any
individual interest in it; he is a well-educated and
liberal-minded man, and generally esteemed. I have
no particular acquaintance with him myself, though
we speak together. He is at this very moment sitting on the outside of the bar of our Supreme Court,
within which I am fagging as a clerk; but as he is
hearing the opinion of the judges upon an action for
augmentation of stipend to him and to his brethren,
it would not, I conceive, be a very favourable time
to canvass a literary topic. But you are quite safe
with him; and having so much command of scriptural language, which appears to me essential to the
devotional poetry of Christians, I am sure you can
assist his purpose much more than any man alive.

" I think those hymns which do not immediately
recall the warm and exalted language of the Bible
are apt to be, however elegant, rather cold and flat
for the purposes of devotion. You will readily believe
that I do not approve of the vague and indiscriminate

Scripture language which the fanatics of old, and the modern Methodists, have adopted, but merely that solemnity and peculiarity of diction, which at once puts the reader and hearer upon his guard as to the purpose of the poetry. To my Gothic ear, indeed, the *Stabat Mater*, the *Dies Iræ*, and some of the other hymns of the Catholic Church, are more solemn and affecting than the fine classical poetry of Buchanan; the one has the gloomy dignity of a Gothic church, and reminds us instantly of the worship to which it is dedicated; the other is more like a Pagan temple, recalling to our memory the classical and fabulous deities.* This is, probably, all referable to the association of ideas — that is, if the ' association of ideas' continues to be the universal pick-lock of all metaphysical difficulties, as it was when I studied moral philosophy — or to any other more fashionable universal solvent which may have succeeded to it in reputation. Adieu, my dear sir,— I hope you and your family will long enjoy all happiness and prosperity. Never be discouraged from the constant use of your charming talent. The opinions of reviewers are really too contradictory to found anything upon them, whether they are favourable or otherwise; for it is usually their principal object to display the abilities of the writers of the critical lu-

* See Life of Dryden, Scott's Miscellaneous Prose Works, vol. i. p. 293.

cubrations themselves. Your ' Tales' are universally admired here. I go but little out, but the few judges whose opinions I have been accustomed to look up to, are unanimous. Ever yours, most truly,

WALTER SCOTT."

" *To Walter Scott, Esq., Edinburgh.*

" My Dear Sir,

" Law, then, is your profession — I mean a profession you give your mind and time to — but how ' fag as a *clerk ?*' Clerk is a name for a learned person, I know, in our Church; but how the same hand which held the pen of Marmion, holds that with which a clerk fags, unless a clerk means something vastly more than I understand — is not to be comprehended. I wait for elucidation. Know you, dear sir, I have often thought I should love to read *reports* — that is, brief histories of extraordinary cases, with the judgments. If that is what is meant by *reports*, such reading must be pleasant; but, probably, I entertain wrong ideas, and could not understand the books I think so engaging. Yet I conclude there are *histories of cases*, and have often thought of consulting Hatchard whether he knew of such kind of reading, but hitherto I have rested in ignorance. . . . . Yours truly,

GEORGE CRABBE."

" To the Rev. George Crabbe.

" My Dear Sir,

" I have too long delayed to thank you for the most kind and acceptable present of your three volumes. Now am I doubly armed, since I have a set for my cabin at Abbotsford as well as in town; and, to say truth, the auxiliary copy arrived in good time, for my original one suffers as much by its general popularity among my young people, as a popular candidate from the hugs and embraces of his democratical admirers. The clearness and accuracy of your painting, whether natural or moral, renders, I have often remarked, your works generally delightful to those whose youth might render them insensible to the other beauties with which they abound. There are a sort of pictures—surely the most valuable, were it but for that reason—which strike the uninitiated as much as they do the connoisseur, though the last alone can render reason for his admiration. Indeed our old friend Horace knew what he was saying when he chose to address his ode, ' *Virginibus puerisque,*' and so did Pope when he told somebody he had the mob on the side of his version of Homer, and did not mind the high-flying critics at Button's. After all, if a faultless poem could be produced, I am satisfied it would tire the critics themselves, and annoy the whole reading world with the spleen.

" You must be delightfully situated in the Vale of Belvoir—a part of England for which I entertain a special kindness, for the sake of the gallant hero, Robin Hood, who, as probably you will readily guess, is no small favourite of mine; his indistinct ideas concerning the doctrine of *meum* and *tuum* being no great objection to an outriding Borderer. I am happy to think that your station is under the protection of the Rutland family, of whom fame speaks highly. Our lord of the ' cairn and the scaur,' waste wilderness and hungry hills, for many a league around, is the Duke of Buccleuch, the head of my clan ; a kind and benevolent landlord, a warm and zealous friend, and the husband of a lady—*comme il y en a peu.* They are both great admirers of Mr Crabbe's poetry, and would be happy to know him, should he ever come to Scotland, and venture into the Gothic halls of a Border chief. The early and uniform kindness of this family, with the friendship of the late and present Lord Melville, enabled me, some years ago, to exchange my toils as a barrister, for the lucrative and respectable situation of one of the Clerks of our Supreme Court, which only requires a certain routine of official duty, neither laborious nor calling for any exertion of the mind ; so that my time is entirely at my own command, except when I am attending the Court, which seldom occupies more than two hours of the morning during sitting. I besides hold *in commendam* the Sheriff-dom of Ettrick Forest, which is now no forest; so that I am a pluralist as to law appointments, and have, as Dogberry says, ' two gowns and every thing handsome about me.' *

" I have often thought it is the most fortunate thing for bards like you and me to have an established profession, and professional character, to render us independent of those worthy gentlemen, the retailers, or, as some have called them, the midwives of literature, who are so much taken up with the abortions they bring into the world, that they are scarcely able to bestow the proper care upon young and flourishing babes like ours. That, however, is only a mercantile way of looking at the matter; but did any of my sons show poetical talent, of which, to my great satisfaction, there are no appearances, the first thing I should do would be to inculcate upon him the duty of cultivating some honourable profession, and qualifying himself to play a more respectable part in society than the mere poet. And as the best corollary of my doctrine, I would make him get your tale of ' The Patron' by heart from beginning to end. It is curious enough that you should have republished the ' Village' for the purpose

* *Much ado about Nothing, Act IV. Scene 2.*

of sending your young men to college, and I should
have written the Lay of the Last Minstrel for the
purpose of buying a new horse for the Volunteer
Cavalry. I must now send this scrawl into town
to get a frank, for, God knows, it is not worthy of
postage. With the warmest wishes for your health,
prosperity, and increase of fame—though it needs
not — I remain most sincerely and affectionately
yours,   WALTER SCOTT."*

The contrast of the two poets' epistolary styles is
highly amusing; but I have introduced these specimens less on that account, than as marking the
cordial confidence which a very little intercourse
was sufficient to establish between men so different
from each other in most of the habits of life. It
will always be considered as one of the most pleasing peculiarities in Scott's history, that he was the
friend of every great contemporary poet: Crabbe,
as we shall see more largely in the sequel, was no
exception to the rule: yet I could hardly name
one of them who, manly principles and the cultivation of literature apart, had many points of resemblance to him; and surely not one who had fewer
than Crabbe.

* Several of these letters having been enclosed in franked
covers, which have perished, I am unable to affix the exact dates
to them.

Scott continued, this year, his care for the Edinburgh Annual Register—the historical department of which was again supplied by Mr Southey.   The poetical miscellany owed its opening piece, the Ballad of Polydore, to the readiness with which Scott entered into correspondence with its author, who sent it to him anonymously, with a letter which, like the verses, might well have excited much interest in his mind, even had it not concluded with stating the writer's age to be *fifteen*.   Scott invited the youth to visit him in the country, was greatly pleased with the modesty of his manners and the originality of his conversation, and wrote to Joanna Baillie, that, " though not one of the crimps for the muses," he thought he could hardly be mistaken in believing that in the boyish author of Polydore he had discovered a true genius.   When I mention the name of my friend William Howison of Clydegrove, it will be allowed that he prognosticated wisely.   He continued to correspond with this young gentleman and his father, and gave both much advice, for which both were most grateful.   There was inserted in the same volume a set of beautiful stanzas, inscribed to Scott by Mr Wilson, under the title of the " Magic Mirror," in which that enthusiastic young poet also bears a lofty and lasting testimony to the gentle kindness with which his earlier efforts had been encouraged by him whom he designates, for the first

time, by what afterwards became one of his standing
titles, that of " The Great Magician."

" Onwards a figure came, with stately brow,
    And, as he glanced upon the ruin'd pile
A look of regal pride, ' Say, who art thou
    (His countenance bright'ning with a scornful smile,
He sternly cried), ' whose footsteps rash profane
The wild romantic realm where I have willed to reign ?'

" But ere to these proud words I could reply,
    How changed that scornful face to soft and mild !
A witching frenzy glitter'd in his eye,
    Harmless, withal, as that of playful child.
And when once more the gracious vision spoke,
    I felt the voice familiar to mine ear ;
While many a faded dream of earth awoke,
    Connected strangely with that unknown seer,
Who now stretch'd forth his arm, and on the sand
A circle round me traced, as with magician's wand," &c. &c.

Scott's own chief contribution to this volume was
a brief account of the Life and Poems (hitherto un-
published)* of Patrick Carey, whom he pronounces
to have been not only as stout a cavalier, but almost
as good a poet as his contemporary Lovelace.   That

* The Rev. Alexander Dyce informs me, that *nine* of Carey's
pieces were printed in 1771, for J. Murray of Fleet Street, in a
quarto of thirty-five pages, entitled " Poems from a MS. written
in the time of Oliver Cromwell." This rare tract had never fallen
into Scott's hands. [1839.]

Essay was expanded, and prefixed to an edition of
Carey's " Trivial Poems and Triolets," which Scott
published in 1820; but its circulation in either shape
has been limited: and I believe I shall be gratifying
the majority of my readers by here transcribing some
paragraphs of his beautiful and highly characteristic
introduction of this forgotten poet of the 17th century.

" The present age has been so distinguished for research into
poetical antiquities, that the discovery of an unknown bard is, in
certain chosen literary circles, held as curious as an augmentation
of the number of fixed stars would be esteemed by astronomers.
It is true, these ' blessed twinklers of the night' are so far removed from us, that they afford no more light than serves barely
to evince their existence to the curious investigator ; and in like
manner the pleasure derived from the revival of an obscure poet
is rather in proportion to the rarity of his volume than to its merit ; yet this pleasure is not inconsistent with reason and principle.
We know by every day's experience the peculiar interest which
the lapse of ages confers upon works of human art.   The clumsy
strength of the ancient castles, which, when raw from the hand
of the builder, inferred only the oppressive power of the barons
who reared them, is now broken by partial ruin into proper subjects for the poet or the painter ; and as Mason has beautifully
described the change,

————' Time
Has mouldered into beauty many a tower,
Which, when it frowned with all its battlements,
Was only terrible '———

" The monastery, too, which was at first but a fantastic monument of the superstitious devotion of monarchs, or of the purple
pride of fattened abbots, has gained by the silent influence of an-

tiquity, the power of impressing awe and devotion. Even the
stains and weather-taints upon the battlements of such buildings
add, like the scars of a veteran, to the affecting impression:

> ' For time has softened what was harsh when new,
> And now the stains are all of sober hue;
> The living stains which nature's hand alone,
> Profuse of life, pours forth upon the stone.'—*Crabbe.*

" If such is the effect of Time in adding interest to the labours
of the architect, if partial destruction is compensated by the additional interest of that which remains, can we deny his exerting a
similar influence upon those subjects which are sought after by
the bibliographer and poetical antiquary? The obscure poet,
who is detected by their keen research, may indeed have possessed
but a slender portion of that spirit which has buoyed up the works
of distinguished contemporaries during the course of centuries,
yet still his verses shall, in the lapse of time, acquire an interest,
which they did not possess in the eyes of his own generation.
The wrath of the critic, like that of the son of Ossian, flies from
the foe that is low. Envy, base as she is, has one property of
the lion, and cannot prey on carcases; she must drink the blood
of a sentient victim, and tear the limbs that are yet warm with
vital life. Faction, if the ancient has suffered her persecution,
serves only to endear him to the recollection of posterity, whose
generous compassion overpays him for the injuries he sustained
while in life. And thus freed from the operation of all unfavourable prepossessions, his merit, if he can boast any, has more than
fair credit with his readers. This, however, is but part of his
advantages. The mere attribute of antiquity is of itself sufficient
to interest the fancy, by the lively and powerful train of associations which it awakens. Had the pyramids of Egypt, equally
disagreeable in form and senseless as to utility, been the work of
any living tyrant, with what feelings, save those of scorn and de-
rision, could we have regarded such a waste of labour? But the
sight, nay the very mention of these wonderful monuments, is

associ.ted with the dark and sublime ideas which vary their tinge according to the favourite hue of our studies. The Christian divine recollects the land of banishment and of refuge; to the eyes of the historian's fancy, they excite the shades of Pharaohs and of Ptolemies, of Cheops and Merops, and Sesostris drawn in triumph by his sceptred slaves; the philosopher beholds the first rays of moral truth as they dawned on the hieroglyphic sculptures of Thebes and Memphis; and the poet sees the fires of magic blazing upon the mystic altars of a land of incantation. Nor is the grandeur of size essential to such feelings, any more than the properties of grace and utility. Even the rudest remnant of a feudal tower, even the obscure and almost indistinguishable vestige of an altogether unknown edifice, has power to awaken such trains of fancy. We have a fellow interest with the ' son of the winged days,' over whose fallen habitation we tread:

> ' The massy stones, though hewn most roughly, show
> The hand of man had once at least been there.'— *Wordsworth.*

" Similar combinations give a great part of the delight we receive from ancient poetry. In the rude song of the Scald, we regard less the strained imagery and extravagance of epithet, than the wild impressions which it conveys of the dauntless resolution, savage superstition, rude festivity, and ceaseless depredation of the ancient Scandinavians. In the metrical romance, we pardon the long, tedious, and bald enumeration of trifling particulars; the reiterated sameness of the eternal combats between knights and giants; the overpowering languor of the love speeches, and the merciless length and similarity of description — when Fancy whispers to us, that such strains may have cheered the sleepless pillow of the Black Prince on the memorable eves of Cressy or Poictiers. There is a certain romance of Ferumbras, which Robert the Bruce read to his few followers to divert their thoughts from the desperate circumstances in which they were placed, after an unsuccessful attempt to rise against the English. Is there a true

Scotsman who, being aware of this anecdote, would be disposed to yawn over the romance of Ferumbras? Or, on the contrary, would not the image of the dauntless hero, inflexible in defeat, beguiling the anxiety of his war-worn attendants by the lays of the minstrel, give to these rude lays themselves an interest beyond Greek and Roman fame?"

The year 1812 had the usual share of minor literary labours—such as contributions to the journals; and before it closed, the Romance of Rokeby was finished. Though it had been long in hand, the MS. sent to the printer bears abundant evidence of its being the *prima cura:* three cantos at least reached Ballantyne through the Melrose post — written on paper of various sorts and sizes — full of blots and interlineations — the closing couplets of a despatch now and then encircling the page, and mutilated by the breaking of the seal.

According to the recollection of Mr Cadell, though James Ballantyne read the poem, as the sheets were advancing through the press, to his usual circle of literary *dilettanti,* their whispers were far from exciting in Edinburgh such an intensity of expectation as had been witnessed in the case of The Lady of the Lake. He adds, however, that it was looked for with undiminished anxiety in the south. " Send me *Rokeby,*" Byron writes to Murray on seeing it advertised, — " Who the devil is he? No matter—

he has good connexions, and will be well introduced." *   Such, I suppose, was the general feeling
in London. I well remember, being in those days a
young student at Oxford, how the booksellers' shops
there were beleaguered for the earliest copies, and
how he that had been so fortunate as to secure one,
was followed to his chambers by a tribe of friends,
all as eager to hear it read as ever horse-jockeys
were to see the conclusion of a match at Newmar-
ket; and indeed not a few of those enthusiastic
academics had bets depending on the issue of the
struggle, which they considered the elder favourite
as making, to keep his own ground against the fiery
rivalry of Childe Harold.

The poem was published a day or two before Scott
returned to Edinburgh from Abbotsford, between
which place and Mertoun he had divided his Christmas vacation. On the 9th and 10th of January
1813, he thus addresses his friends at Sunninghill
and Hampstead : —

" *To George Ellis, Esq.*

" My Dear Ellis,
    " I am sure you will place it to anything rather
than want of kindness that I have been so long silent
—so very long, indeed, that I am not quite sure

* Byron's Life and Works, vol. ii. p. 169.

whether the fault is on my side or yours — but, be it what it may, it can never, I am sure, be laid to forgetfulness in either. This comes to train you on to the merciful reception of a Tale of the Civil Wars; not political, however, but merely a pseudo-romance of pseudo-chivalry. I have converted a lusty buccanier into a hero with some effect; but the worst of all my undertakings is, that my rogue always, in despite of me, turns out my hero. I know not how this should be — I am myself, as Hamlet says, ' indifferent honest;' and my father, though an attorney (as you will call him), was one of the most honest men, as well as gentlemanlike, that ever breathed. I am sure I can bear witness to that — for if he had at all *smacked*, or *grown to*, like the son of Lancelot Gobbo, he might have left us all as rich as Crœsus, besides having the pleasure of taking a fine primrose path himself, instead of squeezing himself through a tight gate and up a steep ascent, and leaving us the decent competence of an honest man's children. As to our more ancient pedigree, I should be loath to vouch for them. My grandfather was a horse-jockey and cattle-dealer, and made a fortune; my great-grandfather a Jacobite and traitor (as the times called him), and lost one; and after him intervened one or two half-starved lairds, who rode a lean horse, and were followed by leaner greyhounds; gathered with difficulty a hundred pounds from a

hundred tenants; fought duels; cocked their hats,
—and called themselves gentlemen.   Then we come
to the old Border times, cattle-driving, halters, and
so forth, for which, in the matter of honesty, very
little I suppose can be said—at least in modern ac-
ceptation of the word.   Upon the whole, I am inclined to think it is owing to the earlier part of this
inauspicious generation that I uniformly find myself
in the same scrape in my fables, and that, in spite of
the most obstinate determination to the contrary, the
greatest rogue in my canvass always stands out as
the most conspicuous and prominent figure.   All
this will be a riddle to you, unless you have received
a certain packet, which the Ballantynes were to have
sent under Freeling's or Croker's cover, so soon as
they could get a copy done up.

"And now let me gratulate you upon the reno-
vated vigour of your fine old friends the Russians.
By the Lord, sir! it is most famous this campaign
of theirs.   I was not one of the very sanguine persons who anticipated the actual capture of Buonaparte — a hope which rather proceeded from the
ignorance of those who cannot conceive that military
movements, upon a large scale, admit of such a force
being accumulated upon any particular point as may,
by abandonment of other considerations, always ensure the escape of an individual.   But I had no
hope, in my time, of seeing the dry bones of the

Continent so warm with life again, as this revivification of the Russians proves them to be. I look
anxiously for the effect of these great events on
Prussia, and even upon Saxony; for I think Boney
will hardly trust himself again in Germany, now
that he has been plainly shown, both in Spain and
Russia, that protracted stubborn unaccommodating
resistance will foil those grand exertions in the long-
run. All laud be to Lord Wellington, who first
taught that great lesson.

" Charlotte is with me just now at this little
scrub habitation, where we weary ourselves all day
in looking at our projected improvements, and then
slumber over the fire, I pretending to read, and she
to work trout-nets, or cabbage-nets, or some such
article. What is Canning about? Is there any
chance of our getting him in? Surely Ministers cannot hope to do without him. Believe me, Dear
Ellis, ever truly yours,   W. SCOTT.

" Abbotsford, 9th January 1813."

" *To Miss Joanna Baillie.*

" Abbotsford, January 10, 1813.

" Your kind encouragement, my dear friend, has
given me spirits to complete the lumbering quarto,
which I hope has reached you by this time. I have

gone on with my story *forth right,* without troubling myself excessively about the development of the plot and other critical matters—

> ' But shall we go mourn for that, my dear?
> The pale moon shines by night;
> And when we wander here and there,
> We then do go most right.'

I hope you will like Bertram to the end; he is a Caravaggio sketch, which, I may acknowledge to you — but tell it not in Gath — I rather pique myself upon; and he is within the keeping of Nature, though critics will say to the contrary. It may be difficult to fancy that any one should take a sort of pleasure in bringing out such a character, but I suppose it is partly owing to bad reading, and ill-directed reading, when I was young. No sooner had I corrected the last sheet of Rokeby, than I escaped to this Patmos as blythe as bird on tree, and have been ever since most decidedly idle—that is to say, with busy idleness. I have been banking, and securing, and dyking against the river, and planting willows, and aspens, and weeping birches, around my new old well, which I think I told you I had constructed last summer. I have now laid the foundations of a famous back-ground of copse, with pendant trees in front; and I have only to beg a few years to see how my colours will come out of the canvass. Alas! who can promise that ?   But somebody will take my place —and enjoy them, whether I do or no.   My old friend and pastor, Principal Robertson (the historian), when he was not expected to survive many weeks, still watched the setting of the blossom upon some fruit trees in the garden with as much interest as if it was possible he could have seen the fruit come to maturity, and moralized on his own conduct, by observing that we act upon the same inconsistent motive throughout life.   It is well we do so for those that are to come after us.   I could almost dislike the man who refuses to plant walnut-trees, because they do not bear fruit till the second generation ; and so —many thanks to our ancestors, and much joy to our successors, and truce to my fine and very new strain of morality.   Yours ever,   W. S."

The following letter lets us completely behind the scenes at the publication of Rokeby.   The "horrid story" it alludes to was that of a young woman found murdered on New Year's Day in the highway between Greta Bridge and Barnard Castle — a crime, the perpetrator of which was never discovered.   The account of a parallel atrocity in Galloway, and the mode of its detection, will show the reader from what source Scott drew one of the most striking incidents in his Guy Mannering : —

" *To J. B. S. Morritt, Esq., Rokeby Park.*

" Edinburgh, 12th January 1813.

" Dear Morritt,

" Yours I have just received in mine office at the Register-House, which will excuse this queer sheet of paper. The publication of Rokeby was delayed till Monday, to give the London publishers a fair start. My copies, that is, my friends', were all to be got off about Friday or Saturday; but yours may have been a little later, as it was to be what they call a picked one. I will call at Ballantyne's as I return from this place, and close the letter with such news as I can get about it there. The book has gone off here very bobbishly; for the impression of 3000 and upwards is within two or three score of being exhausted, and the demand for these continuing faster than they can be boarded. I am heartly glad of this, for now I have nothing to fear but a bankruptcy in the Gazette of Parnassus; but the loss of five or six thousand pounds to my good friends and school-companions would have afflicted me very much. I wish we could whistle you here to-day. Ballantyne always gives a christening dinner, at which the Duke of Buccleuch, and a great many of my friends, are formally feasted. He has always the best singing that can be heard in Edinburgh, and we have usually

a very pleasant party, at which your health as patron
and proprietor of Rokeby will be faithfully and
honourably remembered.

" Your horrid story reminds me of one in Galloway, where the perpetrator of a similar enormity on
a poor idiot girl, was discovered by means of the
print of his foot which he left upon the clay floor
of the cottage in the death-struggle. It pleased
Heaven (for nothing short of a miracle could have
done it) to enlighten the understanding of an old
ram-headed sheriff, who was usually nick-named
Leather-head. The steps which he took to discover the murderer were most sagacious. As the
poor girl was pregnant (for it was not a case of
violation), it was pretty clear that her paramour
had done the deed, and equally so that he must be
a native of the district. The sheriff caused the
minister to advertise from the pulpit that the girl
would be buried on a particular day, and that all
persons in the neighbourhood were invited to attend
the funeral, to show their detestation of such an
enormous crime, as well as to evince their own in-
nocence. This was sure to bring the murderer to
the funeral. When the people were assembled in
the kirk, the doors were locked by the sheriff's
order, and the shoes of all the men were examined;
that of the murderer was detected by the measure
of the foot, tread, &c., and a peculiarity in the mode

in which the sole of one of them had been patched. The remainder of the curious chain of evidence upon which he was convicted will suit best with twilight, or a blinking candle, being too long for a letter. The fellow bore a most excellent character, and had committed this crime for no other reason that could be alleged, than that, having been led accidentally into an intrigue with this poor wretch, his pride revolted at the ridicule which was likely to attend the discovery.

" On calling at Ballantyne's, I find, as I had anticipated, that your copy, being of royal size, requires some particular nicety in hot-pressing. It will be sent by the Carlisle mail *quam primum.* Ever yours, WALTER SCOTT.

" P. S.—Love to Mrs Morritt. John Ballantyne says he has just about eighty copies left, out of 3250, this being the second day of publication, and the book a two-guinea one."

It will surprise no one to hear that Mr Morritt assured his friend he considered Rokeby as the best of all his poems. The admirable, perhaps the unique fidelity of the local descriptions, might alone have swayed, for I will not say it perverted, the judgment of the lord of that beautiful and thenceforth classical domain; and, indeed, I must admit that I never

understood or appreciated half the charm of this
poem until I had become familiar with its scenery.
But Scott himself had not designed to rest his
strength on these descriptions. He said to James
Ballantyne while the work was in progress (September 2), " I hope the thing will do, chiefly because
the world will not expect from *me* a poem of which
the interest turns upon *character;*" and in another
letter (October 28, 1812), " I think you will see
the same sort of difference taken in all my former
poems, — of which I would say, if it is fair for me
to say anything, that the force in the Lay is thrown
on style — in Marmion, on description — and in the
Lady of the Lake, on incident."* I suspect some
of these distinctions may have been matters of after-
thought; but as to Rokeby there can be no mistake.
His own original conceptions of some of its principal characters have been explained in letters already cited; and I believe no one who compares
the poem with his novels will doubt that, had he
undertaken their portraiture in prose, they would

---

* Several letters to Ballantyne on the same subject are quoted
in the notes to the last edition of Rokeby. See Scott's Poetical
Works, 1834, vol. ix. pp. 1–3; and especially the note on p. 300.
from which it appears that the closing stanza was added, in deference to Ballantyne and Erskine, though the author retained
his own opinion that " it spoiled one effect without producing
another."

have come forth with effect hardly inferior to any
of all the groupes he ever created   As it is, I question whether even in his prose there is anything
more exquisitely wrought out, as well as fancied,
than the whole contrast of the two rivals for the
love of the heroine in Rokeby; and that heroine
herself, too, has a very particular interest attached
to her.   Writing to Miss Edgeworth five years after this time (10th March 1818), he says, " I have
not read one of my poems since they were printed,
excepting last year the Lady of the Lake, which I
liked better than I expected, but not well enough
to induce me to go through the rest — so I may truly
say with Macbeth —

> ' I am afraid to think of what I've done —
> Look on't again I dare not.'

" This much of *Matilda* I recollect — (for that is
not so easily forgotten) — that she was attempted
for the existing person of a lady who is now no
more, so that I am particularly flattered with your
distinguishing it from the others, which are in general
mere shadows."   I can have no doubt that the lady
he here alludes to, was the object of his own unfortunate first love ; and as little, that in the romantic
generosity, both of the youthful poet who fails to
win her higher favour, and of his chivalrous com-

petitor, we have before us something more than " a
mere shadow."

In spite of these graceful characters, the inimitable scenery on which they are presented, and the
splendid vivacity and thrilling interest of several
chapters in the story—such as the opening inter-
view of Bertram and Wycliff—the flight up the
cliff on the Greta—the first entrance of the cave
at Brignall—the firing of Rokeby Castle—and the
catastrophe in Eglistone Abbey;—in spite certainly
of exquisitely happy lines profusely scattered throughout the whole composition, and of some detached
images—that of the setting of the tropical sun,*
for example—which were never surpassed by any
poet; in spite of all these merits, the immediate
success of Rokeby was greatly inferior to that of
the Lady of the Lake; nor has it ever since been

---

* " My noontide, India may declare;
    Like her fierce sun, I fired the air!
    Like him, to wood and cave bid fly
    Her natives, from mine angry eye.
    And now, my race of terror run,
    Mine be the eve of tropic sun!
    No pale gradations quench his ray,
    No twilight dews his wrath allay;
    With disk like battle-target red,
    He rushes to his burning bed.
    Dyes the wide wave with bloody light,
    Then sinks at once—and all is night."—*Canto* vi. 21.

so much a favourite with the public at large as any
other of his poetical romances. He ascribes this
failure, in his introduction of 1830, partly to the
radically unpoetical character of the Round-heads;
but surely their character has its poetical side also,
had his prejudices allowed him to enter upon its
study with impartial sympathy; and I doubt not,
Mr Morritt suggested the difficulty on this score,
when the outline of the story was as yet undeter-
mined, from consideration rather of the poet's peculiar feelings, and powers as hitherto exhibited, than
of the subject absolutely. Partly he blames the sa-
tiety of the public ear, which had had so much of
his rhythm, not only from himself, but from dozens
of mocking birds, male and female, all more or
less applauded in their day, and now all equally forgotten.* This circumstance, too, had probably no
slender effect; the more that, in defiance of all the
hints of his friends, he now, in his narrative, repeated (with more negligence) the uniform octo-

---

* " Scott found peculiar favour and imitation among the fair
sex. There was Miss Holford, and Miss Mitford, and Miss
Francis; but, with the greatest respect be it spoken, none of his
imitators did much honour to the original except Hogg, the Ettrick Shepherd, until the appearance of ' The Bridal of Triermain'
and ' Harold the Dauntless,' which, in the opinion of some,
equalled if not surpassed him; and, lo! after three or four years
they turned out to be the master's own compositions."—BYRON,
vol. xv. p. 96.

syllabic couplets of the Lady of the Lake, instead
of recurring to the more varied cadence of the Lay
or Marmion. It is fair to add that, among the
London circles at least, some sarcastic flings in Mr
Moore's "Twopenny Post Bag" must have had an
unfavourable influence on this occasion.* But the
cause of failure which the poet himself places last,
was unquestionably the main one. The deeper and
darker passion of Childe Harold, the audacity of its
morbid voluptuousness, and the melancholy majesty
of the numbers in which it defied the world, had
taken the general imagination by storm; and Rokeby,
with many beauties and some sublimities, was pitched,
as a whole, on a key which seemed tame in the comparison.

I have already adverted to the fact that Scott felt
it a relief, not a fatigue, to compose the Bridal of
Triermain *pari passu* with Rokeby. In answer, for

---

* See, for instance, the Epistle of Lady Corke — or that of
Messrs Lackington, booksellers, to one of their dandy authors —

   "Should you feel any touch of *poetical* glow,
    We've a scheme to suggest—Mr Scott, you must know
    (Who, we're sorry to say it, now works for the *Row*),
    Having quitted the Borders to seek new renown,
    Is coming by long Quarto stages to town,
    And beginning with Rokeby (the job's sure to pay),
    Means to do all the gentlemen's seats on the way.
    Now the scheme is, though none of our hackneys can beat him,
    To start a new Poet through Highgate to meet him;
    Who by means of quick proofs—no revises—long coaches—
    May do a few Villas before Scott approaches;
    Indeed if our Pegasus be not curst shabby,
    He'll reach without foundering, at least Woburn-Abbey." &c. &c.

example, to one of James Ballantyne's letters, urging
accelerated speed with the weightier romance, he
says, " I fully share in your anxiety to get forward
the grand work ; but, I assure you, I feel the more
confidence from coquetting with the guerilla."

The quarto of Rokeby was followed, within two
months, by the small volume which had been designed for a twin-birth ; — the MS. had been trans-
cribed by one of the Ballantynes themselves, in order
to guard against any indiscretion of the press-people ;
and the mystification, aided and abetted by Erskine,
in no small degree heightened the interest of its reception.   Except Mr Morritt, Scott had, so far as
I am aware, no English confidant upon this occasion.
Whether any of his daily companions in the Parliament House were in the secret, I have never heard ;
but I can scarcely believe that any of those intimate
friends, who had known him and Erskine from their
youth upwards, could have for a moment believed
the latter capable either of the invention or the
execution of this airy and fascinating romance in
little.   Mr Jeffrey, for whom chiefly " the trap had
been set," was far too sagacious to be caught in it ;
but, as it happened, he made a voyage that year to
America, and thus lost the opportunity of immediately expressing his opinion either of Rokeby or
of the Bridal of Triermain.   The writer in the
Quarterly Review (July 1813) seems to have been

completely deceived — " We have already spoken of
it," says the critic, " as an imitation of Mr Scott's
style of composition; and if we are compelled to
make the general approbation more precise and spe-
cific, we should say, that if it be inferior in vigour
to some of his productions, it equals or surpasses
them in elegance and beauty; that it is more uniformly tender, and far less infected with the unna-
tural prodigies and coarseness of the earlier romances.
In estimating its merits, however, we should forget
that it is offered as an imitation. The diction undoubtedly reminds us of a rhythm and cadence we
have heard before; but the sentiments, descriptions,
and characters, have qualities that are native and un-
borrowed."

If this writer was, as I suppose, Ellis, he probably
considered it as a thing impossible that Scott should
have engaged in such a scheme without giving him
a hint of it; but to have admitted into the secret
any one who was likely to criticise the piece, would
have been to sacrifice the very object of the device.
Erskine's own suggestion, that " perhaps a quizzical
review might be got up," led, I believe, to nothing
more important than a paragraph in one of the
Edinburgh newspapers. He may be pardoned for
having been not a little flattered to find it generally
considered as not impossible that he should have
written such a poem; and I have heard James

Ballantyne say, that nothing could be more amusing than the style of his coquetting on the subject while it was yet fresh; but when this first excitement was over, his natural feeling of what was due to himself, as well as to his friend, dictated many a remonstrance; and, though he ultimately acquiesced in permitting another minor romance to be put forth in the same manner, he did so reluctantly, and was far from acting his part so well.

Scott says, in the Introduction to the Lord of the Isles, " As Mr Erskine was more than suspected of a taste for poetry, and as I took care, in several places, to mix something that might resemble (as far as was in my power) my friend's feeling and manner, the train easily caught, and two large editions were sold." Among the passages to which he here alludes, are no doubt those in which the character of the minstrel Arthur is shaded with the colourings of an almost effeminate gentleness. Yet, in the midst of them, the " mighty minstrel" himself, from time to time, escapes; as, for instance, where the lover bids Lucy, in that exquisite picture of crossing a mountain stream, trust to his " stalwart arm"—

 " Which could yon oak's prone trunk uprear."

Nor can I pass the compliment to Scott's own fair patroness, where Lucy's admirer is made to con-

fess, with some momentary lapse of gallantry, that
he

> " Ne'er won—best meed to minstrel true —
> One favouring smile from fair Buccleuch;"

nor the burst of genuine Borderism,—

> " Bewcastle now must keep the bold,
>   Speir-Adam's steeds must bide in stall;
> Of Hartley-burn the bowmen bold
>   Must only shoot from battled wall;
> And Liddesdale may buckle spur,
>   And Teviot now may belt the brand,
> Tarras and Ewes keep nightly stir,
>   And Eskdale foray Cumberland."—

But, above all, the choice of the scenery, both of the
Introductions and of the story itself, reveals the
early and treasured predilections of the poet. For
who that remembers the circumstances of his first
visit to the vale of St John, but must see throughout
the impress of his own real romance? I own I am
not without a suspicion that, in one passage, which
always seemed to me a blot upon the composition —
that in which Arthur derides the military coxcom-
bries of his rival—

> " Who comes in foreign trashery
>   Of tinkling chain and spur,
> A walking haberdashery
>   Of feathers, lace, and fur;

In Rowley's antiquated phrase,
Horse-milliner of modern days "—

there is a sly reference to the incidents of a certain
ball, of August 1797, at the Gilsland Spa.*

Among the more prominent Erskinisms, are the
eulogistic mention of Glasgow, the scene of Erskine's
education ; and the lines on Collins — a supplement
to whose Ode on the Highland Superstitions is, as
far as I know, the only specimen that ever was published of Erskine's verse.†

As a whole, the Bridal of Triermain appears to
me as characteristic of Scott as any of his larger
poems. His genius pervades and animates it beneath
a thin and playful veil, which perhaps adds as much
of grace as it takes away of splendour. As Words-
worth says of the eclipse on the lake of Lugano—

" 'Tis sunlight sheathed and gently charmed ;"

and I think there is at once a lightness and a polish
of versification beyond what he has elsewhere attained.
If it be a miniature, it is such a one as a Cooper
might have hung fearlessly beside the masterpieces
of Vandyke.

* See *ante*, vol. i. p. 366.
† It is included in the Border Minstrelsy. Scott's Poetical
Works, vol. i. p. 270.

The Introductions contain some of the most exquisite passages he ever produced; but their general
effect has always struck me as unfortunate.   No art
can reconcile us to contemptuous satire of the merest
frivolities of modern life — some of them already, in
twenty years, grown obsolete — interlaid between
such bright visions of the old world of romance,
when

> " Strength was gigantic, valour high,
>   And wisdom soared beyond the sky,
>   And beauty had such matchless beam
>   As lights not now a lover's dream."

The fall is grievous, from the hoary minstrel of
Newark, and his feverish tears on Killiecrankie, to
a pathetic swain, who can stoop to denounce as objects of his jealousy—

> " The landaulet and four blood bays—
>   The Hessian boot and pantaloon."

Before Triermain came out, Scott had taken wing
for Abbotsford; and indeed he seems to have so
contrived it in his earlier period, that he should not
be in Edinburgh when any unavowed work of his
was published; whereas, from the first, in the case of
books that bore his name on the title-page, he walked
as usual to the Parliament House, and bore all the
buzz and tattle of friends and acquaintance with an
air of good-humoured equanimity, or rather total

apparent indifference. The following letter, which contains some curious matter of more kinds than one, was written partly in town and partly in the country :—

"*To Miss Joanna Baillie, Hampstead.*

"Edinburgh, March 13th, 1813.

" My Dearest Friend,

   " The pinasters have arrived safe, and I can hardly regret, while I am so much flattered by, the trouble you have had in collecting them. I have got some wild larch trees from Loch Katrine, and both are to be planted next week, when, God willing, I shall be at Abbotsford to superintend the operation. I have got a little corner of ground laid out for a nursery, where I shall rear them carefully till they are old enough to be set forth to push their fortune on the banks of Tweed.—What I shall finally make of this villa-work I don't know, but in the mean-time it is very entertaining. I shall have to resist very flattering invitations this season ; for I have received hints, from more quarters than one, that my bow would be acceptable at Carlton House in case I should be in London, which is very flattering, especially as there were some prejudices to be got over in that quarter. I should be in some danger

of giving new offence, too; for, although I utterly
disapprove of the present rash and ill-advised course
of the princess, yet, as she always was most kind
and civil to me, I certainly could not, as a gentleman,
decline obeying any commands she might give me
to wait upon her, especially in her present adversity.
So, though I do not affect to say I should be sorry
to take an opportunity of peeping at the splendours
of royalty, prudence and economy will keep me
quietly at home till another day.   My great amusement here this some time past has been going almost
nightly to see John Kemble, who certainly is a great
artist.   It is a pity he shows too much of his machinery.   I wish he could be double-capped, as they
say of watches; — but the fault of too much study
certainly does not belong to many of his tribe.   He
is, I think, very great in those parts especially where
character is tinged by some acquired and systematic
habits, like those of the Stoic philosophy in Cato
and Brutus, or of misanthropy in Penruddock: but
sudden turns and natural bursts of passion are not
his forte.   I saw him play Sir Giles Overreach (the
Richard III. of middling life) last night; but he
came not within a hundred miles of Cooke, whose
terrible visage, and short, abrupt, and savage utterance, gave a reality almost to that extraordinary
scene in which he boasts of his own successful vil-
lany to a nobleman of worth and honour, of whose

alliance he is ambitious.   Cooke contrived somehow
to impress upon the audience the idea of such a
monster of enormity as had learned to pique himself
even upon his own atrocious character.   But Kemble
was too handsome, too plausible, and too smooth, to
admit its being probable that he should be blind to
the unfavourable impression which these extraordinary vaunts are likely to make on the person whom
he is so anxious to conciliate.

" Abbotsford, 21st March.

" This letter, begun in Edinburgh, is to take wing
from Abbotsford.   John Winnos (now John Winnos
is the sub-oracle of Abbotsford, the principal being
Tom Purdie)—John Winnos pronounces that the
pinaster seed ought to be raised at first on a hot-bed,
and thence transplanted to a nursery : so to a hot-
bed they have been carefully consigned, the upper
oracle not objecting, in respect his talent lies in
catching a salmon, or finding a hare sitting—on
which occasions (being a very complete Scrub) he
solemnly exchanges his working jacket for an old
green one of mine, and takes the air of one of Robin
Hood's followers.   His more serious employments
are ploughing, harrowing, and overseeing all my
premises ; being a complete jack-of-all-trades, from
the carpenter to the shepherd, nothing comes strange
to him ; and being extremely honest, and somewhat

of a humourist, he is quite my right hand. I cannot help singing his praises at this moment, because I have so many odd and out-of-the-way things to do, that I believe the conscience of many of our jog-trot countrymen would revolt at being made my instrument in sacrificing good corn-land to the visions of Mr Price's theory. Mr Pinkerton, the historian, has a play coming out at Edinburgh; it is by no means bad poetry, yet I think it will not be popular; the people come and go, and speak very notable things in good blank verse, but there is no very strong interest excited : the plot also is disagreeable, and liable to the objections (though in a less degree) which have been urged against the Mysterious Mother : it is to be acted on Wednesday; I will let you know its fate. P., with whom I am in good habits, showed the MS., but I referred him, with such praise as I could conscientiously bestow, to the players and the public. I don't know why one should take the task of damning a man's play out of the hands of the proper tribunal. Adieu, my dear friend. I have scarce room for love to Miss, Mrs, and Dr B.   W. SCOTT."

To this I add a letter to Lady Louisa Stuart, who had sent him a copy of these lines, found by Lady Douglas on the back of a tattered bank-note—

" Farewell, my note, and wheresoe'er ye wend,
  Shun gaudy scenes, and be the poor man's friend.
  You've left a poor one ; go to one as poor,
  And drive despair and hunger from his door."

It appears that these noble friends had adopted, or
feigned to adopt, the belief that the Bridal of
Triermain was a production of Mr R. P. Gillies—
who had about this time published an imitation of
Lord Byron's *Romaunt*, under the title of " Childe
Alarique."

" *To the Lady Louisa Stuart, Bothwell Castle.*

                         " Abbotsford, 28th April 1813.
" Dear Lady Louisa,
    " Nothing can give me more pleasure than to
hear from you, because it is both a most acceptable
favour to me, and also a sign that your own spirits
are recovering their tone.   Ladies are, I think, very
fortunate in having a resource in work at a time
when the mind rejects intellectual amusement.   Men
have no resource but striding up and down the room,
like a bird that beats itself to pieces against the bars
of its cage ; whereas needle-work is a sort of seda-
tive, too mechanical to worry the mind by distracting
it from the points on which its musings turn, yet
gradually assisting it in regaining steadiness and

composure; for so curiously are our bodies and minds
linked together, that the regular and constant employment of the former on any process, however
dull and uniform, has the effect of tranquillizing,
where it cannot disarm, the feelings of the other.
I am very much pleased with the lines on the guinea
note, and if Lady Douglas does not object, I would
willingly mention the circumstance in the Edinburgh
Annual Register. I think it will give the author
great delight to know that his lines had attracted
attention, and *had* sent the paper on which they were
recorded, ' heaven-directed, to the poor.' Of course
I would mention no names. There was, as your
Ladyship may remember, some years since, a most
audacious and determined murder committed on a
porter belonging to the British Linen Company's
Bank at Leith, who was stabbed to the heart in
broad daylight, and robbed of a large sum in notes.*
If ever this crime comes to light, it will be through
the circumstance of an idle young fellow having
written part of a playhouse song on one of the
notes, which, however, has as yet never appeared in
circulation.

" I am very glad you like Rokeby, which is nearly
out of fashion and memory with me. It has been

---

* This murder, perpetrated in November 1806, remains a mys-
tery in 1836. The porter's name was Begbie.

wonderfully popular, about ten thousand copies having walked off already, in about three months, and
the demand continuing faster than it can be supplied.
As to my imitator, the Knight of Triermain, I will
endeavour to convey to Mr Gillies *(puisque Gillies
il est)* your Ladyship's very just strictures on the
Introduction to the second Canto.   But if he takes
the opinion of a hacked old author like myself, he
will content himself with avoiding such bevues in
future, without attempting to mend those which are
already made.   There is an ominous old proverb
which says, *confess and be hanged;* and truly if an
author acknowledges his own blunders, I do not know
who he can expect to stand by him; whereas, let
him confess nothing, and he will always find some
injudicious admirers to vindicate even his faults.   So
that I think after publication the effect of criticism
should be prospective, in which point of view I dare
say Mr G. will take your friendly hint, especially as
it is confirmed by that of the best judges who have
read the poem.—Here is beautiful weather for April!
an absolute snow-storm mortifying me to the core
by retarding the growth of all my young trees and
shrubs.—Charlotte begs to be most respectfully remembered to your Ladyship and Lady D.   We are
realizing the nursery tale of the man and his wife
who lived in a vinegar bottle, for our only sitting
room is just twelve feet square, and my Eve alleges

that I am too big for our paradise. To make amends, I have created a tolerable garden, occupying about an English acre, which I begin to be very fond of. When one passes forty, an addition to the quiet occupations of life becomes of real value, for I do not hunt and fish with quite the relish I did ten years ago. Adieu, my dear Lady Louisa, and all good attend you.

WALTER SCOTT."

CHAPTER XXVI.

1813.

ABOUT a month after the publication of the Bridal
of Triermain, the affairs of the Messrs Ballantyne,

which had never apparently been in good order since
the establishment of the bookselling firm, became so
embarrassed as to call for Scott's most anxious efforts
to disentangle them.   Indeed, it is clear that there
had existed some very serious perplexity in the
course of the preceding autumn ; for Scott writes to
John Ballantyne, while Rokeby was in progress
(August 11, 1812)—" I have a letter from James,
very anxious about your health and state of spirits.
If you suffer the present inconveniences to depress
you too much, you are wrong ; and if you conceal
any part of them, are very unjust to us all.   I am
always ready to make any sacrifices to do justice to
engagements, and would rather sell any thing, or
every thing, than be less than true men to the
world."

I have already, perhaps, said enough to account
for the general want of success in this publishing
adventure ; but Mr James Ballantyne sums up the
case so briefly in his death-bed paper, that I may
here quote his words.   " My brother," he says,
" though an active and pushing, was not a cautious
bookseller, and the large sums received never formed
an addition to stock.   In fact, they were all expended
by the partners, who, being then young and sanguine
men, not unwillingly adopted my brother's hasty
results.   By May 1813, in a word, the absolute
throwing away of our own most valuable publica-

tions, and the rash adoption of some injudicious speculations of Mr Scott, had introduced such losses and embarrassments, that after a very careful consideration, Mr Scott determined to dissolve the concern." He adds, — " This became a matter of less difficulty, because time had in a great measure worn away the differences between Mr Scott and Mr Constable, and Mr Hunter was now out of Constable's concern.* A peace, therefore, was speedily made up, and the old habits of intercourse were restored."

How reluctantly Scott had made up his mind to open such a negotiation with Constable, as involved a complete exposure of the mismanagement of John Ballantyne's business as a publisher, will appear from a letter dated about the Christmas of 1812, in which he says to James, who had proposed asking Constable to take a share both in Rokeby and in the Annual Register, " You must be aware, that in stating the objections which occur to me to taking in Constable, I think they ought to give way either to absolute necessity or to very strong grounds of advantage. But I *am* persuaded nothing ultimately good can be expected from any connexion with that house, unless for those who have a mind to be hewers of wood and drawers of water. We will talk the matter coolly over, and in the mean while, perhaps you could see

* Mr. Hunter died in March 1812.

W. Erskine, and learn what impression this odd union
is like to make among your friends.   Erskine is
sound-headed, and quite to be trusted with *your
whole story.*   I must own I can hardly think the
purchase of the Register is equal to the loss of credit
and character which your surrender will be conceived
to infer." At the time when he wrote this, Scott
no doubt anticipated that Rokeby would have success not less decisive than the Lady of the Lake ; but
in this expectation—though 10,000 copies in three
months would have seemed to any other author a
triumphant sale — he had been disappointed. And
mean while the difficulties of the firm accumulating
from week to week, had reached by the middle of
May, a point which rendered it absolutely necessary
for him to conquer all his scruples.

Mr Cadell, then Constable's partner, says in his
Memoranda, — " Prior to this time the reputation
of John Ballantyne and Co. had been decidedly on the
decline.   It was notorious in the trade that their general speculations had been unsuccessful ; they were
known to be grievously in want of money.   These
rumours were realized to the full by an application
which Messrs. B. made to Mr Constable in May 1813,
for pecuniary aid, accompanied by an offer of some of
the books they had published since 1809, as a purchase, along with various shares in Mr Scott's own
poems.   Their difficulties were admitted, and the ne-

gotiation was pressed urgently ; so much so, that a
pledge was given, that if the terms asked were ac-
ceded to, John Ballantyne and Co. would endeavour to
wind up their concerns, and cease as soon as possible
to be publishers." Mr Cadell adds :—" I need hardly
remind you that this was a period of very great general difficulty in the money market. It was the crisis of the war. The public expenditure had reached
an enormous height ; and even the most prosperous
mercantile houses were often pinched to sustain their
credit. It may easily, therefore, be supposed that the
Messrs Ballantyne had during many months besieged
every banker's door in Edinburgh, and that their
agents had done the like in London."

The most important of the requests which the labouring house made to Constable was, that he should
forthwith take entirely to himself the stock, copyright, and future management of the Edinburgh
Annual Register. Upon examining the state of this
book, however, Constable found that the loss on it
had never been less than £1000 per annum, and he
therefore declined that matter for the present. He
promised, however, to consider seriously the means
he might have of ultimately relieving them from the
pressure of the Register, and, in the mean time,
offered to take 300 sets of the stock on hand. The
other purchases he finally made on the 18th of May,
were considerable portions of Weber's unhappy Beau-

mont and Fletcher—of an edition of De Foe's novels
in twelve volumes—of a collection entitled Tales
of the East in three large volumes, 8vo, double
columned—and of another in one volume, called
Popular Tales — about 800 copies of the Vision
of Don Roderick—and a fourth of the remaining
copyright of Rokeby, price £700. The immediate
accommodation thus received amounted to £2000;
and Scott, who had personally conducted the latter
part of the negotiation, writes thus to his junior partner, who had gone a week or two earlier to London
in quest of some similar assistance there :—

" *To Mr John Ballantyne, care of Messrs
Longman & Co., London.*

"Printing-Office, May 18th, 1813.

" Dear John,

" After many *offs* and *ons*, and as many *projets*
and *contre-projets* as the treaty of Amiens, I have at
length concluded a treaty with Constable, in which I
am sensible he has gained a great advantage ;* but
what could I do amidst the disorder and pressure of

* " These and after purchases of books from the stock of
J. Ballantyne and Co. were resold to the trade by Constable's
firm, at less than one half and one third of the prices at which
they were thus obtained."—*Note from Mr R. Cadell.*

so many demands ? The arrival of your long-dated bills decided my giving in, for what could James or I do with them ? I trust this sacrifice has cleared our way, but many rubs remain ; nor am I, after these hard skirimishes, so able to meet them by my proper credit. Constable, however, will be a zealons ally ; and for the first time these many weeks I shall lay my head on a quiet pillow, for now I do think that, by our joint exertions, we shall get well through the storm, save Beaumont from depreciation, get a partner in our heavy concerns, reef our topsails, and move on securely under an easy sail. And if, on the one hand, I have sold my gold too cheap, I have, on the other, turned my lead to gold. Brewster* and Singers† are the only heavy things to which I have not given a blue eye. Had your news of Cadell's sale‡ reached us here, I could not have harpooned my grampus so deeply as I have done, as nothing but Rokeby would have barbed the hook.

" Adieu, my dear John. I have the most sincere regard for you, and you may depend on my considering your interest with quite as much attention as my own. If I have ever expressed myself with irritation

---

* Dr Brewster's edition of Ferguson's Astronomy, 2 vols. 8vo. with plates, 4to, Edin. 1811. 36s.

† Dr Singers' General View of the County of Dumfries, 8vo. Edin. 1812. 18s.

‡ A trade sale of Messrs Cadell and Davies in the Strand.

in speaking of this business, you must impute it to the sudden, extensive, and unexpected embarrassments in which I found myself involved all at once. If to your real goodness of heart and integrity, and to the quickness and acuteness of your talents, you added habits of more universal circumspection, and, above all, the courage to tell disagreeable truths to those whom you hold in regard, I pronounce that the world never held such a man of business. These it must be your study to add to your other good qualities. Mean time, as some one says to Swift, I love you with all your failings. Pray make an effort and love me with all mine. Yours truly, W. S."

Three days afterwards, Scott resumes the subject as follows :—

" *To Mr John Ballantyne, London.*

"Edinburgh, 21st May 1813.
" Dear John,
" Let it never escape your recollection, that shutting your own eyes, or blinding those of your friends, upon the actual state of business, is the high road to ruin. Meanwhile, we have recovered our legs for a week or two. Constable will, I think, come in to the Register. He is most anxious to maintain the printing-office; he sees most truly that

the more we print the less we publish; and for the same reason he will, I think, help us off with our heavy quire-stock.

" I was aware of the distinction between the *state* and the *calendar* as to the latter including the printing-office bills, and I summed and docked them (they are marked with red ink), but there is still a difference of £2000 and upwards on the calendar against the business. I sometimes fear that, between the long dates of your bills, and the tardy settlements of the Edinburgh trade, some difficulties will occur even in June; and July I always regard with deep anxiety. As for loss, if I get out without public exposure, I shall not greatly regard the rest. Radcliffe the physician said, when he lost £2000 on the South-Sea scheme, it was only going up 2000 pair of stairs; I say, it is only writing 2000 couplets, and the account is balanced. More of this hereafter. Yours truly,　　　　　　　　　　W. SCOTT.

" P. S. — James has behaved very well during this whole transaction, and has been most steadily attentive to business. I am convinced that the more he works the better his health will be. One or other of you will need to be constantly in the printing-office henceforward — it is the sheet-anchor."

The allusion in this *postscript* to James Ballantyne's health reminds me that Scott's letters to himself are full of hints on that subject, even from a very early period of their connexion; and these hints are all to the same effect. James was a man of lazy habits, and not a little addicted to the more solid, and perhaps more dangerous, part of the indulgencies of the table. One letter (dated Ashestiel, 1810) will be a sufficient specimen:—

" To Mr James Ballantyne.

" My Dear James,

" I am very sorry for the state of your health, and should be still more so, were I not certain that I can prescribe for you as well as any physician in Edinburgh. You have naturally an athletic constitution and a hearty stomach, and these agree very ill with a sedentary life and the habits of indolence which it brings on. Your stomach thus gets weak; and from those complaints of all others arise most certainly flatulence, hypochondria, and all the train of unpleasant feelings connected with indigestion. We all know the horrible sensation of the nightmare arises from the same cause which gives those waking nightmares commonly called the blue devils. You must positively put yourself on a regimen as to eating, not for a month or two, but for a year at least, and take regular exercise — and my life for yours.

I know this by myself, for if I were to eat and drink in town as I do here, it would soon finish me, and yet I am sensible I live too genially in Edinburgh as it is. Yours very truly, W. SCOTT."

Among Scott's early pets at Abbotsford there was a huge raven, whose powers of speech were remarkable, far beyond any parrot's that he had ever met with; and who died in consequence of an excess of the kind to which James Ballantyne was addicted. Thenceforth, Scott often repeated to his old friend, and occasionally scribbled by way of postscript to his notes on business—

> " When you are craving,
> Remember the Raven."

Sometimes the formula is varied to—

> " When you've dined half,
> Think on poor Ralph!"

His preachments of regularity in book-keeping to John, and of abstinence from good cheer to James Ballantyne, were equally vain; but on the other hand it must be allowed that they had some reason for displeasure—(the more felt because they durst not, like him, express their feelings) *—when they found

---

* Since this work was first published, I have been compelled to examine very minutely the details of Scott's connexion with the Ballantynes, and one result is, that both James and John had

that scarcely had these " hard skirmishes" terminated in the bargain of May 18th, before Scott was preparing fresh embarrassments for himself, by commencing a negotiation for a considerable addition to his property at Abbotsford. As early as the 20th of June he writes to Constable as being already aware of this matter, and alleges his anxiety " to close at once with a very capricious person," as the only reason that could have induced him to make up his mind to sell the whole copyright of an as yet unwritten poem, to be entitled " The Nameless Glen." This copyright he then offered to dispose of to Constable for £5000; adding, " this is considerably less in proportion than I have already made on the share of Rokeby sold to yourself, and surely that is no unfair admeasurement."   A long correspondence ensued, in the course of which Scott mentions " the Lord of the Isles," as a title which had suggested itself to him in place of " the Nameless Glen ;" but as the negotiation did not succeed, I may pass its details. The new property which Scott was so eager

---

trespassed so largely, for their private purposes, on the funds of the Companies, that, Scott being, as their letters distinctly state, the only " monied partner," and his over-advances of capital having been very extensive, any inquiry on their part as to his uncommercial expenditure must have been entirely out of the question. To avoid misrepresentation, however, I leave my text as it was. — [1839.]

to acquire, was that hilly tract stretching from the old Roman road near Turn-again towards the Cauld-shiels Loch: a then desolate and naked mountain-mere, which he likens, in a letter of this summer (to Lady Louisa Stuart), to the Lake of the Genie and the Fisherman in the Arabian Tale. To obtain this lake at one extremity of his estate, as a contrast to the Tweed at the other, was a prospect for which hardly any sacrifice would have appeared too much; and he contrived to gratify his wishes in the course of that July, to which he had spoken of himself in May as looking forward " with the deepest anxiety."

Nor was he, I must add, more able to control some of his minor tastes. I find him writing to Mr Terry, on the 20th of June, about " that splendid lot of ancient armour, advertised by Winstanley," a celebrated auctioneer in London, of which he had the strongest fancy to make his spoil, though he was at a loss to know where it should be placed when it reached Abbotsford; and on the 2d of July, this acquisition also having been settled, he says to the same correspondent — " I have written to Mr Win-stanley. My bargain with Constable was otherwise arranged, but Little John is to find the needful article, and I shall take care of Mr Winstanley's interest, who has behaved too handsomely in this matter to be trusted to the mercy of our little friend

the Picaroon, who is, notwithstanding his many excellent qualities, a little on the score of old Gobbo—
doth somewhat smack — somewhat grow to.* We
shall be at Abbotsford on the 12th, and hope soon
to see you there. I am fitting up a small room above
Peter-house, where an unceremonious bachelor may
consent to do penance, though the place is a cock-
loft, and the access that which leads many a bold
fellow to his last nap — a ladder."† And a few
weeks later, he says, in the same sort, to his sister-
in-law, Mrs Thomas Scott — " In despite of these
hard times, which affect my patrons the booksellers
very much, I am buying old books and old armour
as usual, and adding to what your old friend‡ Burns
calls—

> " A fouth of auld nick-nackets,
>   Rusty airn caps and jingling jackets,
>   Wad haud the Lothians three in tackets
>   A towmont gude,
>   And parritch-pats and auld saut-backets,
>   Before the flude.' "

---

* *Merchant of Venice, Act II. Scene 2.*

† The court of offices, built on the *haugh* at Abbotsford in
1812, included a house for the faithful coachman, Peter Mathie-
son. One of Scott's Cantabrigian friends, Mr W. S. Rose, gave
the whole pile soon afterwards the name, which it retained to the
end, of *Peter-House.* The loft at Peter-House continued to be
occupied by occasional bachelor guests until the existing mansion
was completed.

‡ Mrs Thomas Scott had met Burns frequently in early life at

Notwithstanding all this, it must have been with a most uneasy mind that he left Edinburgh to establish himself at Abbotsford that July. The assistance of Constable had not been granted, indeed it had not been asked, to an extent at all adequate for the difficulties of the case; and I have now to transcribe, with pain and reluctance, some extracts from Scott's letters, during the ensuing autumn, which speak the language of anxious, and indeed humiliating distress; and give a most lively notion of the incurable recklessness of his younger partner.

" *To Mr John Ballantyne.*

" Abbotsford, Saturday, 24th July.

" Dear John,

" I sent you the order, and have only to hope it arrived safe and in good time. I waked the boy at three o'clock myself, having slept little, less on account of the money than of the time. Surely you should have written, three or four days before, the probable amount of the deficit, and, as on former occasions, I would have furnished you with means of meeting it. These expresses, besides every other inconvenience, excite surprise in my family and in

---

Dumfries. Her brother, the late Mr David MacCulloch, was a great favourite with the poet, and the best singer of his songs that I ever heard.

the neighbourhood. I know no justifiable occasion for them but the unexpected return of a bill. I do not consider you as answerable for the success of plans, but I do and must hold you responsible for giving me, in distinct and plain terms, your opinion as to any difficulties which may occur, and that in such time that I may make arrangements to obviate them if possible.

" Of course if anything has gone wrong you will come out here to-morrow. But if, as I hope and trust, the cash arrived safe, you will write to me, under cover to the Duke of Buccleuch, Drumlanrig Castle, Dumfries-shire. I shall set out for that place on Monday morning early.   W. S."

" *To Mr James Ballantyne.*

" Abbotsford, 25th July 1813.

" Dear James,

" I address the following jobation for John to you, that you may see whether I do not well to be angry, and enforce upon him the necessity of constantly writing his fears as well as his hopes. You should rub him often on this point, for his recollection becomes rusty the instant I leave town and am not in the way to rack him with constant questions. I hope the presses are doing well, and that you are quite stout again. Yours truly,   W. S."

(ENCLOSURE.)

" To Mr John Ballantyne.

" My good friend John,

" The post brings me no letter from you, which I am much surprised at, as you must suppose me anxious to learn that your express arrived. I think he must have reached you before post-hours, and James or you *might* have found a minute to say so in a single line. I once more request that you will be a business-like correspondent, and state your provisions for every week prospectively. I do not expect you to *warrant them,* which you rather perversely seem to insist is my wish, but I do want to be aware of their nature and extent, that I may provide against the possibility of miscarriage. The calendar, to which you refer me, tells me what sums are due, but cannot tell your shifts to pay them, which are naturally altering with circumstances, and of which alterations I request to have due notice. You say you *could not suppose* Sir W. Forbes would have refused the long dated bills; but that you *had* such an apprehension is clear, both because in the calendar these bills were rated two months lower, and because, three days before, you wrote me an enigmatical expression of your apprehensions, in-

stead of saying plainly there was a chance of your
wanting £350, when I would have sent you an order
to be used conditionally.

" All I desire is unlimited confidence and frequent
correspondence, and that you will give me weekly at
least the fullest anticipation of your resources, and
the probability of their being effectual. I may be
disappointed in my own, of which you shall have
equally timeous notice. Omit no exertions to procure the use of money, even for a month or six
weeks, for time is most precious. The large balance due in January from the trade, and individuals, which I cannot reckon at less than £4000,
will put us finally to rights; and it will be a shame
to founder within sight of harbour. The greatest
risk we run is from such ill-considered despatches
as those of Friday. Suppose that I had gone to
Drumlanrig—suppose the poney had set up—suppose a thousand things—and we were ruined for
want of your telling your apprehensions in due time.
Do not plague yourself to vindicate this sort of
management; but if you have escaped the consequences (as to which you have left me uncertain),
thank God, and act more cautiously another time. It
was quite the same to me on what day I sent that
draft; indeed it must have been so if I had the
money in my cash account, and if I had not, the
more time given me to provide it the better.

" Now, do not affect to suppose that my displeasure arises from your not having done your utmost to realize funds, and that utmost having failed. It is one mode, to be sure, of exculpation, to suppose one's self accused of something they are not charged with, and then to make a querulous or indignant defence, and complain of the injustice of the accuser. The head and front of your offending is precisely your not writing explicitly, and I request this may not happen again. It is your fault, and I believe arises either from an ill-judged idea of smoothing matters to me — as if I were not behind the curtain — or a general reluctance to allow that any danger is near, until it is almost unparriable. I shall be very sorry if anything I have said gives you pain; but the matter is too serious for all of us, to be passed over without giving you my explicit sentiments. To-morrow I set out for Drumlanrig, and shall not hear from you till Tuesday or Wednesday. Make yourself master of the post-town — Thornhill, probably, or Sanquhar. As Sir W. F. & Co. have cash to meet my order, nothing, I think, can have gone wrong, unless the boy perished by the way. Therefore, in faith and hope, and — that I may lack none of the Christian virtues — in charity with your dilatory worship, I remain very truly yours, W. S.'

Scott proceeded, accordingly, to join a gay and festive circle, whom the Duke of Buccleuch had assembled about him on first taking possession of the magnificent Castle of Drumlanrig, in Nithsdale, the principal messuage of the dukedom of Queensberry, which had recently lapsed into his family. But, *post equitem sedet atra cura* — another of John Ballantyne's unwelcome missives, rendered necessary by a neglect of precisely the same kind as before, reached him in the midst of this scene of rejoicing.　On the 31st, he again writes : —

> " *To Mr John Ballantyne, Bookseller, Edinburgh.*
>
> > " Drumlanrig, Friday.
>
> " Dear John,
>
> " I enclose the order.　Unfortunately, the Drumlanrig post only goes thrice a-week ; but the Marquis of Queensberry, who carries this to Dumfries, has promised that the guard of the mail-coach shall deliver it by five to-morrow.　I was less anxious, as your note said you could clear this month. It is a cruel thing, that no State you furnish excludes the arising of such unexpected claims as this for the taxes on the printing-office.　What unhappy management, to suffer them to run ahead in such a manner !—but it is in vain to complain.　Were it

not for your strange concealments, I should anticipate no difficulty in winding up these matters.   But
who can reckon upon a State where claims are kept
out of view until they are in the hands of a *writer?*
If you have no time to say that *this* comes safe to
hand, I suppose James may favour me so far.   Yours
truly,   W. S.

" Let the guard be rewarded.

" Let me know exactly what you *can* do and
hope to do for next month; for it signifies nothing
raising money for you, unless I see it is to be of
real service.   Observe, I make you responsible for
nothing but a fair statement.*   The guard is known
to the Marquis, who has good-naturedly promised to
give him this letter with his own hand; so it must
reach you in time, though probably past five on Saturday."

Another similar application reached Scott the day
after the guard delivered his packet.   He writes
thus, in reply :—

---

* John Ballantyne had embarked no capital — not a shilling —
in the business; and was bound by the contract to limit himself
to an allowance of £300 a-year, in consideration of his *management*, until there should be an overplus of profits ! — [1839.]

" *To Mr John Ballantyne.*

" Drumlanrig, Sunday.

" Dear John,

" I trust you got my letter yesterday by five, with the draft enclosed. I return your draft accepted. On Wednesday I think of leaving this place, where, but for these damned affairs, I should have been very happy.   W. S."

Scott had been for some time under an engagement to meet the Marquis of Abercorn at Carlisle, in the first week of August, for the transaction of some business connected with his brother Thomas's late administration of that nobleman's Scottish affairs; and he had designed to pass from Drumlanrig to Carlisle for this purpose, without going back to Abbotsford. In consequence of these repeated harassments, however, he so far altered his plans as to cut short his stay at Drumlanrig, and turn homewards for two or three days, where James Ballantyne met him with such a statement as in some measure relieved his mind.

He then proceeded to fulfil his engagement with Lord Abercorn, whom he encountered travelling in a rather peculiar style between Carlisle and Longtown. The ladies of the family and the household occupied four or five carriages, all drawn by the

Marquis's own horses, while the noble Lord himself
brought up the rear, mounted on horseback, and
decorated with the ribbon of the order of the
Garter. On meeting the cavalcade, Scott turned
with them, and he was not a little amused when
they reached the village of Longtown, which he
had ridden through an hour or two before, with the
preparations which he found there made for the dinner of the party. The Marquis's major-domo and
cook had arrived there at an early hour in the
morning, and everything was now arranged for his
reception in the paltry little public-house, as nearly
as possible in the style usual in his own lordly man-
sions. The ducks and geese that had been dabbling
three or four hours ago in the village-pond were
now ready to make their appearance under number-
less disguises as *entrées;* a regular bill-of-fare flanked
the noble Marquis's allotted cover ; every huckaback
towel in the place had been pressed to do service as
a napkin; and, that nothing might be wanting to
the mimicry of splendour, the landlady's poor remnants of crockery and pewter had been furbished
up, and mustered in solemn order on a crazy old
beauffet, which was to represent a sideboard worthy
of Lucullus. I think it worth while to preserve this
anecdote, which Scott delighted in telling, as perhaps
the last relic of a style of manners now passed away,
and never likely to be revived among us.

Having despatched this dinner and his business,
Scott again turned southwards, intending to spend
a few days with Mr Morritt at Rokeby; but on
reaching Penrith, the landlord there, who was his
old acquaintance (Mr Buchanan), placed a letter in
his hands: *ecce iterum* — it was once more a cry
of distress from John Ballantyne. He thus answered
it :—

" *To Mr John Ballantyne.*

" Penrith, Aug. 10, 1813.

" Dear John,

" I enclose you an order for £350. I shall
remain at Rokeby until Saturday or Sunday, and be
at Abbotsford on Wednesday at latest.

" I hope the printing-office is going on well. I
fear, from the state of accompts between the companies, restrictions on the management and expense
will be unavoidable, which may trench upon James's
comforts. I cannot observe hitherto that the printing-office is paying off, but rather adding to its
embarrassments; and it cannot be thought that I
have either means or inclination to support a losing
concern at the rate of £200 a-month. If James
could find a monied partner, an active man who
understood the commercial part of the business, and
would superintend the conduct of the cash, it might
be the best for all parties; for I really am not ade-

quate to the fatigue of mind which these affairs
occasion me, though I must do the best to struggle
through them.   Believe me yours, &c.   W. S."

At Brough he encountered a messenger who
brought him such a painful account of Mrs Morritt's
health, that he abandoned his intention of proceeding
to Rokeby; and, indeed, it was much better that he
should be at Abbotsford again as soon as possible,
for his correspondence shows a continued succession,
during the three or four ensuing weeks, of the same
annoyances that had pursued him to Drumlanrig and
to Penrith.   By his desire, the Ballantynes had, it
would seem, before the middle of August, laid a
statement of their affairs before Constable.   Though
the statement was not so clear and full as Scott had
wished it to be, Constable, on considering it, at once
assured them, that to go on raising money in driblets
would never effectually relieve them; that, in short,
one or both of the companies must stop, unless Mr
Scott could find means to lay his hand, without
farther delay, on at least £4000; and I gather that,
by way of inducing Constable himself to come forward with part at least of this supply, John Bal-
tyne again announced his intention of forthwith
abandoning the bookselling business altogether, and
making an effort to establish himself — on a plan
which Constable had shortly before suggested — as

an auctioneer in Edinburgh. The following letters
need no comment :—

" *To Mr John Ballantyne.*

" Abbotsford, Aug. 16, 1813.

" Dear John,

" I am quite satisfied it is impossible for J. B.
and Co. to continue business longer than is absolutely necessary for the sale of stock and extrication
of their affairs. The fatal injury which their credit
has sustained, as well as your adopting a profession
in which I sincerely hope you will be more fortunate, renders the closing of the bookselling business
inevitable. With regard to the printing, it is my
intention to retire from that also so soon as I can
possibly do so with safety to myself, and with the
regard I shall always entertain for James's interest.
Whatever loss I may sustain will be preferable to
the life I have lately led, when I seem surrounded
by a sort of magic circle, which neither permits me
to remain at home in peace, nor to stir abroad with
pleasure. Your first exertion as an auctioneer may
probably be on ' that distinguished, select, and inimitable collection of books, made by an amateur of
this city retiring from business.' I do not feel either
health or confidence in my own powers sufficient to
authorize me to take a long price for a new poem,
until these affairs shall have been in some measure
digested. This idea has been long running in my

head, but the late fatalities which have attended this business have quite decided my resolution. I will write to James to-morrow, being at present annoyed with a severe headache. Yours truly,

W. Scott."

Were I to transcribe all the letters to which these troubles gave rise, I should fill a volume before I had reached the end of another twelvemonth. The two next I shall quote are dated on the same day (the 24th August), which may, in consequence of the answer the second of them received, be set down as determining the *crisis* of 1813.

" *To Mr James Ballantyne.*

" Abbotsford, 24th August 1813.

" Dear James,

" Mr Constable's advice is, as I have always found it, sound, sensible, and friendly—and I shall be guided by it. But I have no wealthy friend who would join in security with me to such an extent; and to apply in quarters where I might be refused, would ensure disclosure. I conclude John has shown Mr C. the state of the affairs; if not, I would wish him to do so directly. If the proposed accommodation could be granted to the firm on my personally joining in the security, the whole matter would be quite safe, for I have to receive in the course of the

winter some large sums from my father's estate.[*]
Besides which, I shall certainly be able to go to press
in November with a new poem; or, if Mr Constable's additional security would please the bankers
better, I could ensure Mr C. against the possibility
of loss, by assigning the copyrights, together with
that of the new poem, or even my library, in his relief. In fact, if he looks into the affairs, he will I
think see that there is no prospect of any eventual
loss to the creditors, though I may be a loser myself.
My property here is unincumbered; so is my house
in Castle Street; and I have no debts out of my own
family, excepting a part of the price of Abbotsford,
which I am to retain for four years. So that, literally,
I have no claims upon me unless those arising out of
this business; and when it is
considered that my income is
above £2000 a-year, even if
the printing-office pays nothing, I should hope no one
can possibly be a loser by me.

Clerkship,	£1300
Sheriffdom,	300
Mrs Scott,	200
Interest,	100
Somers, (say)	200
	£2100

I am sure I would strip my-
self to my shirt rather than it should be the case;
and my only reason for wishing to stop the concern
was to do open justice to all persons. It must have
been a bitter pill to me. I can more confidently
expect some aid from Mr Constable, or from Long-

* He probably alludes to the final settlement of accounts with
the Marquis of Abercorn.

man's house, because they can look into the concern and satisfy themselves how little chance there is of their being losers, which others cannot do. Perhaps between them they might manage to assist us with the credit necessary, and go on in winding up the concern by occasional acceptances.

" An odd thing has happened. I have a letter, by order of the Prince Regent, offering me the laureate-ship in the most flattering terms. Were I my own man, as you call it, I would refuse this offer (with all gratitude); but, as I am situated, £300 or £400 a-year is not to be sneezed at upon a point of poetical honour—and it makes me a better man to that ex-tent. I have not yet written, however. I will say little about Constable's handsome behaviour, but shall not forget it. It is needless to say I shall wish him to be consulted in every step that is taken. If I should lose all I advanced to this business, I should be less vexed than I am at this moment. I am very busy with Swift at present, but shall certainly come to town if it is thought necessary ; but I should first wish Mr Constable to look into the affairs to the bot-tom. Since I have personally superintended them, they have been winding up very fast, and we are now almost within sight of harbour. I will also own it was partly ill-humour at John's blunder last week that made me think of throwing things up. Yours truly,   W. S."

After writing and despatching this letter, an idea occurred to Scott that there was a quarter, not hitherto alluded to in any of these anxious epistles, from which he might consider himself as entitled to ask assistance, not only with little, if any, chance of a refusal, but (owing to particular circumstances) without incurring any very painful sense of obligation. On the 25th he says to John Ballantyne— " After some meditation, last night, it occurred to me I had some title to ask the Duke of Buccleuch's guarantee to a cash-account for £4000, as Constable proposes. I have written to him accordingly, and have very little doubt that he will be my surety. If this cash-account be in view, Mr Constable will certainly *assist us* until the necessary writings are made out—I beg your pardon—I dare say I am very stupid; but very often you don't consider that I can't follow details which would be quite obvious to a man of business—for instance, you tell me daily, 'that *if* the sums I count upon *are* forthcoming, the results must be as I suppose.' But— in a week—the scene is changed, and all I can do, and more, is inadequate to bring about these results. I protest I don't know if at this moment £4000 *will* clear us out. After all, you are vexed, and so am I; and it is needless to wrangle who has a right to be angry. Commend me to James. Yours truly,

W. S."

Having explained to the Duke of Buccleuch the position in which he stood—obliged either to procure some guarantee which would enable him to raise £4000, or to sell abruptly all his remaining interest in the copyright of his works; and repeated the statement of his personal property and income, as given in the preceding letter to James Ballantyne —Scott says to his noble friend:—" I am not asking nor desiring any loan from your Grace, but merely the honour of your sanction to my credit as a good man for £4000; and the motive of your Grace's interference would be sufficiently obvious to the London Shylocks, as your constant kindness and protection is no secret to the world. Will your Grace consider whether you can do what I propose, in conscience and safety, and favour me with your answer?—I have a very flattering offer from the Prince Regent, of his own free motion, to make me poet-laureate; I am very much embarrassed by it. I am, on the one hand, afraid of giving offence where no one would willingly offend, and perhaps losing an opportunity of smoothing the way to my youngsters through life; on the other hand, the office is a ridiculous one, somehow or other—they and I should be well quizzed,—yet that I should not mind. My real feeling of reluctance lies deeper—it is, that favoured as I have been by the public, I should be considered, with some justice, I fear, as engrossing

a petty emolument which might do real service to
some poorer brother of the Muses. I shall be most
anxious to have your Grace's advice on this subject.
There seems something churlish, and perhaps con-
ceited, in repelling a favour so handsomely offered
on the part of the Sovereign's representative—and
on the other hand, I feel much disposed to shake
myself free from it. I should make but a bad cour-
tier, and an ode-maker is described by Pope as a
poet out of his way or out of his senses. I will find
some excuse for protracting my reply till I can have
the advantage of your Grace's opinion; and remain,
in the mean time, very truly

Your obliged and grateful

WALTER SCOTT.

" P. S.—I trust your Grace will not suppose me
capable of making such a request as the enclosed,
upon any idle or unnecessary speculation; but, as I
stand situated, it is a matter of deep interest to me
to prevent these copyrights from being disposed of
either hastily or at under prices. I could have half
the booksellers in London for my sureties, on a hint
of a new poem; but bankers do not like people in
trade, and my brains are not ready to spin another
web. So your Grace must take me under your
princely care, as in the days of lang syne; and I
think I can say, upon the sincerity of an honest

man, there is not the most distant chance of your having any trouble or expense through my means."

The Duke's answer was in all respects such as might have been looked for from the generous kindness and manly sense of his character.

" *To Walter Scott, Esq., Abbotsford.*

" Drumlanrig Castle, August 28th, 1813.
" My Dear Sir,

" I received yesterday your letter of the 24th. I shall with pleasure comply with your request of guaranteeing the £4000. You must, however, furnish me with the form of a letter to this effect, as I am completely ignorant of transactions of this nature.

" I am never willing to *offer* advice, but when my opinion is asked by a friend I am ready to give it. As to the offer of his Royal Highness to appoint you laureate, I shall frankly say that I should be mortified to see you hold a situation which, by the general concurrence of the world, is stamped ridiculous. There is no good reason why this should be so ; but so it is. *Walter Scott, Poet Laureate,* ceases to be the Walter Scott of the Lay, Marmion, &c. Any future poem of yours would not come forward with the same probability of a successful reception. The poet laureate would stick to you and your productions like a piece of *court plaster*. Your muse has hitherto been independent — don't put her into harness. We know how lightly she trots along when left to her natural paces, but do not try driving. I would write frankly and openly to His Royal Highness, but with respectful gratitude, for he *has* paid you a compliment. I would not fear to state that you had hitherto written when in poetic mood, but feared to trammel yourself with a fixed periodical exertion ; and I cannot but conceive that His Royal Highness, who has much taste, will at once see the many objections which you must have to his proposal, but which you cannot write. Only think of being chaunted and recitatived by a parcel of hoarse and squeaking choristers on a birthday, for the edification of the bishops, pages, maids of honour, and gentlemen-pensioners ! Oh, horrible, thrice horrible ! Yours sincerely,

BUCCLEUCH, &c."

The letter which first announced the Prince Regent's proposal, was from his Royal Highness's librarian, Dr James Stanier Clarke ; but before Scott answered it he had received a more formal notification from the late Marquis of Hertford, then Lord Chamberlain. I shall transcribe both these documents.

" *To Walter Scott, Esq., Edinburgh.*

" Pavilion, Brighton, August 18, 1813.

" My Dear Sir,

" Though I have never had the honour of being introduced to you, you have frequently been pleased to convey to me very kind and flattering messages, * and I trust, therefore, you will allow me, without any further ceremony, to say — That I took an early opportunity this morning of seeing the Prince Regent, who arrived here late yesterday ; and I then delivered to his Royal Highness my earnest wish and anxious desire that the vacant situation of poet laureate might be conferred on you. The Prince replied, ' that you had already been written to, and that if you wished it, everything would be settled as I could desire.'

" I hope, therefore, I may be allowed to congratulate you on this event. You are the man to whom it ought first to have been offered, and it gave me sincere pleasure to find that those sentiments of high approbation which my Royal Master had so often expressed towards you in private, were now so openly and honourably displayed in public. Have the goodness, dear sir, to receive this intrusive letter

* The Royal librarian had forwarded to Scott presentation copies of his successive publications—The Progress of Maritime Discovery — Falconer's Shipwreck, with a Life of the Author — Naufragia—A Life of Nelson, in two quarto volumes, &c. &c. &c.

with your accustomed courtesy, and believe me, yours very sincerely,   J. S. CLARKE,

Librarian to H. R. H. the Prince Regent."

" *To Walter Scott, Esq., Edinburgh.*

"Ragley, 31st August 1813.

" Sir,

" I thought it my duty to his Royal Highness the Prince Regent, to express to him my humble opinion that I could not make so creditable a choice as in your person for the office, now vacant, of poet laureate. I am now authorized to offer it to you, which I would have taken an earlier opportunity of doing, but that, till this morning, I have had no occasion of seeing his Royal Highness since Mr Pye's death. I have the honour to be, sir, your most obedient, humble servant,

INGRAM HERTFORD."

The following letters conclude this matter :—

" *To the Most Noble the Marquis of Hertford, &c. &c. Ragley, Warwickshire.*

"Abbotsford, 4th Sept.

" My Lord,

" I am this day honoured with your Lordship's

letter of the 31st August, tendering for my acceptance
the situation of poet laureate in the Royal Household. I shall always think it the highest honour of
my life to have been the object of the good opinion
implied in your Lordship's recommendation, and in
the gracious acquiescence of his Royal Highness the
Prince Regent. I humbly trust I shall not forfeit
sentiments so highly valued, although I find myself
under the necessity of declining, with every acknow-
ledgement of respect and gratitude, a situation above
my deserts, and offered to me in a manner so very
flattering. The duties attached to the office of poet
laureate are not indeed very formidable, if judged of
by the manner in which they have sometimes been
discharged. But an individual selected from the
literary characters of Britain, upon the honourable
principle expressed in your Lordship's letter, ought
not, in justice to your Lordship, to his own reputation, but above all to his Royal Highness, to accept
of the office, unless he were conscious of the power
of filling it respectably, and attaining to excellence
in the execution of the tasks which it imposes. This
confidence I am so far from possessing, that, on the
contrary, with all the advantages which do now, and
I trust ever will, present themselves to the poet
whose task it may be to commemorate the events of
his Royal Highness's administration, I am certain I
should feel myself inadequate to the fitting discharge

of the regularly recurring duty of periodical composition, and should thus at once disappoint the expectation of the public, and, what would give me still more pain, discredit the nomination of his Royal Highness.

" Will your Lordship permit me to add, that though far from being wealthy, I already hold two official situations in the line of my profession, which afford a respectable income. It becomes me, therefore, to avoid the appearance of engrossing one of the few appointments which seem specially adapted for the provision of those whose lives have been dedicated exclusively to literature, and who too often derive from their labours more credit than emolument.

" Nothing could give me greater pain than being thought ungrateful to his Royal Highness's goodness, or insensible to the honourable distinction his undeserved condescension has been pleased to bestow upon me. I have to trust to your Lordship's kindness for laying at the feet of his Royal Highness, in the way most proper and respectful, my humble, grateful, and dutiful thanks, with these reasons for declining a situation which, though every way superior to my deserts, I should chiefly have valued as a mark of his Royal Highness's approbation.

For your Lordship's unmerited goodness, as well as for the trouble you have had upon this occasion,

I can only offer you my respectful thanks, and entreat that you will be pleased to believe me, my Lord Marquis, your Lordship's much obliged and much honoured humble servant,

WALTER SCOTT."

" *To His Grace the Duke of Buccleuch, &c.*
Drumlanrig Castle.

" Abbotsford, Sept. 5, 1813.
" My Dear Lord Duke,
    " Good advice is easily followed when it jumps with our own sentiments and inclinations. I no sooner found mine fortified by your Grace's opinion than I wrote to Lord Hertford, declining the laurel in the most civil way I could imagine. I also wrote to the Prince's librarian, who had made himself active on the occasion, dilating at somewhat more length than I thought respectful to the Lord Chamberlain, my reasons for declining the intended honour. My wife has made a copy of the last letter, which I enclose for your Grace's perusal — there is no occasion either to preserve or return it — but I am desirous you should know what I have put my apology upon, for I may reckon on its being misrepresented. I certainly should never have survived the recitative described by your Grace — it is a part of

the etiquette I was quite unprepared for, and should have sunk under it. It is curious enough that Drumlanrig should always have been the refuge of bards who decline court promotion. Gay, I think, refused to be a gentleman-usher, or some such post;* and I am determined to abide by my post of Grand Ecuyer Trenchant of the Chateau, varied for that of taleteller of an evening.

" I will send your Grace a copy of the letter of guarantee when I receive it from London. By an arrangement with Longman and Co., the great booksellers in Paternoster-row, I am about to be enabled to place their security, as well as my own, between your Grace and the possibility of hazard. But your kind readiness to forward a transaction which is of such great importance both to my fortune and comfort, can never be forgotten—although it can scarce make me more than I have always been, my dear Lord, your Grace's much obliged and truly faithful

WALTER SCOTT."

---

* Poor Gay — " In wit a man, simplicity a child,"—was insulted, on the accession of George II., by the offer of a gentleman-ushership to one of the royal infants. His prose and verse largely celebrate his obligations to Charles third Duke of Queensberry, and the charming Lady Catharine Hyde, his Duchess—under whose roof the poet spent the latter years of his life.

(COPY — ENCLOSURE.)

" *To the Rev. J. S. Clarke, &c. &c. &c.*
Pavilion, Brighton.

" Abbotsford, 4th September 1813.

" Sir,

" On my return to this cottage, after a short excursion, I was at once surprised and deeply interested by the receipt of your letter. I shall always consider it as the proudest incident of my life that his Royal Highness the Prince Regent, whose taste in literature is so highly distinguished, should have thought of naming me to the situation of poet laureate. I feel, therefore, no small embarrassment lest I should incur the suspicion of churlish ingratitude in declining an appointment in every point of view so far above my deserts, but which I should chiefly have valued as conferred by the unsolicited generosity of his Royal Highness, and as entitling me to the distinction of terming myself an immediate servant of his Majesty. But I have to trust to your goodness in representing to his Royal Highness, with my most grateful, humble, and dutiful acknowledgements, the circumstances which compel me to decline the honour which his undeserved favour has proposed for me. The poetical pieces I have hitherto

composed have uniformly been the hasty production
of impulses, which I must term fortunate, since they
have attracted his Royal Highness's notice and approbation. But I strongly fear, or rather am absolutely certain, that I should feel myself unable to
justify, in the eye of the public, the choice of his
Royal Highness, by a fitting discharge of the duties
of an office which requires stated and periodical
exertion. And although I am conscious how much
this difficulty is lessened under the government of his
Royal Highness, marked by paternal wisdom at home
and successes abroad which seem to promise the
liberation of Europe, I still feel that the necessity of
a regular commemoration would trammel my powers
of composition at the very time when it would be
equally my pride and duty to tax them to the utter-
most. There is another circumstance which weighs
deeply in my mind while forming my present resolution. I have already the honour to hold two appointments under Government, not usually conjoined, and
which afford an income, far indeed from wealth, but
amounting to decent independence. I fear, therefore,
that in accepting one of the few situations which our
establishment holds forth as the peculiar provision of
literary men, I might be justly censured as availing
myself of his Royal Highness's partiality to engross
more than my share of the public revenue, to the
prejudice of competitors equally meritorious at least,

and otherwise unprovided for; and as this calculation will be made by thousands who know that I have reaped great advantages by the favour of the public, without being aware of the losses which it has been my misfortune to sustain, I may fairly reckon that it will terminate even more to my prejudice than if they had the means of judging accurately of my real circumstances. I have thus far, sir, frankly exposed to you, for his Royal Highness's favourable consideration, the feelings which induce me to decline an appointment offered in a manner so highly calculated to gratify, I will not say my vanity only, but my sincere feelings of devoted attachment to the crown and constitution of my country, and to the person of his Royal Highness, by whom its government has been so worthily administered. No consideration on earth would give me so much pain as the idea of my real feelings being misconstrued on this occasion, or that I should be supposed stupid enough not to estimate the value of his Royal Highness's favour, or so ungrateful as not to feel it as I ought. And you will relieve me from great anxiety if you will have the goodness to let me know if his Royal Highness is pleased to receive favourably my humble and grateful apology.

" I cannot conclude without expressing my sense of your kindness and of the trouble you have had upon this account, and I request you will believe me, sir, your obliged humble servant,

WALTER SCOTT."

" To Robert Southey, Esq., Keswick.

" Abbotsford, 4th September 1813.

" My Dear Southey,

" On my return here I found, to my no small surprise, a letter tendering me the laurel vacant by the death of the poetical Pye. I have declined the appointment, as being incompetent to the task of annual commemoration; but chiefly as being provided for in my professional department, and unwilling to incur the censure of engrossing the emolument attached to one of the few appointments which seems proper to be filled by a man of literature who has no other views in life. Will you forgive me, my dear friend, if I own I had you in my recollection. I have given Croker the hint, and otherwise endeavoured to throw the office into your option. I am uncertain if you will like it, for the laurel has certainly been tarnished by some of its wearers, and, as at present managed, its duties are inconvenient and somewhat liable to ridicule. But the latter matter might be amended, as I think the Regent's good sense would lead him to lay aside these regular commemorations;

and as to the former point, it has been worn by Dryden of old, and by Warton in modern days. If you quote my own refusal against me, I reply — first, I have been luckier than you in holding two offices not usually conjoined; secondly, I did not refuse it from any foolish prejudice against the situation, otherwise how durst I mention it to you, my elder brother in the muse? — but from a sort of internal hope that they would give it to you, upon whom it would be so much more worthily conferred. For I am not such an ass as not to know that you are my better in poetry, though I have had, probably but for a time, the tide of popularity in my favour. I have not time to add ten thousand other reasons, but I only wished to tell you how the matter was, and to beg you to think before you reject the offer which I flatter myself will be made to you. If I had not been, like Dogberry, a fellow with two gowns already, I should have jumped at it like a cock at a gooseberry. Ever yours most truly,   WALTER SCOTT."

Immediately after Mr Croker received Scott's letter here alluded to, Mr Southey was invited to accept the vacant laurel. But, as the birthday ode had been omitted since the illness of King George III., and the Regent had good sense and good taste enough to hold that ancient custom as " more honoured in the breach than the observance," the whole fell completely into disuse.* The office was thus relieved from the burden of ridicule which had, in spite of so many illustrious names, adhered to it; and though its emoluments did not in fact amount to more than a quarter of the sum at which Scott rated them when he declined it, they formed no unacceptable addition to Mr Southey's income. Scott's answer to his brother poet's affectionate and grateful letter on the conclusion of this affair, is as follows:—

" *To R. Southey, Esq., Keswick.*

" Edinburgh, November 13, 1813.

" I do not delay, my dear Southey, to say my *gratulor*. Long may you live, as Paddy says, to rule over us, and to redeem the crown of Spenser and of Dryden to its pristine dignity. I am only discontented with the extent of your royal revenue, which I thought had been £400, or £300 at the very least. Is there no getting rid of that iniquitous modus, and requiring the *butt* in kind? I would have you think of it; I know no man so well entitled to Xeres sack as yourself, though many bards would

* See the Preface to the third volume of the late Collective Edition of Mr Southey's Poems, p. xii., where he corrects a trivial error I had fallen into in the first edition of these Memoirs, and adds, " Sir Walter's conduct was, as it always was, characteristically generous, and in the highest degree friendly."—[1839.]

make a better figure at drinking it. I should think
that in due time a memorial might get some relief in
this part of the appointment — it should be at least
£100 wet and £100 dry. When you have carried
your point of discarding the ode, and my point of
getting the sack, you will be exactly in the situation
of Davy in the farce, who stipulates for more wages,
less work, and the key of the ale-cellar.* I was greatly
delighted with the circumstances of your investiture.
It reminded me of the porters at Calais with Dr
Smollett's baggage, six of them seizing upon one
small portmanteau, and bearing it in triumph to his
lodgings. You see what it is to laugh at the superstitions of a gentleman-usher, as I think you do
somewhere. ' The whirligig of time brings in his
revenges.'†

" Adieu, my dear Southey; my best wishes attend all that you do, and my best congratulations
every good that attends you — yea even this, the
very least of Providence's mercies, as a poor clergyman said when pronouncing grace over a herring.
I should like to know how the Prince received
you; his address is said to be excellent, and his
knowledge of literature far from despicable. What
a change of fortune even since the short time when
we met! The great work of retribution is now roll-

* Garrick's *Bon Ton, or High Life Above Stairs.*
† *Twelfth Night, Act V. Scene 1.*

ing onward to consummation, yet am I not fully satisfied—*pereat iste !*—there will be no permanent peace in Europe till Buonaparte sleeps with the tyrants of old. My best compliments attend Mrs Southey and your family. Ever yours,

WALTER SCOTT."

To avoid returning to the affair of the laureate-ship, I have placed together such letters concerning it as appeared important. I regret to say that, had I adhered to the chronological order of Scott's correspondence, ten out of every twelve letters between the date of his application to the Duke of Buccleuch, and his removal to Edinburgh on the 12th of November, would have continued to tell the same story of pecuniary difficulty, urgent and almost daily applications for new advances to the Ballantynes, and endeavours, more or less successful, but in no case effectually so, to relieve the pressure on the book-selling firm by sales of its heavy stock to the great publishing houses of Edinburgh and London. Whatever success these endeavours met with, appears to have been due either directly or indirectly to Mr Constable; who did a great deal more than prudence would have warranted, in taking on himself the results of its unhappy adventures,—and, by his sagacious advice, enabled the distressed partners to procure similar assistance at the hands of others, who did not partake his own feelings of personal kindness and sympathy. " I regret to learn," Scott writes to him on the 16th October, " that there is great danger of your exertions in our favour, which once promised so fairly, proving finally abortive, or at least being too tardy in their operation to work out our relief. If anything more can be honourably and properly done to avoid a most unpleasant shock, I shall be most willing to do it; if not — God's will be done! There will be enough of property, including my private fortune, to pay every claim; and I have not used prosperity so ill, as greatly to fear adversity. But these things we will talk over at meeting; meanwhile believe me, with a sincere sense of your kindness and friendly views, very truly yours, W. S."—I have no wish to quote more largely from the letters which passed during this crisis between Scott and his partners. The pith and substance of his, to John Ballantyne at least, seems to be summed up in one brief *postscript:*—" For God's sake treat me as a man, and not as a milch-cow!"

The difficulties of the Ballantynes were by this time well known throughout the commercial circles not only of Edinburgh, but of London; and a report of their actual bankruptcy, with the addition that Scott was engaged as their surety to the extent of £20,000, found its way to Mr Morritt about the beginning of November. This dear friend wrote to

him, in the utmost anxiety, and made liberal offers
of assistance in case the catastrophe might still be
averted; but the term of Martinmas, always a critical
one in Scotland, had passed before this letter reached
Edinburgh, and Scott's answer will show symptoms
of a clearing horizon.   I think also there is one
expression in it which could hardly have failed to
convey to Mr Morritt that his friend was involved,
more deeply than he had ever acknowledged, in the
concerns of the Messrs Ballantyne.

" To J. B. S. Morritt, Esq., Rokeby Park.

" Edinburgh, 20th November 1813.

" I did not answer your very kind letter, my dear
Morritt, until I could put your friendly heart to rest
upon the report you have heard, which I could not
do entirely until this term of Martinmas was passed.
I have the pleasure to say that there is no truth
whatever in the Ballantynes' reported bankruptcy.
They have had severe difficulties for the last four
months to make their resources balance the demands
upon them, and I, having the price of Rokeby, and
other monies in their hands, have had considerable
reason for apprehension, and no slight degree of
plague and trouble.   They have, however, been so
well supported, that I have got out of hot water

upon their account.   They are winding up their
bookselling concern with great regularity, and are to
abide hereafter by the printing-office, which, with its
stock, &c., will revert to them fairly.

"I have been able to redeem the offspring of my
brain, and they are like to pay me like grateful children. This matter has set me a thinking about money
more seriously than ever I did in my life, and I have
begun by insuring my life for £4000, to secure some
ready cash to my family should I slip girths suddenly.
I think my other property, library, &c., may be worth
about £12,000, and I have not much debt.

"Upon the whole, I see no prospect of any loss
whatever.   Although in the course of human events
I may be disappointed, there certainly *can* be none to
vex your kind and affectionate heart on my account.
I am young, with a large official income, and if I lose
anything now, I have gained a great deal in my day.
I cannot tell you, and will not attempt to tell you,
how much I was affected by your letter—so much,
indeed, that for several days I could not make my
mind up to express myself on the subject.   Thank
God! all real danger was yesterday put over—and
I will write, in two or three days, a funny letter,
without any of these vile cash matters, of which it
may be said there is no living with them nor without
them.   Ever yours, most truly,

WALTER SCOTT."

All these annoyances produced no change whatever in Scott's habits of literary industry. During these anxious months of September, October, and November, he kept feeding James Ballantyne's press, from day to day, both with the annotated text of the closing volumes of Swift's works, and with the MS. of his Life of the Dean. He had also proceeded to mature in his own mind the plan of the Lord of the Isles, and executed such a portion of the First Canto as gave him confidence to renew his negotiation with Constable for the sale of the whole, or part of its copyright. It was, moreover, at this period, that, looking into an old cabinet in search of some fishing-tackle, his eye chanced to light once more on the Ashestiel fragment of *Waverley.* — He read over those introductory chapters — thought they had been undervalued — and determined to finish the story.

All this while, too, he had been subjected to those interruptions from idle strangers, which from the first to the last imposed so heavy a tax on his celebrity; and he no doubt received such guests with all his usual urbanity of attention. Yet I was not surprised to discover, among his hasty notes to the Ballantynes, several of tenour akin to the following specimens : —

" Sept. 2d, 1813.

" My temper is really worn to a hair's breadth.

The intruder of yesterday hung on me till twelve
to-day. When I had just taken my pen, he was
relieved, like a sentry leaving guard, by two other
lounging visitors; and their post has now been supplied by some people on real business."

Again—

" *Monday Evening.*

" Oh James! oh James! Two Irish dames
   Oppress me very sore;
  I groaning send one sheet I've penned—
   For, hang them! there's no more."

A scrap of nearly the same date to his brother
Thomas may be introduced, as belonging to the same
state of feeling—" Dear Tom, I observe what you
say as to Mr * * * *; and as you may often be
exposed to similar requests, which it would be difficult to parry, you can sign such letters of introduction as relate to persons whom you do not delight to
honour short, *T. Scott;* by which abridgement of
your name I shall understand to limit my civilities."

It is proper to mention, that, in the very agony of
these perplexities, the unfortunate Maturin received
from him a timely succour of £50, rendered doubly
acceptable by the kind and judicious letter of advice
in which it was enclosed; and I have before me
ample evidence that his benevolence had been ex-

tended to other struggling brothers of the trade, even when he must often have had actual difficulty to meet the immediate expenditure of his own family. All this, however, will not surprise the reader.

Nor did his general correspondence suffer much interruption; and, as some relief after so many painful details, I shall close the narrative of this anxious year by a few specimens of his miscellaneous communications : —

" *To Miss Joanna Baillie, Hampstead.*

" Abbotsford, Sept. 12, 1813.
" My Dear Miss Baillie,

" I have been a vile lazy correspondent, having been strolling about the country, and indeed a little way into England, for the greater part of July and August; in short, ' aye skipping here and there,' like the Tanner of Tamworth's horse. Since I returned, I have had a gracious offer of the laurel on the part of the Prince Regent. You will not wonder that I have declined it, though with every expression of gratitude which such an unexpected compliment demanded. Indeed, it would be high imprudence in one having literary reputation to maintain, to accept of an offer which obliged him to produce a poetical exercise on a given theme twice a-year; and besides, as my loyalty to the royal family is very sincere, I would not wish to have it thought mercenary. The public has done its part by me very well, and so has Government: and I thought this little literary provision ought to be bestowed on one who has made literature his sole profession. If the Regent means to make it respectable, he will abolish the foolish custom of the annual odes, which is a drudgery no person of talent could ever willingly encounter—or come clear off from, if he was so rash. And so, peace be with the laurel,

'Profaned by Cibber and contemned by Gray.'

"I was for a fortnight at Drumlanrig, a grand old chateau, which has descended, by the death of the late Duke of Queensberry, to the Duke of Buccleuch. It is really a most magnificent pile, and when embosomed amid the wide forest scenery, of which I have an infantine recollection, must have been very romantic. But old Q. made wild devastation among the noble trees, although some fine ones are still left, and a quantity of young shoots are, in despite of the want of every kind of attention, rushing up to supply the places of the fathers of the forest from whose stems they are springing. It will now I trust be in better hands, for the reparation of the castle goes hand in hand with the rebuilding of all the cottages, in which an aged race of pensioners of Duke Charles, and his pious wife, — ' Kitty, blooming, young and gay,' — have, during the last reign, been pining into rheumatisms and agues, in neglected poverty.

" All this is beautiful to witness ; the indoor work does not please me so well, though I am aware that, to those who are to inhabit an old castle, it becomes often a matter of necessity to make alterations by which its tone and character are changed for the worse. Thus a noble gallery, which ran the whole length of the front, is converted into bedrooms — very comfortable, indeed, but not quite so magnificent ; and as grim a dungeon as ever knave or honest man was confined in, is in some danger of being humbled into a wine-cellar. It is almost impossible to draw your breath, when you recollect that this, so many feet under ground, and totally bereft of air and light, was built for the imprisonment of human beings, whether guilty, suspected, or merely unfortunate. Certainly, if our frames are not so hardy, our hearts are softer than those of our forefathers, although probably a few years of domestic war, or feudal oppression, would bring us back to the same case-hardening both in body and sentiment.

" I meant to have gone to Rokeby, but was prevented by Mrs Morritt being unwell, which I very much regret, as I know few people that deserve better health. I am very glad you have known them, and I pray you to keep up the acquaintance in winter. I am glad to see by this day's paper that our friend Terry has made a favourable impression on his first appearance at Covent-Garden — he has got a very good engagement there for three years, at twelve guineas a-week, which is a handsome income. — This little place comes on as fast as can be reasonably hoped; and the pinasters are all above the ground, but cannot be planted out for twelve months. My kindest compliments — in which Mrs Scott always joins—attend Miss Agnes, the Doctor, and his family. Ever, my dear friend, yours most faithfully,

WALTER SCOTT."

" *To Daniel Terry, Esq., London.*

" Abbotsford, 20th October 1813.'

" Dear Terry,

" You will easily believe that I was greatly pleased to hear from you. I had already learned from The Courier (what I had anticipated too strongly to doubt for one instant) your favourable impression on the London public. I think nothing can be more judicious in the managers than to exercise the various powers you possess, in their various extents. A man of genius is apt to be limited to one single style, and to become per force a mannerist, merely because the public is not so just to its own amusement as to give him an opportunity of throwing himself into different lines; and doubtless the exercise of our talents in one unvaried course, by degrees renders them incapable of any other, as the over use of any one limb of our body gradually impoverishes the rest. I shall be anxious to hear that you have played *Malvolio*, which is, I think, one of your *coups-de-maître*, and in which envy itself cannot affect to trace an imitation. That same charge of imitation, by the way, is one of the surest scents upon which dunces are certain to open. Undoubtedly, if the same character is well performed by two individuals, their acting must bear a general resemblance — it could not be well performed by both were it otherwise. But this general resemblance, which arises from both following nature and their author, can as little be termed imitation as the river in Wales can be identified with that of Macedon. Never mind these dunderheads, but go on your own way, and scorn to laugh on the right side of your mouth, to make a difference from some ancient comedian who, in the same part, always laughed on the left. Stick to the public—be uniform in your exertions to study even those characters which have little in them, and to give a grace which you cannot find in the author. Audiences are always grateful for this—or rather—for gratitude is as much out of the question in the Theatre, as Bernadotte says to Boney it is amongst sovereigns—or rather, the au-

dience is gratified by receiving pleasure from a part
which they had no expectation would afford them
any. It is in this view that, had I been of your
profession, and possessed talents, I think I should
have liked often those parts with which my brethren
quarrelled, and studied to give them an effect which
their intrinsic merit did not entitle them to. I have
some thoughts of being in town in spring (not re-
solutions by any means); and it will be an additional
motive to witness your success, and to find you as
comfortably established as your friends in Castle Street
earnestly hope and trust you will be.

" The summer—an uncommon summer in beauty
and serenity—has glided away from us at Abbotsford, amidst our usual petty cares and petty pleasures.
The children's garden is in apple-pie order, our own
completely cropped and stocked, and all the trees
flourishing like the green bay of the Psalmist. I
have been so busy about our domestic arrangements,
that I have not killed six hares this season. Besides,
I have got a cargo of old armour, sufficient to excite
a suspicion that I intend to mount a squadron of
cuirassiers. I only want a place for my armoury;
and, thank God, I can wait for that, these being no
times for building. And this brings me to the loss
of poor Stark, with whom more genius has died than
is left behind among the collected universality of
Scottish architects. O, Lord!—but what does it

signify?—Earth was born to bear, and man to pay (that is, lords, nabobs, Glasgow traders, and those who have wherewithal)—so wherefore grumble at great castles and cottages, with which the taste of the latter contrives to load the back of Mother Terra?—I have no hobby-horsical commissions at present, unless if you meet the Voyages of Captain Richard, or Robert Falconer, in one volume—'cowheel, quoth Sancho'—I mark them for my own. Mrs Scott, Sophia, Anne, and the boys, unite in kind remembrances.   Ever yours truly,

W. SCOTT."

" *To the Right Hon. Lord Byron, 4 Bennet Street, St James's, London.*

" Abbotsford, 6th Nov. 1813.
" My Dear Lord,
   " I was honoured with your Lordship's letter of the 27th September,* and have sincerely to regret that there is such a prospect of your leaving Britain, without my achieving your personal acquaintance. I heartily wish your Lordship had come down to Scotland this season, for I have never seen a finer,

---

* The letter in question has not been preserved in Scott's collection of correspondence. This leaves some allusions in the answer obscure.

and you might have renewed all your old associations with Caledonia, and made such new ones as were likely to suit you. I dare promise you would have liked me well enough—for I have many properties of a Turk—never trouble myself about futurity— am as lazy as the day is long—delight in collecting silver-mounted pistols and ataghans, and go out of my own road for no one—all which I take to be attributes of your good Moslem. Moreover, I am somewhat an admirer of royalty, and in order to maintain this part of my creed, I shall take care never to be connected with a court, but stick to the *ignotum pro mirabili.*

" The author of the Queen's Wake will be delighted with your approbation. He is a wonderful creature for his opportunities, which were far inferior to those of the generality of Scottish peasants. Burns, for instance—(not that their extent of talents is to be compared for an instant)—had an education not much worse than the sons of many gentlemen in Scotland. But poor Hogg literally could neither read nor write till a very late period of his life; and when he first distinguished himself by his poetical talent, could neither spell nor write grammar. When I first knew him, he used to send me his poetry, and was both indignant and horrified when I pointed out to him parallel passages in authors whom he had never read, but whom all the world would have sworn he had copied. An evil fate has hitherto attended him, and baffled every attempt that has been made to place him in a road to independence. But I trust he may be more fortunate in future.

" I have not yet seen Southey in the Gazette as Laureate. He is a real poet, such as we read of in former times, with every atom of his soul and every moment of his time dedicated to literary pursuits, in which he differs from almost all those who have divided public attention with him. Your Lordship's habits of society, for example, and my own professional and official avocations, must necessarily connect us much more with our respective classes in the usual routine of pleasure or business, than if we had not any other employment than *vacare musis*. But Southey's ideas are all poetical, and his whole soul dedicated to the pursuit of literature. In this respect, as well as in many others, he is a most striking and interesting character.

" I am very much interested in all that concerns your Giaour, which is universally approved of among our mountains. I have heard no objection except by one or two geniuses, who run over poetry as a cat does over a harpischord, and they affect to complain of obscurity. On the contrary, I hold every real lover of the art is obliged to you for condensing the narrative, by giving us only those striking scenes which you have shown to be so susceptible of poetic ornament, and leaving to imagination the says I's and says he's, and all the minutiæ of detail which might be proper in giving evidence before a court of justice. The truth is, I think poetry is most striking when the mirror can be held up to the reader, and the same kept constantly before his eyes; it requires most uncommon powers to support a direct and downright narration; nor can I remember many instances of its being successfully maintained even by our greatest bards.

" As to those who have done me the honour to take my rhapsodies for their model, I can only say they have exemplified the ancient adage, ' one fool makes many;' nor do I think I have yet had much reason to suppose I have given rise to anything of distinguished merit. The worst is, it draws on me letters and commendatory verses, to which my sad and sober thanks in humble prose are deemed a most unmeet and ungracious reply. Of this sort of plague your Lordship must ere now have had more than your share, but I think you can hardly have met with so original a request as concluded the letter of a bard I this morning received, who limited his demands to being placed in his due station on Parnassus—*and* invested with a post in the Edinburgh Custom House.

" What an awakening of dry bones seems to be taking place on the Continent! I could as soon have

believed in the resurrection of the Romans as in that
of the Prussians—yet it seems a real and active
renovation of national spirit. It will certainly be
strange enough if that tremendous pitcher, which
has travelled to so many fountains, should be at
length broken on the banks of the Saale ; but from
the highest to the lowest we are the fools of fortune.
Your Lordship will probably recollect where the
Oriental tale occurs, of a Sultan who consulted So-
lomon on the proper inscription for a signet-ring,
requiring that the maxim which it conveyed should
be at once proper for moderating the presumption of
prosperity and tempering the pressure of adversity.
The apophthegm supplied by the Jewish sage was,
I think, admirably adapted for both purposes, being
comprehended in the words ' And this also shall pass
away.'

" When your Lordship sees Rogers, will you remember me kindly to him ? I hope to be in London
next spring, and renew my acquaintance with my
friends there. It will be an additional motive if I
could flatter myself that your Lordship's stay in the
country will permit me the pleasure of waiting upon
you. I am, with much respect and regard, your
Lordship's truly honoured and obliged humble servant,   WALTER SCOTT.

" I go to Edinburgh next week, *multum gemens*."

" *To Miss Joanna Baillie, Hampstead.*

" Edinburgh, 10th Dec. 1813.

" Many thanks, my dear friend, for your kind token of remembrance, which I yesterday received. I ought to blush, if I had grace enough left, at my long and ungenerous silence : but what shall I say ? The habit of procrastination, which had always more or less a dominion over me, does not relax its sway as I grow older and less willing to take up the pen. I have not written to dear Ellis this age, — yet there is not a day that I do not think of you and him, and one or two other friends in your southern land. I am very glad the whisky came safe : do not stint so laudable an admiration for the liquor of Caledonia, for I have plenty of right good and sound Highland Ferintosh, and I can always find an opportunity of sending you up a bottle.

" We are here almost mad with the redemption of Holland, which has an instant and gratifying effect on the trade of Leith, and indeed all along the east coast of Scotland. About £100,000 worth of various commodities, which had been dormant in cellars and warehouses, was sold the first day the news arrived, and Orange ribbons and *Orange Boven* was the order of the day among all ranks. It is a most miraculous revivification which it has been our fate to witness. Though of a tolerably sanguine temper, I had fairly adjourned all hopes and expectations of the kind till another generation: the same power, however, that opened the windows of heaven and the fountains of the great deep, has been pleased to close them, and to cause his wind to blow upon the face of the waters, so that we may look out from the ark of our preservation, and behold the re-appearance of the mountain crests, and old, beloved, and well-known landmarks, which we had deemed swallowed up for ever in the abyss: the dove with the olive branch would complete the simile, but of that I see little hope. Buonaparte is that desperate gambler, who will not rise while he has a stake left; and, indeed, to be King of France would be a poor pettifogging enterprise, after having been almost Emperor of the World. I think he will drive things on, till the fickle and impatient people over whom he rules get tired of him and shake him out of the saddle. Some circumstances seem to intimate his having become jealous of the Senate; and indeed anything like a representative body, however imperfectly constructed, becomes dangerous to a tottering tyranny. The sword displayed on both frontiers may, like that brandished across the road of Balaam, terrify even dumb and irrational subjection into utterance: but enough of politics, though now a more cheerful subject than they have been for many years past.

" I have had a strong temptation to go to the
Continent this Christmas; and should certainly have
done so, had I been sure of getting from Amsterdam
to Frankfort, where, as I know Lord Aberdeen and
Lord Cathcart, I might expect a welcome. But
notwithstanding my earnest desire to see the allied
armies cross the Rhine, which I suppose must be one
of the grandest military spectacles in the world, I
should like to know that the roads were tolerably
secure, and the means of getting forward attainable.
In spring, however, if no unfortunate change takes
place, I trust to visit the camp of the allies, and see
all the pomp and power and circumstance of war,
which I have so often imagined, and sometimes attempted to embody in verse.——Johnnie Richardson is
a good, honourable, kind-hearted little fellow as lives
in the world, with a pretty taste for poetry, which he
has wisely kept under subjection to the occupation of
drawing briefs and revising conveyances. It is a
great good fortune to him to be in your neighbourhood, as he is an idolator of genius, and where could
he offer up his worship so justly? And I am sure
you will like him, for he is really ' officious, inno-
cent, sincere.'* Terry, I hope, will get on well; he
is industrious, and zealous for the honour of his art.

* Scott's old friend, Mr. John Richardson, had shortly before
this time taken a house in Miss Baillie's neighbourhood, on
Hampstead Heath.

Ventidius must have been an excellent part for him, hovering between tragedy and comedy, which is precisely what will suit him. We have a woful want of him here, both in public and private, for he was one of the most easy and quiet chimney-corner companions that I have had for these two or three years past.

 " I am very glad if anything I have written to you could give pleasure to Miss Edgeworth, though I am sure it will fall very short of the respect which I have for her brilliant talents. I always write to you *à la volée*, and trust implicitly to your kindness and judgment upon all occasions where you may choose to communicate any part of my letters.* As to the taxing men, I must battle them as I can: they are worse than the great Emathian conqueror, who

> ' bade spare
> The house of Pindarus, when temple and tower
> Went to the ground.' †

Your pinasters are coming up gallantly in the nursery-bed at Abbotsford. I trust to pay the whole establishment a Christmas visit, which will be, as Robinson Crusoe says of his glass of rum, ' to mine exceeding refreshment.' All Edinburgh have been

---

 * Miss Baillie had apologized to him for having sent an extract of one of his letters to her friend at Edgeworthstown.

 † Milton — *Sonnet No. VIII.*

on tiptoe to see Madame de Staël, but she is now not likely to honour us with a visit, at which I cannot prevail on myself to be very sorry; for as I tired of some of her works, I am afraid I should disgrace my taste by tiring of the authoress too. All my little people are very well, learning, with great pain and diligence, much which they will have forgotten altogether, or nearly so, in the course of twelve years hence; but the habit of learning is something in itself, even when the lessons are forgotten.

" I must not omit to tell you that a friend of mine, with whom that metal is more plenty than with me, has given me some gold mohurs to be converted into a ring for enchasing King Charles' hair; but this is not to be done until I get to London, and get a very handsome pattern. Ever, most truly and sincerely, yours, W. SCOTT."

The last sentence of this letter refers to a lock of the hair of Charles I., which, at Dr Baillie's request, Sir Henry Halford had transmitted to Scott when the royal martyr's remains were discovered at Windsor, in April 1813. Sir John Malcolm had given him some Indian coins to supply virgin gold for the setting of this relic; and for some years he constantly wore the ring, which is a massive and beautiful one, with the word REMEMBER surrounding it in highly relieved black-letter.

The poet's allusion to " taxing men" may require
another word of explanation. To add to his troubles
during this autumn of 1813, a demand was made
on him by the commissioners of the income-tax, to
return in one of their schedules an account of the
profits of his literary exertions during the three last
years. He demurred to this, and took the opinion of
high authorities in Scotland, who confirmed him in
his impression that the claim was beyond the statute.
The grounds of his resistance are thus briefly stated
in one of his letters to his legal friend in London:—

" *To John Richardson, Esq., Fludyer Street,*
Westminster.

" My Dear Richardson,
    " I have owed you a letter this long time, but
perhaps my debt might not yet be discharged, had I
not a little matter of business to trouble you with.
I wish you to lay before either the King's counsel,
or Sir Samuel Romilly and any other you may approve, the point whether a copyright, being sold for
the term during which Queen Anne's act warranted
the property to the author, the price is liable in pay-
ment of the property-tax. I contend it is not so
liable, for the following reasons:— 1*st,* It is a patent
right, expected to produce an annual, or at least an

incidental profit, during the currency of many years; and surely it was never contended that if a man sold a theatrical patent, or a patent for machinery, property-tax should be levied in the first place on the full price as paid to the seller, and then on the profits as purchased by the buyer. I am not very expert at figures, but I think it clear that a double taxation takes place. 2*d*, It should be considered that a book may be the work not of one year, but of a man's whole life; and as it has been found, in a late case of the Duke of Gordon, that a fall of timber was not subject to property-tax because it comprehended the produce of thirty years, it seems at least equally fair that mental exertions should not be subjected to a harder principle of measurement. 3*d*, The demand is, so far as I can learn, totally new and unheard of. 4*th*, Supposing that I died and left my manuscripts to be sold publicly along with the rest of my library, is there any ground for taxing what might be received for the written book, any more than any rare printed book which a speculative bookseller might purchase with a view to re-publication? You will know whether any of these things ought to be suggested in the brief. David Hume, and every lawyer here whom I have spoken to, consider the demand as illegal. Believe me truly yours,

WALTER SCOTT."

Mr Richardson having prepared a case, obtained upon it the opinions of Mr Alexander (afterwards Sir William Alexander and Chief Baron of the Exchequer) and of the late Sir Samuel Romilly. These eminent lawyers agreed in the view of their Scotch brethren; and after a tedious correspondence, the Lords of the Treasury at last decided that the Income-Tax Commissioners should abandon their claim upon the produce of literary labour. I have thought it worth while to preserve some record of this decision, and of the authorities on which it rested, in case such a demand should ever be renewed hereafter.

In the beginning of December, the Town-Council of Edinburgh resolved to send a deputation to congratulate the Prince Regent on the prosperous course of public events, and they invited Scott to draw up their address, which, on its being transmitted for previous inspection to Mr William Dundas, then Member for the City, and through him shown privately to the Regent, was acknowledged to the penman, by his Royal Highness's command, as " the most elegant congratulation a sovereign ever received, or a subject offered." *   The Lord Provost of Edinburgh presented it accordingly at the levee of

* Letter from the Right Hon. W. Dundas, dated 6th December 1813.

the 10th, and it was received most graciously. On returning to the north, the Magistrates expressed their sense of Scott's services on this occasion by presenting him with the freedom of his native city, and also with a piece of plate,—which the reader will find alluded to, among other matters of more consequence, in a letter to be quoted presently.

At this time Scott further expressed his patriotic exultation in the rescue of Europe, by two songs for the anniversary of the death of Pitt; one of which has ever since, I believe, been chaunted at that celebration : —

" O dread was the time and more dreadful the omen,
    When the brave on Marengo lay slaughter'd in vain,"* &c.

* See Scott's Poetical Works, vol xi. p. 309.   Edition 1834.

CHAPTER XXVII.

Insanity of Henry Weber—Letters on the Abdication of Napoleon, &c.—Publication of Scott's Life and Edition of Swift—Essays for the Supplement to the Encyclopædia Britannica—Completion and Publication of Waverley.

1814.

I HAVE to open the year 1814 with a melancholy story.   Mention has been made, more than once, of Henry Weber, a poor German scholar, who escaping to this country in 1804, from misfortunes in his own, excited Scott's compassion, and was thenceforth furnished, through his means, with literary employment of various sorts.   Weber was a man of considerable learning; but Scott, as was his custom, appears to have formed an exaggerated notion of his capacity, and certainly countenanced him, to his own

severe cost, in several most unfortunate undertakings.
When not engaged on things of a more ambitious
character, he had acted for ten years as his protector's amanuensis, and when the family were in Edinburgh, he very often dined with them. There was
something very interesting in his appearance and
manners : he had a fair, open countenance, in which
the honesty and the enthusiasm of his nation were
alike visible ; his demeanour was gentle and modest ;
and he had not only a stock of curious antiquarian
knowledge, but the reminiscences, which he detailed
with amusing simplicity, of an early life chequered
with many strange-enough adventures. He was, in
short, much a favourite with Scott and all the household ; and was invited to dine with them so frequently, chiefly because his friend was aware that he
had an unhappy propensity to drinking,. and was
anxious to keep him away from places where he
might have been more likely to indulge it. This
vice, however, had been growing on him ; and of late
Scott had found it necessary to make some rather
severe remonstrances about habits which were at
once injuring his health, and interrupting his literary
industry.

They had, however, parted kindly when Scott left
Edinburgh at Christmas 1813, — and the day after
his return, Weber attended him as usual in his library, being employed in transcribing extracts during

several hours, while his friend, seated over against
him, continued working at the Life of Swift.   The
light beginning to fail, Scott threw himself back in
his chair, and was about to ring for candles, when
he observed the German's eyes fixed upon him with
an unusual solemnity of expression.   " Weber," said
he, " what's the matter with you ?"   " Mr Scott,"
said Weber rising, " you have long insulted me, and
I can bear it no longer.   I have brought a pair of
pistols with me, and must insist on your taking one
of them instantly ;" and with that he produced the
weapons, which had been deposited under his chair,
and laid one of them on Scott's manuscript.   " You
are mistaken, I think," said Scott, " in your way of
setting about this affair — but no matter.   It can,
however, be no part of your object to annoy Mrs
Scott and the children ; therefore, if you please, we
will put the pistols into the drawer till after dinner,
and then arrange to go out together like gentlemen."
Weber answered with equal coolness, " I believe that
will be better," and laid the second pistol also on the
table.   Scott locked them both in his desk, and said,
" I am glad you have felt the propriety of what I
suggested — let me only request further, that nothing
may occur while we are at dinner to give my wife
any suspicion of what has been passing."   Weber
again assented, and Scott withdrew to his dressing-
room, from which he immediately despatched a mes-

sage to one of Weber's intimate companions, — and
then dinner was served, and Weber joined the family
circle as usual. He conducted himself with perfect
composure, and everything seemed to go on in the
ordinary way, until whisky and hot water being produced, Scott, instead of inviting his guest to help
himself, mixed two moderate tumblers of toddy, and
handed one of them to Weber, who, upon that, start-
ed up with a furious countenance, but instantly sat
down again, and when Mrs Scott expressed her fear
that he was ill, answered placidly that he was liable
to spasms, but that the pain was gone. He then
took the glass, eagerly gulped down its contents,
and pushed it back to Scott. At this moment the
friend who had been sent for made his appearance,
and Weber, on seeing him enter the room, rushed
past him and out of the house, without stopping to
put on his hat. The friend, who pursued instantly,
came up with him at the end of the street, and did
all he could to soothe his agitation, but in vain. The
same evening he was obliged to be put into a strait
waistcoat; and though, in a few days, he exhibited
such symptoms of recovery that he was allowed to
go by himself to pay a visit in the North of England,
he there soon relapsed, and continued ever afterwards
a hopeless lunatic, being supported to the end of his
life, in June 1818, at Scott's expense in an asylum
at York.

The reader will now appreciate the gentle delicacy of the following letter :—

To J. B. S. Morritt, Esq., Rokeby, Greta Bridge.

"Edinburgh, 7th January 1814.

" Many happy New-years to you and Mrs Morritt.

" My Dear Morritt,

"I have postponed writing a long while, in hopes to send you the Life of Swift. But I have been delayed by an odd accident. Poor Weber, whom you may have heard me mention as a sort of grinder of mine, who assisted me in various ways, has fallen into a melancholy state. His habits, like those of most German students, were always too convivial—this, of course, I guarded against while he was in my house, which was always once a-week at least ; but unfortunately he undertook a long walk through the Highlands of upwards of 2000 miles, and, I suppose, took potations pottle deep to support him through the fatigue. His mind became accordingly quite unsettled, and after some strange behaviour here, he was fortunately prevailed upon to go to * * * * who resides in Yorkshire. It is not unlikely, from something that dropped from him, that he may take it into his head to call at Rokeby, in which case you must parry any visit, upon the score

of Mrs Morritt's health.   If he were what he used to
be, you would be much pleased with him ; for besides
a very extensive general acquaintance with literature,
he was particularly deep in our old dramatic lore, a
good modern linguist, a tolerable draughtsman and
antiquary, and a most excellent hydrographer.   I
have not the least doubt that if he submits to the
proper regimen of abstinence and moderate exercise,
he will be quite well in a few weeks or days—if not,
it is miserable to think what may happen.   The being
suddenly deprived of his services in this melancholy
way, has flung me back at least a month with Swift,
and left me no time to write to my friends, for all
my memoranda, &c. were in his hands, and had to be
new-modelled, &c. &c.

" Our glorious prospects on the Continent called
forth the congratulations of the City of Edinburgh
among others.   The Magistrates asked me to draw
their address, which was presented by the Lord Provost in person, who happens to be a gentleman of
birth and fortune.*   The Prince said some very
handsome things respecting the address, with which
the Magistrates were so much elated, that they have
done the genteel thing (as Winifred Jenkins says) by
their literary adviser, and presented me with the
freedom of the city, and a handsome piece of plate.

* The late Sir John Marjoribanks of Lees, Bart.

I got the freedom at the same time with Lord Dal-
housie and Sir Thomas Graham, and the Provost
gave a very brilliant entertainment.　About 150 gentlemen dined at his own house, all as well served as if
there had been a dozen.　So if one strikes a cuff on
the one side from ill-will, there is a pat on the other
from kindness, and the shuttlecock is kept flying.
To poor Charlotte's great horror, I chose my plate
in the form of an old English tankard, an utensil for
which I have a particular respect, especially when
charged with good ale, cup, or any of these potables.
I hope you will soon see mine.*

" Your little friends, Sophia and Walter, were at
a magnificent party on Twelfth Night at Dalkeith,
where the Duke and Duchess entertained all Edinburgh.　I think they have dreamed of nothing since

---

* The inscription for this tankard was penned by the late celebrated Dr. James Gregory, Professor of the Practice of Physic
in the University of Edinburgh; and I therefore transcribe it.

GUALTERUM SCOTT

DE ABBOTSFORD

VIRUM SUMMI INGENII

SCRIPTOREM ELEGANTEM

POETARUM SUI SECULI FACILE PRINCIPEM

PATRIÆ DECUS

OB VARIA ERGA IPSAM MERITA

IN CIVIUM SUORUM NUMERUM

GRATA ADSCRIPSIT CIVITAS EDINBURGENSIS

ET HOC CANTHARO DONAVIT

A. D. M.DCCC.XIII.

but Aladdin's lamp and the palace of Haroun Alraschid. I am uncertain what to do this spring. I would fain go on the continent for three or four weeks, if it be then safe for non-combatants. If not, we will have a merry meeting in London, and, like Master Silence,

> ' Eat, drink, and make good cheer,
>   And praise heaven for the merry year.' *

I have much to say about Triermain. The fourth edition is at press. The Empress-Dowager of Russia has expressed such an interest in it, that it will be inscribed to her, in some doggrel sonnet or other, by the unknown author. This is funny enough. — Love a thousand times to dear Mrs Morritt, who, I trust, keeps pretty well. Pray write soon — a modest request from   WALTER SCOTT."

The last of Weber's literary productions were the analyses of the Old German Poems of the *Helden Buch*, and the *Nibelungen Lied*, which appeared in a massive quarto, entitled Illustrations of Northern Antiquities, published in the summer of 1814, by his and Scott's friend, Mr Robert Jameson. Scott avowedly contributed to this collection an account of the Eyrbiggia Saga, which has since been included in his Prose Miscellanies (Vol. V., edition 1834); but

* *2d King Henry IV. Act V. Scene 3.*

any one who examines the share of the work which
goes under Weber's name, will see that Scott had a
considerable hand in that also.   The rhymed versions
from the Nibelungen Lied came, I can have no doubt,
from his pen ; but he never reclaimed these, or any
other similar benefactions, of which I have traced
not a few ;   nor, highly curious and even beautiful
as many of them are, could they be intelligible, if
separated from the prose narrative on which Weber
embroidered them, in imitation of the style of Ellis's
Specimens of Metrical Romance.

The following letters, on the first abdication of
Napoleon, are too characteristic to be omitted here.
I need not remind the reader how greatly Scott had
calmed his opinions, and softened his feelings, respecting the career and fate of the most extraordinary man
of our age, before he undertook to write his history.

> " *To J. B. S. Morritt, Esq., Portland Place,*
> *London.*

> " Abbotsford, 30th April 1814.

" ' Joy—joy in London now!'— and in Edinburgh, moreover, my dear Morritt; for never did
you or I see, and never again shall we see, according
to all human prospects, a consummation so truly
glorious, as now bids fair to conclude this long and
eventful war.   It is startling to think that, but for

the preternatural presumption and hardness of heart displayed by the arch-enemy of mankind, we should have had a hollow and ominous truce with him, instead of a glorious and stable peace with the country over which he tyrannized, and its lawful ruler. But Providence had its own wise purposes to answer — and such was the deference of France to the ruling power—so devoutly did they worship the Devil for possession of his burning throne, that, it may be, nothing short of his rejection of every fair and advantageous offer of peace could have driven them to those acts of resistance which remembrance of former convulsions had rendered so fearful to them. Thank God! it is done at last: and—although I rather grudge him even the mouthful of air which he may draw in the Isle of Elba—yet I question whether the moral lesson would have been completed either by his perishing in battle, or being torn to pieces (which I should greatly have preferred), like the De Witts, by an infuriated crowd of conscripts and their parents. Good God! with what strange feelings must that man retire from the most unbounded authority ever vested in the hands of one man, to the seclusion of privacy and restraint! We have never heard of one good action which he did, at least for which there was not some selfish or political reason; and the train of slaughter, pestilence, and famine and fire, which his ambition has occasioned, would have outweighed five

hundredfold the private virtues of a Titus. These
are comfortable reflections to carry with one to privacy.   If he writes his own history, as he proposes,
we may gain something; but he must send it here
to be printed.   Nothing less than a neck-or-nothing
London bookseller, like John Dunton of yore, will
venture to commit to the press his strange details
uncastrated.   I doubt if he has *stamina* to undertake such a labour; and yet, in youth, as I know
from the brothers of Lauriston, who were his school-
companions, Buonaparte's habits were distinctly and
strongly literary.   Spain, the Continental System,
and the invasion of Russia he may record as his three
leading blunders—an awful lesson to sovereigns that
morality is not so indifferent to politics as Machiave-
lians will assert. *Res nolunt diu male administrari.*
Why can we not meet to talk over these matters
over a glass of claret? and when shall that be? Not
this spring, I fear, for time wears fast away, and I
have remained here nailed among my future oaks,
which I measure daily with a foot-rule.   Those which
were planted two years ago, begin to look very gaily,
and a venerable plantation of four years old looks as
bobbish as yours at the dairy by Greta side.   Besides,
I am arranging this cottage a little more conveniently,
to put off the plague and expense of building another
year; and I assure you, I expect to spare Mrs Morritt
and you a chamber in the wall, with a dressing-room

and everything handsome about you. You will not stipulate, of course, for many square feet. You would be surprised to hear how the Continent is awakening from its iron sleep. The utmost eagerness seems to prevail about English literature. I have had several voluntary epistles from different parts of Germany, from men of letters, who are eager to know what we have been doing, while they were compelled to play at blind man's buff with the *ci-devant Empereur*. The feeling of the French officers, of whom we have many in our vicinity, is very curious, and yet natural.* Many of them, companions of Buonaparte's victories, and who hitherto have marched with him from conquest to conquest, disbelieve the change entirely. This is all very stupid to write to you, who are in the centre of these wonders; but what else can I say, unless I should send you the measure of the future fathers of the forest? Mrs Scott is with me here—the children in Edinburgh. Our kindest love attends Mrs Morritt. I hope to hear soon that her health continues to gain ground.

" I have a letter from Southey, in high spirits on the glorious news. What a pity this last battle† was

* A good many French officers, prisoners of war, had been living on *parole* in Melrose, and the adjoining villages; and Mr and Mrs Scott had been particularly kind and hospitable to them.

† The battle of Thoulouse.

fought.   But I am glad the rascals were beaten once
more.   Ever yours,   WALTER SCOTT."

" To Robert Southey, Esq., Keswick.

" Edinburgh, 17th June 1814.

" My Dear Southey,
        " I suspended writing to thank you for the
Carmen Triumphale—(a happy omen of what you
can do to immortalize our public story)—until the
feverish mood of expectation and anxiety should be
over.   And then, as you truly say, there followed a
stunning sort of listless astonishment and complica-
tion of feeling, which if it did not lessen enjoyment,
confused and confounded one's sense of it.   I remember the first time I happened to see a launch, I
was neither so much struck with the descent of the
vessel, nor with its majestic sweep to its moorings,
as with the blank which was suddenly made from the
withdrawing so large an object, and the prospect
which was at once opened to the opposite side of
the dock crowded with spectators.   Buonaparte's fall
strikes me something in the same way : the huge
bulk of his power, against which a thousand arms
were hammering, was obviously to sink when its
main props were struck away —and yet now—when
it has disappeared—the vacancy which it leaves in
our minds and attention, marks its huge and prepon-

derating importance more strongly than even its presence. Yet I so devoutly expected the termination, that in discussing the matter with Major Philips, who seemed to partake of the doubts which prevailed during the feverish period preceding the capture of Paris, when he was expressing his apprehensions that the capital of France would be defended to the last, I hazarded a prophecy that a battle would be fought on the heights of Mont Martre—(no great sagacity, since it was the point where Marlborough proposed to attack, and for which Saxe projected a scheme of defence)—and that if the allies were successful, which I little doubted, the city would surrender, and the Senate proclaim the dethronement of Buonaparte. But I never thought nor imagined that he would have *given in* as he has done. I always considered him as possessing the genius and talents of an Eastern conqueror; and although I never supposed that he possessed, allowing for some difference of education, the liberality of conduct and political views which were sometimes exhibited · by old Hyder Ally, yet I did think he might have shown the same resolved and dogged spirit of resolution which induced Tippoo Saib to die manfully upon the breach of his capital city with his sabre clenched in his hand. But this is a poor devil, and cannot play the tyrant so rarely as Bottom the Weaver proposed to do. I think it is Strap in Roderick Random, who seeing a highwayman that had lately robbed him, disarmed and bound, fairly offers to box him for a shilling. One has really the same feeling with respect to Buonaparte, though if he go out of life after all in the usual manner, it will be the strongest proof of his own insignificance, and the liberality of the age we live in. Were I a son of Palm or Hoffer, I should be tempted to take a long shot at him in his retreat to Elba. As for coaxing the French by restoring all our conquests, it would be driving generosity into extravagance: most of them have been colonized with British subjects, and improved by British capital; and surely we owe no more to the French nation than any well-meaning individual might owe to a madman, whom—at the expense of a hard struggle, black eyes, and bruises —he has at length overpowered, knocked down, and by the wholesome discipline of a bull's pizzle and strait jacket, brought to the handsome enjoyment of his senses. I think with you, what we return to them should be well paid for; and they should have no Pondicherry to be a nest of smugglers, nor Mauritius to nurse a hornet-swarm of privateers. In short, draw teeth, and pare claws, and leave them to fatten themselves in peace and quiet, when they are deprived of the means of indulging their restless spirit of enterprise.

" —— The above was written at Abbotsford last

month, but left in my portfolio there till my return
some days ago; and now, when I look over what I
have written, I am confirmed in my opinion that we
have given the rascals too good an opportunity to
boast that they have got well off.   An intimate
friend of mine,* just returned from a long captivity
in France, witnessed the entry of the King, guarded
by the Imperial Guards, whose countenances be-
tokened the most sullen and ferocious discontent.
The mob, and especially the women, pelted them
for refusing to cry ' Vive le Roi.'   If Louis is well
advised, he will get rid of these fellows gradually,
but as soon as possible.   ' Joy, joy in London now!'
What a scene has been going on there! I think you
may see the Czar appear on the top of one of your
stages one morning.   He is a fine fellow, and has
fought the good fight.   Yours affectionately,

WALTER SCOTT."

On the 1st of July 1814, Scott's Life and Edition
of Swift, in nineteen volumes 8vo, at length issued
from the press.   This adventure, undertaken by
Constable in 1808, had been proceeded in during
all the variety of their personal relations, and now
came forth when author and publisher felt more
warmly towards each other than perhaps they had

* Sir Adam Fergusson, who had been taken prisoner in the
course of the Duke of Wellington's retreat from Burgos.

VOL. IV.   L

ever before done. The impression was of 1250
copies; and a reprint of similar extent was called
for in 1824. The Life of Swift has subsequently
been included in the author's Miscellanies, and has
obtained a very wide circulation.

By his industrious enquiries, in which, as the
preface gratefully acknowledges, he found many zealous assistants, especially among the Irish literati,*
Scott added to this edition many admirable pieces,
both in prose and verse, which had never before
been printed, and still more which had escaped notice amidst old bundles of pamphlets and broadsides.
To the illustration of these and of all the better
known writings of the Dean, he brought the same
qualifications which had, by general consent, distinguished his Dryden, " uniting," as the Edinburgh
Review expresses it, " to the minute knowledge
and patient research of the Malones and Chalmerses,
a vigour of judgment and a vivacity of style to which
they had no pretensions." His biographical narrative, introductory essays, and notes on Swift, show,
indeed, an intimacy of acquaintance with the ob-
scurest details of the political, social, and literary
history of the period of Queen Anne, which it is

* The names which he particularly mentions, are those of the
late Matthew Weld Hartstonge, Esq., of Dublin, Theophilus
Swift, Esq., Major Tickell, Thomas Steele, Esq., Leonard
Macnally, Esq., and the Rev. M. Berwick.

impossible to consider without feeling a lively regret
that he never accomplished a long-cherished purpose of preparing a Life and Edition of Pope on a
similar scale. It has been specially unfortunate for
that "true deacon of the craft," as Scott often called
Pope, that first Goldsmith, and then Scott, should
have taken up, only to abandon it, the project of
writing his life and editing his works.

The Edinburgh Reviewer thus characterises Scott's
Memoir of the Dean of St Patrick's :—

"It is not everywhere extremely well written, in a literary
point of view, but it is drawn up in substance with great intelligence, liberality, and good feeling. It is quite fair and moderate
in politics; and perhaps rather too indulgent and tender towards
individuals of all descriptions — more full, at least, of kindness
and veneration for genius and social virtue, than of indignation
at baseness and profligacy. Altogether, it is not much like the
production of a mere man of letters, or a fastidious speculator in
sentiment and morality; but exhibits throughout, and in a very
pleasing form, the good sense and large toleration of a man of
the world, with much of that generous allowance for the

‘ Fears of the brave and follies of the wise,’

which genius too often requires, and should therefore always be
most forward to show. It is impossible, however, to avoid noticing that Mr Scott is by far too favourable to the personal character of his author, whom we think it would really be injurious
to the cause of morality to allow to pass either as a very dignified,
or a very amiable person. The truth is, we think, that he was
extremely ambitious, arrogant, and selfish; of a morose, vindic-
tive, and haughty temper; and though capable of a sort of patro-

nising generosity towards his dependents, and of some attachment towards those who had long known and flattered him, his general demeanour, both in public and private life, appears to have been far from exemplary; destitute of temper and magnanimity, and we will add, of principle, in the former; and in the latter, of tenderness, fidelity, or compassion."—*Edinburgh Review*, vol. xvii. p. 9.

I have no desire to break a lance in this place in defence of the personal character of Swift. It does not appear to me that he stands at all distinguished among politicians (least of all, among the politicians of his time) for laxity of principle; nor can I consent to charge his private demeanour with the absence either of tenderness, or fidelity, or compassion. But who ever dreamed — most assuredly not Scott — of holding up the Dean of St Patrick's as on the whole an " exemplary character?" The biographer felt, whatever his critic may have thought on the subject, that a vein of morbid humour ran through Swift's whole existence, both mental and physical, from the beginning. " He early adopted," says Scott, " the custom of observing his birthday, as a term not of joy but of sorrow, and of reading, when it annually recurred, the striking passage of Scripture in which Job laments and execrates the day upon which it was said in his father's house *that a man-child was born;*" and I should have expected that any man who had considered the black close of

the career thus early clouded, and read the entry of
Swift's diary on the funeral of Stella, his epitaph
on himself, and the testament by which he disposed
of his fortune, would have been willing, like Scott,
to dwell on the splendour of his immortal genius,
and the many traits of manly generosity " which
he unquestionably exhibited," rather than on the
faults and foibles of nameless and inscrutable disease,
which tormented and embittered the far greater part
of his earthly being. What the critic says of the
practical and business-like style of Scott's biography,
appears very just — and I think the circumstance
eminently characteristic — nor, on the whole, could
his edition, as an edition, have been better dealt with
than in the Essay which I have quoted. It was, by
the way, written by Mr Jeffrey, at Constable's particular request. " It was, I think, the first time I
ever asked such a thing of him," the bookseller said
to me; " and I assure you the result was no encouragement to repeat such petitions." Mr Jeffrey
attacked Swift's whole character at great length, and
with consummate dexterity; and, in Constable's opinion, his article threw such a cloud on the Dean, as
materially checked, for a time, the popularity of his
writings. Admirable as the paper is, in point of
ability, I think Mr Constable may have considerably
exaggerated its effects; but in those days it must
have been difficult for him to form an impartial

opinion upon such a question; for, as Johnson said
of Cave, that " he could not spit over his window
without thinking of The Gentleman's Magazine," I
believe Constable allowed nothing to interrupt his
paternal pride in the concerns of his Review, until
the Waverley Novels supplied him with another
periodical publication still more important to his
fortunes.

And this consummation was not long delayed: a
considerable addition having by that time been made
to the original fragment, there appeared in The
Scot's Magazine, for February 1st, 1814, an an-
nouncement, that " Waverley; or, 'tis Sixty Years
Since, a novel, in 3 vols. 12mo," would be published
in March. And before Scott came into Edinburgh,
at the close of the Christmas vacation, on the 12th
of January, Mr Erskine had perused the greater
part of the first volume, and expressed his decided
opinion that Waverley would prove the most popular of all his friend's writings.* The MS. was forth-

* Entertaining one night a small party of friends, Erskine read
the proof sheets of this volume after supper, and was confirmed
in his opinion by the enthusiastic interest they excited in his
highly intelligent circle. Mr James Simpson and Mr Norman
Hill, advocates, were of this party, and from the way in which
their host spoke, they both inferred that they were listening to
the first effort of some unknown aspirant. They all pronounced
the work one of the highest classical merit. The sitting was
protracted till daybreak. — [1839.]

with copied by John Ballantyne, and sent to press.
As soon as a volume was printed, Ballantyne conveyed it to Constable, who did not for a moment
doubt from what pen it proceeded, but took a few
days to consider of the matter, and then offered
£700 for the copyright.   When we recollect what
the state of novel literature in those days was, and
that the only exceptions to its mediocrity, the Irish
Tales of Miss Edgeworth, however appreciated in
refined circles, had a circulation so limited that she
had never realized a tithe of £700 by the best of
them — it must be allowed that Constable's offer was
a liberal one.   Scott's answer, however, transmitted
through the same channel, was, that £700 was too
much, in case the novel should not be successful,
and too little in case it should.   He added, " If our
fat friend had said £1000, I should have been stag-
gered."   John did not forget to hint this last circumstance to Constable, but the latter did not choose
to act upon it; and he ultimately published the
work, on the footing of an equal division of profits
between himself and the author.   There was a considerable pause between the finishing of the first
volume and the beginning of the second.   Constable
had, in 1812, acquired the copyright of the Encyclopædia Britannica, and was now preparing to publish the valuable *Supplement* to that work, which
has since, with modifications, been incorporated into

its text. He earnestly requested Scott to undertake a few articles for the Supplement; he agreed
— and, anxious to gratify the generous bookseller,
at once laid aside his tale until he had finished two
essays — those on Chivalry and the Drama. They
appear to have been completed in the course of
April and May, and he received for each of them
—(as he did subsequently for that on Romance)—
£100.

The two next letters will give us, in more exact
detail than the author's own recollection could supply
in 1830, the history of the completion of Waverley.
It was published on the 7th of July; and two days
afterwards he thus writes :—

" *To J. B. S. Morritt, Esq., M. P., London.*

" Edinburgh, 9th July 1814.
" My Dear Morritt,
" I owe you many apologies for not sooner
answering your very entertaining letter upon your
Parisian journey. I heartily wish I had been of
your party, for you have seen what I trust will not
be seen again in a hurry; since, to enjoy the delight
of a restoration, there is a necessity for a previous
bouleversement of everything that is valuable in mo-
rals and policy, which seems to have been the case

in France since 1790.* The Duke of Buccleuch told me yesterday of a very good reply of Louis to some of his attendants, who proposed shutting the doors of his apartments to keep out the throng of people. ' Open the door,' he said, ' to John Bull; he has suffered a great deal in keeping the door open for me.'

" Now, to go from one important subject to another, I must account for my own laziness, which I do by referring you to a small anonymous sort of a novel, in three volumes, Waverley, which you will receive by the mail of this day. It was a very old attempt of mine to embody some traits of those characters and manners peculiar to Scotland, the last remnants of which vanished during my own youth, so that few or no traces now remain. I had written great part of the first volume, and sketched other passages, when I mislaid the MS., and only found it by the merest accident as I was rummaging the drawers of an old cabinet; and I took the fancy of finishing it, which I did so fast, that the last two volumes were written in three weeks. I had a great deal of fun in the accomplishment of this task, though I do not expect that it will be popular in the south,

* Mr. Morritt had, in the spring of this year, been present at the first levee held at the Tuileries by Monsieur, (afterwards Charles X.), as representative of his brother Louis XVIII. Mr. M. had not been in Paris till that time since 1789.

as much of the humour, if there be any, is local, and
some of it even professional. You, however, who are
an adopted Scotchman, will find some amusement in
it. It has made a very strong impression here, and
the good people of Edinburgh are busied in tracing
the author, and in finding out originals for the portraits it contains. In the first case, they will probably
find it difficult to convict the guilty author, although
he is far from escaping suspicion. Jeffrey has offered
to make oath that it is mine, and another great critic
has tendered his affidavit *ex contrario ;* so that these
authorities have divided the Gude Town. However,
the thing has succeeded very well, and is thought
highly of. I don't know if it has got to London
yet. I intend to maintain my *incognito.* Let me
know your opinion about it. I should be most happy
if I could think it would amuse a painful thought at
this anxious moment. I was in hopes Mrs Morritt
was getting so much better, that this relapse affects
me very much. Ever yours truly,

W. Scott.

" P. S. — As your conscience has very few things
to answer for, you must still burthen it with the
secret of the Bridal. It is spreading very rapidly,
and I have one or two little fairy romances, which
will make a second volume, and which I would wish
published, but not with my name. The truth is,

that this sort of muddling work amuses me, and I am something in the condition of Joseph Surface, who was embarrassed by getting himself too good a reputation; for many things may please people well enough anonymously, which, if they have me in the title-page, would just give me that sort of ill name which precedes hanging — and that would be in many respects inconvenient if I thought of again trying a *grande opus*."

This statement of the foregoing letter (repeated still more precisely in the following one), as to the time occupied in the composition of the second and third volumes of Waverley, recalls to my memory a trifling anecdote, which, as connected with a dear friend of my youth, whom I have not seen for many years, and may very probably never see again in this world, I shall here set down, in the hope of affording him a momentary, though not an unmixed pleasure, when he may chance to read this compilation on a distant shore — and also in the hope that my humble record may impart to some active mind in the rising generation a shadow of the influence which the reality certainly exerted upon his. Happening to pass through Edinburgh in June 1814, I dined one day with the gentleman in question (now the Honourable William Menzies, one of the Supreme Judges at the Cape of Good Hope), whose residence was then in George Street, situated very near to, and at right angles with, North Castle Street. It was a party of very young persons, most of them, like Menzies and myself, destined for the Bar of Scotland, all gay and thoughtless, enjoying the first flush of manhood, with little remembrance of the yesterday, or care of the morrow. When my companion's worthy father and uncle, after seeing two or three bottles go round, left the juveniles to themselves, the weather being hot, we adjourned to a library which had one large window looking northwards. After carousing here for an hour or more, I observed that a shade had come over the aspect of my friend, who happened to be placed immediately opposite to myself, and said something that intimated a fear of his being unwell. " No," said he, " I shall be well enough presently, if you will only let me sit where you are, and take my chair ; for there is a confounded hand in sight of me here, which has often bothered me before, and now it won't let me fill my glass with a good will." I rose to change places with him accordingly, and he pointed out to me this hand which, like the writing on Belshazzar's wall, disturbed his hour of hilarity. " Since we sat down," he said, " I have been watching it — it fascinates my eye — it never stops — page after page is finished and thrown on that heap of MS., and still it goes on unwearied — and so it will be till candles are brought in, and God knows how long after that. It is the same every night — I can't stand a sight of it when I am not at my books."—"Some stupid, dogged, engrossing clerk, probably," exclaimed myself, or some other giddy youth in our society. "No, boys," said our host, "I well know what hand it is—'tis Walter Scott's." This was the hand that, in the evenings of three summer weeks, wrote the two last volumes of Waverley. Would that all who that night watched it, had profited by its example of diligence as largely as William Menzies!

In the next of these letters Scott enclosed to Mr Morritt the Prospectus of a new edition of the old poems of the Bruce and the Wallace, undertaken by the learned lexicographer, Dr John Jamieson; and he announces his departure on a sailing excursion round the north of Scotland. It will be observed, that when Scott began his letter, he had only had Mr Morritt's opinion of the first volume of Waverley, and that before he closed it, he had received his friend's honest criticism on the work as a whole, with the expression of an earnest hope that he would drop his *incognito* on the titlepage of a second edition.

"*J. B. S. Morritt, Esq., M.P., Portland Place, London.*

"Abbotsford, July 24, 1814.

"My Dear Morritt,

"I am going to say my *vales* to you for some

weeks, having accepted an invitation from a committee of the Commissioners for the Northern Lights (I don't mean the Edinburgh Reviewers, but the *bonâ fide* Commissioners for the Beacons), to accompany them upon a nautical tour round Scotland, visiting all that is curious on continent and isle. The party are three gentlemen with whom I am very well acquainted, William Erskine being one. We have a stout cutter, well fitted up and manned for the service by Government; and to make assurance double sure, the admiral has sent a sloop of war to cruise in the dangerous points of our tour, and sweep the sea of the Yankee privateers, which sometimes annoy our northern latitudes. I shall visit the Clephanes in their solitude — and let you know all that I see that is rare and entertaining, which, as we are masters of our time and vessel, should add much to my stock of knowledge.

" As to Waverley, I will play Sir Fretful for once, and assure you that I left the story to flag in the first volume on purpose; the second and third have rather more bustle and interest. I wished (with what success Heaven knows) to avoid the ordinary error of novel writers, whose first volume is usually their best. But since it has served to amuse Mrs Morritt and you *usque ab initio*, I have no doubt you will tolerate it even unto the end. It may really boast to be a tolerably faithful portrait of Scottish manners, and has been recognised as such in Edinburgh. The

first edition of a thousand instantly disappeared, and
the bookseller informs me that the second, of double
the quantity, will not supply the market long. — As
I shall be very anxious to know how Mrs Morritt is,
I hope to have a few lines from you on my return,
which will be about the end of August or beginning
of September. I should have mentioned that we have
the celebrated engineer, Stevenson, along with us.
I delight in these professional men of talent; they
always give you some new lights by the peculiarity of
their habits and studies, so different from the people
who are rounded, and smoothed, and ground down for
conversation, and who can say all that every other
person says, and — nothing more.

" What a miserable thing it is that our royal family
cannot be quiet and decent at least, if not correct and
moral in their deportment. Old farmer George's
manly simplicity, modesty of expense, and domestic
virtue, saved this country at its most perilous crisis ;
for it is inconceivable the number of persons whom
these qualities united in his behalf, who would have
felt but feebly the abstract duty of supporting a crown
less worthily worn.

" — I had just proceeded thus far when your kind
favour of the 21st reached Abbotsford. I am heartily
glad you continued to like Waverley to the end. The
hero is a sneaking piece of imbecility ; and if he had
married Flora, she would have set him up upon the

chimneypiece, as Count Borowlaski's wife used to do
with him.* I am a bad hand at depicting a hero
properly so called, and have an unfortunate propensity for the dubious characters of borderers,
buccaneers, Highland robbers, and all others of a
Robin-Hood description. I do not know why it
should be, as I am myself, like Hamlet, indifferent
honest; but I suppose the blood of the old cattle-
drivers of Teviotdale continues to stir in my veins.

" I shall *not* own Waverley; my chief reason is,
that it would prevent me of the pleasure of writing
again. David Hume, nephew of the historian, says
the author must be of a jacobite family and predilections, a yeoman-cavalry man, and a Scottish lawyer,
and desires me to guess in whom these happy attri-

---

* *Count Borowlaski* was a Polish dwarf, who, after realizing
some money as an itinerant object of exhibition, settled, married,
and died (Sept. 5, 1837) at Durham. He was a well-bred
creature, and much noticed by the clergy and other gentry of
that city. Indeed, even when travelling the country as a show,
he had always maintained a sort of dignity. I remember him
as going from house to house, when I was a child, in a sedan
chair, with a servant in livery following him, who took the fee —
M. le Comte himself (dressed in a scarlet coat and bag wig)
being ushered into the room like any ordinary visitor.
    The Count died in his 99th year —

" A SPIRIT brave, yet gentle, has dwelt, as it appears,
    Within three feet of flesh for near one hundred years;
    Which causes wonder, like his constitution, strong,
    That one *so short alive* should be *alive so long !*"
                        Bentley's Miscellany for November 1837

butes are united.   I shall not plead guilty, however;
and as such seems to be the fashion of the day, I
hope charitable people will believe my *affidavit* in
contradiction to all other evidence.   The Edinburgh
faith now is, that Waverley is written by Jeffrey, having
been composed to lighten the tedium of his late transatlantic voyage.   So you see the unknown infant is
like to come to preferment.   In truth, I am not sure
it would be considered quite decorous for me as a
Clerk of Session, to write novels.   Judges being monks,
Clerks are a sort of lay brethren, from whom some
solemnity of walk and conduct may be expected.   So,
whatever I may do of this kind, ' I shall whistle it
down the wind, and let it prey at fortune.'*   I will
take care, in the next edition, to make the corrections you recommend.   The second is, I believe,
nearly through the press.   It will hardly be printed
faster than it was written; for though the first
volume was begun long ago, and actually lost for a
time, yet the other two were begun and finished
between the 4th June and the 1st July, during all
which I attended my duty in Court, and proceeded
without loss of time or hinderance of business.

" I wish, for poor auld Scotland's sake,† and for
the manes of Bruce and Wallace, and for the living

---

* *Othello, Act III. Scene 3.*
† Burns — lines " On my early days."

comfort of a very worthy and ingenious dissenting clergyman, who has collected a library and medals of some value, and brought up, I believe, sixteen or seventeen children (his wife's ambition extended to twenty) upon about £150 a-year — I say I wish, for all these reasons, you could get me among your wealthy friends a name or two for the enclosed proposals. The price is, I think, too high; but the booksellers fixed it two guineas above what I proposed. I trust it will be yet lowered to five guineas, which is a more come-at-able sum than six. The poems themselves are great curiosities, both to the philologist and antiquary; and that of Bruce is invaluable even to the historian. They have been hitherto wretchedly edited.

"I am glad you are not to pay for this scrawl. Ever yours,   WALTER SCOTT.

"P. S.—I do not see how my silence can be considered as imposing on the public. If I give my name to a book without writing it, unquestionably that would be a trick. But, unless in the case of his averring facts which he may be called upon to defend or justify, I think an author may use his own discretion in giving or withholding his name. Harry Mackenzie never put his name in a titlepage till the last edition of his works; and Swift only owned one out of his thousand and one publications. In point of emolument, everybody knows that I sacrifice much money by withholding my name; and what should I gain by it, that any human being has a right to consider as an unfair advantage?   In fact, only the freedom of writing trifles with less personal responsibility, and perhaps more frequently than I otherwise might do.   W. S."

I am not able to give the exact date of the following reply to one of John Ballantyne's expostulations on the subject of *the secret:*—

> " No, John, I will not own the book—
>   I won't, you Piccaroon.
>   When next I try St. Grubby's brook,
>   The A. of Wa— shall bait the hook—
>   And flat-fish bite as soon,
>   As if before them they had got
>   The worn-out wriggler
>   WALTER SCOTT."

CHAPTER XXVIII.

Voyage to the Shetland Isles, &c. — *Scott's Diary kept on board the Lighthouse Yacht.*

JULY AND AUGUST 1814.

THE gallant composure with which Scott, when he had dismissed a work from his desk, awaited the decision of the public—and the healthy elasticity of spirit with which he could meanwhile turn his whole zeal upon new or different objects—are among the features in his character which will always, I believe, strike the student of literary history as most remarkable.   We have now seen him before the fate of Waverley had been determined—before he had heard a word about its reception in England, except from one partial confidant—preparing to start on a voyage to the northern isles, which was likely to occupy the best part of two months, and in the course of which he could hardly expect to receive any intel-

ligence from his friends in Edinburgh. The diary
which he kept during this expedition, is—thanks to
the leisure of a landsman on board—a very full one;
and, written without the least notion probably that
it would ever be perused except in his own family
circle, it affords such a complete and artless portraiture of the man, as he was in himself, and as
he mingled with his friends and companions, at one
of the most interesting periods of his life, that I
am persuaded every reader will be pleased to see it
printed in its original state. A few extracts from
it were published by himself, in one of the Edinburgh
Annual Registers—he also drew from it some of the
notes to his Lord of the Isles, and the substance of
several others for his romance of the Pirate.   But
the recurrence of these detached passages will not
be complained of—expounded and illustrated as the
reader will find them by the personal details of the
context.

I have been often told by one of the companions
of this voyage, that heartily as Scott entered throughout into their social enjoyments, they all perceived
him, when inspecting for the first time scenes of remarkable grandeur, to be in such an abstracted and
excited mood, that they felt it would be the kindest
and discreetest plan to leave him to himself. " I
often," said Lord Kinnedder, " on coming up from
the cabin at night, found him pacing the deck ra-

pidly, muttering to himself—and went to the fore-castle, lest my presence should disturb him. I remember, that at Loch Corriskin, in particular, he seemed quite overwhelmed with his feelings; and we all saw it, and retiring unnoticed, left him to roam and gaze about by himself, until it was time to muster the party and be gone." Scott used to mention the surprise with which he himself witnessed Erskine's emotion on first entering the Cave of Staffa—" Would you believe it?" he said—" my poor Willie sat down and wept like a woman!" Yet his own sensibilities, though betrayed in a more masculine and sterner guise, were perhaps as keen as well as deeper than his amiable friend's.

The poet's Diary, contained in five little paper-books, is as follows:—

" VACATION, 1814.

" *Voyage in the Lighthouse Yacht to Nova Zembla, and the Lord knows where.*

" *July* 29*th*, 1814.—Sailed from Leith about one o'clock on board the Lighthouse Yacht, conveying six guns, and ten men, commanded by Mr Wilson. The company — Commissioners of the Northern Lights; Robert Hamilton, Sheriff of Lanarkshire;

William Erskine, Sheriff of Orkney and Zetland; Adam Duff, Sheriff of Forfarshire. Non-commissioners—Ipse Ego; Mr David Marjoribanks, son to John Marjoribanks, Provost of Edinburgh, a young gentleman; Rev. Mr Turnbull, minister of Tingwall, in the presbytery of Shetland. But the official chief of the expedition is Mr Stevenson, the Surveyor-Viceroy over the Commissioners—a most gentleman-like and modest man, and well known by his scientific skill.

" Reached the Isle of May in the evening; went ashore, and saw the light—an old tower, and much in the form of a border-keep, with a beacon-grate on the top. It is to be abolished for an oil revolving-light, the grate-fire only being ignited upon the leeward side when the wind is very high. *Quære*— Might not the grate revolve ? The isle had once a cell or two upon it. The vestiges of the chapel are still visible. Mr Stevenson proposed demolishing the old tower, and I recommended *ruining* it *à la picturesque*—*i. e.* demolishing it partially. The island might be made a delightful residence for sea-bathers.

" On board again in the evening: watched the progress of the ship round Fifeness, and the revolving motion of the now distant Bell-Rock light until the wind grew rough, and the landsmen sick. To bed at eleven, and slept sound.

" *30th July.*—Waked at six by the steward : summoned to visit the Bell-Rock, where the beacon is well worthy attention. Its dimensions are well known ; but no description can give the idea of this slight, solitary, round tower, trembling amid the billows, and fifteen miles from Arbroath, the nearest shore. The fitting up within is not only handsome, but elegant. All work of wood (almost) is wainscot ; all hammer-work brass ; in short, exquisitely fitted up. You enter by a ladder of rope, with wooden steps, about thirty feet from the bottom, where the mason-work ceases to be solid, and admits of round apartments.   The lowest is a storehouse for the people's provisions, water, &c.; above that a storehouse for the lights, of oil, &c.; then the kitchen of the people, three in number; then their sleeping chamber; then the saloon or parlour, a neat little room ; above all, the lighthouse; all communicating by oaken ladders, with brass rails, most handsomely and conveniently executed.   Breakfasted in the parlour.*   On board

---

* On being requested, while at breakfast, to inscribe his name in the album of the tower, Scott penned immediately the following lines : —

" Pharos Loquitur.

" Far in the bosom of the deep,
O'er these wild shelves my watch I keep;
A ruddy gem of changeful light,
Bound on the dusky brow of night,
The seaman bids my lustre hail,
And scorns to strike his timorous sail."

again at nine, and run down, through a rough sea, to Aberbrothock, vulgarly called Arbroath. All sick, even Mr Stevenson. God grant this occur seldom! Landed and dined at Arbroath, where we were to take up Adam Duff. We visited the appointments of the lighthouse establishment—a handsome tower, with two wings. These contain the lodgings of the keepers of the light—very handsome, indeed, and very clean. They might be thought too handsome, were it not of consequence to give those men, intrusted with a duty so laborious and slavish, a consequence in the eyes of the public and in their own. The central part of the building forms a single tower, corresponding with the lighthouse. As the keepers' families live here, they are apprised each morning by a signal that *all is well.* If this signal be not made, a tender sails for the rock directly. I visited the abbey church for the third time, the first being— *eheu!* *—the second with T. Thomson. Dined at Arbroath, and came on board at night, where I made up this foolish journal, and now beg for wine and water. So the vessel is once more in motion.

" 31*st July.*—Waked at seven; vessel off Fowlsheugh and Dunnottar. Fair wind, and delightful day; glide enchantingly along the coast of Kincardineshire, and open the bay of Nigg about ten. At

* This is, without doubt, an allusion to some happy day's excursion when his *first love* was of the party.

eleven, off Aberdeen; the gentlemen go ashore to
Girdle-Ness, a projecting point of rock to the east
of the harbour of Fort-Dee.   There the magistrates
of Aberdeen wish to have a fort and beacon-light.
The Oscar, whaler, was lost here last year, with all
her hands, excepting two; about forty perished.
Dreadful, to be wrecked so near a large and populous
town! The view of Old and New Aberdeen from the
sea is quite beautiful.   About noon, proceed along
the coast of Aberdeenshire, which, to the northwards,
changes from a bold and rocky to a low and sandy
character.   Along the bay of Belhelvie, a whole
parish was swallowed up by the shifting sands, and
is still a desolate waste.   It belonged to the Earls
of Errol, and was rented at £500 a-year at the time.
When these sands are past, the land is all arable.
Not a tree to be seen; nor a grazing cow, or sheep,
or even a labour-horse at grass, though this be Sunday.   The next remarkable object was a fragment of
the old castle of Slains, on a precipitous bank, over-
looking the sea.   The fortress was destroyed when
James VI. marched north [A. D. 1594], after the
battle of Glenlivat, to reduce Huntly and Errol to
obedience.   The family then removed to their present
mean habitation, for such it seems, a collection of
low houses forming a quadrangle, one side of which
is built on the very verge of the precipice that over-
hangs the ocean.   What seems odd, there are no

stairs down to the beach.   Imprudence, or ill fortune
as fatal as the sands of Belhelvie, has swallowed up
the estate of Errol, excepting this dreary mansion-
house, and a farm or two adjoining.   We took to
the boat, and running along the coast, had some
delightful sea-views to the northward of the castle.
The coast is here very rocky; but the rocks, being
rather soft, are wasted and corroded by the constant
action of the waves,—and the fragments which remain, where the softer parts have been washed away,
assume the appearance of old Gothic ruins.   There
are open arches, towers, steeples, and so forth.   One
part of this scaur is called *Dun Buy*, being coloured
yellow by the dung of the sea-fowls, who build there
in the most surprising numbers.   We caught three
young gulls.   But the most curious object was the
celebrated Buller of Buchan, a huge rocky cauldron,
into which the sea rushes through a natural arch of
rock.   I walked round the top; in one place the
path is only about two feet wide, and a monstrous
precipice on either side.   We then rowed into the
cauldron or buller from beneath, and saw nothing
around us but a regular wall of black rock, and
nothing above but the blue sky.   A fishing hamlet
had sent out its inhabitants, who, gazing from the
brink, looked like sylphs looking down upon gnomes.
In the side of the cauldron opens a deep black
cavern.   Johnson says it might be a retreat from

storms, which is nonsense. In a high gale the waves rush in with incredible violence. An old fisher said he had seen them flying over the natural wall of the buller, which cannot be less than 200 feet high. Same old man says Slains is now inhabited by a Mr Bowles, who comes so far from the southward that naebody kens whare he comes frae. ' Was he frae the Indies?'—' Na; he did not think he came that road. He was far frae the southland. Naebody ever heard the name of the place; but he had brought more guid out o' Peterhead than a' the Lords he had seen in Slains, and he had seen three.' About half-past five we left this interesting spot, and after a hard pull, reached the yacht. Weather falls hazy, and rather calm; but at sea we observe vessels enjoying more wind. Pass Peterhead, dimly distinguishing two steeples, and a good many masts. Mormounthill said to resemble a coffin—a likeness of which we could not judge, Mormount being for the present invisible. Pass Rattray-Head: near this cape are dangerous shelves, called the Bridge of Rattray. Here the wreck of the Doris merchant vessel came on shore, lost last year with a number of passengers for Shetland. We lie off all night.

" 1st *August.*—Off Frasersburgh—a neat little town. Mr Stevenson and the Commissioners go on shore to look at a light maintained there upon an old castle, on a cape called Kinnaird's Head. The

morning being rainy, and no object of curiosity
ashore, I remain on board, to make up my journal,
and write home.

" The old castle, now bearing the light, is a picturesque object from the sea. It was the baronial
mansion of the Frasers, now Lords Saltoun—an old
square tower with a minor fortification towards the
landing-place on the sea-side. About eleven, the
Commissioners came off, and we leave this town, the
extreme point of the Moray Firth, to stretch for
Shetland—salute the castle with three guns, and
stretch out with a merry gale. See Mormount, a
long flattish-topped hill near to the West Troup-
head, and another bold cliff promontory projecting
into the frith. Our gale soon failed, and we are
now all but becalmed; songs, ballads, recitations,
backgammon, and piquet, for the rest of the day.
Noble sunset and moon rising; we are now out of
sight of land.

" 2d *August.*—At sea in the mouth of the Moray
Frith. This day almost a blank—light baffling airs,
which do us very little good; most of the landsmen
sick, more or less; piquet, backgammon, and chess,
the only resources.—*P. M.* A breeze, and we begin
to think we have passed the Fair Isle, lying between
Shetland and Orkney, at which it was our intention to have touched. In short, like one of Sinbad's
adventures, we have run on till neither captain nor

pilot know exactly where we are. The breeze increases—weather may be called rough; worse and worse after we are in our berths, nothing but booming, trampling, and whizzing of waves about our ears, and ever and anon, as we fall asleep, our ribs come in contact with those of the vessel; hail Duff and the Udaller* in the after-cabin, but they are too sick to answer. Towards morning, calm (comparative), and a nap.

" 3d August.—At sea as before; no appearance of land; proposed that the Sheriff of Zetland do issue a *meditatione fugæ* warrant against his territories, which seem to fly from us. Pass two whalers; speak the nearest, who had come out of Lerwick, which is about twenty miles distant; stand on with a fine breeze. About nine at night, with moonlight and strong twilight, we weather the point of Bardhead, and enter a channel about three-quarters of a mile broad, which forms the southern entrance to the harbour of Lerwick, where we cast anchor about half past ten, and put Mr Turnbull on shore.

" 4th August. — Harbour of Lerwick. Admire the excellence of this harbour of the metropolis of Shetland. It is a most beautiful place, screened on all sides from the wind by hills of a gentle elevation. The town, a fishing village built irregularly upon a

---

* Erskine —Sheriff of Shetland and Orkney

hill ascending from the shore, has a picturesque appearance. On the left is Fort Charlotte, garrisoned
of late by two companies of veterans. The Green-
landmen, of which nine fine vessels are lying in the
harbour, add much to the liveliness of the scene. Mr
Duncan, sheriff-substitute, came off to pay his respects to his principal; he is married to a daughter
of my early acquaintance, Walter Scott of Scots-
hall. We go ashore. Lerwick, a poor-looking place,
the streets flagged instead of being causewayed, for
there are no wheel-carriages. The streets full of
drunken riotous sailors, from the whale-vessels. It
seems these ships take about 1000 sailors from Zetland every year, and return them as they come back
from the fishery. Each sailor may gain from £20
to £30, which is paid by the merchants of Lerwick,
who have agencies from the owners of the whalers
in England. The whole return may be between
£25,000 and £30,000. These Zetlanders, as they
get a part of this pay on landing, make a point of
treating their English messmates, who get drunk of
course, and are very riotous. The Zetlanders themselves do *not* get drunk, but go straight home to
their houses, and reserve their hilarity for the winter
season, when they spend their wages in dancing and
drinking. Erskine finds employment as Sheriff, for
the neighbourhood of the fort enables him to make
main forte, and secure a number of the rioters. We

visit F. Charlotte, which is a neat little fort mounting ten heavy guns to the sea, but only one to the
land.   Major F. the Governor, showed us the fort ;
it commands both entrances of the harbour : the
north entrance is not very good, but the south
capital.   The water in the harbour is very deep, as
frigates of the smaller class lie almost close to the
shore.   Take a walk with Captain M'Diarmid, a
gentlemanlike and intelligent officer of the garrison ;
we visit a small fresh-water loch called *Cleik-him-
in ;* it borders on the sea, from which it is only
divided by a sort of beach, apparently artificial :
though the sea lashes the outside of this beach, the
water of the lake is not brackish.   In this lake are
the remains of a Picts' Castle, but ruinous.   The
people think the Castle has not been built on a natural island, but on an artificial one formed by a heap
of stones.   These Duns or Picts' Castles are so
small, it is impossible to conceive what effectual
purpose they could serve excepting a temporary refuge
for the chief.— Leave *Cleik - him - in,* and proceed
along the coast.   The ground is dreadfully encumbered with stones ;   the patches which have been
sown with oats and barley, bear very good crops, but
they are mere *patches,* the cattle and ponies feeding
amongst them, and secured by tethers.   The houses
most wretched, worse than the worst herd's house I
ever saw.   It would be easy to form a good farm by

enclosing the ground with Galloway dykes, which would answer the purpose of clearing it at the same time of stones ; and as there is plenty of lime-shell, marle, and alga-marina, manure could not be wanting. But there are several obstacles to improvement, chiefly the undivided state of the properties, which lie *run-rig;* then the claims of Lord Dundas, the lord of the country, and above all, perhaps, the state of the common people, who, dividing their attention between the fishery and the cultivation, are not much interested in the latter, and are often absent at the proper times of labour. Their ground is chiefly dug with the spade, and their ploughs are beyond description awkward. An odd custom prevails — any person, without exception (if I understand rightly) who wishes to raise a few kail, fixes upon any spot he pleases, encloses it with a dry stone wall, uses it as a kail-yard till he works out the soil, then deserts it and makes another. Some dozen of these little enclosures, about twenty or thirty feet square, are in sight at once. They are called *planty-cruives;* and the Zetlanders are so far from reckoning this an invasion, or a favour on the part of the proprietor, that their most exaggerated description of an avaricious person is one who would refuse liberty for a *planty-cruive ;* or to infer the greatest contempt of another, they will say, they would not hold a *planty-cruive* of him. It is needless to notice how much this licence must interfere with cultivation.

"Leaving the *cultivated* land, we turn more inland, and pass two or three small lakes. The muirs are mossy and sterile in the highest degree; the hills are clad with stunted heather, intermixed with huge great stones; much of an astringent root with a yellow flower, called *Tormentil*, used by the islanders in dressing leather in lieu of the oak bark. We climbed a hill, about three miles from Lerwick, to a cairn which presents a fine view of the indented coast of the island, and the distant isles of Mousa and others. Unfortunately the day is rather hazy — return by a circuitous route, through the same sterile country. These muirs are used as a commonty by the proprietors of the parishes in which they lie, and each, without any regard to the extent of his peculiar property, puts as much stock upon them as he chooses. The sheep are miserable looking, hairy-legged creatures, of all colours, even to sky-blue. I often wondered where Jacob got speckled lambs; I think now they must have been of the Shetland stock. In our return, pass the upper end of the little lake of *Cleik-him-in,* which is divided by a rude causeway from another small loch, communicating with it, however, by a sluice, for the purpose of driving a mill. But such a mill! The wheel is horizontal, with the cogs turned diagonally to the water; the beam stands upright, and is inserted in a stone-quern of the old-fashioned construction. This simple machine is enclosed in a hovel about the size of a pig-stye—and there is the mill!* There are about 500 such mills in Shetland, each incapable of grinding more than a sack at a time.

" I cannot get a distinct account of the nature of the land rights. The Udal proprietors have ceased to exist, yet proper feudal tenures seem ill understood. Districts of ground are in many instances understood to belong to Townships or Communities, possessing what may be arable by patches, and what is muir as a commonty, *pro indiviso*. But then individuals of such a Township often take it upon them to grant feus of particular parts of the property thus possessed *pro indiviso*. The town of Lerwick is built upon a part of the commonty of Sound, the proprietors of the houses having feu-rights from different heritors of that Township, but why from one rather than another, or how even the whole Township combining (which has not yet been attempted) could grant such a right upon principle, seems altogether uncertain. In the mean time the chief stress is laid upon occupance. I should have supposed, upon principle, that Lord Dundas, as superior, possessed the *dominium eminens*, and ought to be resorted to as the source of land rights. But

* Here occurs a rude scratch of drawing.

it is not so. It has been found that the heritors of
each Township hold directly of the Crown, only
paying the *Scat*, or Norwegian land-tax, and other
duties to his lordship, used and wont. Besides, he
has what are called property lands in every Township, or in most, which he lets to his tenants. Lord
Dundas is now trying to introduce the system of
leases and a better kind of agriculture.* Return
home and dine at Sinclair's, a decent inn — Captain
M'Diarmid and other gentlemen dine with us. —
Sleep at the inn on a straw couch.

" *5th August* 1814. — Hazy disagreeable morning; — Erskine trying the rioters — notwithstanding which, a great deal of rioting still in the town.
The Greenlanders, however, only quarrelled among
themselves, and the Zetland sailors seemed to exert
themselves in keeping peace. They are, like all
the other Zetlanders I have seen, a strong, clear-
complexioned, handsome race, and the women are
very pretty. The females are rather slavishly employed,
however, and I saw more than one carrying home
the heavy sea-chests of their husbands, brothers, or
lovers, discharged from on board the Greenlanders.
The Zetlanders are, however, so far provident, that
when they enter the navy they make liberal allowance
of their pay for their wives and families. Not less
than £15,000 a-year has been lately paid by the Ad-

* Lord Dundas was created Earl of Zetland in 1838, and died
in February 1839.

miralty on this account; yet this influx of money,
with that from the Greenland fishery, seems rather
to give the means of procuring useless indulgences
than of augmenting the stock of productive labour.
Mr Collector Ross tells me, that from the King's
books it appears that the quantity of spirits, tea,
coffee, tobacco, snuff, and sugar, imported annually
into Lerwick for the consumption of Zetland, ave-
rages at sale price, £20,000 yearly, at the least.
Now the inhabitants of Zetland, men, women, and
children, do not exceed 22,000 in all, and the proportion of foreign luxuries seems monstrous, unless
we allow for the habits contracted by the seamen in
their foreign trips. Tea, in particular, is used by
all ranks, and porridge quite exploded.

" We parade Lerwick. The most remarkable
thing is, that the main street being flagged, and all
the others very narrow lanes descending the hill by
steps, anything like a cart, of the most ordinary and
rude construction, seems not only out of question
when the town was built, but in its present state
quite excluded. A road of five miles in length, on
the line between Lerwick and Scalloway, has been
already made — upon a very awkward and expensive
plan, and ill-lined as may be supposed. But it is
proposed to extend this road by degrees : carts will
then be introduced, and by crossing the breed of
their ponies judiciously, they will have Galloways

to draw them. The streets of Lerwick (as one
blunder perpetrates another) will then be a bar to
improvement, for till the present houses are greatly
altered, no cart can approach the quay. In the garden of Captain Nicolson, R.N., which is rather in a
flourishing state, he has tried various trees, almost
all of which have died except the willow. But the
plants seem to me to be injured in their passage;
seeds would perhaps do better. We are visited
by several of the notables of the island, particularly
Mr Mowat, a considerable proprietor, who claims
acquaintance with me as the friend of my father, and
remembers me as a boy. The day clearing up, Duff
and I walk with this good old gentleman to *Cleik-
him-in*, and with some trouble drag a boat off the
beach into the fresh-water loch, and go to visit the
Picts' castle. It is of considerable size, and consists
of three circular walls, of huge natural stones admirably combined without cement. The outer circuit
seems to have been simply a bounding wall or bulwark; the second or interior defence contains lodgements such as I shall describe. This inner circuit
is surrounded by a wall of about sixteen or eighteen
feet thick, composed, as I said, of huge massive stones
placed in layers with great art, but without mortar
or cement. The wall is not perpendicular, but the
circle lessens gradually towards the top, as an old-
fashioned pigeon-house. Up the interior of this

wall there proceeds a circular winding gallery ascending in the form of an inclined plane, so as to gain the top by circling round like a cork-screw within the walls. This is enlightened by little apertures (about two feet by three) into the inside, and also, it is said, by small slits — of which I saw none. It is said there are marks of galleries within the circuit, running parallel to the horizon; these I saw no remains of; and the interior gallery, with its apertures, is so extremely low and narrow, being only about three feet square, that it is difficult to conceive how it could serve the purpose of communication. At any rate, the size fully justifies the tradition prevalent here as well as in the south of Scotland, that the Picts were a diminutive race. More of this when we see the more perfect specimen of a Pict castle in Mousa, which we resolve to examine, if it be possible. Certainly I am deeply curious to see what must be one of the most ancient houses in the world, built by a people who, while they seem to have bestowed much pains on their habitations, knew neither the art of cement, of arches, or of stairs. The situation is wild, dreary, and impressive. On the land side are huge sheets and fragments of rocks, interspersed with a stinted vegetation of grass and heath, which bears no proportion to the rocks and stones. From the top of his tower the Pictish Monarch might look out upon a stormy sea, washing a succession of rocky capes, reaches, and headlands, and immediately around him was the deep fresh-water loch on which his fortress was constructed. It communicates with the land by a sort of cause-way, formed, like the artificial islet itself, by heaping together stones till the pile reached the surface of the water. This is usually passable, but at present overflooded. — Return and dine with Mr Duncan, Sheriff-substitute — are introduced to Dr Edmonstone, author of a History of Shetland, who proposes to accompany us to-morrow to see the Cradle of Noss. I should have mentioned that Mr Stevenson sailed this morning with the yacht to survey some isles to the northward; he returns on Saturday, it is hoped.

" *6th August.* — Hire a six-oared boat, whaler-built, with a taper point at each end, so that the rudder can be hooked on either at pleasure. These vessels look very frail, but are admirably adapted to the stormy seas, where they live when a ship's boat stiffly and compactly built must necessarily perish. They owe this to their elasticity and lightness. Some of the rowers wear a sort of coats of dressed sheep leather, sewed together with thongs. We sailed out at the southern inlet of the harbour, rounding suc-cessively the capes of the Hammer, Kirkubus, the Ving, and others, consisting of bold cliffs, hollowed into caverns, or divided into pillars and arches of fantastic appearance, by the constant action of the waves. As we passed the most northerly of these capes, called, I think, the Ord, and turned into the open sea, the scenes became yet more tremendously sublime. Rocks upwards of three or four hundred feet in height, presented themselves in gigantic succession, sinking perpendicularly into the main, which is very deep even within a few fathoms of their base. One of these capes is called the Bard-head; a huge projecting arch is named the Giant's Leg.

‘ Here the lone sea-bird wakes its wildest cry.’*

Not lone, however, in one sense, for their numbers and the variety of their tribes are immense, though I think they do not quite equal those of Dunbuy, on the coast of Buchan. Standing across a little bay, we reached the Isle of Noss, having hitherto coasted the shore of Bressay. Here we see a detached and precipitous rock, or island, being a portion rent by a narrow sound from the rest of the cliff, and called the Holm. This detached rock is wholly inaccessible, unless by a pass of peril, entitled the Cradle of Noss, which is a sort of wooden chair, travelling from precipice to precipice on rings, which run upon two cables stretched across over the gulf. We viewed this extraordinary contrivance from beneath, at the distance of perhaps one hundred fathoms

* Campbell — *Pleasures of Hope.*

at least. The boatmen made light of the risk of
crossing it, but it must be tremendous to a brain
disposed to be giddy. Seen from beneath, a man in
the basket would resemble a large crow or raven
floating between rock and rock. The purpose of
this strange contrivance is to give the tenant the
benefit of putting a few sheep upon the Holm, the
top of which is level, and affords good pasture. The
animals are transported in the cradle by one at a
time, a shepherd holding them upon his knees. The
channel between the Holm and the isle is passable
by boats in calm weather, but not at the time when
we saw it. Rowing on through a heavy tide, and
nearer the breakers than any but Zetlanders would
have ventured, we rounded another immensely high
cape, called by the islanders the Noup of Noss, but
by sailors Hang-cliff, from its having a projecting
appearance. This was the highest rock we had yet
seen, though not quite perpendicular. Its height
has never been measured : I should judge it exceeds
600 feet; it has been conjectured to measure 800
and upwards. Our steersman had often descended
this precipitous rock, having only the occasional
assistance of a rope, one end of which he secured
from time to time round some projecting cliff. The
collecting sea-fowl for their feathers was the object,
and he might gain five or six dozen, worth eight or
ten shillings, by such an adventure. These huge
precipices abound with caverns, many of which run

much farther into the rock than any one has ventured to explore. We entered (with much hazard to our boat) one called the Orkney-man's Harbour, because an Orkney vessel run in there some years since to escape a French privateer. The entrance was lofty enough to admit us without striking the mast, but a sudden turn in the direction of the cave would have consigned us to utter darkness if we had gone in farther. The dropping of the sea-fowl and cormorants into the water from the sides of the cavern, when disturbed by our approach, had something in it wild and terrible.

" After passing the Noup, the precipices become lower, and sink into a rocky shore with deep indentations, called by the natives, *Gios.* Here we would fain have landed to visit the Cradle from the top of the cliff, but the surf rendered it impossible. We therefore rowed on like Thalaba in ' Allah's name,' around the Isle of Noss, and landed upon the opposite side of the small sound which divides it from Bressay. Noss exactly resembles in shape Salisbury crags, supposing the sea to flow down the valley called the Hunter's bog, and round the foot of the precipice. The eastern part of the isle is fine smooth pasture, the best I have seen in these isles, sloping upwards to the verge of the tremendous rocks which form its western front.

" As we are to dine at Gardie-House (the seat of

young Mr Mowat), on the Isle of Bressay, Duff and
I—who went together on this occasion—resolve to
walk across the island, about three miles, being by
this time thoroughly wet. Bressay is a black and
heathy isle, full of little lochs and bogs. Through
storm and shade, and dense and dry, we find our
way to Gardie, and have then to encounter the
sublunary difficulties of wanting the keys of our
portmanteaus, &c., the servants having absconded
to see the Cradle. These being overcome, we are
most hospitably treated at Gardie. Young Mr Mowat,
son of my old friend, is an improver, and a *moderate* one. He has got a ploughman from Scotland,
who acts as *grieve*, but as yet with the prejudices
and inconveniences which usually attach themselves
to the most salutary experiments. The ploughman
complains that the Zetlanders work as if a spade or
hoe burned their fingers, and that though they only
got a shilling a-day, yet the labour of three of them
does not exceed what one good hand in Berwick-
shire would do for 2s. 6d. The islanders retort,
that a man can do no more than he can; that they
are not used to be taxed to their work so severely;
that they will work as their fathers did, and not
otherwise; and at first the landlord found difficulty
in getting hands to work under his Caledonian task-
master. Besides, they find fault with his *ho*, and
gee, and *wo*, when ploughing. ' He speaks to the

horse,' they say, ' and they gang — and there's
something no canny about the man.' In short, between the prejudices of laziness and superstition,
the ploughman leads a sorry life of it; yet these
prejudices are daily abating, under the steady and
indulgent management of the proprietor. Indeed,
nowhere is improvement in agriculture more necessary. An old-fashioned Zetland plough is a real
curiosity. It had but one handle, or stilt, and a
coulter, but no sock; it ripped the furrow, therefore, but did not throw it aside. When this precious
machine was in motion, it was dragged by four little
bullocks yoked a-breast, and as many ponies har-
nessed, or rather strung, to the plough by ropes
and thongs of raw hide. One man went before
walking backward, with his face to the bullocks, and
pulling them forward by main strength. Another
held down the plough by its single handle, and made
a sort of slit in the earth, which two women, who
closed the procession, converted into a furrow, by
throwing the earth aside with shovels. An antiquary
might be of opinion that this was the very model
of the original plough invented by Triptolemus;
and it is but justice to Zetland to say, that these
relics of ancient agricultural art will soon have
all the interest attached to rarity. We could only
hear of one of these ploughs within three miles of
Lerwick.

" This and many other barbarous habits to which
the Zetlanders were formerly wedded, seem only to
have subsisted because their amphibious character of
fishers and farmers induced them to neglect agricultural arts.   A Zetland farmer looks to the sea
to pay his rent ; if the land finds him a little meal
and kail, and (if he be a very clever fellow) a few
potatoes, it is very well.   The more intelligent part
of the landholders are sensible of all this, but argue
like men of good sense and humanity on the subject.
To have good farming, you must have a considerable
farm, upon which capital may be laid out to advantage.   But to introduce this change suddenly would
turn adrift perhaps twenty families, who now occupy
small farms *pro indiviso*, cultivating by patches, or
rundale and *runrig*, what part of the property is
arable, and stocking the pasture as a common upon
which each family turns out such stock as they can
rear, without observing any proportion as to the
number which it can support.   In this way many
townships, as they are called, subsist indeed, but in
a precarious and indigent manner.   Fishing villages
seem the natural resource for this excess of population ; but, besides the expense of erecting them, the
habits of the people are to be considered, who, with
‘ one foot on land and one on sea,’ would be with
equal reluctance confined to either element.   The
remedy seems to be, that the larger proprietors

should gradually set the example of better cultivation, and introduce better implements. They will, by degrees, be imitated by the inferior proprietors, and by their tenants ; and, as turnips and hay crops become more general, a better and heavier class of stock will naturally be introduced.

" The sheep in particular might be improved into a valuable stock, and would no doubt thrive, since the winters are very temperate. But I should be sorry that extensive pasture farms were introduced, as it would tend to diminish a population invaluable for the supply of our navy. The improvement of the arable land, on the contrary, would soon set them beyond the terrors of famine with which the islanders are at present occasionally visited; and, combined with fisheries, carried on not by farmers, but by real fishers, would amply supply the inhabitants, without diminishing the export of dried fish. This separation of trades will in time take place, and then the prosperous days of Zetland will begin. The proprietors are already upon the alert, studying the means of gradual improvement, and no humane person would wish them to drive it on too rapidly, to the distress and perhaps destruction of the numerous tenants who have been bred under a different system.

" I have gleaned something of the peculiar superstitions of the Zetlanders, which are numerous and

potent. Witches, fairies, &c., are as numerous as
ever they were in Teviotdale. The latter are called
Trows, probably from the Norwegian *Dwärg* (or
dwarf) the D being readily converted into T. The
dwarfs are the prime agents in the machinery of
Norwegian superstition. The *trows* do not differ
from the fairies of the Lowlands, or *Sighean* of the
Highlanders. They steal children, dwell within, the
interior of green hills, and often carry mortals into
their recesses. Some, yet alive, pretend to have
been carried off in this way, and obtain credit for
the marvels they tell of the subterranean habitations
of the trows. Sometimes, when a person becomes
melancholy and low-spirited, the trows are supposed
to have stolen the real being, and left a moving
phantom to represent him. Sometimes they are said
to steal only the heart—like Lancashire witches.
There are cures in each case. The party's friends
resort to a cunning man or woman, who hangs about
the neck a triangular stone in the shape of a heart,
or conjures back the lost individual, by retiring to
the hills and employing the necessary spells. A
common receipt, when a child appears consumptive
and puny, is, that the conjurer places a bowl of
water on the patient's head, and pours melted lead
into it through the wards of a key. The metal assumes of course a variety of shapes, from which he
selects a portion, after due consideration, which is

sewn into the shirt of the patient. Sometimes no part of the lead suits the seer's fancy. Then the operation is recommenced, until he obtains a fragment of such a configuration as suits his mystical purpose. Mr Duncan told us he had been treated in this way when a boy.

"A worse and most horrid opinion prevails, or did prevail, among the fishers—namely, that he who saves a drowning man will receive at his hands some deep wrong or injury. Several instances were quoted to-day in company, in which the utmost violence had been found necessary to compel the fishers to violate this inhuman prejudice. It is conjectured to have arisen as an apology for rendering no assistance to the mariners as they escaped from a shipwrecked vessel, for these isles are infamous for plundering wrecks. A story is told of the crew of a stranded vessel who were warping themselves ashore by means of a hawser which they had fixed to the land. The islanders (of Unst, as I believe) watched their motions in silence, till an old man reminded them that if they suffered these sailors to come ashore, they would consume all their winter stock of provisions. A Zetlander cut the hawser, and the poor wretches, twenty in number, were all swept away. This is a tale of former times—the cruelty would not now be *active;* but I fear that even yet the drowning mariner would in some places receive no assistance in his exertions, and certainly he would in most be plundered to the skin upon his landing. The gentlemen do their utmost to prevent this infamous practice. It may seem strange that the natives should be so little affected by a distress to which they are themselves so constantly exposed. But habitual exposure to danger hardens the heart against its consequences, whether to ourselves or others. There is yet living a man — if he can be called so — to whom the following story belongs : — He was engaged in catching sea-fowl upon one of the cliffs, with his father and brother. All three were suspended by a cord, according to custom, and overhanging the ocean at the height of some hundred feet. This man being uppermost on the cord, observed that it was giving way, as unable to support their united weight. He called out to his brother who was next to him — ' Cut away a nail below, Willie,' meaning he should cut the rope beneath, and let his father drop. Willie refused, and bid him cut himself, if he pleased. He did so, and his brother and father were precipitated into the sea. He never thought of concealing or denying the adventure in all its parts. We left Gardie-House late ; being on the side of the Isle of Bressay, opposite to Lerwick, we were soon rowed across the bay. A laugh with Hamilton,* whose

* Robert Hamilton, Sheriff of Lanarkshire, and afterwards one of the Clerks of Session, was a particular favourite of Scott —

gout keeps him stationary at Lerwick, but whose good-humour defies gout and every other provocation, concludes the evening.

" 7th August 1814. — Being Sunday, Duff, Erskine, and I, rode to Tingwall upon Zetland ponies, to breakfast with our friend Parson Turnbull, who had come over in our yacht. An ill-conducted and worse-made road served us four miles on our journey. This *Via Flaminia* of Thule terminates, like its prototype, in a bog. It is, however, the only road in these isles, except about half a mile made by Mr Turnbull. The land in the interior much resembles the Peel-heights, near Ashestiel; but, as you approach the other side of the island, becomes better. Tingwall is rather a fertile valley, up which winds a loch of about two miles in length. The kirk and manse stand at the head of the loch, and command a view down the valley to another

---

first, among many other good reasons, because he had been a soldier in his youth, had fought gallantly and been wounded severely in the American war, and was a very Uncle Toby in military enthusiasm; 2dly, because he was a brother antiquary of the genuine Monkbarns breed ; 3dly (last not least), because he was, in spite of the example of the head of his name and race, a steady Tory. Mr Hamilton sent for Scott when upon his deathbed in 1831, and desired him to choose and carry off as a parting memorial, any article he liked in his collection of arms. Sir Walter (by that time sorely shattered in his own health) selected the sword with which his good friend had been begirt at Bunker's Hill.

lake beyond the first, and thence over another reach of land, to the ocean, indented by capes and studded with isles; among which, that of St Ninian's, abruptly divided from the mainland by a deep chasm, is the most conspicuous. Mr Turnbull is a Jedburgh man by birth, but a Zetlander by settlement and inclination. I have reason to be proud of my countryman; —he is doing his best, with great patience and judgment, to set a good example both in temporals and spirituals, and is generally beloved and respected among all classes. His glebe is in far the best order of any ground I have seen in Zetland. It is enclosed chiefly with dry-stone, instead of the useless turf-dikes; and he has sown grass, and has a hay-stack, and a second crop of clover, and may claim well-dressed fields of potatoes, barley, and oats. The people around him are obviously affected by his example. He gave us an excellent discourse and remarkably good prayers, which are seldom the excellence of the Presbyterian worship.* The congregation were numerous, decent, clean, and well-dressed. The men have all the air of seamen, and are a good-looking hardy race. Some of the old fellows had got faces much resembling Tritons; if they had had conchs to blow, it would have completed them.

* During the winter of 1837–8, this worthy clergyman's wife, his daughter, and a servant, perished within sight of the manse, from a flaw in the ice on the loch — which they were crossing as the nearest way home. — [1839.]

After church, ride down the loch to Scalloway — the country wild but pleasant, with sloping hills of good pasturage, and patches of cultivation on the lower ground. Pass a huge standing stone or pillar. Here, it is said, the son of an old Earl of the Orkneys met his fate. He had rebelled against his father, and fortified himself in Zetland. The Earl sent a party to dislodge him, who, not caring to proceed to violence against his person, failed in the attempt. The Earl then sent a stronger force, with orders to take him dead or alive. The young Absalom's castle was stormed — he himself fled across the loch, and was overtaken and slain at this pillar. The Earl afterwards executed the perpetrators of this slaughter, though they had only fulfilled his own mandate.

" We reach Scalloway, and visit the ruins of an old castle, composed of a double tower or keep, with turrets at the corners. It is the principal, if not the only ruin of Gothic times in Zetland, and is of very recent date, being built in 1600. It was built by Patrick Stewart, Earl of Orkney, afterwards deservedly executed at Edinburgh for many acts of tyranny and oppression. It was this rapacious Lord who imposed many of those heavy duties still levied from the Zetlanders by Lord Dundas. The exactions by which he accomplished this erection were represented as grievous. He was so dreaded, that upon his trial one Zetland witness refused to say a word till he was assured that there was no chance of the

Earl returning to Scalloway. Over the entrance of
the castle are his arms, much defaced, with the uni-
corns of Scotland for supporters, the assumption of
which was one of the articles of indictment. There
is a Scriptural inscription also above the door, in
Latin, now much defaced —

'PATRICIUS ORCHADIÆ ET ZETLANDIÆ COMES. A. D. 1600.
CUJUS FUNDAMEN SAXUM EST, DOMUS ILLA MANEBIT
STABILIS: E CONTRA, SI SIT ARENA, PERIT.'

"This is said to have been furnished to Earl
Patrick by a Presbyterian divine, who slily couched
under it an allusion to the evil practices by which
the Earl had established his power. He perhaps
trusted that the language might disguise the import
from the Earl.*   If so, the Scottish nobility are im-

* In his reviewal of Pitcairn's Trials (1831), Scott says—"In
erecting this Earl's Castle of Scalloway, and other expensive edi-
fices, the King's tenants were forced to work in quarries, transport
stone, dig, delve, climb, and build, and submit to all possible
sorts of servile and painful labour, without either meat, drink,
hire, or recompense of any kind. ' My father,' said Earl Patrick,
' built his house at Sumburgh on the sand, and it has given way
already; this of mine on the rock shall abide and endure.' He
did not or would not understand that the oppression, rapacity
and cruelty by means of which the house arose, were what the
clergyman really pointed to in his recommendation of a motto.
Accordingly, the huge tower remains wild and desolate — its
chambers filled with sand, and its rifted walls and dismantled battlements giving unrestrained access to the roaring sea blast."—
For more of Earl Patrick, see Scott's Miscellaneous Prose Works,
vol. xxi. pp. 230, 233; vol. xxiii. pp. 327, 329.

proved in literature, for the Duke of Gordon pointed
out an error in the Latinity.

" Scalloway has a beautiful and very safe harbour,
but as it is somewhat difficult of access, from a com-
plication of small islands, it is inferior to Lerwick.
Hence, though still nominally the capital of Zetland,
for all edictal citations are made at Scalloway, it has
sunk into a small fishing hamlet. The Norwegians
made their original settlement in this parish of Tingwall.   At the head of this loch, and just below the
manse, is a small round islet accessible by stepping-
stones, where they held their courts ; hence the islet
is called Law-ting — Ting, or Thing, answering to
our word business, exactly like the Latin *negotium.*
It seems odd that in Dumfries-shire, and even in the
Isle of Man, where the race and laws were surely
Celtic, we have this Gothic word Ting and Ting-
wald applied in the same way. We dined with Mr
Scott of Scalloway, who, like several families of this
name in Shetland, is derived from the house of Scotstarvet.   They are very clannish, marry much among
themselves, and are proud of their descent.   Two
young ladies, daughters of Mr Scott's, dined with
us — they were both Mrs Scotts, having married
brothers — the husband of one was lost in the unfortunate Doris. They were pleasant, intelligent
women, and exceedingly obliging. Old Mr Scott
seems a good country gentleman. He is negotiating

an exchange with Lord Dundas, which will give him
the Castle of Scalloway and two or three neighbouring islands : the rest of the archipelago (seven I
think in number) are already his own. He will thus
have command of the whole fishing and harbour, for
which he parts with an estate of more immediate
value, lying on the other side of the mainland. I
found my name made me very popular in this family,
and there were many enquiries after the state of the
Buccleuch family, in which they seemed to take
much interest. I found them possessed of the remarkable circumstances attending the late projected
sale of Ancrum, and the death of Sir John Scott,
and thought it strange that, settled for three generations in a country so distant, they should still take
an interest in those matters. I was loaded with
shells and little curiosities for my young people.

" There was a report (January was two years)
of a kraken or some monstrous fish being seen off
Scalloway. The object was visible for a fortnight,
but nobody dared approach it, although I should have
thought the Zetlanders would not have feared the
devil if he came by water. They pretended that the
suction, when they came within a certain distance,
was so great as to endanger their boats. The object
was described as resembling a vessel with her keel
turned upmost in the sea, or a small ridge of rock or
island. Mr Scott thinks it might have been a ves-

sel overset, or a large whale: if the latter, it seems odd they should not have known it, as whales are the intimate acquaintances of all Zetland sailors.   Whatever it was, it disappeared after a heavy gale of wind, which seems to favour the idea that it was the wreck of a vessel.   Mr Scott seems to think Pontopiddan's narrations and descriptions are much more accurate than we inland men suppose ; and I find most Zetlanders of the same opinion.   Mr Turnbull, who is not credulous upon these subjects, tells me that this year a parishioner of his, a well-informed and veracious person, saw an animal, which, if his description was correct, must have been of the species of sea-snake, driven ashore on one of the Orkneys two or three years ago.   It was very long, and seemed about the thickness of a Norway log, and swam on the top of the waves, occasionally lifting and bending its head.   Mr T. says he has no doubt of the veracity of the narrator, but still thinks it possible it may have been a mere log or beam of wood, and that the spectator may have been deceived by the motion of the waves, joined to the force of imagination. . This for the Duke of Buccleuch.

" At Scalloway my curiosity was gratified by an account of the sword-dance, now almost lost, but still practised in the Island of Papa, belonging to Mr Scott.   There are eight performers, seven of whom represent the Seven Champions of Christendom, who enter one by one with their swords drawn, and are presented to the eighth personage, who is not named. Some rude couplets are spoken (in *English*, not *Norse*), containing a sort of panegyric upon each champion as he is presented. They then dance a sort of cotillion, as the ladies described it, going through a number of evolutions with their swords. One of my three Mrs Scotts readily promised to procure me the lines, the rhymes, and the form of the dance. I regret much that young Mr Scott was absent during this visit; he is described as a reader and an enthusiast in poetry. Probably I might have interested him in preserving the dance, by causing young persons to learn it. A few years since, a party of Papa-men came to dance the sword-dance at Lerwick as a public exhibition with great applause. The warlike dances of the northern people, of which I conceive this to be the only remnant in the British dominions,* are repeatedly alluded to by their poets and historians. The introduction of the Seven Champions savours of a later period, and was probably ingrafted upon the dance when *mysteries* and *mo-*

---

* Mr W. S. Rose informs me, that when he was at school at Winchester, the morris-dancers there used to exhibit a sword-dance resembling that described at Camacho's wedding in Don Quixote; and Mr Morritt adds, that similar dances are even yet performed in the villages about Rokeby every Christmas.

ralities (the first scenic representations) came into fashion. In a stall pamphlet, called the history of Buckshaven, it is said those fishers sprung from Danes, and brought with them their *war-dance* or *sword-dance*, and a rude wooden cut of it is given. We resist the hospitality of our entertainers, and return to Lerwick despite a most downright fall of rain. My pony stumbles coming down hill; saddle sways round, having but one girth and that too long, and lays me on my back. *N. B.* The bogs in Zetland as soft as those in Liddisdale. Get to Lerwick about ten at night. No yacht has appeared.

" *8th August.*—No yacht, and a rainy morning; bring up my journal. Day clears up, and we go to pay our farewell visits of thanks to the hospitable Lerwegians, and at the Fort. Visit kind old Mr Mowat, and walk with him and Collector Ross to the point of Quaggers, or Twaggers, which forms one arm of the southern entrance to the sound of Bressay. From the eminence a delightful sea view, with several of those narrow capes and deep reaches or inlets of the sea, which indent the shores of that land. On the right hand a narrow bay, bounded by the isthmus of Sound, with a house upon it resembling an old castle. In the indenture of the bay, and divided from the sea by a slight causeway, the lake of *Cleik-him-in*, with its Pictish castle. Beyond this the bay opens another yet; and, behind

all, a succession of capes, headlands, and islands, as
far as the cape called Sumburgh-head, which is the
furthest point of Zetland in that direction.   Inland,
craggy, and sable muirs, with cairns, among which
we distinguish the Wart or Ward of Wick, to which
we walked on the 4th.   On the left the island of
Bressay, with its peaked hill called the Wart of
Bressay.   Over Bressay see the top of Hang-cliff.
Admire the Bay of Lerwick, with its shipping,
widening out to the northwards, and then again contracted into a narrow sound, through which the
infamous Bothwell was pursued by Kirkaldy of
Grange, until he escaped through the dexterity of
his pilot, who sailed close along a sunken rock, upon
which Kirkaldy, keeping the weather-gage, struck,
and sustained damage.   The rock is visible at low
water, and is still called the Unicorn, from the name
of Kirkaldy's vessel.   Admire Mr Mowat's little farm.
of about thirty acres, bought about twenty years since
for £75, and redeemed from the miserable state of
the surrounding country, so that it now bears excellent corn; here also was a hay crop.   With Mr
Turnbull's it makes two.   Visit Mr Ross, collector
of the customs, who presents me with the most
superb collection of the stone axes (or adzes, or
whatever they are), called *celts*. The Zetlanders
call them *thunderbolts*, and keep them in their
houses as a receipt against thunder; but the Col-

lector has succeeded in obtaining several. We are
now to dress for dinner with the Notables of Lerwick, who give us an entertainment in their Town-
hall. Oho!

" Just as we were going to dinner, the yacht appeared, and Mr Stevenson landed. He gives a most
favourable account of the isles to the northward, particularly Unst. I believe Lerwick is the worst part
of Shetland. Are hospitably received and entertained
by the Lerwick gentlemen. They are a quick intelligent race — chiefly of Scottish birth, as appears
from their names Mowat, Gifford, Scott, and so
forth. These are the chief proprietors. The Norwegian or Danish surnames, though of course the
more ancient, belong, with some exceptions, to the
lower ranks. The Veteran Corps expects to be dis-
banded, and the officers and Lerwegians seem to part
with regret. Some of the officers talk of settling
here. The price of everything is moderate, and the
style of living unexpensive. Against these con-
veniences are to be placed a total separation from
public life, news, and literature; and a variable and
inhospitable climate. Lerwick will suffer most severely if the Fort is not occupied by some force or
other; for, between whisky and frolic, the Greenland
sailors will certainly burn the little town. We have
seen a good deal, and heard much more, of the pranks
of these unruly guests. A gentleman of Lerwick,

who had company to dine with him, observed beneath his window a party of sailors eating a leg of roast mutton, which he witnessed with philanthropic satisfaction, till he received the melancholy information, that that individual leg of mutton, being the very sheet-anchor of his own entertainment, had been violently carried off from his kitchen, spit and all, by these honest gentlemen, who were now devouring it. Two others having carried off a sheep, were apprehended, and brought before a Justice of the Peace, who questioned them respecting the fact. The first denied he had taken the sheep, but said he had seen it taken away by a fellow with a red nose and a black wig—(this was the Justice's description) —' Don't you think he was like his honour, Tom?' he added, appealing to his comrade. ' By G—, Jack,' answered Tom, ' I believe it was the very man!' Erskine has been busy with these facetious gentlemen, and has sent several to prison, but nothing could have been done without the soldiery. We leave Lerwick at eight o'clock, and sleep on board the yacht.

" *9th August* 1814.—Waked at seven, and find the vessel has left Lerwick harbour, and is on the point of entering the sound which divides the small island of Mousa (or Queen's island) from Coningsburgh, a very wild part of the main island so called. Went ashore, and see the very ancient castle of

Mousa, which stands close on the sea-shore. It is a Pictish fortress, the most entire probably in the world. In form it resembles a dice-box, for the truncated cone is continued only to a certain height, after which it begins to rise perpendicularly, or rather with a tendency to expand outwards. The building is round, and has been surrounded with an outer-wall, of which hardly the slightest vestiges now remain. It is composed of a layer of stones, without cement; they are not of large size, but rather small and thin. To give a vulgar comparison, it resembles an old ruinous pigeon-house. Mr Stevenson took the dimensions of this curious fort, which are as follows:—Outside diameter at the base is fifty-two feet; at the top thirty-eight feet. The diameter of the interior at the base is nineteen feet six inches; at the top twenty-one feet; the curve in the inside being the reverse of the outside, or nearly so. The thickness of the walls at the base seventeen feet; at the top eight feet six inches. The height outside forty-two feet; the inside thirty-four feet. The door or entrance faces the sea, and the interior is partly filled with rubbish. When you enter you see, in the inner wall, a succession of small openings like windows, directly one above another, with broad flat stones, serving for lintels; these are about nine inches thick. The whole resembles a ladder. There were four of these perpendicular rows of windows

or apertures, the situation of which corresponds with
the cardinal points of the compass. You enter the
galleries contained in the thickness of the wall by
two of these apertures, which have been broken
down. These interior spaces are of two descriptions: one consists of a winding ascent, not quite
an inclined plane, yet not by any means a regular
stair; but the edges of the stones, being suffered to
project irregularly, serve for rude steps — or a kind
of assistance. Through this narrow staircase, which
winds round the building, you creep up to the top
of the castle, which is partly ruinous. But besides
the staircase, there branch off at irregular intervals
horizontal galleries, which go round the whole building, and receive air from the holes I formerly mentioned. These apertures vary in size, diminishing
as they run, from about thirty inches in width by
eighteen in height, till they are only about a foot
square. The lower galleries are full man height, but
narrow. They diminish both in height and width
as they ascend, and as the thickness of the wall in
which they are enclosed diminishes. The uppermost
gallery is so narrow and low, that it was with great
difficulty I crept through it. The walls are built
very irregularly, the sweep of the cone being different on the different sides.

" It is said by Torfæus that this fort was repaired
and strengthened by Erlind, who, having forcibly

carried off the mother of Harold Earl of the Orkneys, resolved to defend himself to extremity in this place against the insulted Earl.   How a castle could be defended which had no opening to the outside for shooting arrows, and which was of a capacity to be pulled to pieces by the assailants, who could advance without annoyance to the bottom of the wall (unless it were battlemented upon the top), does not easily appear.   But to Erlind's operations the castle of Mousa possibly owes the upper and perpendicular, or rather overhanging, part of its elevation, and also its rude staircase.   In these two particulars it seems to differ from all other Picts' castles, which are ascended by an inclined plane, and generally, I believe, terminate in a truncated cone, without that strange counterpart of the perpendicular or projecting part of the upper wall.   Opposite to the castle of Mousa are the ruins of another Pictish fort: indeed, they all communicate with each other through the isles. The island of Mousa is the property of a Mr Piper, who has improved it considerably, and values his castle.   I advised him to clear out the interior, as he tells us there are three or four galleries beneath those now accessible, and the difference of height between the exterior and interior warrants his assertion.

" We get on board, and in time, for the wind freshens, and becomes contrary.   We beat down to Sumburgh-head, through rough weather.   This is the extreme south-eastern point of Zetland; and as the Atlantic and German oceans unite at this point, a frightful tide runs here, called Sumburgh-rost. The breeze, contending with the tide, flings the breakers in great style upon the high broken cliffs of Sumburgh-head. They are all one white foam, ascending to a great height. We wished to double this point, and lie by in a bay between that and the northern or north-western cape, called Fitful-head, and which seems higher than Sumburgh itself—and tacked repeatedly with this view; but a confounded islet, called *The Horse*, always baffled us, and, after three heats, fairly distanced us. So we run into a roadstead, called Quendal bay, on the south-eastern side, and there anchor for the night. We go ashore with various purposes—Stevenson to see the site of a proposed lighthouse on this tremendous cape — Marjoribanks to shoot rabbits—and Duff and I to look about us.

" I ascended the head by myself, which is lofty, and commands a wild sea-view. Zetland stretches away, with all its projecting capes and inlets, to the north-eastward. Many of those inlets approach each other very nearly; indeed, the two opposite bays at Sumburgh-head seem on the point of joining, and rendering that cape an island. The two creeks from those east and western seas are only divided by a low isthmus of blowing sand, and simi-

lar to that which wastes part of the east coast of
Scotland. It has here blown like the deserts of
Arabia, and destroyed some houses, formerly the
occasional residences of the Earls of Orkney. The
steep and rocky side of the cape, which faces the
west, does not seem much more durable. These
lofty cliffs are all of sand-flag, a very loose and
perishable kind of rock, which slides down in immense masses, like avalanches, after every storm.
The rest lies so loose, that, on the very brow of the
loftiest crag, I had no difficulty in sending down a
fragment as large as myself: he thundered down in
tremendous style, but splitting upon a projecting
cliff, descended into the ocean like a shower of
shrapnel shot. The sea beneath rages incessantly
among a thousand of the fragments which have fallen
from the peaks, and which assume an hundred strange
shapes. It would have been a fine situation to
compose an ode to the Genius of Sumburgh-head,
or an Elegy upon a Cormorant—or to have written
and spoken madness of any kind in prose or poetry.
But I gave vent to my excited feelings in a more
simple way; and sitting gently down on the steep
green slope which led to the beach, I e'en slid down
a few hundred feet, and found the exercise quite an
adequate vent to my enthusiasm. I recommend this
exercise (time and place suiting) to all my brother
scribblers, and I have no doubt it will save much

effusion of Christian ink. Those slopes are covered
with beautiful short herbage. At the foot of the
ascent, and towards the isthmus, is the old house
of Sumburgh, in appearance a most dreary mansion.
I found, on my arrival at the beach, that the hospitality of the inhabitants had entrapped my companions. I walked back to meet them, but escaped
the gin and water. On board about nine o'clock at
night. A little schooner lies between us and the
shore, which we had seen all day buffeting the tide
and breeze like ourselves. The wind increases, and
the ship is made SNUG — a sure sign the passengers
will not be so.

" 10*th August* 1814. — The omen was but too
true — a terrible combustion on board, among plates,
dishes, glasses, writing-desks, &c. &c.; not a wink
of sleep. We weigh and stand out into that delightful current called *Sumburgh-rost*, or *rust*. This
tide certainly owes us a grudge, for it drove us to
the eastward about thirty miles on the night of the
first, and occasioned our missing the Fair Isle, and
now it has caught us on our return. All the landsmen sicker than sick, and our Viceroy, Stevenson,
qualmish. This is the only time that I have felt
more than temporary inconvenience, but this morning I have headach and nausea; these are trifles,
and in a well-found vessel, with a good pilot, we
have none of that mixture of danger which gives

dignity to the traveller. But he must have a stouter
heart than mine, who can contemplate without horror the situation of a vessel of an inferior description
caught among these headlands and reefs of rocks,
in the long and dark winter nights of these regions.
Accordingly, wrecks are frequent. It is proposed to
have a light on Sumburgh-head, which is the first
land made by vessels coming from the eastward;
Fitful-head is higher, but is to the west, from which
quarter few vessels come.

" We are now clear of Zetland, and about ten
o'clock reach the Fair Isle;* one of their boats
comes off, a strange-looking thing without an entire
plank in it, excepting one on each side, upon the
strength of which the whole depends, the rest being
patched and joined. This trumpery skiff the men
manage with the most astonishing dexterity, and
row with remarkable speed; they have two banks,
that is, two rowers on each bench, and use very
short paddles. The wildness of their appearance,
with long elf-locks, striped worsted caps, and shoes
of raw hide—the fragility of their boat—and their
extreme curiosity about us and our cutter, give them
a title to be distinguished as *natives*. One of our
people told their steersman, by way of jeer, that he

---

* This is a solitary island, lying about half-way between Orkney and Zetland.

must have great confidence in Providence to go to
sea in such a vehicle; the man very sensibly replied,
that without the same confidence he would not go
to sea in the best *tool* in England. We take to our
boat, and row for about three miles round the coast,
in order to land at the inhabited part of the island.
This coast abounds with grand views of rocks and
bays. One immense portion of rock is (like the
Holm of Noss) separated by a chasm from the mainland. As it is covered with herbage on the top,
though a literal precipice all round, the natives contrive to ascend the rock by a place which would make
a goat dizzy, and then drag the sheep up by ropes,
though they sometimes carry a sheep up on their
shoulders. The captain of a sloop of war, being
ashore while they were at this work, turned giddy
and sick while looking at them. This immense precipice is several hundred feet high, and is perforated below by some extraordinary apertures, through
which a boat might pass; the light shines distinctly
through these hideous chasms.

" After passing a square bay called the North-
haven, tenanted by sea-fowl and seals (the first we
have yet seen), we come in view of the small harbour.
Land, and breakfast, for which, till now, none of us
felt inclination. In front of the little harbour is the
house of the tacksman, Mr Strong, and in view are
three small assemblages of miserable huts, where the

inhabitants of the isle live. There are about thirty families and 250 inhabitants upon the *Fair Isle*. It merits its name, as the plain upon which the hamlets are situated, bears excellent barley, oats, and potatoes, and the rest of the isle is beautiful pasture, excepting to the eastward, where there is a moss, equally essential to the comfort of the inhabitants, since it supplies them with peats for fuel. The Fair Isle is about three miles long and a mile and a half broad. Mr Strong received us very courteously. He lives here, like Robinson Crusoe, in absolute solitude as to society, unless by a chance visit from the officers of a man-of-war. There is a signal-post maintained on the island by Government, under this gentleman's inspection; when any ship appears that cannot answer his signals, he sends off to Lerwick and Kirkwall to give the alarm. Rogers* was off here last year, and nearly cut off one of Mr Strong's express-boats, but the active islanders outstripped his people by speed of rowing. The inhabitants pay Mr Strong for the possessions which they occupy under him as sub-tenants, and cultivate the isle in their own way, *i. e.* by digging instead of ploughing (though the ground is quite open and free from rocks, and they have several scores of ponies), and by raising alternate crops of barley, oats, and potatoes; the first and

* An American Commodore.

last are admirably good.   They rather over-manure
their crops; the possessions lie runrig, that is, by
alternate ridges, and the outfield or pasture ground
is possessed as common to all their cows and ponies.
The islanders fish for Mr Strong at certain fixed
rates, and the fish is his property, which he sends to
Kirkwall, Lerwick, or elsewhere, in a little schooner,
the same which we left in Quendal bay, and about
the arrival of which we found them anxious.   An
equal space of rich land on the Fair Isle, situated in
an inland county of Scotland, would rent for £3000
a-year at the very least.   To be sure it would not be
burdened with the population of 250 souls, whose
bodies (fertile as it is) it cannot maintain in bread,
they being supplied chiefly from the mainland.   Fish
they have plenty, and are even nice in their choice.
Skate they will not touch; dog-fish they say is only
food for Orkney-men, and when they catch them,
they make a point of tormenting the poor fish for
eating off their baits from the hook, stealing the haddocks from their lines, and other enormities.   These
people, being about half-way between Shetland and
Orkney, have unfrequent connexion with either archipelago, and live and marry entirely among themselves.   One lad told me, only five persons had left
the island since his remembrance, and of those, three
were pressed for the navy.   They seldom go to
Greenland; but this year five or six of their young

men were on board the whalers. They seemed extremely solicitous about their return, and repeatedly
questioned us about the names of the whalers which
were at Lerwick, a point on which we could give
little information.

" The manners of these islanders seem primitive
and simple, and they are sober, good-humoured, and
friendly — but *jimp* honest. Their comforts are, of
course, much dependent on *their master's* pleasure ;
for so they call Mr Strong. But they gave him the
highest character for kindness and liberality, and
prayed to God he might long be their ruler. After
mounting the signal-post hill, or Malcolm's Head.
which is faced by a most tremendous cliff, we separated on our different routes. The Sheriff went to
rectify the only enormity on the island, which existed
in the person of a drunken schoolmaster; Marchie *
went to shoot sea-fowl, or rather to frighten them,
as his calumniators allege. Stevenson and Duff
went to inspect the remains or vestiges of a Danish
lighthouse upon a distant hill, called, as usual, the
Ward, or Ward-hill, and returned with specimens
of copper ore. Hamilton went down to cater fish
for our dinner, and see it properly cooked — and I
to see two remarkable indentures in the coast called
Rivas, perhaps from their being rifted or *riven*.

* Mr Marjoribanks.

They are exactly like the Buller of Buchan, the sea rolling into a large open basin within the land through a natural archway. These places are close to each other — one is oblong, and it is easy to descend into it by a rude path; the other gulf is inaccessible from the land, unless to a *crags-man*, as these venturous climbers call themselves. I sat for about an hour upon the verge, like the cormorants around me, hanging my legs over the precipice; but I could not get free of two or three well-meaning islanders, who held me fast by the skirts all the time — for it must be conceived, that our numbers and appointments had drawn out the whole population to admire and attend us. After we separated, each, like the nucleus of a comet, had his own distinct train of attendants. — Visit the capital town, a wretched assemblage of the basest huts, dirty without, and still dirtier within; pigs, fowls, cows, men, women, and children, all living promiscuously under the same roof, and in the same room — the brood-sow making (among the more opulent) a distinguished inhabitant of the mansion. The compost, a liquid mass of utter abomination, is kept in a square pond of seven feet deep; when I censured it, they allowed it might be dangerous to the *bairns;* but appeared unconscious of any other objection. I cannot wonder they want meal, for assuredly they waste it. A great *bowie* or wooden vessel of por-

ridge is made in the morning; a child comes and
sups a few spoonfuls; then Mrs Sow takes her
share; then the rest of the children or the parents,
and all at pleasure; then come the poultry when
the mess is more cool; the rest is flung upon the
dunghill — and the goodwife wonders and complains
when she wants meal in winter.   They are a long-
lived race, notwithstanding utter and inconceivable
dirt and sluttery.   A man of sixty told me his father
died only last year, aged ninety-eight; nor was this
considered as very unusual.

" The clergyman of Dunrossness, in Zetland, visits
these poor people once a-year, for a week or two
during summer.   In winter this is impossible, and
even the summer visit is occasionally interrupted for
two years.   Marriages and baptisms are performed,
as one of the Isles-men told me, *by the slump*, and
one of the children was old enough to tell the clergyman who sprinkled him with water, ' Deil be in
your fingers.'   Last time, four couple were married;
sixteen children baptised.   The schoolmaster reads
a portion of Scripture in the church each Sunday,
when the clergyman is absent; but the present man
is unfit for this part of his duty.   The women knit
worsted stockings, night-caps, and similar trifles,
which they exchange with any merchant vessels that
approach their lonely isle.   In these respects they
greatly regret the American war; and mention with

unction the happy days when they could get from an American trader a bottle of peach-brandy or rum in exchange for a pair of worsted-stockings or a dozen of eggs. The humanity of their *master* interferes much with the favourite but dangerous occupation of the islanders, which is *fowling*, that is, taking the young sea-fowl from their nests among these tremendous crags. About a fortnight before we arrived, a fine boy of fourteen had dropped from the cliff, while in prosecution of this amusement, into a roaring surf, by which he was instantly swallowed up. The unfortunate mother was labouring at the peat-moss at a little distance. These accidents do not, however, strike terror into the survivors. They regard the death of an individual engaged in these desperate exploits, as we do the fate of a brave relation who falls in battle, when the honour of his death furnishes a balm to our sorrow. It therefore requires all the tacksman's authority to prevent a practice so pregnant with danger. Like all other precarious and dangerous employments, the occupation of the crags-men renders them unwilling to labour at employments of a more steady description. The Fair Isle inhabitants are a good-looking race, more like Zetlanders than Orkneymen. Evenson, and other names of a Norwegian or Danish derivation, attest their Scandinavian descent. Return and dine at Mr Strong's, having sent our cookery ashore, not to overburthen his hospitality. In this place, and perhaps in the very cottage now inhabited by Mr Strong, the Duke of Medina Sidonia, Commander-in-Chief of the Invincible Armada, wintered, after losing his vessel to the eastward of the island. It was not till he had spent some weeks in this miserable abode, that he got off to Norway. Independently of the moral consideration, that, from the pitch of power in which he stood a few days before, the proudest peer of the proudest nation in Europe found himself dependent on the jealous and scanty charity of these secluded islanders, it is scarce possible not to reflect with compassion on the change of situation from the palaces of Estramadura to the hamlet of the Fair Isle —

'Dost thou wish for thy deserts, O Son of Hodeirah?
Dost thou long for the gales of Arabia?' *

" Mr Strong gave me a curious old chair belonging to Quendale, a former proprietor of the Fair Isle, and which a more zealous antiquary would have dubbed ' the Duke's chair.' I will have it refitted for Abbotsford, however. About eight o'clock we take boat, amid the cheers of the inhabitants, whose minds, subdued by our splendour, had been secured by our munificence, which consisted in a moderate

* Thalaba, Book VIII.

benefaction of whisky and tobacco, and a few shillings laid out on their staple commodities. They
agreed no such day had been seen in the isle. The
signal - post displayed its flags, and to recompense
these distinguished marks of honour, we hung out
our colours, stood into the bay, and saluted with
three guns,

' Echoing from a thousand caves,'

and then bear away for Orkney, leaving, if our
vanity does not deceive us, a very favourable impression on the mind of the inhabitants of the Fair
Isle. The tradition of the Fair Isle is unfavourable to those shipwrecked strangers, who are said to
have committed several acts of violence to extort
the supplies of provision, given them sparingly and
with reluctance by the islanders, who were probably
themselves very far from being well supplied.

" I omitted to say we were attended in the morning by two very sportive whales, but of a kind, as
some of our crew who had been on board Green-
land-men assured us, which it was very dangerous
to attack. There were two Gravesend smacks fishing off the isle. Lord, what a long draught London
makes !

" 11*th August* 1814. — After a sound sleep to
make amends for last night, we find, at awaking, the
vessel off the Start of Sanda, the first land in the

Orkneys which we could make. There a lighthouse has been erected lately upon the best construction. Landed and surveyed it. All in excellent
order, and the establishment of the keepers in the
same style of comfort and respectability as elsewhere,
far better than the house of the master of the Fair
Isle, and rivalling my own baronial mansion of Abbotsford. Go to the top of the tower and survey
the island, which, as the name implies, is level, flat,
and sandy, quite the reverse of those in Zetland: it
is intersected by creeks and small lakes, and, though
it abounds with shell marle, seems barren. There
is one dreadful inconvenience of an island life, of
which we had here an instance. The keeper's wife
had an infant in her arms — her first-born, too, of
which the poor woman had been delivered without
assistance. Erskine told us of a horrid instance
of malice which had been practised in this island
of Sanda. A decent tenant, during the course of
three or four successive years, lost to the number
of twenty-five cattle, stabbed as they lay in their
fold by some abominable wretch. What made the
matter stranger was, that the poor man could not
recollect any reason why he should have had the
ill-will of a single being, only that in taking up
names for the *militia,* a duty imposed upon him by
the Justices, he thought he might possibly have given

some unknown offence. The villain was never discovered.

" The wrecks on this coast were numerous before
the erection of the lighthouse. It was not uncommon to see five or six vessels on shore at once.
The goods and chattels of the inhabitants are all
said to savour of *Flotsome* and *Jetsome*, as the
floating wreck and that which is driven ashore are
severally called. Mr Stevenson happened to observe
that the boat of a Sanda farmer had bad sails — ' If
it had been His (*i. e.* God's) will that you hadna
built sae many lighthouses hereabout' — answered
the Orcadian, with great composure — ' I would
have had new sails last winter.' Thus do they talk
and think upon these subjects ; and so talking and
thinking, I fear the poor mariner has little chance
of any very anxious attempt to assist him. There
is one wreck, a Danish vessel, now aground under
our lee. These Danes are the stupidest seamen, by
all accounts, that sail the sea. When this light upon
the Start of Sanda was established, the Commissioners, with laudable anxiety to extend its utility, had
its description and bearings translated into Danish
and sent to Copenhagen. But they never attend
to such trifles. The Norwegians are much better
liked, as a clever, hardy, sensible people. I forgot
to notice there was a Norwegian prize lying in the

Sound of Lerwick, sent in by one of our cruisers. This was a queer-looking, half-decked vessel, all tattered and torn, and shaken to pieces, looking like Coleridge's Spectre Ship. It was pitiable to see such a prize. Our servants went aboard, and got one of their loaves, and gave a dreadful account of its composition. I got and cut a crust of it; it was rye-bread, with a slight mixture of pine-fir bark or sawings of deal. It was not good, but (as Charles XII. said) might be eaten. But after all, if the people can be satisfied with such bread as this, it seems hard to interdict it to them. What would a Londoner say if, instead of his roll and muffins, this black bread, relishing of tar and turpentine, were presented for his breakfast? I would to God there could be a Jehovah-jireh, ' a ram caught in the thicket,' to prevent the sacrifice of that people.

" The few friends who may see this Journal are much indebted for these pathetic remarks to the situation under which they are recorded; for since we left the lighthouse we have been struggling with adverse wind (pretty high too), and a very strong tide, called the Rost of the Start, which, like Sumburgh Rost, bodes no good to our roast and boiled. The worst is that this struggle carries us past a most curious spectacle, being no less than the carcasses of two hundred and sixty-five whales, which have been driven ashore in Taftsness bay, now lying close under us. With all the inclination in the world, it is impossible to stand in close enough to verify this massacre of Leviathans with our own eyes, as we do not care to run the risk of being drawn ashore ourselves among the party. In fact, this species of spectacle has been of late years very common among the isles. Mr Stevenson saw upwards of a hundred and fifty whales lying upon the shore in a bay at Unst, in his northward trip. They are not large, but are decided whales, measuring perhaps from fifteen to twenty-five feet. They are easily mastered, for the first that is wounded among the sounds and straits so common in the isles, usually runs ashore. The rest follow the blood, and, urged on by the boats behind, run ashore also. A cut with one of the long whaling knives under the back-fin is usually fatal to these huge animals. The two hundred and sixty-five whales, now lying within two or three miles of us, were driven ashore by seven boats only.

" *Five o'clock.*—We are out of the *Rost* (I detest that word), and driving fast through a long sound among low green islands, which hardly lift themselves above the sea—not a cliff or hill to be seen— what a contrast to the land we have left! We are standing for some creek or harbour, called Lingholm-bay, to lie to or anchor for the night; for to pursue our course by night, and that a thick one, among these isles, and islets, and sandbanks, is out of the question—clear moonlight might do. Our sea is now moderate. But, oh gods and men! what misfortunes have travellers to record! Just as the quiet of the elements had reconciled us to the thought of dinner, we learn that an unlucky sea has found its way into the galley during the last infernal combustion, when the lee-side and bolt-sprit were constantly under water; so our soup is poisoned with salt water —our cod and haddocks, which cost ninepence this blessed morning, and would have been worth a couple of guineas in London, are soused in their primitive element—the curry is undone—and all gone to the devil. We all apply ourselves to comfort our Lord High Admiral Hamilton, whose despair for himself and the public might edify a patriot. His good-humour—which has hitherto defied every incident, aggravated even by the gout—supported by a few bad puns, and a great many fair promises on the part of the steward and cook, fortunately restores his equilibrium.

" *Eight o'clock.*—Our supplemental dinner proved excellent, and we have glided into an admirable roadstead or harbour, called Lingholm-bay, formed by the small island of Lingholm embracing a small basin dividing that islet from the larger isle of Stronsay. Both, as well as Sanda, Eda, and others which we have passed, are low, green, and sandy. I have seen nothing to-day worth marking, except the sporting

of a very large whale at some distance, and H.'s face
at the news of the disaster in the cook-room.   We
are to weigh at two in the morning, and hope to
reach Kirkwall, the capital of Orkney, by breakfast
to-morrow.   I trust there are no *rusts* or *rosts* in
the road.   I shall detest that word even when used
to signify verd-antique or patina in the one sense, or
roast venison in the other.   Orkney shall begin a
new volume of these exquisite memoranda.

" OMISSION.—At Lerwick the Dutch fishers had
again appeared on their old haunts.   A very interesting meeting took place between them and the
Lerwegians, most of them being old acquaintances.
They seemed very poor, and talked of having been
pillaged of everything by the French, and expected
to have found Lerwick ruined by the war.   They
have all the careful, quiet, and economical habits of
their country, and go on board their busses with
the utmost haste so soon as they see the Greenland
sailors, who usually insult and pick quarrels with
them.   The great amusement of the Dutch sailors is
to hire the little ponies, and ride up and down upon
them.   On one occasion, a good many years ago, an
English sailor interrupted this cavalcade, frightened
the horses, and one or two Dutchmen got tumbles.
Incensed at this beyond their usual moderation, they
pursued the cause of their overthrow, and wounded

him with one of their knives. The wounded man went on board his vessel, the crew of which, about fifty strong, came ashore with their long flinching knives with which they cut up the whales, and falling upon the Dutchmen, though twice their numbers, drove them all into the sea, where such as could not swim were in some risk of being drowned. The instance of aggression, or rather violent retaliation, on their part, is almost solitary. In general they are extremely quiet, and employ themselves in bartering their little merchandise of gin and gingerbread for Zetland hose and night-caps."

CHAPTER XXIX.

Diary on Board the Lighthouse Yacht continued—The Orkneys—Kirkwall—Hoy—The Standing Stones of Stennis, &c.

AUGUST 1814.

" 12*th August* 1814.—With a good breeze and calm sea we weighed at two in the morning, and worked by short tacks up to Kirkwall bay, and find ourselves in that fine basin upon rising in the morning. The town looks well from the sea, but is chiefly indebted to the huge old cathedral that rises out of the centre. Upon landing we find it but a poor and dirty place, especially towards the harbour. Farther up the town are seen some decent old-fashioned houses, and the Sheriff's interest secures us good lodgings. Marchie goes to hunt for a pointer. The morning, which was rainy, clears up pleasantly, and Hamilton, Erskine, Duff, and I, walk to Malcolm Laing's, who has a pleasant house about half-a-mile

from the town. Our old acquaintance, though an
invalid, received us kindly; he looks very poorly,
and cannot walk without assistance, but seems to retain all the quick, earnest, and vivacious intelligence
of his character and manner. After this visit the
antiquities of the place, viz. the Bishop's palace,
the Earl of Orkney's castle, and the cathedral, all
situated within a stone-cast of each other. The two
former are ruinous. The most prominent part of
the ruins of the Bishop's palace is a large round
tower, similar to that of Bothwell in architecture,
but not equal to it in size. This was built by Bishop
Reid, *tempore Jacobi V.*, and there is a rude statue
of him in a niche in the front. At the north-east
corner of the building is a square tower of greater
antiquity, called the Mense or Mass Tower; but, as
well as a second and smaller round tower, it is quite
ruinous. A suite of apartments of different sizes
fills up the space between these towers, all now
ruinous. The building is said to have been of great
antiquity, but was certainly in a great measure re-
edified in the sixteenth century.

" Fronting this castle or palace of the Bishop,
and about a gun-shot distant, is that of the Earl
of Orkney. The Earl's palace was built by Patrick
Stewart, Earl of Orkney, the same who erected
that of Scalloway, in Shetland. It is an elegant
structure, partaking at once of the character of a

palace and castle. The building forms three sides
of an oblong square, but one of the sides extends
considerably beyond the others.   The great hall
must have been remarkably handsome, opening into
two or three huge rounds or turrets, the lower part
of which is divided by stone shafts into three windows. It has two immense chimneys, the arches
or lintels of which are formed by a flat arch, as at
Crichton Castle.   There is another very handsome
apartment communicating with the hall like a modern
drawing-room, and which has, like the former, its
projecting turrets.   The hall is lighted by a fine
Gothic-shafted window at one end, and by others on
the sides. It is approached by a spacious and elegant
staircase of three flights of steps.   The dimensions
may be sixty feet long, twenty broad, and fourteen
high, but doubtless an arched roof sprung from the
side walls, so that fourteen feet was only the height
from the ground to the arches.   Any modern architect, wishing to emulate the real Gothic architecture,
and apply it to the purposes of modern splendour,
might derive excellent hints from this room.   The
exterior ornaments are also extremely elegant.   The
ruins, once the residence of this haughty and oppressive Earl, are now so disgustingly nasty, that it
required all the zeal of an antiquary to prosecute the
above investigation. Architecture seems to have
been Earl Patrick's prevailing taste. Besides this

castle and that of Scalloway, he added to or en-
larged the old castle of Bressay. To accomplish
these objects, he oppressed the people with severities
unheard-of even in that oppressive age, drew down
on himself a shameful though deserved punishment,
and left these dishonoured ruins to hand down to
posterity the tale of his crimes and of his fall. We
may adopt, though in another sense, his own pre-
sumptuous motto—*Sic Fuit, Est, et Erit.*

" We visit the cathedral, dedicated to St Magnus,
which greeted the Sheriff's approach with a merry
peal. Like that of Glasgow, this church has escaped
the blind fury of Reformation. It was founded in
1138, by Ronald, Earl of Orkney, nephew of the
Saint. It is of great size, being 260 feet long, or
thereabout, and supported by twenty-eight Saxon
pillars, of good workmanship. The round arch pre-
dominates in the building, but I think not exclusively.
The steeple (once a very high spire) rises upon four
pillars of great strength, which occupy each angle
of the nave. Being destroyed by lightning, it was
rebuilt upon a low and curtailed plan. The appearance of the building is rather massive and gloomy
than elegant, and many of the exterior ornaments,
carving around the door-ways, &c., have been injured
by time. We entered the cathedral, the whole of
which is kept locked, swept, and in good order,
although only the eastern end is used for divine

worship. We walked some time in the nave and
western end, which is left unoccupied, and has a very
solemn effect as the avenue to the place of worship.
There were many tombstones on the floor and elsewhere; some, doubtless, of high antiquity. One, I
remarked, had the shield of arms hung by the corner,
with a helmet above it of a large proportion, such
as I have seen on the most ancient seals. But we
had neither time nor skill to decipher what noble
Orcadian lay beneath. The church is as well fitted
up as could be expected; much of the old carved
oak remains, but with a motley mixture of modern
deal pews. All, however, is neat and clean, and
does great honour to the kirk-session who maintain
its decency. I remarked particularly Earl Patrick's
seat, adjoining to that of the magistrates, but sur-
mounting it and every other in the church; it is
surrounded with a carved screen of oak, rather elegant, and bears his arms and initials, and the motto
I have noticed. He bears the royal arms *without
any mark of bastardy* (his father was a natural son of
James V.) quarterly, with a lymphad or galley, the
ancient arms of the county. This circumstance was
charged against him on his trial.* I understand the

* " This noted oppressor was finally brought to trial, and be-
headed at the Cross of Edinburgh [6th February 1614.] It is
said that the King's mood was considerably heated against him
by some ill-chosen and worse written Latin inscriptions with

late Mr Gilbert Laing Meason left the interest of
£1000 to keep up this cathedral.

" There are in the street facing the cathedral the
ruins of a much more ancient castle ; a proper feudal
fortress belonging to the Earls of Orkney, but called
the King's Castle. It appears to have been very
strong, being situated near the harbour, and having,
as appears from the fragments, very massive walls.
While the wicked Earl Patrick was in confinement,
one of his natural sons defended this castle to extremity against the King's troops, and only surren-
dered when it was nearly a heap of ruins, and then
under condition he should not be brought in evidence
against his father.

" We dine at the inn, and drink the Prince Regent's health, being that of the day—Mr Baikie of
Tankerness dines with us.

" 13th August 1814.—A bad morning, but clears
up. No letters from Edinburgh. The country about

which his father and himself had been unlucky enough to decorate
some of their insular palaces. In one of these, Earl Robert, the
father, had given his own designation thus: — ' Orcadiæ Comes
Rex Jacobi Quinti Filius.' In this case he was not, perhaps,
guilty of anything worse than bad Latin. But James VI., who
had a keen nose for puzzling out treason, and with whom an as-
sault and battery upon Priscian ranked in nearly the same degree of crime, had little doubt that the use of the nominative
Rex, instead of the genitive Regis, had a treasonable savour."—
Scott's Miscellaneous Prose Works, vol. xxiii. p. 232.

Kirkwall is flat, and tolerably cultivated. We see oxen generally wrought in the small country carts, though they have a race of ponies, like those of Shetland, but larger. Marchie goes to shoot on a hill called Whiteford, which slopes away about two or three miles from Kirkwall. The grouse is abundant, for the gentleman who chaperons Marchie killed thirteen brace and a half, with a snipe. There are no partridges nor hares. The soil of Orkney is better, and its air more genial than Shetland; but it is far less interesting, and possesses none of the wild and peculiar character of the more northern archipelago. All vegetables grow here freely in the gardens, and there are one or two attempts at trees where they are sheltered by walls. How ill they succeed may be conjectured from our bringing with us a quantity of brushwood, commissioned by Malcolm Laing from Aberbrothock, to be sticks to his pease. This trash we brought two hundred miles. I have little to add, except that the Orkney people have some odd superstitions about a stone on which they take oaths to Odin. Lovers often perform this ceremony in pledge of mutual faith, and are said to account it a sacred engagement.—It is agreed that we go on board after dinner, and sail with the next tide. The magistrates of Kirkwall present us with the freedom of their ancient burgh; and Erskine, instead of being cumbered with drunken sailors, as at

Lerwick, or a drunken schoolmaster, as at Fair Isle,
is annoyed by his own Substitute.   This will occasion
his remaining two days at Kirkwall, during which
time it is proposed we shall visit the lighthouse upon
the dangerous rocks called the Skerries, in the Pentland Frith; and then, returning to the eastern side
of Pomona, take up the counsellor at Stromness.   It
is further settled that we leave Marchie with Erskine
to get another day's shooting.   On board at ten
o'clock, after a little bustle in expediting our do-
mestics, washerwomen, &c.

" 14th August 1814.—Sail about four, and in
rounding the mainland of Orkney, called Pomona,
encounter a very heavy sea; about ten o'clock, get
into the Sound of Holm or Ham, a fine smooth current meandering away between two low green islands,
which have little to characterise them.   On the right
of the Sound is the mainland, and a deep bay called
Scalpa Flow indents it up to within two miles of
Kirkwall.   A canal through this neck of the island
would be of great consequence to the burgh.   We
see the steeple and church of Kirkwall across the
island very distinctly.   Getting out of the Sound of
Holm, we stand in to the harbour or roadstead of
Widewall, where we find seven or eight foreign vessels bound for Ireland, and a sloop belonging to the
lighthouse service.   These roadsteads are common
all through the Orkneys, and afford excellent shelter

for small vessels.   The day is pleasant and sunny,
but the breeze is too high to permit landing at the
Skerries.   Agree, therefore, to stand over for the
mainland of Scotland, and visit Thurso.   Enter the
Pentland Frith, so celebrated for the strength and
fury of its tides, which is boiling even in this pleasant
weather ; we see a large ship battling with this heavy
current, and though with all her canvass set and a
breeze, getting more and more involved.   See the
two Capes of Dungsby or Duncansby, and Dunnet-
head, between which lies the celebrated John o'Groat's
house, on the north-eastern extremity of Scotland.
The shores of Caithness rise bold and rocky before
us, a contrast to the Orkneys, which are all low,
excepting the Island of Hoy.   On Duncansby-head
appear some remarkable rocks, like towers, called
the Stacks of Duncansby.   Near this shore runs the
remarkable breaking tide called the *Merry Men of
Mey*, whence Mackenzie takes the scenery of a
poem—

> ' Where the dancing Men of Mey,
>   Speed the current to the land.' *

Here, according to his locality, the Caithness man
witnessed the vision, in which was introduced the

* Henry Mackenzie's Introduction to " The Fatal Sisters."—
Works, 1808, vol. viii. p. 63.

song translated by Gray, under the title of the Fatal
Sisters.   On this subject, Mr Baikie told me the
following remarkable circumstance:—A clergyman
told him, that while some remnants of the Norse
were yet spoken in North Ronaldsha, he carried
thither the translation of Mr Gray, then newly published, and read it to some of the old people as referring to the ancient history of their islands.   But
so soon as he had proceeded a little way, they exclaimed they knew it very well in the original, and
had often sung it to himself when he asked them for
an old Norse song; they called it *The Enchantresses.*
—— The breeze dies away between two wicked little
islands called Swona and Stroma, the latter belonging
to Caithness, the former to Orkney.—*Nota Bene.*
The inhabitants of the rest of the Orcades despise
those of Swona for eating limpets, as being the last
of human meannesses.   Every land has its fashions.
The Fair-Islesmen disdain Orkney-men for eating
dog-fish.   Both islands have dangerous reefs and
whirlpools, where, even, in this fine day, the tide
rages furiously.   Indeed, the large high unbroken
billows, which at every swell hide from our deck
each distant object, plainly intimate what a dreadful
current this must be when vexed by high or adverse
winds.   Finding ourselves losing ground in the tide,
and unwilling to waste time, we give up Thurso—
run back into the roadstead or bay of Long-Hope,

and anchor under the fort. The bay has four entrances and safe anchorage in most winds, and having become a great rendezvous for shipping (there are nine vessels lying here at present), has been an object of attention with Government.

" Went ashore after dinner, and visited the fort, which is only partly completed; it is a *flêche* to the sea, with eight guns, twenty-four pounders, but without any land defences; the guns are mounted *en barbette*, without embrasures, each upon a kind of moveable stage, which stage wheeling upon a pivot in front, and traversing by means of wheels behind, can be pointed in any direction that may be thought necessary. Upon this stage, the gun-carriage moves forward and recoils, and the depth of the parapet shelters the men even better than an embrasure; at a little distance from this battery they are building a Martello tower, which is to cross the fire of the battery, and also that of another projected tower upon the opposite point of the bay. The expedience of these towers seems excessively problematical. Supposing them impregnable, or nearly so, a garrison of fourteen or fifteen men may be always blockaded by a very trifling number, while the enemy dispose of all in the vicinity at their pleasure. In the case of Long-Hope, for instance, a frigate might disembark 100 men, take the fort in the rear, where it is undefended even by a palisade, destroy the magazines,

spike and dismount the cannon, carry off or cut out
any vessels in the roadstead, and accomplish all the
purposes that could bring them to so remote a spot,
in spite of a serjeant's party in the Martello tower,
and without troubling themselves about them at all.
Meanwhile, Long-Hope will one day turn out a
flourishing place; there will soon be taverns and
slop-shops, where sailors rendezvous in such numbers;
then will come quays, docks, and warehouses; and
then a thriving town.   Amen, so be it.   This is the
first fine day we have enjoyed to an end since Sunday, 31st ult.   Rainy, cold, and hazy, have been our
voyages around these wild islands; I hope the weather begins to mend, though Mr Wilson, our master,
threatens a breeze to-morrow.   We are to attempt
the Skerries, if possible; if not, we will, I believe,
go to Stromness.

" 15th August 1814.— Fine morning; we get
again into the Pentland Frith, and with the aid of a
pilot-boat belonging to the lighthouse service, from
South Ronaldsha, we attempt the Skerries.   Notwithstanding the fair weather, we have a specimen of
the violence of the flood-tide, which forms whirlpools
on the shallow sunken rocks by the islands of Swona
and Stroma, and in the deep water makes strange,
smooth, whirling, and swelling eddies, called by the
sailors, *wells*.   We run through the *wells of Tuftile*
in particular, which, in the least stress of weather,

wheel a large ship round and round, without respect
either to helm or sails. Hence the distinction of
wells and *waves* in old English; the *well* being that
smooth, glassy, oily-looking eddy, the force of which
seems to the eye almost resistless. The bursting of
the waves in foam around these strange eddies has a
bewildering and confused appearance, which it is impossible to describe. Get off the Skerries about ten
o'clock, and land easily; it is the first time a boat
has got there for several days. The *Skerries*** is an
island about sixty acres, of fine short herbage, belonging to Lord Dundas; it is surrounded by a reef
of precipitous rocks, not very high, but inaccessible,
unless where the ocean has made ravines among
them, and where stairs have been cut down to the
water for the lighthouse service. Those inlets have
a romantic appearance, and have been christened by
the sailors, the Parliament House, the Seals' Lying-
in-Hospital, &c. The last inlet, after rushing through
a deep chasm, which is open overhead, is continued
under ground, and then again opens to the sky in
the middle of the island: in this hole the seals bring
out their whelps; when the tide is high, the waves
rise up through this aperture in the middle of the
isle—like the blowing of a whale in noise and appearance. There is another round cauldron of solid

* " A Skerrie means a flattish rock which the sea does not
overflow."—*Edmondstone's View of the Zetlands.*

rock, to which the waves have access through a natural arch in the rock, having another and lesser arch rising just above it; in hard weather, the waves rush through both apertures with a horrid noise; the workmen called it the Carron Blast, and indeed, the variety of noises which issued from the abyss, somewhat reminded me of that engine. Take my rifle, and walk round the cliffs in search of seals, but see none, and only disturb the digestion of certain aldermen-cormorants, who were sitting on the points of the crags after a good fish breakfast; only made one good shot out of four. The lighthouse is too low, and on the old construction, yet it is of the last importance. The keeper is an old man-of-war's-man, of whom Mr Stevenson observed that he was a great swearer when he first came; but after a year or two's residence in this solitary abode, became a changed man. There are about fifty head of cattle on the island; they must be got in and off with great danger and difficulty. There is no water upon the isle, except what remains after rain in some pools; these sometimes dry in summer, and the cattle are reduced to great straits. Leave the isle about one; and the wind and tide being favourable, crowd all sail, and get on at the rate of fourteen miles an hour. Soon reach our old anchorage at the Long-Hope, and passing, stand to the north-westward, up the sound of Hoy, for Stromness.

" I should have mentioned, that in going down the Pentland Frith this morning, we saw Johnnie Groat's house, or rather the place where it stood, now occupied by a storehouse. Our pilot opines there was no such man as Johnnie Groat, for, he says, he cannot hear that anybody *ever saw him.* This reasoning would put down most facts of antiquity. They gather shells on the shore, called *Johnnie Groat's buckies,* but I cannot procure any at present. I may also add, that the interpretation given to *wells* may apply to the *Wells of Slain,* in the fine ballad of Clerk Colvill; such eddies in the romantic vicinity of Slains Castle would be a fine place for a mermaid. *

" Our wind fails us, and what is worse, becomes westerly ; the Sound has now the appearance of a fine land-locked bay, the passages between the several islands being scarce visible. We have a superb view of Kirkwall Cathedral, with a strong gleam of sunshine upon it. Gloomy weather begins to collect

---

* Clerk Colvill falls a sacrifice to a meeting with " a fair Mermaid," whom he found washing her " Sark of Silk" on this romantic shore. He had been warned by his " gay lady" in these words :—

> " O promise me now, Clerk Colvill,
>   Or it will cost ye muckle strife,
> Ride never by the Wells of Slane,
>   If ye wad live and brook your life."

around us, particularly on the island of Hoy, which, covered with gloom and vapour, now assumes a majestic mountainous character. On Pomona we pass the Hill of Orphir, which reminds me of the clergyman of that parish, who was called to account for some of his inaccuracies to the General Assembly; one charge he held particularly cheap, viz., that of drunkenness. 'Reverend Moderator,' said he, in reply, ' I *do* drink, as other gentlemen do.' This Orphir of the north must not be confounded with the Ophir of the south. From the latter came gold, silver, and precious stones; the former seems to produce little except peats. Yet these are precious commodities, which some of the Orkney Isles altogether want, and lay waste and burn the turf of their land instead of importing coal from Newcastle. The Orcadians seem by no means an alert or active race; they neglect the excellent fisheries which lie under their very noses, and in their mode of managing their boats, as well as in the general tone of urbanity and intelligence, are excelled by the less favoured Zetlanders. I observe they always crowd their boat with people in the bows, being the ready way to send her down in any awkward circumstance. There are remains of their Norwegian descent and language in North Ronaldsha, an isle I regret we did not see. A missionary preacher came ashore there a year or two since, but being a very little black-

bearded unshaved man, the seniors of the isle suspected him of being an ancient Pecht or Pict, and
no canny, of course.   The schoolmaster came down
to entreat our worthy Mr Stevenson, then about to
leave the island, to come up and verify whether the
preacher was an ancient Pecht, yea or no.   Finding
apologies were in vain, he rode up to the house
where the unfortunate preacher, after three nights'
watching, had got to bed, little conceiving under
what odious suspicion he had fallen.   As Mr S. declined disturbing him, his boots were produced,
which being a *little — little — very little* pair, confirmed, in the opinion of all the bystanders, the
suspicion of Pechtism.   Mr S. therefore found it
necessary to go into the poor man's sleeping apartment, where he recognised one Campbell, heretofore
an ironmonger in Edinburgh, but who had put his
hand for some years to the missionary plough ; of
course he warranted his quondam acquaintance to be
no ancient Pecht.   Mr Stevenson carried the same
schoolmaster who figured in the adventure of the
Pecht, to the mainland of Scotland, to be examined
for his office.   He was extremely desirous to see a
tree ; and, on seeing one, desired to know what *girss*
it was that grew at the top on't — the leaves appear-
ing to him to be grass.   They still speak a little
Norse, and indeed I hear every day words of that
language ; for instance, *Ja, kul,* for ' *Yes, sir.*'   We

creep slowly up Hoy Sound, working under the
Pomona shore; but there is no hope of reaching
Stromness till we have the assistance of the evening
tide.   The channel now seems like a Highland loch;
not the least ripple on the waves.   The passage is
narrowed, and (to the eye) blocked up by the inter-
position of the green and apparently fertile isle of
Græmsay, the property of Lord Armadale.*   Hoy
looks yet grander, from comparing its black and
steep mountains with this verdant isle.   To add to
the beauty of the Sound, it is rendered lively by the
successive appearance of seven or eight whaling vessels from Davies' Straits; large strong ships, which
pass successively, with all their sails set, enjoying
the little wind that is.   Many of these vessels display
the *garland;* that is, a wreath of ribbons which the
young fellows on board have got from their sweet-
hearts, or come by otherwise, and which hangs
between the foremast and mainmast, surmounted
sometimes by a small model of the vessel.   This
garland is hung up upon the 1st May, and remains
till they come into port.   I believe we shall dodge
here till the tide makes about nine, and then get
into Stromness: no boatman or sailor in Orkney
thinks of the wind in comparison of the tides and
currents.   We must not complain, though the night

* Sir William Honeyman, Bart.—a Judge of the Court of
Session by the title of Lord Armadale.

gets rainy, and the Hill of Hoy is now completely
invested with vapour and mist. In the forepart of
the day we executed very cleverly a task of considerable difficulty and even danger.

" 16th August 1814. — Get into Stromness bay,
and anchor before the party are up. A most decided
rain all night. The bay is formed by a deep in-
dention in the mainland, or Pomona; on one side
of which stands Stromness — a fishing village and
harbour of *call* for the Davies' Straits whalers, as
Lerwick is for the Greenlanders. Betwixt the vessels we met yesterday, seven or eight which passed
us this morning, and several others still lying in the
bay, we have seen between twenty and thirty of these
large ships in this remote place. The opposite side
of Stromness bay is protected by Hoy, and Græmsay
lies between them; so that the bay seems quite land-
locked, and the contrast between the mountains of
Hoy, the soft verdure of Græmsay, and the swelling
hill of Orphir on the mainland, has a beautiful effect.
The day clears up, and Mr Rae, Lord Armadale's
factor, comes off from his house, called Clestrom,
upon the shore opposite to Stromness, to breakfast
with us. We go ashore with him. His farm is well
cultivated, and he has procured an excellent breed of
horses from Lanarkshire, of which county he is a
native; strong hardy Galloways, fit for labour or
hacks. By this we profited, as Mr Rae mounted

us all, and we set off to visit the Standing Stones of
Stenhouse or Stennis.

" At the upper end of the bay, about half way
between Clestrom and Stromness, there extends a
loch of considerable size, of fresh water, but communicating with the sea by apertures left in a long
bridge or causeway which divides them. After riding
about two miles along this lake, we open another
called the Loch of Harray, of about the same dimensions, and communicating with the lower lake,
as the former does with the sea, by a stream, over
which is constructed a causeway, with openings to
suffer the flow and reflux of the water, as both lakes
are affected by the tide. Upon the tongues of land
which, approaching each other, divide the lakes of
Stennis and Harray, are situated the Standing Stones.
The isthmus on the eastern side exhibits a semicircle
of immensely large upright pillars of unhewn stone,
surrounded by a mound of earth. As the mound is
discontinued, it does not seem that the circle was
ever completed. The flat or open part of the semi-
circle looks up a plain, where, at a distance, is seen
a large tumulus. The highest of these stones may
be about sixteen or seventeen feet, and I think there
are none so low as twelve feet. At irregular dis-
tances are pointed out other unhewn pillars of the
same kind. One, a little to the westward, is perforated with a round hole, perhaps to bind a victim;

or rather, I conjecture, for the purpose of solemnly attesting the deity, which the Scandinavians did by passing their head through a ring, — *vide* Eyrbiggia Saga. Several barrows are scattered around this strange monument. Upon the opposite isthmus is a complete circle, of ninety-five paces in diameter, surrounded by standing stones, less in size than the others, being only from ten or twelve to fourteen feet in height, and four in breadth. A deep trench is drawn around this circle on the outside of the pillars, and four tumuli, or mounds of earth, are regularly placed, two on each side.

" Stonehenge excels these monuments, but I fancy they are otherwise unparalleled in Britain. The idea that such circles were exclusively Druidical is now justly exploded. The northern nations all used such erections to mark their places of meeting, whether for religious purposes or civil policy; and there is repeated mention of them in the Sagas. *See* the Eyrbiggia Saga,* for the establishment of the Helga-fels, or holy mount, where the people held their Comitia, and where sacrifices were offered to Thor and Woden. About the centre of the semi-circle is a broad flat stone, probably once the altar on which human victims were sacrificed. — Mr Rae seems to think the common people have no tradition of the purpose of these stones, but probably he has not enquired particularly. He admits they look upon them with superstitious reverence; and it is evident that those which have fallen down (about half the original number) have been wasted by time, and not demolished. The materials of these monuments lay near, for the shores and bottom of the lake are of the same kind of rock. How they were raised, transported, and placed upright, is a puzzling question. In our ride back, noticed a round entrenchment, or *tumulus*, called the Hollow of Tongue.

" The hospitality of Mrs Rae detained us to an early dinner at Clestrom. About four o'clock took our long-boat and rowed down the bay to visit the Dwarfie Stone of Hoy. We have all day been pleased with the romantic appearance of that island, for though the Hill of Hoy is not very high, perhaps about 1200 feet, yet rising perpendicularly (almost) from the sea, and being very steep and furrowed with ravines, and catching all the mists from the western ocean, it has a noble and pictu-resque effect in every point of view. We land upon the island, and proceed up a long and very swampy valley broken into peatbogs. The one side of this valley is formed by the Mountain of Hoy, the other by another steep hill, having at the top a circular belt of rock; upon the slope of this last hill, and

just where the principal mountain opens into a wide
and precipitous and circular *corrie* or hollow, lies
the Dwarfie Stone.   It is a huge sandstone rock, of
one solid stone, being about seven feet high, twenty-
two feet long, and seventeen feet broad.   The upper
end of this stone is hewn into a sort of apartment
containing two beds of stone and a passage between
them.   The uppermost and largest is five feet eight
inches long, by two feet broad, and is furnished with
a stone pillow.   The lower, supposed for the Dwarf's
Wife, is shorter, and rounded off, instead of being
square at the corners.   The entrance may be about
three feet and a half square.   Before it lies a huge
stone, apparently intended to serve the purpose of a
door, and shaped accordingly.   In the top, over the
passage which divides the beds, there is a hole to
serve for a window or chimney, which was doubtless
originally wrought square with irons, like the rest of
the work, but has been broken out by violence into
a shapeless hole.   Opposite to this stone, and proceeding from it in a line down the valley, are several
small barrows, and there is a very large one on the
same line, at the spot where we landed.   This seems
to indicate that the monument is of heathen times,
and probably was meant as the temple of some
northern edition of the *Dii Manes*.   There are no
symbols of Christian devotion — and the door is to
the westward; it therefore does not seem to have

been the abode of a hermit, as Dr Barry[*] has conjectured. The Orcadians have no tradition on the
subject, excepting that they believe it to be the work
of a dwarf, to whom, like their ancestors, they attribute supernatural powers and malevolent disposition.
They conceive he may be seen sometimes sitting at
the door of his abode, but he vanishes on a nearer
approach. Whoever inhabited this den certainly
enjoyed

‘ Pillow cold and sheets not warm.’

" Duff, Stevenson, and I, now walk along the
skirts of the Hill of Hoy, to rejoin Robert Hamilton,
who in the meanwhile had rode down to the clergyman's house, the wet and boggy walk not suiting his
gout. Arrive at the manse completely wet, and
drink tea there. The clergyman (Mr Hamilton)
has procured some curious specimens of natural history for Bullock's Museum, particularly a pair of
fine eaglets. He has just got another of the golden,
or white kind, which he intends to send him. The
eagle, with every other ravenous bird, abounds
among the almost inaccessible precipices of Hoy,
which afford them shelter, while the moors, abound-
ing with grouse, and the small uninhabited islands
and holms, where sheep and lambs are necessarily

* History of the Orkney Islands, by the Rev. George Barry,
D.D. 4to. Edinburgh: 1805.

left unwatched, as well as the all-sustaining ocean, give these birds of prey the means of support. The clergyman told us, that a man was very lately alive in the island of   , who, when an infant, was transported from thence by an eagle over a broad sound, or arm of the sea, to the bird's nest in Hoy. Pursuit being instantly made, and the eagle's nest being known, the infant was found there playing with the young eaglets. A more ludicrous instance of transportation he himself witnessed. Walking in the fields, he heard the squeaking of a pig for some time, without being able to discern whence it proceeded, until looking up, he beheld the unfortunate grunter in the talons of an eagle, who soared away with him towards the summit of Hoy. From this it may be conjectured, that the island is very thinly inhabited; in fact, we only saw two or three little wigwams. After tea we walked a mile farther, to a point where the boat was lying, in order to secure the advantage of the flood-tide. We rowed with toil across one stream of tide, which set strongly up between Græmsay and Hoy; but, on turning the point of Græmsay, the other branch of the same flood-tide carried us with great velocity alongside our yacht, which we reached about nine o'clock. Between riding, walking, and running, we have spent a very active and entertaining day.

" *Domestic Memoranda* — The eggs on Zetland

and Orkney are very indifferent, having an earthy taste, and being very small. But the hogs are an excellent breed — queer wild-looking creatures, with heads like wild-boars, but making capital bacon."

CHAPTER XXX.

Diary continued — Stromness — Bessy Millie's
Charm — Cape Wrath — Cave of Smowe — The
Hebrides — Scalpa, &c.

1814.

" *Off Stromness, 17th August* 1814. — Went on
shore after breakfast, and found W. Erskine and
Marjoribanks had been in this town all last night,
without our hearing of them or they of us. No
letters from Abbotsford or Edinburgh. Stromness
is a little dirty straggling town, which cannot be
traversed by a cart, or even by a horse, for there are
stairs up and down, even in the principal streets.
We paraded its whole length like turkeys in a string,
I suppose to satisfy ourselves that there was a worse
town in the Orkneys than the metropolis, Kirkwall.
We clomb, by steep and dirty lanes, an eminence

rising above the town, and commanding a fine view. An old hag lives in a wretched cabin on this height, and subsists by selling winds. Each captain of a merchantman, between jest and earnest, gives the old woman sixpence, and she boils her kettle to procure a favourable gale. She was a miserable figure; upwards of ninety, she told us, and dried up like a mummy. A sort of clay-coloured cloak, folded over her head, corresponded in colour to her corpselike complexion. Fine light-blue eyes, and nose and chin that almost met, and a ghastly expression of cunning, gave her quite the effect of Hecate. She told us she remembered *Gow the pirate*, who was born near the House of Clestrom, and afterwards commenced buccanier. He came to his native country about 1725, with a *snow* which he commanded, carried off two women from one of the islands, and committed other enormities. At length, while he was dining in a house in the island of Eda, the islanders, headed by Malcolm Laing's grandfather, made him prisoner, and sent him to London, where he was hanged. While at Stromness, he made love to a Miss Gordon, who pledged her faith to him by shaking hands, an engagement which, in her idea, could not be dissolved without her going to London to seek back again her ' faith and troth,' by shaking hands with him again after execution. We left our Pythoness, who assured us there was

nothing evil in the intercession she was to make
for us, but that we were only to have a fair wind
through the benefit of her prayers.   She repeated a
sort of rigmarole which I suppose she had ready for
such occasions, and seemed greatly delighted and
surprised with the amount of our donation, as every
body gave her a trifle, our faithful Captain Wilson
making the regular offering on behalf of the ship.
So much for buying a wind.   Bessy Millie's habitation is airy enough for Æolus himself, but if she is
a special favourite with that divinity, he has a strange
choice.   In her house I remarked a quern, or hand-
mill.—A cairn, a little higher, commands a beautiful
view of the bay, with its various entrances and islets.
Here we found the vestiges of a bonfire, lighted in
memory of the battle of Bannockburn, concerning
which every part of Scotland has its peculiar traditions.   The Orcadians say that a Norwegian prince,
then their ruler, called by them Harold, brought
1400 men of Orkney to the assistance of Bruce,
and that the King, at a critical period of the engagement, touched him with his scabbard, saying, ' The
day is against us.'—' I trust,' returned the Orcadian,
' your Grace will *venture again ;*' which has given
rise to their motto, and passed into a proverb.   On
board at half-past three, and find Bessy Millie a
woman of her word, for the expected breeze has
sprung up, if it but last us till we double Cape

Wrath. Weigh anchor (I hope) to bid farewell to Orkney.*

" The land in Orkney is, generally speaking, excellent, and what is not fitted for the plough, is admirably adapted for pasture. But the cultivation is very bad, and the mode of using these extensive commons, where they tear up, without remorse, the turf of the finest pasture, in order to make fuel, is absolutely execrable. The practice has already peeled and exhausted much fine land, and must in the end ruin the country entirely. In other respects, their mode of cultivation is to manure for barley and oats, and then manure again, and this without the least idea of fallow or green crops. Mr Rae thinks that his example—and he farms very well—has had no effect upon the natives, except in the article of potatoes, which they now cultivate a little more, but crops of turnips are unknown. For this slovenly labour the Orcadians cannot, like the Shetland men, plead the occupation of fishing, which is wholly neglected by them, excepting that about this time of

* Lord Teignmouth, in his recent " Sketches of the Coasts and Islands of Scotland," says — " The publication of the Pirate satisfied the natives of Orkney as to the authorship of the Waverley Novels. It was remarked by those who had accompanied Sir Walter Scott in his excursions in these Islands, that the vivid descriptions which the work contains were confined to those scenes which he visited."—Vol. i. p. 28.

the year all the people turn out for the dogfish, the liver of which affords oil, and the bodies are a food as much valued here by the lower classes as it is contemned in Shetland. We saw nineteen boats out at this work. But cod, tusk, ling, haddocks, &c., which abound round these isles, are totally neglected. Their inferiority in husbandry is therefore to be ascribed to the prejudices of the people, who are all peasants of the lowest order. On Lord Armadale's estate, the number of tenantry amounts to 300, and the average of rent is about seven pounds each. What can be expected from such a distribution? and how is the necessary restriction to take place, without the greatest immediate distress and hardship to these poor creatures? It is the hardest chapter in Economicks; and if I were an Orcadian laird, I feel I should shuffle on with the old useless creatures, in contradiction to my better judgment. Stock is improved in these islands, and the horses seem to be better bred than in Shetland; at least, I have seen more clever animals. The good horses find a ready sale; Mr Rae gets twenty guineas readily for a colt of his rearing—to be sure, they are very good.

 "*Six o'Clock.*—Our breeze has carried us through the Mouth of Hoy, and so into the Atlantic. The north-western face of the island forms a ledge of high perpendicular cliffs, which might have surprised us more, had we not already seen the Ord of Bres-

say, the Noup of Noss, and the precipices of the
Fair Isle. But these are formidable enough. One
projecting cliff, from the peculiarities of its form,
has acquired the name of the Old Man of Hoy, and
is well known to mariners as marking the entrance
to the Mouth. The other jaw of this mouth is
formed by a lower range of crags, called the Burgh
of Birsa. The access through this strait would be
easy, were it not for the Island of Græmsay, lying
in the very throat of the passage, and two other
islands covering the entrance to the harbour of
Stromness. Græmsay is infamous for shipwrecks,
and the chance of these *God-sends*, as they were
impiously called, is said sometimes to have doubled
the value of the land. In Stromness, I saw many
of the sad relics of shipwrecked vessels applied to
very odd purposes, and indeed to all sorts of occasions. The gates, or *grinds*, as they are here called,
are usually of ship planks and timbers, and so are
their bridges, &c. These casualties are now much
less common since the lights on the Skerries and the
Start have been established. Enough of memoranda
for the present.—We have hitherto kept our course
pretty well; and a King's ship about eighteen guns
or so, two miles upon our lee-boom, has shortened
sail, apparently to take us under her wing, which
may not be altogether unnecessary in the latitude of
Cape Wrath, where several vessels have been taken

by Yankee - Doodle.   The sloop-of-war looks as if
she could bite hard, and is supposed by our folks
to be the Malay.   If we can speak the captain, we
will invite him to some grouse, or send him some,
as he likes best, for Marchie's campaign was very
successful.

   " 18th *August* 1814.— Bessy Millie's charm has
failed us.   After a rainy night, the wind has come
round to the north-west, and is getting almost contrary.   We have weathered Whitten-head, however,
and Cape Wrath, the north-western extremity of
Britain, is now in sight.   The weather gets rainy
and squally.   Hamilton and Erskine keep their berths.
Duff and I sit upon deck, like two great bears, wrapt
in watch-cloaks, the sea flying over us every now
and then.   At length, after a sound buffeting with
the rain, the doubling Cape Wrath with this wind
is renounced as impracticable, and we stand away
for Loch Eribol, a lake running into the extensive
country of Lord Reay.   No sickness; we begin to
get hardy sailors in that particular.   The ground
rises upon us very bold and mountainous, especially
a very high steep mountain, called Ben-y-Hope, at
the head of a lake called Loch Hope.   The weather
begins to mitigate as we get under the lee of the
land.   Loch Eribol opens, running up into a wild
and barren scene of crags and hills.   The proper
anchorage is said to be at the head of the lake, but

to go eight miles up so narrow an inlet would expose us to be wind-bound. A pilot boat comes off from Mr Anderson's house, a principal tacksman of Lord Reay's. After some discussion we anchor within a reef of sunken rocks, nearly opposite to Mr Anderson's house of Rispan; the situation is not, we are given to understand, altogether without danger if the wind should blow hard, but it is now calm. In front of our anchorage a few shapeless patches of land, not exceeding a few yards in diameter, have been prepared for corn by the spade, and bear wretched crops. All the rest of the view is utter barrenness; the distant hills, we are told, contain plenty of deer, being part of a forest belonging to Lord Reay, who is proprietor of all the extensive range of desolation now under our eye. The water has been kinder than the land, for we hear of plenty of salmon, and haddocks, and lobsters, and send our faithful minister of the interior, John Peters, the steward, to procure some of those good things of this very indifferent land, and to invite Mr Anderson to dine with us. Four o'clock,—John has just returned, successful in both commissions, and the evening concludes pleasantly.

" 19th August 1814, Loch Eribol, near Cape Wrath.—Went off before eight A. M. to breakfast with our friend Mr Anderson. His house, invisible from the vessel at her moorings, and, indeed, from

any part of the entrance into Loch Eribol, is a very
comfortable one, lying obscured behind a craggy eminence.   A little creek, winding up behind the crag,
and in front of the house, forms a small harbour,
and gives a romantic air of concealment and snug-
ness.   There we found a ship upon the stocks, built
from the keel by a Highland carpenter, who had
magnanimously declined receiving assistance from
any of the ship-carpenters who happened to be here
occasionally, lest it should be said he could not
have finished his task without their aid.   An ample
Highland breakfast of excellent new-taken herring,
equal to those of Lochfine, fresh haddocks, fresh
eggs, and fresh butter, not forgetting the bottle of
whisky, and bannocks of barley, and oat-cakes, with
the Lowland luxuries of tea and coffee.   After
breakfast, took the long-boat, and under Mr Anderson's pilotage, row to see a remarkable natural
curiosity, called Uamh Smowe, or the Largest Cave.
Stevenson, Marchie, and Duff, go by land.   Take
the fowling-piece, and shoot some sea-fowl and a
large hawk of an uncommon appearance.   Fire four
shots, and kill three times.   After rowing about
three miles to the westward of the entrance from
the sea to Loch Eribol, we enter a creek, between
two ledges of very high rocks, and landing, find
ourselves in front of the wonder we came to see.
The exterior apartment of the cavern opens under

a tremendous rock, facing the creek, and occupies
the full space of the ravine where we landed. From
the top of the rock to the base of the cavern, as we
afterwards discovered by plumb, is eighty feet, of
which the height of the arch is fifty-three feet; the
rest, being twenty-seven feet, is occupied by the
precipitous rock under which it opens; the width
is fully in proportion to this great height, being
110 feet. The depth of this exterior cavern is 200
feet, and it is apparently supported by an interme-
diate column of natural rock. Being open to daylight and the sea air, the cavern is perfectly clean
and dry, and the sides are incrusted with stalactites.
This immense cavern is so well proportioned, that I
was not aware of its extraordinary height and extent, till I saw our two friends, who had somewhat
preceded us, having made the journey by land, ap-
pearing like pigmies among its recesses. Afterwards,
on entering the cave, I climbed up a sloping rock at
its extremity, and was much struck with the prospect, looking outward from this magnificent arched
cavern upon our boat and its crew, the view being
otherwise bounded by the ledge of rocks which
formed each side of the creek. We now propose
to investigate the farther wonders of the cave of
Smowe. In the right or west side of the cave
opens an interior cavern of a different aspect. The
height of this second passage may be about twelve

or fourteen feet, and its breadth about six or eight, neatly formed into a Gothic portal by the hand of nature. The lower part of this porch is closed by a ledge of rock, rising to the height of between five and six feet, and which I can compare to nothing but the hatch-door of a shop. Beneath this hatch a brook finds its way out, forms a black deep pool before the Gothic archway, and then escapes to the sea, and forms the creek in which we landed. It is somewhat difficult to approach this strange pass, so as to gain a view into the interior of the cavern. By clambering along a broken and dangerous cliff, you can, however, look into it; but only so far as to see a twilight space filled with dark-coloured water in great agitation, and representing a subterranean lake, moved by some fearful convulsion of nature. How this pond is supplied with water you cannot see from even this point of vantage, but you are made partly sensible of the truth by a sound like the dashing of a sullen cataract within the bowels of the earth. Here the adventure has usually been abandoned, and Mr Anderson only mentioned two travellers whose curiosity had led them farther. We were resolved, however, to see the adventures of this new cave of Montesinos to an end. Duff had already secured the use of a fisher's boat and its hands, our own long-boat being too heavy and far too valuable to be ventured upon this

Cocytus. Accordingly the skiff was dragged up the brook to the rocky ledge or hatch which barred up the interior cavern, and there, by force of hands, our boat's crew and two or three fishers first raised the boat's bow upon the ledge of rock, then brought her to a level, being poised upon that narrow hatch, and lastly launched her down into the dark and deep subterranean lake within. The entrance was so narrow, and the boat so clumsy, that we, who were all this while clinging to the rock like sea-fowl, and with scarce more secure footing, were greatly alarmed for the safety of our trusty sailors. At the instant when the boat sloped inward to the cave, a Highlander threw himself into it with great boldness and dexterity, and, at the expense of some bruises, shared its precipitate fall into the waters under the earth. This dangerous exploit was to prevent the boat drifting away from us, but a cord at its stern would have been a safer and surer expedient.

" When our *enfant perdu* had recovered breath and legs, he brought the boat back to the entrance, and took us in. We now found ourselves embarked on a deep black pond of an irregular form, the rocks rising like a dome all around us, and high over our heads. The light, a sort of dubious twilight, was derived from two chasms in the roof of the vault, for that offered by the entrance was but trifling. Down one of those rents there poured from the height of eighty feet, in a sheet of foam, the brook, which, after supplying the subterranean pond with water, finds its way out beneath the ledge of rock that blocks its entrance. The other skylight, if I may so term it, looks out at the clear blue sky. It is impossible for description to explain the impression made by so strange a place, to which we had been conveyed with so much difficulty. The cave itself, the pool, the cataract, would have been each separate objects of wonder, but all united together, and affecting at once the ear, the eye, and the imagination, their effect is indescribable. The length of this pond, or loch as the people here call it, is seventy feet over, the breadth about thirty at the narrowest point, and it is of great depth.

" As we resolved to proceed, we directed the boat to a natural arch on the right hand, or west side of the cataract. This archway was double, a high arch being placed above a very low one, as in a Roman aqueduct. The ledge of rock which forms this lower arch is not above two feet and a half high above the water, and under this we were to pass in the boat; so that we were fain to pile ourselves flat upon each other like a layer of herrings. By this judicious disposition we were pushed in safety beneath this low-browed rock into a region of utter darkness. For this, however, we were provided, for we had a tinder-box and lights. The view back upon the twilight

lake we had crossed, its sullen eddies wheeling round
and round, and its echoes resounding to the ceaseless
thunder of the waterfall, seemed dismal enough, and
was aggravated by temporary darkness, and in some
degree by a sense of danger. The lights, however,
dispelled the latter sensation, if it prevailed to any
extent, and we now found ourselves in a narrow cavern, sloping somewhat upward from the water. We
got out of the boat, proceeded along some slippery
places upon shelves of the rock, and gained the dry
land. I cannot say *dry*, excepting comparatively.
We were then in an arched cave, twelve feet high in
the roof, and about eight feet in breadth, which went
winding into the bowels of the earth for about an
hundred feet. The sides, being (like those of the
whole cavern) of limestone rock, were covered with
stalactites, and with small drops of water like dew,
glancing like ten thousand thousand sets of birthday
diamonds under the glare of our lights. In some
places these stalactites branch out into broad and
curious ramifications, resembling coral and the foliage
of submarine plants.

" When we reached the extremity of this passage,
we found it declined suddenly to a horrible ugly gulf,
or well, filled with dark water, and of great depth,
over which the rock closed. We threw in stones,
which indicated great profundity by their sound; and
growing more familiar with the horrors of this den,

we sounded with an oar, and found about ten feet
depth at the entrance, but discovered in the same
manner, that the gulf extended under the rock, deepening as it went, God knows how far.   Imagination
can figure few deaths more horrible than to be sucked
under these rocks into some unfathomable abyss,
where your corpse could never be found to give in-
timation of your fate.   A water kelpy, or an evil
spirit of any aquatic propensities, could not choose a
fitter abode; and, to say the truth, I believe at our
first entrance, and when all our feelings were afloat
at the novelty of the scene, the unexpected plashing
of a seal would have routed the whole dozen of us.
The mouth of this ugly gulf was all covered with
slimy alluvious substances, which led Mr Stevenson
to observe, that it could have no separate source, but
must be fed from the waters of the outer lake and
brook, as it lay upon the same level, and seemed to
rise and fall with them, without having anything to
indicate a separate current of its own.   Rounding this
perilous hole, or gulf, upon the aforesaid alluvious
substances, which formed its shores, we reached the
extremity of the cavern, which there ascends like a
vent, or funnel, directly up a sloping precipice, but
hideously black and slippery from wet and sea-weeds.
One of our sailors, a Zetlander, climbed up a good
way, and by holding up a light, we could plainly
perceive that this vent closed after ascending to a

considerable height; and here, therefore, closed the
adventure of the cave of Smowe, for it appeared utterly impossible to proceed further in any direction
whatever.   There is a tradition, that the first Lord
Reay went through various subterranean abysses,
and at length returned, after ineffectually endeavouring to penetrate to the extremity of the Smowe cave;
but this must be either fabulous, or an exaggerated
account of such a journey as we performed.   And
under the latter supposition, it is a curious instance
how little the people in the neighbourhood of this
curiosity have cared to examine it.

" In returning, we endeavoured to familiarize ourselves with the objects in detail, which, viewed together, had struck us with so much wonder.   The
stalactites, or limy incrustations, upon the walls of
the cavern, are chiefly of a dark-brown colour, and
in this respect, Smowe is inferior, according to Mr
Stevenson, to the celebrated cave of Macallister in
the Isle of Skye.   In returning, the men with the
lights, and the various groups and attitudes of the
party, gave a good deal of amusement.   We now
ventured to clamber along the side of the rock above
the subterranean water, and thus gained the upper
arch, and had the satisfaction to see our admirable
and good-humoured commodore, Hamilton, floated
beneath the lower arch into the second cavern.   His
goodly countenance being illumined by a single

candle, his recumbent posture, and the appearance of
a hard-favoured fellow guiding the boat, made him
the very picture of Bibo, in the catch, when he wakes
in Charon's boat:

> ' When Bibo thought fit from this world to retreat,
> As full of Champagne as an egg's full of meat,
> He waked in the boat, and to Charon he said,
> That he would be row'd back, for he was not yet dead.'

" Descending from our superior station on the
upper arch, we now again embarked, and spent some
time in rowing about and examining this second
cave. We could see our dusky entrance, into which
daylight streamed faint, and at a considerable distance ; and under the arch of the outer cavern stood
a sailor, with an oar in his hand, looking, in the
perspective, like a fairy with his wand. We at length
emerged unwillingly from this extraordinary basin,
and again enjoyed ourselves in the large exterior
cave. Our boat was hoisted with some difficulty
over the ledge, which appears the natural barrier of
the interior apartments, and restored in safety to the
fishers, who were properly gratified for the hazard
which their skiff, as well as one of themselves, had
endured. After this we resolved to ascend the rocks,
and discover the opening by which the cascade was
discharged from above into the second cave. Erskine
and I, by some chance, took the wrong side of the

rocks, and, after some scrambling, got into the face of a dangerous precipice, where Erskine, to my great alarm, turned giddy, and declared he could not go farther. I clambered up without much difficulty, and shouting to the people below, got two of them to assist the Counsellor, who was brought into, by the means which have sent many a good fellow out of, the world—I mean a rope. We easily found the brook, and traced its descent till it precipitates itself down a chasm of the rock into the subterranean apartment, where we first made its acquaintance. Divided by a natural arch of stone from the chasm down which the cascade falls, there is another rent, which serves as a skylight to the cavern, as I already noticed. Standing on a natural foot-bridge, formed by the arch which divides these two gulfs, you have a grand prospect into both. The one is deep, black, and silent, only affording at the bottom a glimpse of the dark and sullen pool which occupies the interior of the cavern. The right-hand rent, down which the stream discharges itself, seems to ring and reel with the unceasing roar of the cataract which envelopes its side in mist and foam. This part of the scene alone is worth a day's journey. After heavy rains, the torrent is discharged into this cavern with astonishing violence; and the size of the chasm being inadequate to the reception of such a volume of water, it is thrown up in spouts like the blowing of a whale.

But at such times the entrance of the cavern is inaccessible.

" Taking leave of this scene with regret, we rowed
back to Loch Eribol. Having yet an hour to spare
before dinner, we rowed across the mouth of the
lake to its shore on the east side. This rises into a
steep and shattered stack of mouldering calcareous
rock and stone, called Whiten Head. It is pierced
with several caverns, the abode of seals and cormorants. We entered one, where our guide promised
to us a grand sight, and so it certainly would have
been to any who had not just come from Smowe.
In this last cave the sea enters through a lofty arch,
and penetrates to a great depth; but the weight of
the tide made it dangerous to venture very far, so
we did not see the extremity of Friskin's Cavern,
as it is called. We shot several cormorants in the
cave, the echoes roaring like thunder at every discharge. We received, however, a proper rebuke
from Hamilton, our commodore, for killing anything which was not fit for *eating.*· It was in vain
I assured him that the Zetlanders made excellent
hare-soup out of these sea-fowl. He will listen to
no subordinate authority, and rules us by the Al-
manach des Gourmands. Mr Anderson showed
me the spot where the Norwegian monarch, Haco,
moored his fleet, after the discomfiture he received
at Largs. He caused all the cattle to be driven

from the hills, and houghed and slain upon a broad flat rock, for the refreshment of his dispirited army. Mr Anderson dines with us, and very handsomely presents us with a stock of salmon, haddocks, and so forth, which we requite by a small present of wine from our sea stores. This has been a fine day; the first fair day here for these eight weeks.

" 20th *August* 1814.—Sail by four in the morning, and by half-past six are off Cape Wrath. All hands ashore by seven, and no time allowed to breakfast, except on beef and biscuit. On this dread Cape, so fatal to mariners, it is proposed to build a lighthouse, and Mr Stevenson has fixed on an advantageous situation. It is a high promontory, with steep sides that go sheer down to the breakers, which lash its feet. There is no landing, except in a small creek about a mile and a half to the eastward. There the foam of the sea plays at long bowls with a huge collection of large stones, some of them a ton in weight, but which these fearful billows chuck up and down as a child tosses a ball. The walk from thence to the Cape was over rough boggy ground, but good sheep pasture. Mr —— Dunlop, brother to the laird of Dunlop, took from Lord Reay, some years since, a large track of sheep-land, including the territories of Cape Wrath, for about £300 a-year, for the period of two-nineteen years and a liferent. It is needless to say, that the tenant has an immense

profit, for the value of pasture is now understood
here. Lord Reay's estate, containing 150,000 square
acres, and measuring eighty miles by sixty, was,
before commencement of the last leases, rented at
£1200 a-year. It is now worth £5000, and Mr
Anderson says he may let it this ensuing year (when
the leases expire) for about £15,000. But then he
must resolve to part with his people, for these rents
can only be given upon the supposition that sheep
are generally to be introduced on the property.   In
an economical, and perhaps in a political point of
view, it might be best that every part of a country
were dedicated to that sort of occupation for which
nature has best fitted it.   But to effect this reform
in the present instance, Lord Reay must turn out
several hundred families who have lived under him
and his fathers for many generations, and the swords
of whose fathers probably won the lands from which
he is now expelling them. He is a good-natured
man, I suppose, for Mr A. says he is hesitating
whether he shall not take a more moderate rise
(£7000 or £8000), and keep his Highland tenantry.
This last war (before the short peace), he levied a
fine fencible corps (the Reay fencibles), and might
have doubled their number. *Wealth* is no doubt
strength in a country, while all is quiet and governed
by law, but on any altercation or internal commotion,
it ceases to be strength, and is only the means of

tempting the strong to plunder the possessors. Much may be said on both sides.*

" Cape Wrath is a striking point, both from the dignity of its own appearance, and from the mental association of its being the extreme cape of Scotland, with reference to the north-west. There is no land in the direct line between this point and America. I saw a pair of large eagles, and if I had had the rifle-gun might have had a shot, for the birds, when I first saw them, were perched on a rock within about sixty or seventy yards. They are, I suppose, little disturbed here, for they showed no great alarm. After the Commissioners and Mr Stevenson had examined the headland, with reference to the site of a lighthouse, we strolled to our boat, and came on board between ten and eleven. Get the boat up upon deck, and set sail for the Lewis with light winds and a great swell of tide. Pass a rocky islet called Gousla. Here a fine vessel was lately wrecked; all her crew perished but one, who got upon the rocks from the boltsprit, and was afterwards brought off. In front of Cape Wrath are some angry breakers, called the *Staggs;* the rocks which occasion them are visible at low water. The country behind Cape

---

* The whole of the immense district called *Lord Reay's country* — the habitation, as far back as history reaches, of the clan Mackay — has passed, since Sir W. Scott's journal was written, into the hands of the noble family of Sutherland.

Wrath swells in high sweeping elevations, but without any picturesque or dignified mountainous scenery.
But on sailing westward a few miles, particularly
after doubling a headland called the Stour of Assint,
the coast assumes the true Highland character, being
skirted with a succession of picturesque mountains
of every variety of height and outline.   These are
the hills of Ross-shire—a waste and thinly-peopled
district at this extremity of the island.   We would
willingly have learned the names of the most remarkable, but they are only laid down in the charts
by the cant names given them by mariners, from their
appearance, as the Sugar-loaf, and so forth.   Our
breeze now increases, and seems steadily favourable,
carrying us on with exhilarating rapidity, at the rate
of eight knots an hour, with the romantic outline of
the mainland under our lee-beam, and the dusky
shores of the Long Island beginning to appear ahead.
We remain on deck long after it is dark, watching
the phosphoric effects occasioned, or made visible,
by the rapid motion of the vessel, and enlightening
her course with a continued succession of sparks and
even flashes of broad light, mingled with the foam
which she flings from her bows and head.   A rizard
haddock and to bed.   Charming weather all day.

   " 21st August 1814.— Last night went out like
a lamb, but this morning came in like a lion, all roar
and tumult.   The wind shifted and became squally;

the mingled and confused tides that run among the
Hebrides got us among their eddies, and gave the
cutter such concussions, that, besides reeling at
every wave, she trembled from head to stern, with
a sort of very uncomfortable and ominous vibration.
Turned out about three, and went on deck; the
prospect dreary enough, as we are beating up a
narrow channel between two dark and disconsolate-
looking islands, in a gale of wind and rain, guided
only by the twinkling glimmer of the light on an
island called Ellan Glas.—Go to bed and sleep
soundly, notwithstanding the rough rocking. Great
bustle about four; the light-keeper having seen our
flag, comes off to be our pilot, as in duty bound.
Asleep again till eight. When I went on deck, I
found we had anchored in the little harbour of Scalpa,
upon the coast of Harris, a place dignified by the
residence of Charles Edward in his hazardous attempt
to escape in 1746. An old man, lately alive here,
called Donald Macleod, was his host and temporary
protector, and could not, until his dying hour, mention the distresses of the adventurer without tears.
From this place, Charles attempted to go to Storno-
way; but the people of the Lewis had taken arms
to secure him, under an idea that he was coming to
plunder the country. And although his faithful
attendant, Donald Macleod, induced them by fair
words, to lay aside their purpose, yet they insisted

upon his leaving the island. So the unfortunate Prince was obliged to return back to Scalpa. He afterwards escaped to South Uist, but was chased in the passage by Captain Fergusson's sloop of war. The harbour seems a little neat secure place of anchorage. Within a small island, there seems more shelter than where we are lying; but it is crowded with vessels, part of those whom we saw in the Long-Hope — so Mr Wilson chose to remain outside. The ground looks hilly and barren in the extreme; but I can say little for it, as an incessant rain prevents my keeping the deck. Stevenson and Duff, accompanied by Marchie, go to examine the lighthouse on Ellan Glas. Hamilton and Erskine keep their beds, having scarce slept last night — and I bring up my journal. The day continues bad, with little intermission of rain. Our party return with little advantage from their expedition, excepting some fresh butter from the lighthouse. The harbour of Scalpa is composed of a great number of little uninhabited islets. The masts of the vessels at anchor behind them have a good effect. To bed early, to make amends for last night, with the purpose of sailing for Dunvegan in the Isle of Skye with daylight."

CHAPTER XXXI.

*Diary continued — Isle of Harris — Monuments of
the Chiefs of Macleod — Isle of Skye — Dunvegan Castle — Loch Corriskin — Macallister's
Cave.*

1814.

" 22d *August* 1814.—Sailed early in the morning
from Scalpa Harbour, in order to cross the Minch,
or Channel, for Dunvegan; but the breeze being
contrary, we can only creep along the Harris shore,
until we shall gain the advantage of the tide. The
east coast of Harris, as we now see it, is of a character which sets human industry at utter defiance,
consisting of high sterile hills, covered entirely with
stones, with a very slight sprinkling of stunted
heather. Within, appear still higher peaks of mountains. I have never seen anything more unpropi-
tious, excepting the southern side of Griban, on the
shores of Loch-na-Gaoil, in the Isle of Mull. We

sail along this desolate coast (which exhibits no
mark of human habitation) with the advantage of
a pleasant day, and a brisk, though not a favourable
gale. *Two o'clock* — Row ashore to see the little
harbour and village of Rowdill, on the coast of
Harris. There is a decent three-storied house,
belonging to the laird, Mr Macleod of the Harris,*
where we were told two of his female relations lived.
A large vessel had been stranded last year, and two
or three carpenters were about repairing her, but
in such a style of Highland laziness that I suppose
she may float next century. The harbour is neat
enough, but wants a little more cover to the eastward.
The ground, on landing, does not seem altogether
so desolate as from the sea. In the former point of
view, we overlook all the retired glens and crevices,
which, by infinite address and labour, are rendered
capable of a little cultivation. But few and evil are
the patches so cultivated in Harris, as far as we have
seen. Above the house is situated the ancient church
of Rowdill. This pile was unfortunately burned
down by accident some years since, by fire taking to
a quantity of wood laid in for fitting it up. It is a
building in the form of a cross, with a rude tower
at the eastern end, like some old English churches.
Upon this tower are certain pieces of sculpture, of a

* The Harris has recently passed into the possession of the
Earl of Dunmore. — [1839.]

kind the last which one would have expected on a
building dedicated to religious purposes. Some have
lately fallen in a storm, but enough remains to asto-
nish us at the grossness of the architect and the age.

" Within the church are two ancient monuments.
The first, on the right hand of the pulpit, presents
the effigy of a warrior completely armed in plate armour, with his hand on his two-handed broadsword.
His helmet is peaked, with a gorget or upper corslet
which seems to be made of mail. His figure lies flat
on the monument, and is in bas relief, of the natural size. The arch which surmounts this monument
is curiously carved with the figures of the apostles.
In the flat space of the wall beneath the arch, and
above the tombstone, are a variety of compartments,
exhibiting the arms of the Macleods, being a galley
with the sails spread, a rude view of Dunvegan Castle,
some saints and religious emblems, and a Latin inscription, of which our time (or skill) was inadequate
to decipher the first line ; but the others announced
the tenant of the monument to be *Alexander, filius
Willielmi MacLeod, de Dunvegan, Anno Dni*
M.CCCC.XXVIII. A much older monument (said also
to represent a Laird of Macleod) lies in the transept,
but without any arch over it. It represents the grim
figure of a Highland chief, not in feudal armour like
the former, but dressed in a plaid — (or perhaps a
shirt of mail) — reaching down below the knees, with

a broad sort of hem upon its lower extremity.   The
figure wears a high-peaked open helmet, or scull-cap,
with a sort of tippet of mail attached to it, which
falls over the breast of the warrior, pretty much as
women wear a handkerchief or short shawl.   This
remarkable figure is bearded most tyrannically, and
has one hand on his long two-handed sword, the
other on his dirk, both of which hang at a broad
belt.   Another weapon, probably his knife, seems to
have been also attached to the baldric.   His feet rest
on his two dogs entwined together, and a similar
emblem is said to have supported his head, but is
now defaced, as indeed the whole monument bears
marks of the unfortunate fire.   A lion is placed at
each end of the stone.   Who the hero was, whom
this martial monument commemorated, we could not
learn.   Indeed, our Cicerone was but imperfect.   He
chanced to be a poor devil of an excise-officer who
had lately made a seizure of a still upon a neighbouring island, after a desperate resistance.   Upon
seeing our cutter, he mistook it, as has often happened to us, for an armed vessel belonging to the
revenue, which the appearance and equipment of the
yacht, and the number of men, make her resemble
considerably.   He was much disappointed when he
found we had nothing to do with the tribute to
Cæsar, and begged us not to undeceive the natives,
who were so much irritated against him that he found

it necessary to wear a loaded pair of pistols in each pocket, which he showed to our Master, Wilson, to convince him of the perilous state in which he found himself while exercising so obnoxious a duty in the midst of a fierce-tempered people, and at many miles distance from any possible countenance or assistance. The village of Rowdill consists of Highland huts of the common construction, *i. e.* a low circular wall of large stones, without mortar, deeply sunk in the ground, surmounted by a thatched roof secured by ropes, without any chimney but a hole in the roof. There may be forty such houses in the village. We heard that the laird was procuring a schoolmaster—he of the parish being ten miles distant—and there was a neatness about the large house which seems to indicate that things are going on well. Adjacent to the churchyard were two eminences, apparently artificial. Upon one was fixed a stone, seemingly the staff of a cross; upon another the head of a cross, with a sculpture of the crucifixion. These monuments (which refer themselves to Catholic times of course) are popularly called, *The Croshlets*—crosslets, or little crosses.

" Get on board at five, and stand across the Sound for Skye with the ebb-tide in our favour. The sunset being delightful, we enjoy it upon deck, admiring the Sound on each side bounded by islands. That of Skye lies in the east, with some very high moun-

tains in the centre, and a bold rocky coast in front,
opening up into several lochs, or arms of the sea ;—
that of Loch Folliart, near the upper end of which
Dunvegan is situated, is opposite to us, but our
breeze has failed us, and the flood-tide will soon set
in, which is likely to carry us to the northward of
this object of our curiosity until next morning. To
the west of us lies Harris, with its variegated ridges
of mountains, now clear, distinct, and free from
clouds. The sun is just setting behind the Island
of Bernera, of which we see one conical hill. North
Uist and Benbecula continue from Harris to the
southerly line of what is called the Long Island.
They are as bold and mountainous, and probably as
barren as Harris—worse they cannot be. Unnum-
bered islets and holms, each of which has its name
and its history, skirt these larger isles, and are
visible in this clear evening as distinct and separate
objects, lying lone and quiet upon the face of the
undisturbed and scarce-rippling sea. To our berths
at ten, after admiring the scenery for some time.

"23d *August* 1814.—Wake under the Castle of
Dunvegan, in the Loch of Folliart. I had sent a
card to the Laird of Macleod in the morning, who
came off before we were dressed, and carried us to
his castle to breakfast. A part of Dunvegan is very
old ; ' its birth tradition notes not.' Another large
tower was built by the same Alaster Macleod whose

burial-place and monument we saw yesterday at
Rowdill. He had a Gaelic surname, signifying the
Hump-backed. Roderick More (knighted by James
VI.) erected a long edifice combining. these two ancient towers : and other pieces of building, forming
a square, were accomplished at different times. The
whole castle occupies a precipitous mass of rock
overhanging the lake, divided by two or three islands
in that place, which form a snug little harbour under
the walls. There is a court-yard looking out upon
the sea, protected by a battery, at least a succession
of embrasures, for only two guns are pointed, and
these unfit for service. The ancient entrance rose
up a flight of steps cut in the rock, and passed into
this court-yard through a portal, but this is now demolished. You land under the castle, and walking
round, find yourself in front of it. This was originally inaccessible, for a brook coming down on the
one side, a chasm of the rocks on the other, and a
ditch in front, made it impervious. But the late
Macleod built a bridge over the stream, and the
present laird is executing an entrance suitable to
the character of this remarkable fortalice, by making
a portal between two advanced towers and an outer
court, from which he proposes to throw a draw-
bridge over to the high rock in front of the castle.
This, if well executed, cannot fail to have a good
and characteristic effect. We were most kindly and

hospitably received by the chieftain, his lady, and his sister ;* the two last are pretty and accomplished young women, a sort of persons whom we have not seen for some time ; and I was quite as much pleased with renewing my acquaintance with them as with the sight of a good field of barley just cut (the first harvest we have seen), not to mention an extensive young plantation and some middle-aged trees, though all had been strangers to mine eyes since I left Leith. In the garden — or rather the orchard which was formerly the garden — is a pretty cascade, divided into two branches, and called Rorie More's Nurse, because he loved to be lulled to sleep by the sound of it. The day was rainy, or at least inconstant, so we could not walk far from the castle. Besides the assistance of the laird himself, who was most politely and easily attentive, we had that of an intelligent gentlemanlike clergyman, Mr Suter, minister of Kilmore, to explain the *carte-de-pays*. Within the castle we saw a remarkable drinking-cup, with an inscription dated A.D. 993, which I have described particularly elsewhere.† I saw also a fairy flag, a pennon of silk, with something like round red rowan-berries wrought upon it. We also saw the drinking-horn of Rorie More, holding about three

---

* Miss Macleod, now Mrs Spencer Perceval.

† See Note, Lord of the Isles, Scott's Poetical Works, vol. x. p. 294.

pints English measure—an ox's horn tipped with silver, not nearly so large as Watt of Harden's bugle. The rest of the curiosities in the castle are chiefly Indian, excepting an old dirk and the fragment of a two-handed sword. We learn that most of the Highland superstitions, even that of the second-sight, are still in force. Gruagach, a sort of tutelary divinity, often mentioned by Martin in his history of the Western Islands, has still his place and credit, but is modernized into a tall man, always a Lowlander, with a long coat and white waistcoat. Passed a very pleasant day. I should have said the fairy-flag had three properties. Produced in battle, it multiplied the numbers of the Macleods—spread on the nuptial bed, it ensured fertility—and lastly, it brought herring into the loch.*

* The following passage, from the last of Scott's Letters on Demonology (written in 1830), refers to the night of this 23d of August 1814. He mentions that twice in his life he had experienced the sensation which the Scotch call *eerie;* gives a night-piece of his early youth in the castle of Glammis, which has already been quoted (*ante,* vol. i. p. 295), and proceeds thus:—" Amid such tales of ancient tradition, I had from Macleod and his lady the courteous offer of the haunted apartment of the castle, about which, as a stranger, I might be supposed interested. Accordingly I took possession of it about the witching hour. Except, perhaps, some tapestry hangings, and the extreme thickness of the walls, which argued great antiquity, nothing could have been more comfortable than the interior of the apartment; but if you looked from the windows, the view was such as to

" 24*th August* 1814.—This morning resist with difficulty Macleod's kind and pressing entreaty to send round the ship, and go to the cave at Airds by land; but our party is too large to be accom-

---

correspond with the highest tone of superstition. An autumnal blast, sometimes clear, sometimes driving mist before it, swept along the troubled billows of the lake, which it occasionally concealed, and by fits disclosed. The waves rushed in wild disorder on the shore, and covered with foam the steep pile of rocks, which, rising from the sea in forms something resembling the human figure, have obtained the name of Macleod's Maidens, and, in such a night, seemed no bad representative of the Norwegian goddesses, called Choosers of the Slain, or Riders of the Storm. There was something of the dignity of danger in the scene; for, on a platform beneath the windows, lay an ancient battery of cannon, which had sometimes been used against privateers even of late years. The distant scene was a view of that part of the Quillen mountains which are called, from their form, Macleod's Dining-Tables. The voice of an angry cascade, termed the Nurse of Rorie Mhor, because that chief slept best in its vicinity, was heard from time to time mingling its notes with those of wind and wave. Such was the haunted room at Dunvegan; and, as such, it well deserved a less sleepy inhabitant. In the language of Dr Johnson, who has stamped his memory on this remote place,— ' I looked around me, and wondered that I was not more affected; but the mind is not at all times equally ready to be moved.' In a word, it is necessary to confess that, of all I heard or saw, the most engaging spectacle was the comfortable bed in which I hoped to make amends for some rough nights on shipboard, and where I slept accordingly without thinking of ghost or goblin, till I was called by my servant in the morning."

modated without inconvenience, and divisions are
always awkward.   Walk and see Macleod's farm.
The plantations seem to thrive admirably, although
I think he hazards planting his trees greatly too
tall.   Macleod is a spirited and judicious improver,
and if he does not hurry too fast, cannot fail to be
of service to his people.   He seems to think and
act much like a chief, without the fanfaronade of the
character.   See a female school patronised by Mrs
M.   There are about twenty girls, who learn reading, writing, and spinning ; and being compelled to
observe habits of cleanliness and neatness when at
school, will probably be the means of introducing
them by degrees at home.   The roads around the
castle are, generally speaking, very good; some are
old, some made under the operation of the late act.
Macleod says almost all the contractors for these
last roads have failed, being tightly looked after by
Government, which I confess I think very right.
If Government is to give relief where a disadvan-
tageous contract has been engaged in, it is plain it
cannot be refused in similar instances, so that all
calculations of expenses in such operations are at an
end.   The day being delightfully fair and warm, we
walk up to the Church of Kilmore.   In a cottage,
at no great distance, we heard the women singing
as they *waulked* the cloth, by rubbing it with their
hands and feet, and screaming all the while in a sort

of chorus. At a distance, the sound was wild and
sweet enough, but rather discordant when you approached too near the performers. In the churchyard (otherwise not remarkable) was a pyramidical
monument erected to the father of the celebrated
Simon, Lord Lovat, who was fostered at Dunvegan.
It is now nearly ruinous, and the inscription has
fallen down. Return to the castle, take our luncheon,
and go aboard at three—Macleod accompanying us
in proper style with his piper. We take leave of
the castle, where we have been so kindly entertained, with a salute of seven guns. The chief returns ashore, with his piper playing ' the Macleod's
gathering,' heard to advantage along the calm and
placid loch, and dying as it retreated from us.

" The towers of Dunvegan, with the banner
which floated over them in honour of their guests,
now showed to great advantage. On the right were
a succession of three remarkable hills, with round
flat tops, popularly called Macleod's Dining-Tables.
Far behind these, in the interior of the island, arise
the much higher and more romantic mountains,
called Quillen, or Cuillin, a name which they have
been said to owe to no less a person than Cuthullin,
or Cuchullin, celebrated by Ossian. I ought, I believe, to notice, that Macleod and Mr Suter have
both heard a tacksman of Macleod's, called Grant,
recite the celebrated Address to the Sun; and an-

other person, whom they named, repeat the description of Cuchullin's car. But all agree as to the gross infidelity of Macpherson as a translator and editor. It ends in the explanation of the Adventures in the cave of Montesinos, afforded to the Knight of La Mancha, by the ape of Gines de Passamonte — some are true and some are false. There is little poetical tradition in this country, yet there should be a great deal, considering how lately the bards and genealogists existed as a distinct order. Macleod's *hereditary* piper is called MacCrimmon, but the present holder of the office has risen above his profession. He is an old man, a lieutenant in the army, and a most capital piper, possessing about 200 tunes and pibrochs, most of which will probably die with him, as he declines to have any of his sons instructed in his art. He plays to Macleod and his lady, but only in the same room, and maintains his minstrel privilege by putting on his bonnet so soon as he begins to play. These MacCrimmons formerly kept a college in Skye for teaching the pipe-music. Macleod's present piper is of the name, but scarcely as yet a deacon of his craft. He played every day at dinner.—After losing sight of the Castle of Dunvegan, we open another branch of the loch on which it is situated, and see a small village upon its distant bank. The mountains of Quillen continue to form a background to the wild

landscape with their variegated and peaked outline.
We approach Dunvegan-head, a bold bluff cape,
where the loch joins the ocean. The weather, hitherto so beautiful that we had dined on deck *en
seigneurs,* becomes overcast and hazy, with little or
no wind. Laugh and lie down.

" *25th August* 1814.—Rise about eight o'clock,
the yacht gliding delightfully along the coast of Skye
with a fair wind and excellent day. On the opposite
side lie the islands of Canna, Rum, and Muick, popularly Muck. On opening the sound between Rum
and Canna, see a steep circular rock, forming one
side of the harbour, on the point of which we can
discern the remains of a tower of small dimensions,
built, it is said, by a King of the Isles to secure a
wife of whom he was jealous. But, as we kept the
Skye side of the Sound, we saw little of these islands
but what our spy-glasses could show us. The coast
of Skye is highly romantic, and at the same time displayed a richness of vegetation on the lower grounds,
to which we have hitherto been strangers. We
passed three salt-water lochs, or deep embayments,
called Loch Bracadale, Loch Eynort, and Loch Britta
—and about eleven o'clock open Loch Scavig. We
were now under the western termination of the high
mountains of Quillen, whose weather-beaten and serrated peaks we had admired at a distance from Dun-
gevan. They sunk here upon the sea, but with the

same bold and peremptory aspect which their distant appearance indicated. They seemed to consist of precipitous sheets of naked rock, down which the torrents were leaping in a hundred lines of foam. The tops, apparently inaccessible to human foot, were rent and split into the most tremendous pinnacles; towards the base of these bare and precipitous crags, the ground, enriched by the soil washed away from them, is verdant and productive. Having passed within the small isle of Soa, we enter Lock Scavig under the shoulder of one of these grisly mountains, and observe that the opposite side of the loch is of a milder character softened down into steep green declivities. From the depth of the bay advanced a headland of high rocks which divided the lake into two recesses, from each of which a brook seemed to issue. Here Macleod had intimated we should find a fine romantic loch, but we were uncertain up what inlet we should proceed in search of it. We chose, against our better judgment, the southerly inlet, where we saw a house which might afford us information. On manning our boat and rowing ashore, we observed a hurry among the inhabitants, owing to our being as usual suspected for *king's men*, although, Heaven knows, we have nothing to do with the revenue but to spend the part of it corresponding to our equipment. We find that there is a lake adjoining to each branch of the bay,

and foolishly walk a couple of miles to see that next
the farm-house, merely because the honest man
seemed jealous of the honour of his own loch, though
we were speedily convinced it was not that which
we had been recommended to examine. It had no
peculiar merit excepting from its neighbourhood to
a very high cliff or mountain of precipitous granite ;
otherwise, the sheet of water does not equal even
Cauldshiels Loch. Returned and re-embarked in our
boat, for our guide shook his head at our proposal to
climb over the peninsula which divides the two bays
and the two lakes. In rowing round the headland,
surprised at the infinite number of sea-fowl, then
busy apparently with a shoal of fish ; at the depth of
the bay, find that the discharge from this second lake
forms a sort of waterfall or rather rapid; round this
place were assembled hundreds of trouts and salmon
struggling to get up into the fresh water; with a
net we might have had twenty salmon at a haul, and
a sailor, with no better hook than a crooked pin,
caught a dish of trouts during our absence.

"Advancing up this huddling and riotous brook,
we found ourselves in a most extraordinary scene :
we were surrounded by hills of the boldest and most
precipitous character, and on the margin of a lake
which seemed to have sustained the constant ravages
of torrents from these rude neighbours. The shores
consisted of huge layers of naked granite, here and

there intermixed with bogs, and heaps of gravel and sand marking the course of torrents. Vegetation there was little or none, and the mountains rose so perpendicularly from the water's edge, that Borrowdale is a jest to them. We proceeded about one mile and a half up this deep, dark, and solitary lake, which is about two miles long, half a mile broad, and, as we learned, of extreme depth. The vapour which enveloped the mountain ridges obliged us by assuming a thousand shapes, varying its veils in all sorts of forms, but sometimes clearing off altogether. It is true it made us pay the penalty by some heavy and downright showers, from the frequency of which, a Highland boy, whom we brought from the farm, told us the lake was popularly called the Water Kettle. The proper name is Loch Corriskin, from the deep *corrie* or hollow in the mountains of Cuillin, which affords the basin for this wonderful sheet of water. It is as exquisite as a savage scene, as Loch Katrine is as a scene of stern beauty. After having penetrated so far as distinctly to observe the termination of the lake, under an immense mountain which rises abruptly from the head of the waters, we returned, and often stopped to admire the ravages which storms must have made in these recesses when all human witnesses were driven to places of more shelter and security. Stones, or rather large massive fragments of rock of a composite kind, perfectly

different from the granite barriers of the lake, lay
upon the rocky beach in the strangest and most precarious situations, as if abandoned by the torrents
which had borne them down from above; some lay
loose and tottering upon the ledges of the natural
rock, with so little security that the slightest push
moved them, though their weight exceeded many
tons. These detached rocks were chiefly what are
called plum-pudding stones. Those which formed
the shore were granite. The opposite side of the
lake seemed quite pathless, as a huge mountain, one
of the detached ridges of the Quillen, sinks in a
profound and almost perpendicular precipice down
to the water. On the left-hand side, which we
traversed, rose a higher and equally inaccessible
mountain, the top of which seemed to contain the
crater of an exhausted volcano. I never saw a spot
on which there was less appearance of vegetation of
any kind; the eye rested on nothing but brown and
naked crags,* and the rocks on which we walked by

* 'Rarely human eye has known
A scene so stern as that dread lake,
  With its dark ledge of barren stone.
Seems that primeval earthquake's sway,
Hath rent a strange and shatter'd way
  Through the rude bosom of the hill;
And that each naked precipice,
Sable ravine and dark abyss,
  Tells of the outrage still.

the side of the loch were as bare as the pavement of Cheapside.   There are one or two spots of islets in the loch which seem to bear juniper, or some such low bushy shrub.

" Returned from our extraordinary walk and went on board.   During dinner, our vessel quitted Loch Scavig, and having doubled its southern cape, opened the bay or salt-water Loch of Sleapin.   There went again on shore to visit the late discovered and much celebrated cavern, called Macallister's Cave.   It opens at the end of a deep ravine running upward from the sea, and the proprietor, Mr Macallister of Strath Aird, finding that visitors injured it, by breaking and

The wildest glen, but this, can show
Some touch of Nature's genial glow ;
On high Benmore green mosses grow,
And heath-bells bud in deep Glencroe,
   And copse on Cruchan-Ben ;
But here—above, around, below,
   On mountain or in glen,
Nor tree, nor shrub, nor plant, nor flower,
Nor aught of vegetative power,
   The weary eye may ken ;
For all is rocks at random thrown,
Black waves, bare crags, and banks of stone,
   As if were here denied
The summer's sun, the spring's sweet dew,
That clothe with many a varied hue
   The bleakest mountain side.'

Lord of the Isles, III. 14.

carrying away the stalactites with which it abounds,
has secured this cavern by an eight or nine feet wall,
with a door.   Upon enquiring for the key, we found
it was three miles up the loch at the laird's house.
It was now late, and to stay until a messenger had
gone and returned three miles, was not to be thought
of, any more than the alternative of going up the
loch and lying there all night.   We therefore, with
regret, resolved to scale the wall, in which attempt,
by the assistance of a rope and some. ancient acquaintance with orchard breaking, we easily succeeded.
The first entrance to this celebrated cave is rude and
unpromising, but the light of the torches with which
we were provided, is soon reflected from roof, floor,
and walls, which seem as if they were sheeted with
marble, partly smooth, partly rough with frost-work
and rustic ornaments, and partly wrought into statuary.   The floor forms a steep and difficult ascent,
and might be fancifully compared to a sheet of water,
which, while it rushed whitening and foaming down
a declivity, had been suddenly arrested and consoli-
dated by the spell of an enchanter.   Upon attaining
the summit of this ascent, the cave descends with
equal rapidity to the brink of a pool of the most
limpid water, about four or five yards broad.   There
opens beyond this pool a portal arch, with beautiful
white chasing upon the sides, which promises a continuation of the cave.   One of our sailors swam

across, for there was no other mode of passing, and informed us (as indeed we partly saw by the light he carried), that the enchantment of Macallister's cave terminated with this portal, beyond which there was only a rude ordinary cavern speedily choked with stones and earth. But the pool, on the brink of which we stood, surrounded by the most fanciful mouldings in a substance resembling white marble, and distinguished by the depth and purity of its waters, might be the bathing grotto of a Naiad. I think a statuary might catch beautiful hints from the fanciful and romantic disposition of the stalactites. There is scarce a form or group that an active fancy may not trace among the grotesque ornaments which have been gradually moulded in this cavern by the dropping of the calcareous water, and its hardening into petrifactions; many of these have been destroyed by the senseless rage of appropriation among recent tourists, and the grotto has lost (I am informed), through the smoke of torches, much of that vivid silver tint which was originally one of its chief distinctions. But enough of beauty remains to compensate for all that may be lost. As the easiest mode of return, I slid down the polished sheet of marble which forms the rising ascent, and thereby injured my pantaloons in a way which my jacket is ill calculated to conceal. Our wearables, after a month's hard service, begin to be frail, and there are

daily demands for repairs. Our eatables also begin
to assume a real nautical appearance—no soft bread
—milk a rare commodity—and those gentlemen
most in favour with John Peters, the steward, who
prefer salt beef to fresh. To make amends, we never
hear of sea-sickness, and the good-humour and har-
mony of the party continue uninterrupted. When
we left the cave we carried off two grandsons of Mr
Macallister's, remarkably fine boys; and Erskine,
who may be called *L'ami des Enfans,* treated them
most kindly, and showed them all the curiosities
in the vessel, causing even the guns to be fired for
their amusement, besides filling their pockets with
almonds and raisins. So that, with a handsome letter
of apology, I hope we may erase any evil impression
Mr Macallister may adopt from our storming the
exterior defences of his cavern. After having sent
them ashore in safety, stand out of the bay with little
or no wind, for the opposite island of Egg."

CHAPTER XXXII.

Diary continued — Cave of Egg — Iona — Staffa — Dunstaffnage — Dunluce Castle — Giant's Causeway — Isle of Arran, &c. — Diary concluded.

AUGUST — SEPTEMBER, 1814.

" *26th August* 1814. — At seven this morning were in the Sound which divides the Isle of Rum from that of Egg. Rum is rude, barren, and mountainous; Egg, although hilly and rocky, and traversed by one remarkable ridge called Scuir-Egg, has, in point of soil, a much more promising appearance. Southward of both lies Muick, or Muck, a low and fertile island, and though the least, yet probably the most valuable of the three. Caverns being still the order of the day, we man the boat and row along the shore of Egg, in quest of that which was the

memorable scene of a horrid feudal vengeance. We
had rounded more than half the island, admiring the
entrance of many a bold natural cave which its rocks
exhibit, but without finding that which we sought,
until we procured a guide. This noted cave has a
very narrow entrance, through which one can hardly
creep on knees and hands. It rises steep and lofty
within, and runs into the bowels of the rock to the
depth of 255 measured feet. The height at the entrance may be about three feet, but rises to eighteen
or twenty, and the breadth may vary in the same
proportion. The rude and stony bottom of this cave
is strewed with the bones of men, women, and children, being the sad relics of the ancient inhabitants
of the island, 200 in number, who were slain on the
following occasion: — The Macdonalds of the Isle
of Egg, a people dependent on Clanranald, had done
some injury to the Laird of Macleod. The tradition
of the isle says, that it was by a personal attack on
the chieftain, in which his back was broken; but
that of the other isles bears that the injury was
offered to two or three of the Macleods, who, landing
upon Egg and using some freedom with the young
women, were seized by the islanders, bound hand and
foot, and turned adrift in a boat, which the winds
and waves safely conducted to Skye. To avenge the
offence given, Macleod sailed with such a body of
men as rendered resistance hopeless. The natives,

fearing his vengeance, concealed themselves in this cavern, and after strict search, the Macleods went on board their galleys, after doing what mischief they could, concluding the inhabitants had left the isle. But next morning they espied from their vessel a man upon the island, and, immediately landing again, they traced his retreat, by means of a light snow on the ground, to this cavern. Macleod then summoned the subterraneous garrison, and demanded that the individuals who had offended him, should be delivered up. This was peremptorily refused. The chieftain thereupon caused his people to divert the course of a rill of water, which, falling over the mouth of the cave, would have prevented his purposed vengeance. He then kindled at the entrance of the cavern a huge fire, and maintained it until all within were destroyed by suffocation. The date of this dreadful deed must have been recent, if one can judge from the fresh appearance of those relics. I brought off, in spite of the prejudices of our sailors, a skull, which seems that of a young woman.

" Before re-embarking, we visit another cave opening to the sea, but of a character widely different, being a large open vault as high as that of a cathedral, and running back a great way into the rock at the same height; the height and width of the opening give light to the whole. Here, after 1745, when the Catholic priests were scarcely tolerated, the

priest of Egg used to perform the Romish service.
A huge ledge of rock, almost half-way up one side
of the vault, served for altar and pulpit; and the
appearance of a priest and Highland congregation
in such an extraordinary place of worship, might
have engaged the pencil of Salvator. Most of the
inhabitants of Egg are still Catholics, and laugh at
their neighbours of Rum, who, having been converted
by the cane of their chieftain, are called *Protestants
of the yellow stick.* The Presbyterian minister and
Catholic priest live upon this little island on very
good terms. The people here were much irritated
against the men of a revenue vessel who had seized
all the stills, &c., in the neighbouring Isle of Muck,
with so much severity as to take even the people's
bedding. We had been mistaken for some time for
this obnoxious vessel. Got on board about two
o'clock, and agreed to stand over for Coll, and to be
ruled by the wind as to what was next to be done.
Bring up my journal.

" *27th August* 1814.— The wind, to which we
resigned ourselves, proves exceedingly tyrannical,
and blows squally the whole night, which, with the
swell of the Atlantic, now unbroken by any islands
to windward, proves a means of great combustion in
the cabin. The dishes and glasses in the steward's
cupboards become locomotive — portmanteaus and
writing-desks are more active than necessary—it is

scarce possible to keep one's self within bed, and impossible to stand upright if you rise. Having crept upon deck about four in the morning, I find we are beating to windward off the Isle of Tyree, with the determination on the part of Mr Stevenson, that his constituents should visit a reef of rocks called *Skerry Vhor*, where he thought it would be essential to have a lighthouse. Loud remonstrances on the part of the Commissioners, who one and all declare they will subscribe to his opinion, whatever it may be, rather than continue this infernal buffeting. Quiet perseverance on the part of Mr S., and great kicking, bouncing, and squabbling upon that of the Yacht, who seems to like the idea of Skerry Vhor as little as the Commissioners. At length, by dint of exertion, come in sight of this long ridge of rocks (chiefly under water), on which the tide breaks in a most tremendous style. There appear a few low broad rocks at one end of the reef, which is about a mile in length. These are never entirely under water, though the surf dashes over them. To go through all the forms, Hamilton, Duff, and I, resolve to land upon these bare rocks in company with Mr Stevenson. Pull through a very heavy swell with great difficulty, and approach a tremendous surf dashing over black pointed rocks. Our rowers, however, get the boat into a quiet creek between two rocks, where we contrive to land well wetted. I saw nothing remarkable in my way, excepting several seals, which we might have shot, but, in the doubtful circumstances of the landing, we did not care to bring guns.   We took possession of the rock in name of the Commissioners, and generously bestowed our own great names on its crags and creeks.   The rock was carefully measured by Mr S.   It will be a most desolate position for a lighthouse—the Bell Rock and Eddystone a joke to it, for the nearest land is the wild island of Tyree, at fourteen miles' distance. So much for the Skerry Vhor.

" Came on board proud of our achievement; and, to the great delight of all parties, put the ship before the wind, and run swimmingly down for Iona.   See a large square-rigged vessel, supposed an American. Reach Iona about five o'clock.   The inhabitants of the isle of Columba, understanding their interest as well as if they had been Deal boatmen, charged two guineas for pilotage, which Captain W. abridged into fifteen shillings, too much for ten minutes' work.   We soon got on shore, and landed in the bay of Martyrs, beautiful for its white sandy beach.   Here all dead bodies are still landed, and laid for a time upon a small rocky eminence, called the Sweyne, before they are interred.   Iona, the last time I saw it, seemed to me to contain the most wretched people I had any where seen.   But either they have got better since I was here, or my eyes, familiarized with the wretchedness of Zetland and the Harris, are less shocked with that of Iona. Certainly their houses are better than either, and the appearance of the people not worse. This little fertile isle contains upwards of 400 inhabitants, all living upon small farms, which they divide and subdivide as their families increase, so that the country is greatly over-peopled, and in some danger of a famine in case of a year of scarcity. Visit the nunnery and Reilig Oran, or burial-place of St Oran, but the night coming on we return on board.

"28th August 1814.—Carry our breakfast ashore —take that repast in the house of Mr Maclean, the schoolmaster and cicerone of the island—and resume our investigation of the ruins of the cathedral and the cemetery. Of these monuments, more than of any other, it may be said with propriety,

> ' You never tread upon them but you set
> Your feet upon some ancient history.'

I do not mean to attempt a description of what is so well-known as the ruins of Iona. Yet I think it has been as yet inadequately performed, for the vast number of carved tombs containing the reliques of the great, exceeds credibility. In general, even in the most noble churches, the number of the vulgar dead exceed in all proportion the few of eminence who are deposited under monuments. Iona is in all respects the reverse ; until lately the inhabitants of

the isle did not presume to mix their vulgar dust
with that of chiefs, reguli, and abbots.   The number,
therefore, of carved and inscribed tombstones, is quite
marvellous, and I can easily credit the story told by
Sacheverell, who assures us that 300 inscriptions had
been collected, and were lost in the troubles of the
17th century.   Even now, many more might be de-
ciphered than have yet been made public, but the
rustic step of the peasants and of Sassenach visitants is
fast destroying these faint memorials of the valiant of
the isles.   A skilful antiquary remaining here a week,
and having (or assuming) the power of raising the
half-sunk monuments, might make a curious collection.   We could only gaze and grieve; yet had the
day not been Sunday, we would have brought our
seamen ashore, and endeavoured to have raised some
of these monuments.   The celebrated ridges called
Jomaire na'n Righrean, or Graves of the Kings,
can now scarce be said to exist, though their site is
still pointed out.   Undoubtedly, the thirst of spoil,
and the frequent custom of burying treasures with
the ancient princes, occasioned their early violation;
nor am I any sturdy believer in their being regularly
ticketed off by inscriptions into the tombs of the
Kings of Scotland, of Ireland, of Norway, and so
forth.   If such inscriptions ever existed, I should
deem them the work of some crafty bishop or abbot,
for the credit of his diocese or convent.   Macbeth

is said to have been the last King of Scotland here buried; sixty preceded him, all doubtless as powerful in their day, but now unknown —*carent quia vate sacro.* A few weeks' labour of Shakspeare, an obscure player, has done more for the memory of Macbeth than all the gifts, wealth, and monuments of this ce- metery of princes have been able to secure to the rest of its inhabitants. It also occurred to me in Iona (as it has on many similar occasions) that the tradi- tional recollections concerning the monks themselves are wonderfully faint, contrasted with the beautiful and interesting monuments of architecture which they have left behind them. In Scotland particularly, the people have frequently traditions wonderfully vivid of the persons and achievements of ancient warriors, whose towers have long been levelled with the soil. But of the monks of Melrose, Kelso, Aberbrothock, Iona, &c. &c. &c., they can tell nothing but that such a race existed, and inhabited the stately ruins of these monasteries. The quiet, slow, and uniform life of those recluse beings, glided on, it may be, like a dark and silent stream, fed from unknown resources, and vanishing from the eye without leaving any marked trace of its course. The life of the chieftain was a mountain torrent thundering over rock and precipice, which, less deep and profound in itself, leaves on the minds of the terrified spectators those deep impres- sions of awe and wonder which are most readily handed down to posterity.

"Among the various monuments exhibited at
Iona, is one where a Maclean lies in the same grave
with one of the Macfies or Macduffies of Colonsay,
with whom he had lived in alternate friendship and
enmity during their lives. ' He lies above him
during death,' said one of Maclean's followers, as
his chief was interred, ' as he was above him during
life.' There is a very ancient monument lying
among those of the Macleans, but perhaps more
ancient than any of them; it has a knight riding on
horseback, and behind him a minstrel playing on a
harp; this is conjectured to be Reginald Macdonald
of the Isles, but there seems no reason for disjoining
him from his kindred who sleep in the cathedral.
A supposed ancestor of the Stewarts, called Paul
Purser, or Paul the Purse-bearer (treasurer to the
King of Scotland), is said to lie under a stone near
the Lords of the Isles. Most of the monuments
engraved by Pennant are still in the same state of
preservation, as are the few ancient crosses which
are left. What a sight Iona must have been, when
360 crosses, of the same size and beautiful workmanship, were ranked upon the little rocky ridge of
eminences which form the background to the cathedral! Part of the tower of the cathedral has fallen
since I was here. It would require a better architect than I am, to say anything concerning the
antiquity of these ruins, but I conceive those of the

nunnery and of the *Reilig nan Oran*, or Oran's chapel, are decidedly the most ancient. Upon the cathedral and buildings attached to it, there are marks of repairs at different times, some of them of a late date, being obviously designed not to enlarge the buildings, but to retrench them. We take a reluctant leave of Iona, and go on board.

" The haze and dullness of the atmosphere seem to render it dubious if we can proceed, as we intended, to Staffa to-day—for mist among these islands is rather unpleasant. Erskine reads prayers on deck to all hands, and introduces a very apt allusion to our being now in sight of the first Christian Church from which Revelation was diffused over Scotland and all its islands. There is a very good form of prayer for the Lighthouse Service, composed by the Rev. Mr Brunton.* A pleasure vessel lies under our lee from Belfast, with an Irish party related to Macneil of Colonsay. The haze is fast degenerating into downright rain, and that right heavy—verifying the words of Collins—

> ' And thither where beneath the *showery west*
> The mighty Kings of three fair realms are laid.' †

After dinner, the weather being somewhat cleared,

---

* The Rev. Alexander Brunton, D.D., now (1836) Professor of Oriental Languages in the University of Edinburgh.

† Ode on the Superstitions of the Highlands.

sailed for Staffa, and took boat. The surf running
heavy up between the island and the adjacent rock,
called Booshala, we landed at a creek near the Cormorant's cave. The mist now returned so thick as
to hide all view of Iona, which was our land-mark;
and although Duff, Stevenson, and I, had been formerly on the isle, we could not agree upon the
proper road to the cave. I engaged myself, with
Duff and Erskine, in a clamber of great toil and
danger, and which at length brought me to the *Can-
non-ball*, as they call a round granite stone moved
by the sea up and down in a groove of rock, which
it has worn for itself, with a noise resembling thunder. Here I gave up my research, and returned to
my companions, who had not been more fortunate.
As night was now falling, we resolved to go aboard
and postpone the adventure of the enchanted cavern
until next day. The yacht came to an anchor with
the purpose of remaining off the island all night,
but the hardness of the ground, and the weather
becoming squally, obliged us to return to our safer
mooring at Y-Columb-Kill.

" *29th August* 1814.—Night squally and rainy
— morning ditto — we weigh, however, and return
toward Staffa, and, very happily, the day clears as
we approach the isle. As we ascertained the situation of the cave, I shall only make this memorandum,
that when the weather will serve, the best landing is

to the lee of Booshala, a little conical islet or rock,
composed of basaltic columns placed in an oblique
or sloping position.   In this way, you land at once
on the flat causeway, formed by the heads of truncated pillars, which leads to the cave.   But if the
state of tide renders it impossible to land under
Booshala, then take one of the adjacent creeks; in
which case, keeping to the left hand along the top
of the ledge of rocks which girdles in the isle, you
find a dangerous and precipitous descent to the
causeway aforesaid, from the table.   Here we were
under the necessity of towing our Commodore,
Hamilton, whose gallant heart never fails him, whatever the tenderness of his toes may do.   He was
successfully lowered by a rope down the precipice,
and proceeding along the flat terrace or causeway
already mentioned, we reached the celebrated cave.
I am not sure whether I was not more affected by
this second, than by the first view of it.   The stupendous columnar side walls—the depth and strength
of the ocean with which the cavern is filled—the
variety of tints formed by stalactites dropping and
petrifying between the pillars, and resembling a sort
of chasing of yellow or cream-coloured marble filling
the interstices of the roof—the corresponding variety
below, where the ocean rolls over a red, and in some
places a violet-coloured rock, the basis of the basaltic
pillars—the dreadful noise of those august billows so

well corresponding with the grandeur of the scene —
are all circumstances elsewhere unparalleled. We
have now seen in our voyage the three grandest
caverns in Scotland, Smowe, Macallister's Cave, and
Staffa; so that, like the Troglodytes of yore, we
may be supposed to know something of the matter.
It is, however, impossible to compare scenes of na-
tures so different, nor, were I compelled to assign
a preference to any of the three, could I do it but
with reference to their distinct characters, which
might affect different individuals in different degrees.
The characteristic of the Smowe cave may in this
case be called the terrific, for the difficulties which
oppose the stranger are of a nature so uncommonly
wild as, for the first time at least, convey an impression of terror — with which the scenes to which
he is introduced fully correspond. On the other
hand, the dazzling whiteness of the incrustations in
Macallister's cave, the elegance of the entablature,
the beauty of its limpid pool, and the graceful
dignity of its arch, render its leading features those
of severe and chastened beauty. Staffa, the third
of these subterraneous wonders, may challenge sub-
limity as its principal characteristic. Without the
savage gloom of the Smowe cave, and investigated
with more apparent ease, though, perhaps, with equal
real danger, the stately regularity of its columns
forms a contrast to the grotesque imagery of Mac-

allister's cave, combining at once the sentiments of
grandeur and beauty. The former is, however, pre-
dominant, as it must necessarily be in any scene of
the kind.

" We had scarce left Staffa when the wind and
rain returned. It was Erskine's object and mine to
dine at Torloisk on Loch Tua, the seat of my valued
friend Mrs Maclean Clephane, and her accomplished
daughters. But in going up Loch Tua between
Ulva and Mull with this purpose,

> ' So thick was the mist on the ocean green,
> Nor cape nor headland could be seen.'*

It was late before we came to anchor in a small bay
presented by the little island of Gometra, which may
be regarded as a continuation of Ulva. We therefore dine aboard, and after dinner, Erskine and I
take the boat and row across the loch under a heavy
rain. We could not see the house of Torloisk, so
very thick was the haze, and we were a good deal
puzzled how and where to achieve a landing; at
length, espying a cart-road, we resolved to trust to
its guidance, as we knew we must be near the house.
We therefore went ashore with our servants, *à la
bonne aventure*, under a drizzling rain. This was
soon a matter of little consequence, for the necessity
of crossing a swollen brook wetted me considerably,

---

* " So thick a haze o'erspreads the sky,
> They cannot see the Sun on high."
> SOUTHEY's *Inchcape Rock.*

and Erskine, whose foot slipped, most completely.
In wet and weary plight we reached the house, after
a walk of a mile, in darkness, dirt, and rain, and it
is hardly necessary to say, that the pleasure of seeing
our friends soon banished all recollection of our unpleasant voyage and journey.

"*30th August* 1814.—The rest of our friends
come ashore by invitation, and breakfast with the
ladies, whose kindness would fain have delayed us
for a few days, and at last condescended to ask for
one day only—but even this could not be, our time
wearing short.   Torloisk is finely situated upon the
coast of Mull, facing Staffa.   It is a good comfortable house, to which Mrs Clephane has made some
additions.   The grounds around have been dressed,
so as to smooth their ruggedness, without destroying
the irregular and wild character peculiar to the scene
and country.   In this, much taste has been displayed.
'At Torloisk, as at Dunvegan, trees grow freely and
rapidly, and the extensive plantations formed by Mrs
C. serve to show that nothing but a little expense
and patience on the part of the proprietors, with
attention to planting in proper places at first, and
in keeping up fences afterward, are awanting to re-
move the reproach of nakedness, so often thrown
upon the Western Isles.   With planting comes shelter, and the proper allotment and division of fields.
With all this Mrs Clephane is busied, and, I trust,
successfully; I am sure, actively and usefully.   Take

leave of my fair friends, with regret that I cannot prolong my stay for a day or two. When we come on board, we learn that Staffa-Macdonald is just come to his house of Ulva; this is a sort of unpleasant dilemma, for we cannot now go there without some neglect towards Mrs Maclean Clephane; and, on the other hand, from his habits with all of us, he may be justly displeased with our quitting his very threshold without asking for him. However, upon the whole matter, and being already under weigh, we judged it best to work out of the loch, and continue our purpose of rounding the northern extremity of Mull, and then running down the Sound between Mull and the mainland. We had not long pursued our voyage before we found it was like to be a very slow one. The wind fell away entirely, and after repeated tacks we could hardly clear the extreme north-western point of Mull by six o'clock — which must have afforded amusement to the ladies whose hospitable entreaties we had resisted, as we were almost all the while visible from Torloisk. A fine evening, but scarce a breath of wind.

" 31st August 1814. — Went on deck between three and four in the morning, and found the vessel almost motionless in a calm sea, scarce three miles advanced on her voyage. We had, however, rounded the north-western side of Mull, and were advancing between the north-eastern side and the rocky and wild shores of Ardnamurchan on the mainland of Scotland. Astern were visible in bright moonlight the distant mountains of Rum; yet nearer, the remarkable ridge in the Isle of Egg, called Scuir-Egg; and nearest of all the low isle of Muick. After enjoying this prospect for some time, returned to my berth. Rise before eight—a delightful day, but very calm, and the little wind there is decidedly against us. Creeping on slowly, we observe, upon the shore of Ardnamurchan, a large old castle called Mingary. It appears to be surrounded with a very high wall, forming a kind of polygon, in order to adapt itself to the angles of a precipice overhanging the sea, on which the castle is founded. Within or beyond the wall, and probably forming part of an inner court, I observed a steep roof and windows, probably of the 17th century. The whole, as seen with a spyglass, seems ruinous. As we proceed, we open on the left hand Loch Sunart, running deep into the mainland, crossed by distant ridges of rocks, and terminating apparently among the high mountains above Strontian. On the right hand we open the Sound of Mull, and pass the Bloody Bay, which acquired that name from a desperate battle fought between an ancient Lord of the Isles and his son. The latter was assisted by the Macleans of Mull, then in the plenitude of their power, but was defeated. This

was a sea-fight ; gallies being employed on each side.
It has bequeathed a name to a famous pibroch.

" Proceeding southward, we open the beautiful
bay of Tobermory, or Mary's Well. The mouth of
this fine natural roadstead is closed by an isle called
Colvay, having two passages, of which only one, the
northerly, is passable for ships. The bay is surrounded by steep hills, covered with copsewood,
through which several brooks seek the sea in a succession of beautiful cascades. The village has been
established as a fishing station by the Society for
British Fisheries. The houses along the quay are
two and three stories high, and well built; the feuars
paying to the Society sixpence per foot of their line
of front. On the top of a steep bank, rising above
the first town, runs another line of second-rate cottages, which pay fourpence per foot; and behind are
huts, much superior to the ordinary sheds of the
country, which pay only twopence per foot. The
town is all built upon a regular plan, laid down by
the Society. The new part is reasonably clean, and
the old not unreasonably dirty. We landed at an
excellent quay, which is not yet finished, and found
the little place looked thriving and active. The people
were getting in their patches of corn; and the shrill
voices of the children, attending their parents in the
field, and loading the little ponies which are used in
transporting the grain, formed a chorus not disagree-

able to those whom it reminds of similar sounds at
home.   The praise of comparative cleanliness does
not extend to the lanes around Tobermory, in one
of which I had nearly been effectually bogged.   But
the richness of the round steep green knolls, clothed
with copse, and glancing with cascades, and a pleasant peep at a small fresh-water loch embosomed
among them—the view of the bay, surrounded and
guarded by the island of Colvay—the gliding of two
or three vessels in the more distant Sound—and the
row of the gigantic Ardnamurchan mountains closing
the scene to the north, almost justify the eulogium
of Sacheverell, who, in 1688, declared the bay of
Tobermory might equal any prospect in Italy.   It is
said that Sacheverell made some money by weighing
up the treasures lost in the Florida, a vessel of the
Spanish Armada, which was wrecked in the harbour.
He himself affirms, that though the use of the diving-
bells was at first successful, yet the attempt was
afterwards disconcerted by bad weather.

   " Tobermory takes its name from a spring dedicated to the Virgin, which was graced by a chapel ;
but no vestiges remain of the chapel, and the spring
rises in the middle of a swamp, whose depth and
dirt discouraged the nearer approach of Protestant
pilgrims.   Mr Stevenson, whose judgment is un-
questionable, thinks that the village should have been
built on the island called Colvay, and united to the

continent by a key, or causeway, built along the southermost channel, which is very shallow. By this means the people would have been much nearer the fishings, than retired into the depth of the bay.

" About three o'clock we get on board, and a brisk and favourable breeze arises, which carries us smoothly down the Sound. We soon pass Arros, with its fragment of a castle, behind which is the house of Mr Maxwell (an odd name for this country), chamberlain to the Duke of Argyle, which reminds me of much kindness and hospitality received from him and Mr Stewart, the sheriff-substitute, when I was formerly in Mull. On the shore of Morven, on the opposite side, pass the ruins of a small fortalice, called Donagail, situated as usual on a precipice overhanging the sea. The ' woody Morven,' though the quantity of shaggy diminutive copse, which springs up where it obtains any shelter, still shows that it must once have merited the epithet, is now, as visible from the Sound of Mull, a bare country—of which the hills towards the sea have a slope much resembling those in Selkirkshire, and accordingly afford excellent pasture, and around several farm-houses well cultivated and improved fields. I think I observe considerable improvement in husbandry, even since I was here last; but there is a difference in coming from Oban and Cape Wrath.— Open Loch Alline, a beautiful salt-water lake, with a narrow outlet to the Sound. It is surrounded by round hills, sweetly fringed with green copse below, and one of which exhibits to the spy-glass ruins of a castle. There is great promise of beauty in its interior, but we cannot see every thing. The land on the southern bank of the entrance slopes away into a sort of promontory, at the extremity of which are the very imperfect ruins of the castle of Ardtornish, to which the Lords of the Isles summoned parliaments, and from whence one of them dated a treaty with the Crown of England as an independent Prince. These ruins are seen to most advantage from the south, where they are brought into a line with one high fragment towards the west predominating over the rest. The shore of the promontory on the south side becomes rocky, and when it slopes round to the west, rises into a very bold and high precipitous bank, skirting the bay on the western side, partly cliffy, partly covered with brushwood, with various streams dashing over it from a great height. Above the old castle of Ardtornish, and about where the promontory joins the land, stands the present mansion, a neat white-washed house, with several well enclosed and well cultivated fields surrounding it.

" The high and dignified character assumed by the shores of Morven after leaving Ardtornish, continues till we open the Loch Linnhe, the commence-

ment of the great chain of inland lakes running up
to Fort-William, and which it is proposed to unite
with Inverness by means of the Caledonian Canal.
The wisdom of the plan adopted in this national
measure seems very dubious.   Had the Canal been
of more moderate depth, and the burdens imposed
upon passing vessels less expensive, there can be no
doubt that the coasters, sloops, and barks, would
have carried on a great trade by means of it.   But
the expense and plague of locks, &c. may prevent
these humble vessels from taking this abridged voyage, while ships above twenty or thirty tons will
hesitate to engage themselves in the intricacies of
a long lake navigation, exposed, without room for
manœuvring, to all the sudden squalls of the mountainous country.   Ahead of us, in the mouth of Loch
Linnhe, lies the low and fertile isle of Lismore,
formerly the appanage of the Bishops of the Isles,
who, as usual, knew where to choose church patri-
mony.   The coast of the Mull, on the right hand
of the Sound, has a black, rugged, and unimproved
character.   Above Scallister bay are symptoms of
improvement.   Moonlight has risen upon us as we
pass Duart castle, now an indistinct mass upon its
projecting promontory.   It was garrisoned for Government so late as 1780, but is now ruinous.   We
see, at about a mile's distance, the fatal shelve on
which Duart exposed the daughter of Argyle, on

which Miss Baillie's play of the Family Legend is
founded, but now,

> ‘ Without either sign or sound of their shock,
> The waves flowed over the Lady's rock.’ *

The placid state of the sea is very different from
what I have seen it, when six stout rowers could
scarce give a boat headway through the conflicting
tides.   These fits of violence so much surprised and
offended a body of the Camerons, who were bound
upon some expedition to Mull, and had been accustomed to the quietness of lake-navigation, that they
drew their dirks, and began to stab the waves —
from which popular tale this run of tide is called
the Men of Lochaber.   The weather being delightfully moderate, we agree to hover hereabout all
night, or anchor under the Mull shore, should it
be necessary, in order to see Dunstaffnage to-morrow morning.   The isle of Kerrera is now in sight,
forming the bay of Oban.   Beyond lie the varied
and magnificent summits of the chain of mountains
bordering Loch Linnhe, as well as those between
Loch Awe and Loch Etive, over which the summit
of Ben Cruachan is proudly prominent.   Walk on
deck, admiring this romantic prospect until ten ;
then below, and turn in.

    " 1*st September* 1814. — Rise betwixt six and
seven, and having discreetly secured our breakfast,

---

* Southey's *Inchcape Rock.*

take boat for the old castle of Dunstaffnage, situated
upon a promontory on the side of Loch Linnhe and
near to Loch Etive.   Nothing could exceed the
beauty of the day and of the prospect.   We coasted
the low, large, and fertile isle of Lismore, where a
Catholic Bishop, Chisholm, has established a semi-
nary of young men intended for priests, and what is
a better thing, a valuable lime-work.   Report speaks
well of the lime, but indifferently of the progress of
the students.   Tacking to the shore of the loch, we
land at Dunstaffnage, once, it is said, the seat of the
Scottish monarchy, till success over the Picts and
Saxons transferred their throne to Scoone, Dun-
fermline, and at length to Edinburgh.   The castle
is still the King's (nominally), and the Duke of
Argyle (nominally also), is hereditary keeper.   But
the real right of property is in the family of the
depute-keeper, to which it was assigned as an appanage, the first possessor being a natural son of an
Earl of Argyle.   The shell of the castle, for little
more now remains, bears marks of extreme antiquity.   It is square in form, with round towers at
three of the angles, and is situated upon a lofty
precipice, carefully scarped on all sides to render
it perpendicular.   The entrance is by a staircase,
which conducts you to a wooden landing-place in
front of the portal-door.   This landing-place could
formerly be raised at pleasure, being of the nature of

a draw-bridge. When raised, the place was inaccessible. You pass under an ancient arch, with a low vault (being the porter's lodge) on the right hand, and flanked by loop-holes, for firing upon any hostile guest who might force his passage thus far. This admits you into the inner-court, which is about eighty feet square. It contains two mean-looking buildings, about sixty or seventy years old; the ancient castle having been consumed by fire in 1715. It is said that the nephew of the proprietor was the incendiary. We went into the apartments, and found they did not exceed the promise of the exterior; but they admitted us to walk upon the battlements of the old castle, which displayed a most splendid prospect. Beneath, and far projected into the loch, were seen the woods and houses of Campbell of Lochnell. A little summer-house, upon an eminence, belonging to this wooded bank, resembles an ancient monument. On the right, Loch Etive, after pouring its waters like a furious cataract over a strait called Connell-ferry, comes between the castle and a round island belonging to its demesne, and nearly insulates the situation. In front is a low rocky eminence on the opposite side of the arm, through which Loch Etive flows into Loch Linnhe. Here was situated *Beregenium*, once, it is said, a British capital city; and, as our informant told us, the largest market-town in Scotland. Of this splendour are no remains but a few trenches and excavations, which the distance did not allow us to examine. The ancient masonry of Dunstaffnage is mouldering fast under time and neglect. The foundations are beginning to decay, and exhibit gaps between the rock and the wall; and the battlements are become ruinous. The inner court is encumbered with ruins. A hundred pounds or two would put this very ancient fortress in a state of preservation for ages, but I fear this is not to be expected. The stumps of large trees, which had once shaded the vicinity of the castle, gave symptoms of decay in the family of Dunstaffnage. We were told of some ancient spurs and other curiosities preserved in the castle, but they were locked up. In the vicinity of the castle is a chapel which had once been elegant, but by the building up of windows, &c. is now heavy enough. I have often observed that the means adopted in Scotland for repairing old buildings are generally as destructive of their grace and beauty, as if that had been the express object. Unfortunately, most churches, particularly, have gone through both stages of destruction, having been first repaired by the building up of the beautiful shafted windows, and then the roof being suffered to fall in, they became ruins indeed, but without any touch of the picturesque farther than their massive walls and columns may afford. Near the chapel of Dunstaffnage is a remarkable echo.

" Re-embarked, and, rowing about a mile and a half or better along the shore of the lake, again landed under the ruins of the old castle of Dunolly. This fortress, which, like that of Dunstaffnage, forms a marked feature in this exquisite landscape, is situated on a bold and precipitous promontory overhanging the lake. The principal part of the ruins now remaining is a square tower or keep of the ordinary size, which had been the citadel of the castle; but fragments of other buildings, overgrown with ivy, show that Dunolly had once been a place of considerable importance. These had enclosed a court-yard, of which the keep probably formed one side, the entrance being by a very steep ascent from the land side, which had formerly been cut across by a deep moat, and defended doubtless by outworks and a drawbridge. Beneath the castle stands the modern house of Dunolly, a decent mansion, suited to the reduced state of the MacDougalls of Lorn, who, from being Barons powerful enough to give battle to and defeat Robert Bruce, are now declined into private gentlemen of moderate fortune.

" This very ancient family is descended from Somerled, Thane, or rather, under that name, *King* of Argyle and the Hebrides. He had two sons, to one of whom he left his insular possessions — and he became founder of the dynasty of the Lords of the Isles, who maintained a stirring independence during the middle ages. The other was founder of the family of the MacDougalls of Lorn. One of them being married to a niece of the Red Cumming, in revenge of his slaughter at Dumfries, took a vigorous part against Robert Bruce in his struggles to maintain the independence of Scotland. At length the King, turning his whole strength towards Mac-Dougall, encountered him at a pass near Loch Awe; but the Highlanders, being possessed of the strong ground, compelled Bruce to retreat, and again gave him battle at Dalry, near Tynedrum, where he had concentrated his forces. Here he was again defeated, and the tradition of the MacDougall family bears, that in the conflict the Lord of Lorn engaged hand to hand with Bruce, and was struck down by that monarch. As they grappled together on the ground, Bruce being uppermost, a vassal of Mac-Dougall, called MacKeoch, relieved his master by pulling Bruce from him. In this close struggle the King left his mantle and brooch in the hands of his enemies, and the latter trophy was long preserved in the family, until it was lost in an accidental fire. Barbour tells the same story, but I think with circumstances somewhat different. When Bruce had gained the throne for which he fought so long, he displayed his resentment against the MacDougalls of Lorn, by depriving them of the greatest part of their domains, which were bestowed chiefly upon

the Steward of Scotland. Sir Colin Campbell, the
Knight of Loch Awe, and the Knight of Glenur-
chy, Sir Dugald Campbell, married daughters of
the Steward, and received with them great portion
of the forfeiture of MacDougall. Bruce even compelled or persuaded the Lord of the Isles to divorce
his wife, who was a daughter of MacDougall, and
take in marriage a relation of his own. The son of
the divorced lady was not permitted to succeed to
the principality of the Isles, on account of his connexion with the obnoxious MacDougall. But a large
appanage was allowed him upon the Mainland, where
he founded the family of Glengarry.

" The family of MacDougall suffered farther reduction during the great civil war, in which they
adhered to the Stewarts, and in 1715 they forfeited
the small estate of Dunolly, which was then all that
remained of what had once been a principality. The
then representative of the family fled to France, and
his son (father of the present proprietor) would have
been without any means of education, but for the
spirit of clanship, which induced one of the name, in
the humble situation of keeper of a public-house at
Dumbarton, to take his young chief to reside with
him, and be at the expense of his education and
maintenance until his fifteenth or sixteenth year. He
proved a clever and intelligent man, and made good
use of the education he received. When the affair

of 1745 was in agitation, it was expected by the south-western clans that Charles Edward would have landed near Oban, instead of which he disembarked at Loch-nan-augh, in Arisaig. Stuart of Appin sent information of his landing to MacDougall, who gave orders to his brother to hold the clan in readiness to rise, and went himself to consult with the chamberlain of the Earl of Breadalbane, who was also in the secret. He found this person indisposed to rise, alleging that Charles had disappointed them both in the place of landing, and the support he had promised. MacDougall then resolved to play cautious, and went to visit the Duke of Argyle, then residing at Roseneath, probably without any determined purpose as to his future proceedings. While he was waiting the Duke's leisure, he saw a horseman arrive at full gallop, and shortly after, the Duke entering the apartment where MacDougall was, with a map in his hand, requested him, after friendly salutations, to point out Loch-nan-augh on that map. MacDougall instantly saw that the secret of Charles's landing had transpired, and resolved to make a merit of being the first who should give details. The persuasions of the Duke determined him to remain quiet, and the reward was the restoration of the little state of Dunolly, lost by his father in 1715. This gentleman lived to a very advanced stage of life, and was succeeded by Peter MacDougall, Esq. now of Dunolly.

I had these particulars respecting the restoration of the estate from a near relation of the family, whom we met at Dunstaffnage.

" The modern house of Dunolly is on the neck of land under the old castle, having on the one hand the lake with its islands and mountains ; on the other, two romantic eminences tufted with copeswood, of which the higher is called Barmore, and is now planted. I have seldom seen a more romantic and delightful situation, to which the peculiar state of the family gave a sort of moral interest. Mrs Mac-Dougall, observing strangers surveying the ruins, met us on our return, and most politely insisted upon our accepting fruit and refreshments. This was a a compliment meant to absolute strangers, but when our names became known to her, the good lady's entreaties that we would stay till Mr. MacDougall returned from his ride, became very pressing. She was in deep mourning for the loss of an eldest son, who had fallen bravely in Spain and under Welling-ton, a death well becoming the descendant of so famed a race. The second son, a lieutenant in the navy, had, upon this family misfortune, obtained leave to visit his parents for the first time after many years' service, but had now returned to his ship. Mrs M. spoke with melancholy pride of the death of her eldest son, with hope and animation of the prospects of the survivor. A third is educated for the law. Declining the hospitality offered us, Mrs M. had the goodness to walk with us along the shore towards Oban, as far as the property of Dunolly extends, and showed us a fine spring, called *Tobar nan Gall,* or the Well of the Stranger, where our sailors supplied themselves with excellent water, which has been rather a scarce article with us, as it soon becomes past a landsman's use on board ship. On the sea-shore, about a quarter of a mile from the castle, is a huge fragment of the rock called *plum-pudding stone,* which art or nature has formed into a gigantic pillar. Here it is said Fion or Fingal tied his dog Bran — here also the celebrated Lord of the Isles tied up his dogs when he came upon a visit to the Lords of Lorn. Hence it is called *Clach nan Con; i.e.* the Dog's Stone. A tree grew once on the top of this bare mass of composite stone, but it was cut down by a curious damsel of the family, who was desirous to see a treasure said to be deposited beneath it. Enjoyed a pleasant walk of a mile along the beach to Oban, a town of some consequence, built in a semicircular form, around a good harbour formed by the opposite isle of Kerrara, on which Mrs M. pointed out the place where Alexander II. died, while, at the head of a powerful armament, he meditated the reduction of the Hebrides. The field is still called Dal-ry — the King's field.

" Having taken leave of Mrs MacDougall, we soon

satisfied our curiosity concerning Oban, which owed
its principal trade to the industry of two brothers,
Messrs Stevenson, who dealt in ship-building.   One
is now dead, the other almost retired from business,
and trade is dull in the place.   Heard of an active
and industrious man, who had set up a nursery of
young trees, which ought to succeed, since at present,
whoever wants plants must send to Glasgow; and
how much the plants suffer during a voyage of such
length, any one may conceive.   Go on board after a
day delightful for the serenity and clearness of the
weather, as well as for the objects we had visited.
I forgot to say, that through Mr MacDougall's absence we lost an opportunity of seeing a bronze figure
of one of his ancestors, called *Bacach*, or the lame,
armed and mounted as for a tournament.   The hero
flourished in the twelfth century.   After a grand
council of war, we determine, as we are so near the
coast of Ulster, that we will stand over and view
the celebrated Giant's Causeway; and Captain Wilson receives directions accordingly.

" *2d September* 1814.—Another most beautiful
day.   The heat, for the first time since we sailed
from Leith, is somewhat incommodious; so we spread
a handsome awning to save our complexions, God
wot, and breakfast beneath it in style.   The breeze
is gentle, and quite favourable.   It has conducted
us from the extreme cape of Mull, called the Black

Head of Mull, into the Sound of Islay. We view
in passing that large and fertile island, the property
of Campbell of Shawfield, who has introduced an admirable style of farming among his tenants. Still
farther behind us retreats the island of Jura, with the
remarkable mountains called the Paps of Jura, which
form a landmark at a great distance. They are very
high, but in our eyes, so much accustomed of late to
immense height, do not excite much surprise. Still
farther astern is the small isle of Scarba, which, as
we see it, seems to be a single hill. In the passage
or sound between Scarba and the extremity of Jura,
is a terrible run of tide, which, contending with the
sunk rocks and islets of that foul channel, occasions
the succession of whirlpools called the Gulf of Corrievreckan. Seen at this distance, we cannot judge
of its terrors. The sight of Corrievreckan and of the
low rocky isle of Colonsay, betwixt which and Islay
we are now passing, strongly recalls to my mind
poor John Leyden and his tale of the Mermaid and
MacPhail of Colonsay.* Probably the name of the
hero should have been MacFie, for to the MacDuffies
(by abridgment MacFies) Colonsay of old pertained.
It is said the last of these MacDuffies was executed
as an oppressor by order of the Lord of the Isles, and
lies buried in the adjacent small island of Oransay,

* See Minstrelsy of the Border — Scott's Poetical Works,
vol. iv., pp. 285–306.

where there is an old chapel with several curious monuments, which, to avoid losing this favourable breeze, we are compelled to leave unvisited. Colonsay now belongs to a gentleman named MacNeil. On the right beyond it, opens at a distance the western coast of Mull, which we already visited in coming from the northward. We see the promontory of Ross, which is terminated by Y-Columb-kill, also now visible. The shores of Loch Tua and Ulva are in the blue distance, with the little archipelago which lies around Staffa. Still farther, the hills of Rum can just be distinguished from the blue sky. We are now arrived at the extreme point of Islay, termed, from the strong tides, the *Runs of Islay.* We here only feel them as a large but soft swell of the sea, the weather being delightfully clear and serene. In the course of the evening we lose sight of the Hebrides, excepting Islay, having now attained the western side of that island.

" *3d September* 1814.—In the morning early, we are of Innistulhan, an islet very like Inchkeith in size and appearance, and, like Inchkeith, displaying a lighthouse. Messrs Hamilton, Duff, and Stevenson, go ashore to visit the Irish lighthouse and compare notes. A fishing-boat comes off with four or five stout lads, without neckerchiefs or hats, and the best of whose joint garments selected would hardly equip an Edinburgh beggar. Buy from this specimen of Paddy in his native land some fine John Dories for threepence each. The mainland of Ireland adjoining to this island (being part of the county of Donegal) resembles Scotland, and though hilly, seems well cultivated upon the whole. A brisk breeze directly against us. We beat to windward by assistance of a strong tide-stream, in order to weather the head of Innishowen, which covers the entrance of Lough Foyle, with the purpose of running up the loch to see Londonderry, so celebrated for its siege in 1689. But short tacks and long tacks were in vain, and at dinner-time, having lost our tide, we find ourselves at all disadvantage both against wind and sea. Much combustion at our meal, and the manœuvres by which we attempted to eat and drink remind me of the enchanted drinking-cup in the old ballad, —

> ' Some shed it on their shoulder,
> Some shed it on their thigh ;
> And he that did not hit his mouth
> Was sure to hit his eye.'

In the evening, backgammon and cards are in great request. We have had our guns shotted all this day for fear of the Yankees—a privateer having been seen off Tyree Islands, and taken some vessels—as is reported.—About nine o'clock weather the Innishowen head, and enter the Lough, and fire a gun as a signal for a pilot. The people here are great smugglers ; and at the report of the gun, we see

several lights on shore disappear.—About the middle
of the day too, our appearance (much resembling a
revenue cutter) occasioned a smoke being made in
the midst of a very rugged cliff on the shore — a
signal probably to any of the smugglers' craft that
might be at sea. Come to anchor in eight fathom
water, expecting our pilot.

" *4th September* 1814.—Waked in the morning
with good hope of hearing service in Derry Cathedral, as we had felt ourselves under weigh since
daylight; but these expectations vanished when, going
on deck, we found ourselves only half-way up Lough
Foyle, and at least ten miles from Derry. Very
little wind, and that against us; and the navigation
both shoally and intricate. Called a council of war;
and after considering the difficulty of getting up to
Derry, and the chance of being wind-bound when we
do get there, we resolve to renounce our intended
visit to that town. We had hardly put the ship
about, when the Irish Æolus shifted his trumpet,
and opposed our exit, as he had formerly been unfavourable to our progress up the lake. At length,
we are compelled to betake ourselves to towing, the
wind fading into an absolute calm. This gives us
time enough to admire the northern, or Donegal,
side of Lough Foyle—the other being hidden from
us by haze and distance. Nothing can be more favourable than this specimen of Ireland.— A beautiful
variety of cultivated slopes, intermixed with banks

of wood; rocks skirted with a distant ridge of heathy
hills, watered by various brooks; the glens or banks
being, in general, planted or covered with copse;
and finally, studded by a succession of villas and
gentlemen's seats, good farm-houses, and neat white-
washed cabins. Some of the last are happily situated
upon the verge of the sea, with banks of copse or a
rock or two rising behind them, and the white sand
in front. The land, in general, seems well cultivated
and enclosed — but in some places the enclosures
seem too small, and the ridges too crooked, for proper farming. We pass two gentlemen's seats, called
White Castle and Red Castle; the last a large good-
looking mansion, with trees, and a pretty vale sloping
upwards from the sea. As we approach the termination of the Lough, the ground becomes more
rocky and barren, and the cultivation interrupted by
impracticable patches, which have been necessarily
abandoned. Come in view of Green Castle, a large
ruinous castle, said to have belonged to the Mac-
Williams. The remains are romantically situated
upon a green bank sloping down to the sea, and are
partly covered with ivy. From their extent, the
place must have been a chieftain's residence of the
very first consequence. Part of the ruins appear to
be founded upon a high red rock, which the eye at
first blends with the masonry. To the east of the
ruins, upon a cliff overhanging the sea, are a modern
fortification and barrack-yard, and beneath, a large

battery for protection of the shipping which may
enter the Lough; the guns are not yet mounted.
The Custom-house boat boards us and confirms the
account that American cruisers are upon the coast.
Drift out of the Lough, and leave behind us this fine
country, all of which belongs in property to Lord
Donegal; other possessors only having long leases,
as sixty years, or so forth. Red Castle, however,
before distinguished as a very good-looking house,
is upon a perpetual lease. We discharge our pilot—
the gentlemen go ashore with him in the boat, in
order to put foot on Irish land. I shall defer that
pleasure till I can promise myself something to see.
When our gentlemen return, we read prayers on
deck. After dinner go ashore at the small fishing-
village of Port Rush, pleasantly situated upon a
peninsula, which forms a little harbour. Here we
are received by Dr Richardson, the inventor of the
fiorin-grass (or of some of its excellencies.) He
cultivates this celebrated vegetable on a very small
scale, his whole farm not exceeding four acres. Here
I learn, with inexpressible surprise and distress, the
death of one of the most valued of the few friends
whom these memoranda might interest.* She was,
indeed, a rare example of the soundest good sense,
and the most exquisite purity of moral feeling, united
with the utmost grace and elegance of personal

* Harriet, Duchess of Buccleuch, died Aug. 24, 1814.

beauty, and with manners becoming the most dignified rank in British society. There was a feminine
softness in all her deportment, which won universal
love, as her firmness of mind and correctness of
principle commanded veneration. To her family her
loss is inexpressibly great. I know not whether it
was the purity of her mind, or the ethereal cast of
her features and form, but I could never associate in
my mind her idea and that of mortality; so that the
shock is the more heavy, as being totally unexpected. God grant comfort to the afflicted survivor
and his family!

" *5th September* 1814.—Wake, or rather rise at
six, for I have waked the whole night, or fallen into
broken sleeps only to be hag-ridden by the nightmare. Go ashore with a heavy heart, to see sights
which I had much rather leave alone. Land under
Dunluce, a ruined castle built by the MacGilligans,
or MacQuillens, but afterwards taken from them by
a Macdonnell, ancestor of the Earls of Antrim, and
destroyed by Sir John Perrot, Lord-Lieutenant in
the reign of Queen Elizabeth. This Macdonnell
came from the Hebrides at the head of a Scottish
colony. The site of the castle much resembles
Dunnottar, but it is on a smaller scale. The ruins
occupy perhaps more than an acre of ground, being
the level top of a high rock advanced into the sea,
by which it is surrounded on three sides, and divided
from the mainland by a deep chasm. The access

was by a narrow bridge, of which there now remains but a single rib, or ledge, forming a doubtful and a precarious access to the ruined castle. On the outer side of the bridge are large remains of outworks, probably for securing cattle, and for domestic offices —and the vestiges of a chapel. Beyond the bridge are an outer and inner gateway, with their defences. The large gateway forms one angle of the square enclosure of the fortress, and at the other landward angle is built a large round tower. There are vestiges of similar towers occupying the angles of the precipice overhanging the sea. These towers were connected by a curtain, on which artillery seems to have been mounted. Within this circuit are the ruins of an establishment of feudal grandeur on the large scale. The great hall, forming, it would seem, one side of the inner court, is sixty paces long, lighted by windows which appear to have been shafted with stone, but are now ruined. Adjacent are the great kitchen and ovens, with a variety of other buildings, but no square tower, or keep. The most remarkable part of Dunluce, however, is, that the whole mass of plum-pudding rock on which the fort is built is completely perforated by a cave sloping downwards from the inside of the moat or dry-ditch beneath the bridge, and opening to the sea on the other side. It might serve the purpose of a small harbour, especially if they had, as is believed, a descent to the cave from within the castle. It is difficult to conceive the use of the aperture to the land, unless it was in some way enclosed and defended. Above the ruinous castle is a neat farm-house. Mrs More, the good-wife, a Scoto-Hibernian, received us with kindness and hospitality which did honour to the nation of her birth, as well as of her origin, in a house whose cleanliness and neatness might have rivalled England. Her churn was put into immediate motion on our behalf, and we were loaded with all manner of courtesy, as well as good things. We heard here of an armed schooner having been seen off the coast yesterday, which fired on a boat that went off to board her, and would seem therefore to be a privateer, or armed smuggler.

" Return on board for breakfast, and then again take boat for the Giant's Causeway — having first shotted the guns, and agreed on a signal, in case this alarming stranger should again make his appearance. Visit two caves, both worth seeing, but not equal to those we have seen; one, called Port Coon, opens in a small cove, or bay — the outer reach opens into an inner cave, and that again into the sea. The other, called Down Kerry, is a sea-cave, like that on the eastern side of Loch Eribol — a high arch up which the sea rolls: — the weather being quiet we sailed in very nearly to the upper end. We then rowed on to the celebrated Causeway, a platform composed of basaltic pillars, projecting into the sea

like the pier of a harbour.   As I was tired, and had
a violent headache, I did not land, but could easily
see that the regularity of the columns was the same
as at Staffa; but that island contains a much more
extensive and curious specimen of this curious phe-
nomenon.

" Row along the shores of this celebrated point,
which are extremely striking as well as curious.
They open into a succession of little bays, each of
which has precipitous banks graced with long ranges
of the basaltic pillars, sometimes placed above each
other, and divided by masses of interweaving strata,
or by green sloping banks of earth of extreme steep-
ness. These remarkable ranges of columns are in
some places chequered by horizontal strata of a red
rock or earth, of the appearance of ochre; so that
the green of the grassy banks, the dark-grey or black
appearance of the columns, with those red seams and
other varieties of the interposed strata, have most
uncommon and striking effects. The outline of these
cliffs is as singular as their colouring. In several
places the earth has wasted away from single columns,
and left them standing insulated and erect, like the
ruined colonnade of an ancient temple, upon the
verge of the precipice. In other places, the disposition of the basaltic ranges presents singular appearances, to which the guides give names agreeable
to the images which they are supposed to represent.

Each of the little bays or inlets has also its appropriate name. One is called the Spanish Bay, from one of the Spanish Armada having been wrecked there. Thus our voyage has repeatedly traced the memorable remnants of that celebrated squadron. The general name of the cape adjacent to the Causeway, is Bengore Head. To those who have seen Staffa, the peculiar appearance of the Causeway itself will lose much of its effect; but the grandeur of the neighbouring scenery will still maintain the reputation of Bengore Head. The people ascribe all these wonders to Fin MacCoul, whom they couple with a Scottish giant called Ben-an something or other. The traveller is plied by guides, who make their profit by selling pieces of crystal, agate, or chalcedony, found in the interstices of the rocks. Our party brought off some curious joints of the columns, and, had I been quite as I am wont to be, I would have selected four to be capitals of a rustic porch at Abbotsford. But, alas! alas! I am much out of love with vanity at this moment. From what we hear at the Causeway, we have every reason to think that the pretended privateer has been a gentleman's pleasure-vessel. — Continue our voyage southward, and pass between the Main of Ireland and the Isle of Rachrin, a rude heathy-looking island, once a place of refuge to Robert Bruce. This is said, in ancient times, to have been the abode of banditti, who plun-

dered the neighbouring coast. At present it is under
a long lease to a Mr Gage, who is said to maintain
excellent order among the islanders. Those of bad
character he expels to Ireland, and hence it is a
phrase among the people of Rachrin, when they wish
ill to any one, ' *May Ireland be his hinder end.*'
On the Main we see the village of Ballintry, and a
number of people collected, the remains of an Irish
fair. Close by is a small island, called Sheep Island.
We now take leave of the Irish coast, having heard
nothing of its popular complaints, excepting that the
good lady at Dunluce made a heavy moan against
the tithes, which had compelled her husband to
throw his whole farm into pasture. Stand over toward Scotland, and see the Mull of Cantyre light.

" *6th September* 1814. — Under the lighthouse
at the Mull of Cantyre; situated on a desolate
spot among rocks, like a Chinese pagoda in Indian
drawings. Duff and Stevenson go ashore at six
Hamilton follows, but is unable to land, the sea
having got up. The boat brings back letters, and I
have the great comfort to learn all are well at Abbotsford. About eight the tide begins to run very
strong, and the wind rising at the same time, makes
us somewhat apprehensive for our boat, which had
returned to attend D. and S. We observe them set
off along the hills on foot, to walk, as we understand,
to a bay called Carskey, five or six miles off, but the

nearest spot at which they can hope to re-embark in this state of the weather. It now becomes very squally, and one of our jibsails splits. We are rather awkwardly divided into three parties — the pedestrians on shore, with whom we now observe Captain Wilson, mounted upon a pony—the boat with four sailors, which is stealing along in-shore, unable to row, and scarce venturing to carry any sail — and we in the yacht, tossing about most exceedingly. At length we reach Carskey, a quiet-looking bay, where the boat gets into shore, and fetches off our gentlemen. After this the coast of Cantyre seems cultivated and arable, but bleak and unenclosed, like many other parts of Scotland. We then learn that we have been repeatedly in the route of two American privateers, who have made many captures in the Irish Channel, particularly at Innistruhul, at the back of Islay, and on the Lewis. They are the Peacock, of twenty-two guns, and 165 men, and a schooner of eighteen guns, called the Prince of Neuchatel. These news, added to the increasing inclemency of the weather, induce us to defer a projected visit to the coast of Galloway; and indeed it is time one of us was home on many accounts. We therefore resolve, after visiting the lighthouse at Pladda, to proceed for Greenock. About four drop anchor off Pladda, a small islet lying on the south side of Arran. Go ashore and visit the establish-

ment. When we return on board, the wind being
unfavourable for the mouth of Clyde, we resolve to
weigh anchor and go into Lamlash Bay.

" 7th September 1814.—We had amply room
to repent last night's resolution, for the wind, with
its usual caprice, changed so soon as we had weighed
anchor, blew very hard, and almost directly against
us, so that we were beating up against it by short
tacks, which made a most disagreeable night; as,
between the noise of the wind and the sea, the clat-
tering of the ropes and sails above, and of the move-
ables below, and the eternal ' ready about,' which
was repeated every ten minutes when the vessel was
about to tack, with the lurch and clamour which
succeeds, sleep was much out of the question. We
are not now in the least sick, but want of sleep is
uncomfortable, and I have no agreeable reflections to
amuse waking hours, excepting the hope of again
rejoining my family. About six o'clock went on
deck to see Lamlash Bay, which we have at length
reached after a hard struggle. The morning is fine
and the wind abated, so that the coast of Arran
looks extremely well. It is indented with two deep
bays. That called Lamlash, being covered by an
island with an entrance at either end, makes a secure
roadstead. The other bay, which takes its name
from Brodick Castle, a seat of the Duke of Hamilton, is open. The situation of the castle is very

fine, among extensive plantations, laid out with perhaps too much formality, but pleasant to the eye, as the first tract of plantation we have seen for a long time. One stripe, however, with singular want of taste, runs straight up a finely rounded hill, and turning by an obtuse angle, cuts down the opposite side with equal lack of remorse. This vile habit of opposing the line of the plantation to the natural line and bearing of the ground, is one of the greatest practical errors of early planters. As to the rest, the fields about Brodick, and the lowland of Arran in general, seem rich, well enclosed, and in good cultivation. Behind and around rise an amphitheatre of mountains, the principal a long ridge with fine swelling serrated tops, called Goat-Fell. Our wind now altogether dies away, while we want its assistance to get to the mouth of the Firth of Clyde, now opening between the extremity of the large and fertile Isle of Bute, and the lesser islands called the Cumbrays. The fertile coast of Ayrshire trends away to the south-westward, displaying many villages, and much appearance of beauty and cultivation. On the north-eastward arises the bold and magnificent screen formed by the mountains of Argyleshire and Dumbartonshire, rising above each other in gigantic succession. About noon a favourable breath of wind enables us to enter the mouth of the Clyde, passing between the larger Cumbray and the extremity of

Bute. As we advance beyond the Cumbray, and
open the opposite coast, see Largs, renowned for the
final defeat of the Norwegian invaders by Alexander III. [A. D. 1263.]   The ground of battle was
a sloping, but rather gentle, ascent from the sea,
above the modern Kirk of Largs.   Had Haco gained
the victory, it would have opened all the south-west
of Scotland to his arms.   On Bute, a fine and
well-improved island, we open the Marquis of Bute's
house of Mount Stewart, neither apparently large
nor elegant in architecture, but beautifully situated
among well-grown trees, with an open and straight
avenue to the sea-shore.   The whole isle is prettily
varied by the rotation of crops: and the rocky ridges
of Goat-Fell and other mountains in Arran are now
seen behind Bute as a background.   These ridges
resemble much the romantic and savage outline of
the mountains of Cullin, in Skye.   On the southward of Largs is Kelburn, the seat of Lord Glasgow,
with extensive plantations ; on the northward Skel-
morlie, an ancient seat of the Montgomeries.   The
Firth, closed to appearance by Bute and the Cumbrays, now resembles a long irregular inland lake,
bordered on the one side by the low and rich coast of
Renfrewshire, studded with villages and seats, and
on the other by the Highland mountains.   Our
breeze dies totally away, and leaves us to admire this
prospect till sunset.   I learn incidentally, that, in

the opinion of honest Captain Wilson, I have been myself the cause of all this contradictory weather. ' It is all,' says the Captain to Stevenson, ' owing to the cave at the Isle of Egg,' — from which I had abstracted a skull. Under this odium I may labour yet longer, for assuredly the weather has been doggedly unfavourable. Night quiet and serene, but dead calm — a fine contrast to the pitching, rolling, and walloping of last night.

" 8*th* September. — Waked very much in the same situation — a dead calm, but the weather very serene. With much difficulty, and by the assistance of the tide, we advanced up the Firth, and passing the village of Gourock at length reached Greenock. Took an early dinner, and embarked in the steam-boat for Glasgow. We took leave of our little yacht under the repeated cheers of the sailors, who had been much pleased with their erratic mode of travelling about, so different from the tedium of a regular voyage. After we reached Glasgow — a journey which we performed at the rate of about eight miles an hour, and with a smoothness of motion which probably resembles flying — we supped together and prepared to separate. — Erskine and I go to-morrow to the Advocate's at Killermont, and thence to Edinburgh. So closes my journal. But I must not omit to say, that among five or six persons, some of whom were doubtless different in tastes and pursuits, there

did not occur, during the close communication of
more than six weeks aboard a small vessel, the
slightest difference of opinion. Each seemed anxious
to submit his own wishes to those of his friends.
The consequence was, that by judicious arrangement
all were gratified in their turn, and frequently he who
made some sacrifices to the views of his companions,
was rewarded by some unexpected gratification calculated particularly for his own amusement.   Thus
ends my little excursion, in which, bating one circumstance, which must have made me miserable for
the time wherever I had learned it, I have enjoyed
as much pleasure as in any six weeks of my life.
We had constant exertion, a succession of wild and uncommon scenery, good humour on board, and objects
of animation and interest when we went ashore —

　　‘ Sed fugit interea—fugit irrevocabile tempus.’ ”

CHAPTER XXXIII.

Letter in Verse from Zetland and Orkney—Death
of the Duchess of Buccleuch — Correspondence
with the Duke — Altrive Lake — Negotiation
concerning the Lord of the Isles completed —
Success of Waverley — Contemporaneous Criti-
cisms on the Novel — Letters to Scott from Mr
Morritt — Mr Lewis — and Miss Maclean Cle-
phane — Letter from James Ballantyne to Miss
Edgeworth.

1814.

I QUESTION if any man ever drew his own character
more fully or more pleasingly than Scott has done in
the preceding diary of a six weeks' pleasure voyage.
We have before us, according to the scene and occasion, the poet, the antiquary, the magistrate, the
planter, and the agriculturist; but everywhere the
warm yet sagacious philanthropist — everywhere the

courtesy, based on the unselfishness, of the thorough-
bred gentleman;—and surely never was the tenderness of a manly heart portrayed more touchingly
than in the closing pages.   I ought to mention that
Erskine received the news of the Duchess of Buccleuch's death on the day when the party landed at
Dunstaffnage; but, knowing how it would affect
Scott, took means to prevent its reaching him until
the expedition should be concluded.   He heard the
event casually mentioned by a stranger during dinner
at Port Rush, and was for the moment quite overpowered.

Of the letters which Scott wrote to his friends
during those happy six weeks, I have recovered only
one, and it is, thanks to the leisure of the yacht, in
verse.   The strong and easy heroics of the first sec-
tion prove, I think, that Mr Canning did not err
when he told him that if he chose he might emulate
even Dryden's command of that noble measure; and
the dancing anapæsts of the second, show that he
could with equal facility have rivalled the gay graces
of Cotton, Anstey, or Moore.   This epistle did not
reach the Duke of Buccleuch till his lovely Duchess
was no more; and I shall annex to it some communications relating to that affliction, which afford a
contrast, not less interesting than melancholy, to the
light-hearted glee reflected in the rhymes from the
region of Magnus Troil.

To his Grace the Duke of Buccleuch, &c. &c. &c.

"Lighthouse Yacht in the Sound of Lerwick,
Zetland, 8th August 1814.

" Health to the chieftain from his clansman true !
From her true minstrel, health to fair Buccleuch !
Health from the isles, where dewy Morning weaves
Her chaplet with the tints that Twilight leaves ;
Where late the sun scarce vanished from the sight,
And his bright pathway graced the short-lived night,
Though darker now as autumn's shades extend,
The north winds whistle and the mists ascend !——
Health from the land where eddying whirlwinds toss
The storm-rocked *cradle* of the Cape of Noss ;
On outstretched cords the giddy engine slides,
His own strong arm the bold adventurer guides,
And he that lists such desperate feat to try,
May, like the sea-mew, skim 'twixt surf and sky,
And feel the mid-air gales around him blow,
And see the billows rage five hundred feet below.

" Here by each stormy peak and desert shore,
The hardy islesman tugs the daring oar,
Practised alike his venturous course to keep,
Through the white breakers or the pathless deep,
By ceaseless peril and by toil to gain
A wretched pittance from the niggard main.
And when the worn-out drudge old ocean leaves,
What comfort greets him, and what hut receives ?
Lady ! the worst your presence ere has cheered
(When want and sorrow fled as you appeared)
Were to a Zetlander as the high dome
Of proud Drumlanrig to my humble home.

Here rise no groves, and here no gardens blow,
Here even the hardy heath scarce dares to grow;
But rocks on rocks, in mist and storm arrayed,
Stretch far to sea their giant colonnade,
With many a cavern seam'd, the dreary haunt
Of the dun seal and swarthy cormorant.
Wild round their rifted brows with frequent cry,
As of lament, the gulls and gannets fly,
And from their sable base, with sullen sound,
In sheets of whitening foam the waves rebound.

" Yet even these coasts a touch of envy gain
From those whose land has known oppression's chain;
For here the industrious Dutchman comes once more
To moor his fishing craft by Bressay's shore;
Greets every former mate and brother tar,
Marvels how Lerwick 'scaped the rage of war,
Tells many a tale of Gallic outrage done,
And ends by blessing God and Wellington.
Here too the Greenland tar, a fiercer guest,
Claims a brief hour of riot, not of rest;
Proves each wild frolic that in wine has birth,
And wakes the land with brawls and boisterous mirth.
A sadder sight on yon poor vessel's prow
The captive Norse-man sits in silent wo,
And eyes the flags of Britain as they flow.
Hard fate of war, which bade her terrors sway
His destined course, and seize so mean a prey;
A bark with planks so warp'd and seams so riven,
She scarce might face the gentlest airs of heaven:
Pensive he sits, and questions oft if none
Can list his speech and understand his moan;
In vain — no islesman now can use the tongue
Of the bold Norse, from whom their lineage sprung.

Not thus of old the Norse-men hither came,
Won by the love of danger or of fame;
On every storm-beat cape a shapeless tower
Tells of their wars, their conquests, and their power;
For ne'er for Grecia's vales, nor Latian land,
Was fiercer strife than for this barren strand;
A race severe — the isle and ocean lords,
Loved for its own delight the strife of swords;
With scornful laugh the mortal pang defied,
And blest their gods that they in battle died.

" Such were the sires of Zetland's simple race,
And still the eye may faint resemblance trace
In the blue eye, tall form, proportion fair,
The limbs athletic, and the long light hair—
(Such was the mien, as Scald and Minstrel sings,
Of fair-haired Harold, first of Norway's Kings);
But their high deeds to scale these crags confined,
Their only warfare is with waves and wind.

" Why should I talk of Mousa's castled coast?
Why of the horrors of the Sumburgh Rost?
May not these bald disjointed lines suffice,
Penn'd while my comrades whirl the rattling dice —
While down the cabin skylight lessening shine
The rays, and eve is chased with mirth and wine?
Imagined, while down Mousa's desert bay
Our well-trimm'd vessel urged her nimble way,
While to the freshening breeze she leaned her side,
And bade her bowsprit kiss the foamy tide?

" Such are the lays that Zetland Isles supply;
Drenched with the drizzly spray and dropping sky,
Weary and wet, a sea-sick minstrel I.—— W. Scott."

" POSTSCRIPTUM.

" Kirkwall, Orkney, Aug. 13, 1814.

" In respect that your Grace has commissioned a Kraken,
  You will please be informed that they seldom are taken;
  It is January two years, the Zetland folks say,
  Since they saw the last Kraken in Scalloway bay;
  He lay in the offing a fortnight or more,
  But the devil a Zetlander put from the shore,
  Though bold in the seas of the North to assail
  The morse and the sea-horse, the grampus and whale.
  If your Grace thinks I'm writing the thing that is not,
  You may ask at a namesake of ours, Mr Scott —
  (He's not from our clan, though his merits deserve it,
  But springs, I'm informed, from the Scotts of Scotstarvet;)*
  He questioned the folks who beheld it with eyes,
  But they differed confoundedly as to its size.
  For instance, the modest and diffident swore
  That it seemed like the keel of a ship, and no more —
  Those of eyesight more clear, or of fancy more high,
  Said it rose like an island 'twixt ocean and sky —
  But all of the hulk had a steady opinion
  That 'twas sure a *lire* subject of Neptune's dominion —
  And I think, my Lord Duke, your Grace hardly would wish,
  To cumber your house, such a kettle of fish.
  Had your order related to night-caps or hose,
  Or mittens of worsted, there's plenty of those.
  Or would you be pleased but to fancy a whale?
  And direct me to send it — by sea or by mail?
  The season, I'm told, is nigh over, but still
  I could get you one fit for the lake at Bowhill.

---

* The Scotts of Scotstarvet, and other families of the name in Fife
and elsewhere, claim no kindred with the great clan of the Border —
and their armorial bearings are different.

Indeed, as to whales, there's no need to be thrifty,
Since one day last fortnight two hundred and fifty,
Pursued by seven Orkneymen's boats and no more,
Betwixt Truffness and Luffness were drawn on the shore!
You'll ask if I saw this same wonderful sight;
I own that I did not, but easily might —
For this mighty shoal of leviathans lay
On our lee-beam a mile, in the loop of the bay,
And the islesmen of Sanda were all at the spoil,
And *flinching* (so term it) the blubber to boil;
(Ye spirits of lavender, drown the reflection
That awakes at the thoughts of this odorous dissection.)
To see this huge marvel full fain would we go,
But Wilson, the wind, and the current, said no.
We have now got to Kirkwall, and needs I must stare
When I think that in verse I have once called it *fair;*
'Tis a base little borough, both dirty and mean —
There is nothing to hear, and there's nought to be seen,
Save a church, where, of old times, a prelate harangued,
And a palace that's built by an earl that was hanged.
But farewell to Kirkwall — aboard we are going,
The anchor's a-peak and the breezes are blowing;
Our commodore calls all his band to their places,
And 'tis time to release you — good night to your Graces!"

" *To His Grace the Duke of Buccleuch, &c.*

" Glasgow, Sept. 8, 1814.

" My Dear Lord Duke,

" I take the earliest opportunity, after landing, to discharge a task so distressing to me, that I find reluctance and fear even in making the attempt, and

for the first time address so kind and generous a
friend without either comfort and confidence in myself, or the power of offering a single word of consolation to his affliction.   I learned the late calamitous
news (which indeed no preparation could have greatly
mitigated) quite unexpectedly, when upon the Irish
coast; nor could the shock of an earthquake have
affected me in the same proportion.   Since that time
I have been detained at sea, thinking of nothing but
what has happened, and of the painful duty I am
now to perform.   If the deepest interest in this inexpressible loss could qualify me for expressing myself upon a subject so distressing, I know few whose
attachment and respect for the lamented object of
our sorrows can, or ought to exceed my own, for
never was more attractive kindness and condescension displayed by one of her sphere, or returned with
deeper and more heart-felt gratitude by one in my
own.   But selfish regret and sorrow, while they
claim a painful and unavailing ascendance, cannot
drown the recollection of the virtues lost to the
world, just when their scene of acting had opened
wider, and to her family when the prospect of their
speedy entry upon life rendered her precept and example peculiarly important.   And such an example!
for of all whom I have ever seen, in whatever rank,
she possessed most the power of rendering virtue
lovely—combining purity of feeling and soundness

of judgment with a sweetness and affability which won the affections of all who had the happiness of approaching her. And this is the partner of whom it has been God's pleasure to deprive your Grace, and the friend for whom I now sorrow, and shall sorrow while I can remember any thing. The recollection of her excellencies can but add bitterness, at least in the first pangs of calamity, yet it is impossible to forbear the topic; it runs to my pen as to my thoughts, till I almost call in question, for an instant, the Eternal Wisdom which has so early summoned her from this wretched world, where pain and grief and sorrow is our portion, to join those to whom her virtues, while upon earth, gave her so strong a resemblance. Would to God I could say, *be comforted;* but I feel every common topic of consolation must be, for the time at least, even an irritation to affliction. Grieve then, my dear Lord, or I should say my dear and much honoured friend, for sorrow for the time levels the highest distinctions of rank; but do not grieve as those who have no hope. I know the last earthly thoughts of the departed sharer of your joys and sorrows must have been for your Grace and the dear pledges she has left to your care. Do not, for their sake, suffer grief to take that exclusive possession which disclaims care for the living, and is not only useless to the dead, but is what their wishes would have most earnestly deprecated.   To time, and to God, whose are both time and eternity, belongs the office of future consolation; it is enough to require from the sufferer under such a dispensation to bear his burthen of sorrow with fortitude, and to resist those feelings which prompt us to believe that that which is galling and grievous is therefore altogether beyond our strength to support. Most bitterly do I regret some levity which I fear must have reached you when your distress was most poignant, and most dearly have I paid for venturing to anticipate the time which is not ours, since I received these deplorable news at the very moment when I was collecting some trifles that I thought might give satisfaction to the person whom I so highly honoured, and who, among her numerous excellencies, never failed to seem pleased with what she knew was meant to afford her pleasure.

" But I must break off, and have perhaps already written too much.   I learn by a letter from Mrs Scott, this day received, that your Grace is at Bowhill—in the beginning of next week I will be in the vicinity—and when your Grace can receive me without additional pain, I shall have the honour of waiting upon you.   I remain, with the deepest sympathy, my Lord Duke, your Grace's truly distressed and most grateful servant,

WALTER SCOTT."

The following letter was addressed to Scott by the Duke of Buccleuch, before he received that which the Poet penned on landing at Glasgow. I present it here, because it will give a more exact notion of what Scott's relations with his noble patron really were, than any other single document which I could produce : and to set that matter in its just light, is essential to the business of this narrative. But I am not ashamed to confess that I embrace with satisfaction the opportunity of thus offering to the readers of the present time a most instructive lesson. They will here see what pure and simple virtues and humble piety may be cultivated as the only sources of real comfort in this world and consolation in the prospect of futurity,—among circles which the giddy and envious mob are apt to regard as intoxicated with the pomps and vanities of wealth and rank ; which so many of our popular writers represent systematically as sunk in selfish indulgence—as viewing all below them with apathy and indifference—and last, not least, as upholding, when they do uphold, the religious institutions of their country, merely because they have been taught to believe that their own hereditary privileges and possessions derive security from the prevalence of Christian maxims and feelings among the mass of the people.

" *To Walter Scott, Esq., Post Office, Greenock.*

" Bowhill, Sept. 3, 1814.

" My Dear Sir,

" It is not with the view of distressing you with my griefs, in order to relieve my own feelings, that I address you at this moment. But knowing your attachment to myself, and more particularly the real affection which you bore to my poor wife, I thought that a few lines from me would be acceptable, both to explain the state of my mind at present, and to mention a few circumstances connected with that melancholy event.

" I am calm and resigned. The blow was so severe that it stunned me, and I did not feel that agony of mind which might have been expected. I now see the full extent of my misfortune; but that extended view of it has come gradually upon me. I am fully aware how imperative it is upon me to exert myself to the utmost on account of my children. I must not depress their spirits by a display of my own melancholy feelings. I have many new duties to perform,—or rather, perhaps, I now feel more pressingly the obligation of duties which the unceasing exertions of my poor wife rendered less necessary, or induced me to attend to with less than sufficient accuracy. I have been taught a severe lesson; it may and ought to be a useful one. I feel that my lot, though a hard one, is accompanied by many alleviations denied to others. I have a numerous family, thank God, in health, and profiting, according to their different ages, by the admirable lessons they have been taught. My daughter, Anne, worthy of so excellent a mother, exerts herself to the utmost to supply her place, and has displayed a fortitude and strength of mind beyond her years, and (as I had foolishly thought) beyond her powers. I have most kind friends willing and ready to afford me every assistance. These are my worldly comforts, and they are numerous and great.

" Painful as it may be, I cannot reconcile it to myself to be totally silent as to the last scene of this cruel tragedy. As she had lived, so she died — an example of every noble feeling — of love, attachment, and the total want of everything selfish. Endeavouring to the last to conceal her suffering, she evinced a fortitude, a resignation, a Christian courage, beyond all power of description. Her last injunction was to attend to her poor people. It was a dreadful but instructive moment. I have learned that the most truly heroic spirit may be lodged in the tenderest and the gentlest breast. Need I tell *you* that she expired in the full hope and expectation, nay, in the firmest certainty, of passing to a better world, through a steady reliance on her

Saviour. If ever there was a proof of the efficacy of our religion in moments of the deepest affliction, and in the hour of death, it was exemplified in her conduct. But I will no longer dwell upon a subject which must be painful to you. Knowing her sincere friendship for you, I have thought it would give you pleasure, though a melancholy one, to hear from me that her last moments were such as to be envied by every lover of virtue, piety, and true and genuine religion.

" I will endeavour to do in all things what I know she would wish. I have therefore determined to lay myself open to all the comforts my friends can afford me. I shall be most happy to cultivate their society as heretofore. I shall love them more and more, because I know they loved her. Whenever it suits your convenience I shall be happy to see you here. I feel that it is particularly my duty not to make my house the house of mourning to my children; for I know it was *her* decided opinion that it is most mischievous to give an early impression of gloom to the mind.

" You will find me tranquil, and capable of going through the common occupations of society. Adieu for the present. Yours very sincerely,

BUCCLEUCH, &c."

" *To His Grace the Duke of Buccleuch, &c. &c. &c.*

" Edinburgh, 11th Sept. 1814.

" My Dear Lord Duke,

" I received your letter (which had missed me at Greenock) upon its being returned to this place, and cannot sufficiently express my gratitude for the kindness which, at such a moment, could undertake the task of writing upon such a subject to relieve the feelings of a friend. Depend upon it, I am so far worthy of your Grace's kindness, that, among many proofs of it, this affecting and most distressing one can never be forgotten. It gives me great though melancholy satisfaction, to find that your Grace has had the manly and Christian fortitude to adopt that resigned and patient frame of spirit, which can extract from the most bitter calamity a wholesome mental medicine. I trust in God, that, as so many and such high duties are attached to your station, and as he has blessed you with the disposition that draws pleasure from the discharge of them, your Grace will find your first exertions, however painful, rewarded with strength to persevere, and finally with that comfort which attends perseverance in that which is right. The happiness of hundreds depends upon your Grace almost directly, and the effect of your example in the country, and of your constancy

in support of a constitution daily undermined by the
wicked and designing, is almost incalculable. Justly,
then, and well, has your Grace resolved to sacrifice
all that is selfish in the indulgence of grief, to the
duties of your social and public situation. Long
may you have health and strength to be to your dear
and hopeful family an example and guide in all that
becomes their high rank. It is enough that one
light, and alas, what a light that was! has been re-
called by the Divine Will to another and a better
sphere.

" I wrote a hasty and unconnected letter immediately on landing. I am detained for two days in
this place, but shall wait upon your Grace immediately
on my return to Abbotsford. If my society cannot,
in the circumstances, give much pleasure, it will, I
trust, impose no restraint.

" Mrs Scott desires me to offer her deepest sympathy upon this calamitous occasion. She has much
reason, for she has lost the countenance of a friend
such as she cannot expect the course of human life
again to supply. I am ever, with much and affectionate respect, your Grace's truly faithful humble
servant,   WALTER SCOTT."

" *To J. B. S. Morritt, Esq., M.P., Worthing.*

" Edinburgh, September 14, 1814.

" My Dear Morritt,

" ' At the end of my tour on the 22d August'!!!
Lord help us! — this comes of going to the Levant
and the Hellespont, and your Euxine, and so forth.
A poor devil who goes to Nova Zembla and Thule
is treated as if he had been only walking as far as
Barnard Castle or Cauldshiel's Loch.* I would have

---

* Lord Byron writes to Mr Moore, August 3, 1814 — " Oh!
I have had the most amusing letter from Hogg, the Ettrick
Minstrel and Shepherd. I think very highly of him as a poet,
but he and half of these Scotch and Lake troubadours are spoilt
by living in little circles and petty coteries. London and the
world is the only place to take the conceit out of a man — in the
milling phrase. Scott, he says, is gone to the Orkneys in a gale
of wind, during which wind, he affirms, the said Scott he is sure
is not at his ease, to say the least of it. Lord! Lord! if these
home-keeping minstrels had crossed your Atlantic or my Medi-
terranean, and tasted a little open boating in a white squall — or
a gale in ' the Gut,' — or the bay of Biscay, with no gale at all—
how it would enliven and introduce them to a few of the sensa-
tions! — to say nothing of an illicit amour or two upon shore, in
the way of Essay upon the Passions, beginning with simple adul-
tery, and compounding it as they went along." *Life and Works,*
vol. iii. p. 102. Lord Byron, by the way, had written on July
the 24th to Mr Murray, " Waverley is the best and most interesting novel I have redde since — I don't know when," &c.
Ibid. p. 98.

you to know I only returned on the 10th current, and the most agreeable thing I found was your letter. I am sure you must know I had need of something pleasant, for the news of the death of the beautiful, the kind, the affectionate, and generous Duchess of Buccleuch gave me a shock, which, to speak God's truth, could not have been exceeded unless by my own family's sustaining a similar deprivation. She was indeed a light set upon a hill, and had all the grace which the most accomplished manners and the most affable address could give to those virtues by which she was raised still higher than by rank. As she always distinguished me by her regard and confidence, and as I had many opportunities of seeing her in the active discharge of duties in which she rather resembled a descended angel than an earthly being, you will excuse my saying so much about my own feelings on an occasion where sorrow has been universal. But I will drop the subject. The survivor has displayed a strength and firmness of mind seldom equalled, where the affection has been so strong and mutual, and amidst the very high station and commanding fortune which so often render self-control more difficult, because so far from being habitual. I trust, for his own sake, as well as for that of thousands to whom his life is directly essential, and hundreds of thousands to whom his example is important, that God, as he has given him fortitude

to bear this inexpressible shock, will add strength
of constitution to support him in the struggle. He
has written to me on the occasion in a style becoming
a man and a Christian, submissive to the will of
God, and willing to avail himself of the consolations
which remain among his family and friends. I am
going to see him, and how we shall meet, God
knows; but though ' an iron man of iron mould'
upon many of the occasions of life in which I see
people most affected, and a peculiar contemner of
the commonplace sorrow which I see paid to the
departed, this is a case in which my stoicism will not
serve me. They both gave me reason to think they
loved me, and I returned their regard with the most
sincere attachment — the distinction of rank being,
I think, set apart on all sides. But God's will be
done. I will dwell no longer upon this subject. It
is much to learn that Mrs Morritt is so much better,
and that if I have sustained a severe wound from a
quarter so little expected, I may promise myself the
happiness of your dear wife's recovery.

" I will shortly mention the train of our voyage,
reserving particulars till another day. We sailed
from Leith, and skirted the Scottish coast, visiting
the Buller of Buchan and other remarkable objects
— went to Shetland — thence to Orkney — from
thence round Cape Wrath to the Hebrides, making

descents everywhere, where there was anything to
be seen — thence to Lewis and the Long Island —
to Skye — to Iona — and so forth, lingering among
the Hebrides as long as we could. Then we stood
over to the coast of Ireland, and visited the Giant's
Causeway and Port Rush, where Dr Richardson,
the inventor (discoverer, I would say) of the celebrated fiorin grass, resides. By the way, he is a
chattering charlatan, and his fiorin a mere humbug.
But if he were Cicero, and his invention were potatoes, or anything equally useful, I should detest the
recollection of the place and the man, for it was
there I learned the death of my friend. Adieu, my
dear Morritt; kind compliments to your lady; like
poor Tom, ' I cannot daub it farther.' When I
hear where you are, and what you are doing, I will
write you a more cheerful epistle. Poor Mackenzie,
too, is gone — the brother of our friend Lady Hood
— and another Mackenzie, son to the Man of Feeling. So short time have I been absent, and such
has been the harvest of mortality among those whom
I regarded!

" I will attend to your corrections in Waverley.
My principal employment for the autumn will be re-
ducing the knowledge I have acquired of the localities of the islands into scenery and stage-room for
the ' Lord of the Isles,' of which renowned romance

I think I have repeated some portions to you. It was elder born than Rokeby, though it gave place to it in publishing.

" After all, scribbling is an odd propensity. I don't believe there is any ointment, even that of the Edinburgh Review, which can cure the infected. Once more yours entirely,

WALTER SCOTT."

Before I pass from the event which made August 1814 so black a month in Scott's calendar, I may be excused for once more noticing the kind interest which the Duchess of Buccleuch had always taken in the fortunes of the Ettrick Shepherd, and introducing a most characteristic espistle which she received from him a few months before her death. The Duchess—" fearful" (as she said) " of seeing herself in print"—did not answer the Shepherd, but forwarded his letter to Scott, begging him to explain that circumstances did not allow the Duke to concede what he requested, but to assure him that they both retained a strong wish to serve him whenever a suitable opportunity should present itself. Hogg's letter was as follows:—

" *To her Grace the Duchess of Buccleuch, Dalkeith*
Palace.   Favoured by Messrs Grieve and Scott,
*hatters, Edinburgh.**

" Ettrickbank, March 17, 1814.

" May it please your Grace,

" I have often grieved you by my applications
for this and that.   I am sensible of this, for I have
had many instances of your wishes to be of service
to me, could you have known what to do for that
purpose.   But there are some eccentric characters
in the world, of whom no person can judge or know
what will prove beneficial, or what may prove their
bane.   I have again and again received of your
Grace's private bounty, and though it made me love
and respect you the more, I was nevertheless grieved
at it.   It was never your Grace's money that I
wanted, but the honour of your countenance; indeed my heart could never yield to the hope of being
patronised by any house save that of Buccleuch,
whom I deemed bound to cherish every plant that
indicated anything out of the common way on the
Braes of Ettrick and Yarrow.

" I know you will be thinking that this long
prelude is to end with a request.   No, Madam! I

* Mr Grieve was a man of cultivated mind and generous disposition, and a most kind and zealous friend of the Shepherd.

have taken the resolution of never making another request. I will, however, tell you a story, which is, I believe, founded on a fact:—

" There is a small farm at the head of a water called * * * * * , possessed by a mean fellow named * * * *. A third of it has been taken off and laid into another farm—the remainder is as yet unappropriated. Now, there is a certain poor bard, who has two old parents, each of them upwards of eighty-four years of age; and that bard has no house nor home to shelter those poor parents in, or cheer the evening of their lives. A single line from a certain very great and very beautiful lady, to to a certain Mr Riddle,* would ensure that small pendicle to the bard at once. But she will grant no such thing! I appeal to your Grace if she is not a very bad lady that? I am your Grace's ever obliged and grateful   JAMES HOGG,

THE ETTRICK SHEPHERD."

Though the Duke of Buccleuch would not dismiss a poor tenant merely because Hogg called him " a mean fellow," he had told Scott that if he could find an unappropriated " pendicle," such as this letter referred to, he would most willingly bestow it on the Shepherd. It so happened, that when Scott paid his first visit at Bowhill after the death of the

---

* Major Riddell, the Duke's Chamberlain at Branksome Castle.

Duchess, the Ettrick Shepherd was mentioned :—
" My friend," said the Duke, " I must now consider
this poor man's case as *her* legacy ;" and to this feeling Hogg owed, very soon afterwards, his establishment at Altrive, on his favourite Braes of Yarrow.

As Scott passed through Edinburgh on his return
from his voyage, the negotiation as to the Lord of
the Isles, which had been protracted through several
months, was completed— Constable agreeing to give
fifteen hundred guineas for one half of the copyright,
while the other moiety was retained by the author.
The sum mentioned had been offered by Constable
at an early stage of the affair, but it was not until
now accepted, in consequence of the earnest wish of
Scott and Ballantyne to saddle the publisher of the
new poem with part of their old " quire stock," —
which, however, Constable ultimately persisted in
refusing. It may easily be believed that John Ballantyne's management of money matters during Scott's
six weeks' absence had been such as to render it
doubly convenient for the Poet to have this matter
settled on his arrival in Edinburgh—and it may also
be supposed that the progress of Waverley during
that interval had tended to put the chief parties in
good humour with each other.

In returning to Waverley, I must observe most
distinctly that nothing can be more unfounded than
the statement which has of late years been frequently

repeated in memoirs of Scott's life, that the sale of the first edition of this immortal Tale was slow. It appeared on the 7th of July, and the whole impression (1000 copies) had disappeared within five weeks; an occurrence then unprecedented in the case of an anonymous novel, put forth, at what is called among publishers, *the dead season*. A second edition, of 2000 copies, was at least projected by the 24th of the same month,*—that appeared before the end of August, and it too had gone off so rapidly, that when Scott passed through Edinburgh, on his way from the Hebrides, he found Constable eager to treat, on the same terms as before, for a third of 1000 copies. This third edition was published in October, and when a fourth of the like extent was called for in November, I find Scott writing to John Ballantyne — "I suppose Constable won't quarrel with a work on which he has netted £612 in four months, with a certainty of making it £1000 before the year is out;" and, in fact, owing to the diminished expense of advertising, the profits of this fourth edition were to each party £440. To avoid recurring to these details, I may as well state at once that a fifth edition of 1000 copies appeared in January 1815; a sixth of 1500 in June 1816; a seventh of 2000 in October 1817; an eighth of 2000 in April 1821; that in the collective editions,

* See letter to Mr Morritt, *ante*, p. 245.

prior to 1829, 11,000 were disposed off; and that
the sale of the current edition, with notes, begun in
1829, has already reached 40,000 copies.   Well
might Constable regret that he had not ventured to
offer £1000 for the whole copyright of Waverley!

I must now look back for a moment to the history
of the composition.—The letter of September 1810
was not the only piece of discouragement which
Scott had received, during the progress of Waverley,
from his first confidant.   James Ballantyne, in his
deathbed *memorandum*, says—" When Mr Scott
first questioned me as to my hopes of him as a
novelist, it somehow or other did chance that they
were not very high.   He saw this, and said—
' Well, I don't see why I should not succeed as well
as other people.   At all events, faint heart never won
fair lady—tis only trying.'   When the first volume
was completed, I still could not get myself to think
much of the Waverley-Honour scenes; and in this I
afterwards found that I sympathized with many.   But,
to my utter shame be it spoken, when I reached the
exquisite descriptions of scenes and manners at Tully-Veolan, what did I do but pronounce them at once
to be utterly vulgar!   When the success of the work
so entirely knocked me down as a man of taste, all
that the good-natured author said was—' Well, I
really thought you were wrong about the Scotch.
Why, Burns, by his poetry, had already attracted

universal attention to every thing Scottish, and I confess I could'nt see why I should not be able to keep the flame alive, merely because I wrote Scotch in prose, and he in rhyme.' "—It is, I think, very agreeable to have this manly avowal to compare with the delicate allusion which Scott makes to the affair in his Preface to the Novel.

The only other friends originally intrusted with his secret appear to have been Mr Erskine and Mr Morritt. I know not at what stage the former altered the opinion which he formed on seeing the tiny fragment of 1805. The latter did not, as we have seen, receive the book until it was completed; but he anticipated, before he closed the first volume, the station which public opinion would ultimately assign to Waverley. "How the story may continue," Mr Morritt then wrote, "I am not able to divine; but, as far as I have read, pray let us thank you for the Castle of Tully-Veolan, and the delightful drinking-bout at Lucky Mac-Leary's, for the characters of the Laird of Balmawhapple and the Baron of Bradwardine; and no less for Davie Gelatly, whom I take to be a transcript of William Rose's motley follower, commonly yclept Caliban.*

* This alludes to some mummery in which David Hinves, of merry memory, wore a Caliban-like disguise. He lived more than forty years in the service of Mr W. S. Rose, and died in it last year. Mr Rose was of course extremely young

If the completion be equal to what we have just
devoured, it deserves a place among our standard
works far better than its modest appearance and
anonymous titlepage will at first gain it in these
days of prolific story-telling. Your manner of nar-
rating is so different from the slipshod sauntering
verbiage of common novels, and from the stiff, precise, and prim sententiousness of some of our female
moralists, that I think it can't fail to strike anybody
who knows what style means; but, amongst the

---

when he first picked up Hinves — a bookbinder by trade, and
a preacher among the Methodists. A sermon heard casually
under a tree in the New Forest, had such touches of good feeling
and broad humour, that the young gentleman promoted him to be
his valet on the spot. He was treated latterly more like a friend
than a servant, by his master, and by all his master's intimate
friends. Scott presented him with a copy of all his works; and
Coleridge gave him a corrected (or rather an altered) copy of
Christabelle, with this inscription on the fly-leaf: " Dear Hinves,
— Till this book is concluded, and with it ' Gundimore, a poem,
by the same author,' accept of this *corrected* copy of Christabelle
as a *small* token of regard; yet such a testimonial as I would not
pay to any one I did not esteem, though he were an emperor.
Be assured I shall send you for your private library, every work
I have published (if there be any to be had) and whatever I
shall publish. Keep steady to the FAITH. If the fountainhead be
always full, the stream cannot be long empty. Yours sincerely,
11th Nov. 1816 — Muddeford.   S. T. COLERIDGE."
    Mr Rose imagines that the warning " keep steady to the faith,"
was given in allusion to Ugo Foscolo's "supposed licence in religious opinions." *Rhymes* (Brighton 1837) p. 92. [1839.]

gentle class, who swallow every blue-backed book
in a circulating library for the sake of the story, I
should fear half the knowledge of nature it contains,
and all the real humour, may be thrown away. Sir
Everard, Mrs Rachael, and the Baron, are, I think,
in the first rank of portraits for nature and character ; and I could depone to their likeness in any
court of taste. The ballad of St Swithin, and scraps
of *old songs*, were measures of danger if you meant
to continue your concealment ; but, in truth, you
wear your disguise something after the manner of
Bottom the weaver ; and in spite of you the truth
will soon peep out." And next day he resumes,—
" We have finished Waverley, and were I to tell
you all my admiration, you would accuse me of
complimenting. You have quite attained the point
which your *postscript-preface* mentions as your object—the discrimination of Scottish character, which
had hitherto been slurred over with clumsy national
daubing." He adds, a week or two later,—" After
all, I need not much thank you for your confidence.
How could you have hoped that I should not discover you ? I had heard you tell half the anecdotes
before—some turns you owe to myself ; and no
doubt most of your friends must have the same sort
of thing to say."

Monk Lewis's letter on the subject is so short,
that I must give it as it stands :—

" To Walter Scott, Esq., Abbotsford.

" The Albany, Aug. 17, 1814.

" My Dear Scott,

 " I return some books of yours which you lent me ' *sixty years since* '—and I hope they will reach you safe. I write in great haste; and yet I must mention, that hearing ' Waverley' ascribed to you, I bought it, and read it with all impatience. I am now told it is not yours, but William Erskine's. If this is so, pray tell him from me that I think it excellent in every respect, and that I believe every word of it. Ever yours,   M. G. Lewis."

Another friend (and he had, I think, none more dear), the late Margaret Maclean Clephane of Tor-loisk, afterwards Marchioness of Northampton, writes thus from Kirkness, in Kinross-shire, on the 11th October:—" In this place I feel a sort of pleasure, not unallied to pain, from the many recollections that every venerable tree, and every sunny bank, and every honeysuckle bower, occasions; and I have found something here that speaks to me in the voice of a valued friend—*Waverley.* The question that rises, it is perhaps improper to give utterance to. If so, let it pass as an exclamation.— Is it possible that Mr Erskine can have written it? The poetry

I think, would prove a different descent in any court in Christendom. The turn of the phrases in many places is so peculiarly yours, that I fancy I hear your voice repeating them; and there wants but verse to make all Waverley an enchanting poem — varying to be sure from grave to gay, but with so deepening an interest as to leave an impression on the mind that few — very few poems — could awaken. But, why did not the author allow me to be his Gaelic Dragoman? Oh! Mr ——, whoever you are, you might have safely trusted — M. M. C."

There was one person with whom it would, of course, have been more than vain to affect any concealment. On the publication of the third edition, I find him writing thus to his brother Thomas, who had by this time gone to Canada as paymaster of the 70th regiment: — " Dear Tom, a novel here, called Waverley, has had enormous success. I sent you a copy, and will send you another, with the Lord of the Isles, which will be out at Christmas. The success which it has had, with some other circumstances, has induced people

    ' To lay the bantling at a certain door,
     Where lying store of faults, they'd fain heap more.'

You will guess for yourself how far such a report has credibility; but by no means give the weight of your opinion to the Transatlantic public; for you must know there is also a counter-report, that *you* have written the said Waverley. Send me a novel intermixing your exuberant and natural humour, with any incidents and descriptions of scenery you may see — particularly with characters and traits of manners. I will give it all the cobbling that is necessary, and, if you do but exert yourself, I have not the least doubt it will be worth £500; and, to encourage you, you may, when you send the MS., draw on me for £100, at fifty days' sight — so that your labours will at any rate not be quite thrown away. You have more fun and descriptive talent than most people; and all that you want — *i. e.* the mere practice of composition — I can supply, or the devil's in it. Keep this matter a dead secret, and look knowing when Waverley is spoken of. If you are not Sir John Falstaff, you are as good a man as he, and may therefore face Colville of the Dale. You may believe I don't want to make you the author of a book you have never seen; but if people will, upon their own judgment, suppose so, and also on their own judgment give you £500 to try your hand on a novel, I don't see that you are a pin's-point the worse. Mind that your MS. attends the draft. I am perfectly serious and confident, that in two or three months you might clear the cobs. I beg my compliments to the hero who is afraid of Jeffrey's scalping-knife."

In truth, no one of Scott's intimate friends ever had, or could have had, the slightest doubt as to the parentage of Waverley : nor, although he abstained from communicating the fact formally to most of them, did he ever affect any real concealment in the case of such persons ; nor, when any circumstance arose which rendered the withholding of direct confidence on the subject incompatible with perfect freedom of feeling on both sides, did he hesitate to make the avowal.

Nor do I believe that the mystification ever answered much purpose, among literary men of eminence beyond the circle of his personal acquaintance. But it would be difficult to suppose that he had ever wished that to be otherwise ; it was sufficient for him to set the mob of readers at gaze, and above all, to escape the annoyance of having productions, actually known to be his, made the daily and hourly topics of discussion in his presence.

Mr Jeffrey had known Scott from his youth — and, in reviewing Waverley, he was at no pains to conceal his conviction of its authorship. He quarrelled, as usual, with carelessness of style, and some inartificialities of plot, but rendered justice to the substantial merits of the work, in language which I shall not mar by abridgment. The Quarterly was far less favourable in its verdict. Indeed, the articles on Waverley, and afterwards on Guy Mannering,

which appeared in that journal, will bear the test
of ultimate opinion as badly as any critical pieces
which our time has produced. They are written in
a captious, cavilling strain of quibble, which shows
as complete blindness to the essential interest of
the narrative, as the critic betrays on the subject
of the Scottish dialogue, which forms its liveliest
ornament, when he pronounces that to be " a dark
dialogue of Anglified Erse." With this remarkable
exception, the professional critics were, on the whole,
not slow to confess their belief, that, under a hack-
neyed name and trivial form, there had at last appeared a work of original creative genius, worthy
of being placed by the side of the very few real
masterpieces of prose fiction. Loftier romance was
never blended with easier, quainter humour, by Cer-
vantes himself. In his familiar delineations, he had
combined the strength of Smollett with the native
elegance and unaffected pathos of Goldsmith ; in
his darker scenes, he had revived that real tragedy
which appeared to have left our stage with the age of
Shakspeare ; and elements of interest so diverse had
been blended and interwoven with that nameless
grace, which, more surely perhaps than even the
highest perfection in the command of any one strain
of sentiment, marks the master-mind cast in Nature's
most felicitous mould.

Scott, with the consciousness (avowed long afterwards in his General Preface) that he should never in all likelihood have thought of a Scotch novel had he not read Maria Edgeworth's exquisite pieces of Irish character, desired James Ballantyne to send her a copy of Waverley on its first appearance, inscribed " from the author." Miss Edgeworth, whom Scott had never then seen, though some literary correspondence had passed between them, thanked the nameless novelist, under cover to Ballantyne, with the cordial generosity of kindred genius; and the following answer, not from Scott, but from Ballantyne—(who had kept a copy, now before me)—is not to be omitted:—

" *To Miss Edgeworth, Edgeworthstown, Ireland.*

"Edinburgh, 11th November 1814.

" Madam,

"; I am desired by the Author of Waverley to acknowledge, in his name, the honour you have done him by your most flattering approbation of his work—a distinction which he receives as one of the highest that could be paid him, and which he would have been proud to have himself stated his sense of, only that being *impersonal*, he thought it more respectful to require my assistance than to write an anonymous letter.

" There are very few who have had the opportu-

nities that have been presented to me, of knowing
how very elevated is the admiration entertained by
the Author of Waverley for the genius of Miss
Edgeworth. From the intercourse that took place
betwixt us while the work was going through my
press, *I know* that the exquisite truth and power of
your characters operated on his mind at once to
excite and subdue it. He felt that the success of his
book was to depend upon the characters, much more
than upon the story; and he entertained so just and
so high an opinion of your eminence in the management of both, as to have strong apprehensions of
any comparison which might be instituted betwixt
his picture and story and yours; besides, that there is
a richness and *naïveté* in Irish character and humour,
in which the Scotch are certainly defective, and which
could hardly fail, as he thought, to render his delineations cold and tame by the contrast. ' If I could
but hit Miss Edgeworth's wonderful power of vivify-
ing all her persons, and making them live as *beings* in
your mind, I should not be afraid:'—Often has the
Author of Waverley used such language to me; and
I knew that I gratified him most when I could say,
—' Positively this *is* equal to Miss Edgeworth.'
You will thus judge, Madam, how deeply he must
feel such praise as you have bestowed upon his
efforts. I believe he himself thinks the Baron the
best drawn character in his book — I mean the

Bailie—honest Bailie Macwheeble. He protests it is the most *true*, though from many causes he did not expect it to be the most popular. It appears to me, that amongst so many splendid portraits, all drawn with such strength and truth, it is more easy to say which is your favourite, than which is best. Mr Henry Mackenzie agrees with you in your objection to the resemblance to Fielding. He says, you should never be forced to recollect, *maugre* all its internal evidence to the contrary, that such a work is a work of fiction, and all its fine creations but of air. The character of Rose is less finished than the author had at one period intended; but I believe the characters of humour grew upon his liking, to the prejudice, in some degree, of those of a more elevated and sentimental kind. Yet what can surpass Flora, and her gallant brother?

" I am not authorized to say—but I will not resist my impulse to say to Miss Edgeworth, that another novel, descriptive of more ancient manners still, may be expected ere long from the Author of Waverley. But I request her to observe, that I say this in strict confidence—not certainly meaning to exclude from the knowledge of what will give them pleasure, her respectable family.

" Mr Scott's poem, the Lord of the Isles, promises fully to equal the most admired of his productions. It is, I think, equally powerful, and certainly more uniformly polished and sustained.   I have seen three cantos.   It will consist of six.

" I have the honour to be, Madam, with the utmost admiration and respect,

Your most obedient

and most humble servant,

JAMES BALLANTYNE."

END OF VOL. IV.